ISLA

LOVE SEQUENCE
BOOK 2

DAPHNE LEIGH

MARBLE CITY PRESS

1

I slide off the bed like a boneless jellyfish, desperate not to wake the snoring fucker who fell asleep with his cock still inside me. *Before* he got me there. Asshole.

All I need is a good dicking down every two weeks, and I'm golden, but that's nearly impossible when I depend on tourists to visit this tiny remote island I call my home. And then finding one that knows their way around a woman's body? Not likely.

I gather my clothes and tiptoe straight through the front door of his Airbnb, the brisk April breeze nipping at my ass as I pull on my jeans, sweatshirt, and jacket. What a fucking waste of a good cock. I take one last look at the door, hoping he'll stick his head out, make up some excuse about his sub-par performance, and drag me back inside to change my mind. He doesn't. I gather my hair over my shoulder, braiding it quickly before jamming my helmet over my head. I swing my leg over the bike, stomping on the kick start and revving the engine. I get lost in thought as I take the winding streets back to my house, the full moon casting an ethereal silver glow over the landscape.

If I'm honest with myself, I no longer have the emotional fortitude for this. Becoming a celibate cat lady seems like a far better option.

My stash of toys can keep me happy without dealing with the headache of men. I have too much on my plate anyway. Between my sister-in-law, Charlie, almost ready to give birth, helping my brother with the castle, and rehabbing the bar, I'm lucky to make it home at the end of the day with the energy to wash my face. Thank the gods Charlie's guys like to cook–I would have starved to death by now.

I can taste a hint of summer in the air as I take a deep, calming breath. I tell myself everything will settle down soon. Charlie and the guys will finally find a crew to work on the castle, and I'll book an appointment with the lawyer so James can sign the pub over to me— something I've been putting off for far too long. The dark, hulking shape of the house looms over me as I pull into the driveway. I cut the engine and sigh into the silence. It's too quiet now that Lach and Charlie moved in with Jack. I promise myself that I'll move my stuff to the cottage behind the house first thing tomorrow and list the house online as a holiday rental.

After a good night's sleep—thanks to my battery-operated boyfriend—I roll out of bed, gulp down a protein shake, and spend the day moving into the cottage. I have no idea why I waited so long. I've always loved it. A huge picture window looks out over the sea, an office, a tiny bedroom, and an even tinier kitchen. Perfect for a single gal. All I need now is a cat.

AFTER SPENDING the day moving my belongings and cleaning the house, I work a full shift at the pub.

I fucking hate this place.

No. That's a goddamned lie.

I love it so much that sometimes I can't stand it–like a lover that hangs around so long that you start to feel claustrophobic. I look up at the thick wood beams, scrubbed clean from years of smoke by Charlie and me. James had looked at us like we were crazy, but I could tell he was impressed with the final results.

Tonight, the bar is overflowing with regulars. So regular, I don't even need to think about what they want to eat or drink. I know their wives and their kids, their vices and idiosyncrasies. I also know exactly which ones will bitch and moan when I kick them out promptly at eleven. I lock the door behind them, take the till back to the office, and bag the money to take to the bank in the morning.

"Night, James!" I call as I head toward the back door, wincing as my boots stick to the floor. I'll have to come in extra early to mop tomorrow. "James?" I backtrack toward the bar. Every other night, he's there like clockwork, babying the scarred wood that's provided a good life for him and his family–but it's empty tonight. A low groan has me throwing my shit on the bar and launching myself over it. James is slumped in the corner, drool stringing from the side of his mouth to his shoulder. I curse as I snatch my phone from my back pocket and call an ambulance. I set it on the bar, hitting the speaker button before crouching on the floor. I grab his jacket and pull him onto his side. My legs fold under me as I sit, gently resting his head on my lap. I murmur softly to him as I run my fingers over his thinning gray hair. His breaths are shallow, each one ending in a horrible wheeze.

"James, stay with me. Please stay with me." Why the fuck are they taking so long to get here? I press a hand to my mouth, holding back a sob. He can't die. He's the only father figure I've had since I was barely a teenager. My parents had taken care of me financially before they died, but James gave me the unconditional love that was missing. My siblings had been there for me but were older and had their own lives to worry about. James had swooped in and provided a safe space and a comforting shoulder. I didn't need the money, but I started working for him as soon as I was of legal age just to help him out. He never stopped needing help, so I stayed.

I jump when a stretcher bangs through the kitchen door next to the bar. I stand up, shoving my jacket under James' head before standing, wiping at my cheeks with my sweater. The paramedics ask me a million questions I can't answer. "Just please fucking hurry," I whisper, my heart breaking with each rattling breath. I follow them out, locking the door before I climb into the ambulance.

"Miss, are you family?" a man asks, reaching toward me.

"I'm not fucking leaving him," I spit, swatting his hand away. The man holds both hands up and backs away. "Is he going to be okay?" I ask the woman taking his vitals, my gaze glued to James' face, willing his eyes to open. Desperate to see those sparkling blue eyes one more time.

"I'm not sure," the woman says honestly, fitting an oxygen mask over his face. "I think he may have had a heart attack. His vitals aren't looking good. They'll try to stabilize him at the hospital and then run some tests." I can feel her looking at me, but I can't bear to look at her face and see the truth.

They wheel him away the second we get to the hospital. I wait in the hallway, pacing back and forth for what seems like hours. I've seen this scene too many times in a million different movies, and it never ends well. I slump into a chair and drop my face into my hands. I have to keep myself together. No matter what happens, I'll have to be at the bar tomorrow or the day after. People in our community rely on it—whether it's to drown the sorrows of the past or for a hot dinner and company.

"Miss?"

I look up into the face of a doctor barely older than me.

"Please tell me he's okay," I rasp, blinking back tears.

The doctor shakes his head. "I'm sorry. We tried to stabilize him, but his heart just couldn't keep going."

I wipe away my tears with the back of my hand, forcing myself to take a deep breath.

"Are you the next of kin?"

I shake my head. "His son lives in London."

"Do you have someone that can come pick you up?"

I nod, sniffling. "Yes, I'll call my brother. Thank you for trying." I give him a watery smile and walk away, the sob I've been holding in constricting my chest until it hurts. I text Jay quickly and then burst through the doors, taking deep gulps of the night air.

Then I scream.

I scream for James and the reconciliation he'll never have with his son. I scream for me, for the hole in my chest he used to fill. I scream for the pub and the uncertainty surrounding it now that he's gone. Jack pulls up on his motorcycle, sweeping me into his arms and hugging me tight, my sobs muffled against his chest.

"You're staying at the castle tonight," he says gruffly, leaving no room for argument. Not that I would have argued anyway. I want to be surrounded by people I love. Lord knows I'll need their help to figure everything out come morning.

I stumble up the steps to the castle's front door a few minutes later, falling into Charlie's soft embrace. She squeezes me and kisses my forehead.

"I'm so sorry, Isla. He was a great man." I can only nod, not trusting the tremble in my lip. "Come on, I'll make you something to drink." She pulls me by my hand as she waddles toward the kitchen. "Liquor or cocoa?"

I laugh weakly, dragging in a ragged breath. "Cocoa would be nice."

"Sit." She pushes me into a chair at the table.

Lach and Cam come into the kitchen together, Jack a few steps behind them. Cam squats down next to me, pulling my hand into his. He and Lach were Jack's roommates back in college, and over the years, they've become like brothers to me. Charlie was the one that brought them all back together again. Now she wears three stacked engagement rings and one wedding band on her left hand. I've never seen them happier.

"What can I do?" Cam asked, his fingers squeezing around mine.

"Just being here helps. I don't want to be alone."

"You got it, Bug."

I wrinkle my nose at the nickname, pretending to hate it even though I've grown to love it. Not that I would ever tell any of them that.

Lach sits on my other side and pushes his phone into my hand, a video queued up.

"What's this?" I ask, thankful for the distraction.

"Charlie started making promotional videos for the castle. They're brilliant."

Charlie pauses in the middle of stirring the pot of milk, her eyes sparkling at the praise. "I opened a couple of social media accounts. I'm just experimenting right now."

"Did you find a crew yet?" I ask them.

"Not yet. Everyone's booked up for months. Right now, I think we're just going to do tours," Lach says, sitting next to me.

I raise my eyebrow, looking at Jack, "You're okay with that?" Before meeting Charlie, he treasured privacy the most, so this is a complete surprise.

"I'm more than okay with it. Starting slow is better than not starting at all. I've been hemorrhaging money for years to keep the castle up."

I wince slightly, feeling bad that the castle had fallen into Jack's responsibility by default. I was too young, and our sister Laurel had no interest.

I WATCH THE VIDEO, grinning from the first second to the last. Charlie had made the guys take off their shirts and do a mini-tour. It's possibly the best thing I've ever seen. I wipe tears from my eyes for the tenth time that day, but they're happy tears this time.

"Cocoa is ready!" As the guys grab mugs, Charlie brings the pot and ladle to the table, setting it on the scarred surface.

"What will happen to the pub?" Jack asks, wiping the cocoa from his mustache.

"James told me a million times he would leave it to me, but I don't think he ever actually made it legal." I sigh, wishing I had pushed him to make a will. "It'll go to his son, I guess."

"What will his son do with it? He's some city bigwig, right?"

I nod. "He lives in London. If I could guess, he'll sell it to the highest bidder."

"That's in our favor, then," Jack says.

"True, but I'm not going to overpay for it when the money goes to the person who never once came to visit his only living relative. Fuck him."

Charlie chokes on her cocoa, eyes watering as Lach slaps her on her back. "Just make sure you call him soon, Isla. If he's that cold, he may try to sell it right away."

"That's going to be a fun phone call." I grimace.

"I can call for you," Lach offers.

"No, I need to do it." I yawn, exhaustion settling over me.

"Finish up," Charlie says, gathering empty mugs. "I'll sleep with you tonight."

"Thank you. All of you." I smile at them, failing to smother another yawn.

"G'night, Bug," Lach says, ruffling my hair.

"Night," I murmur, squeezing Cam's hand as he passes.

Jack pulls me into a quick hug. "Let me know if you need anything. Love you."

"Love you, too."

Charlie pulls me out of the chair and down the hall to the guest bedroom. I flop on the bed, descending into sleep almost immediately. I barely feel her untying my boots or easing my jacket off. She had shown up out of the blue a year ago and became the bond that glued our family together. She's my ride-or-die. My best friend. I snuggle into her side and fall into a deep, dreamless sleep.

2

The silence is suffocating as I hoist myself into a seat at the empty bar. I closed the pub yesterday in honor of James, but we're open as usual tonight, and I need to be on my A-game. I know that's what he'd want. I fiddle with my phone, trying to drum up the courage to call James' son. I never let guys intimidate me, but this is different. I thought I would spend my entire life in this pub. It's my home. Now that everything hangs in the balance, I can't stop thinking about what'll happen if he doesn't accept my offer.

I slam my fist on the bar. Fuck this. I punch in his number and hold the phone to my ear. Taking a deep breath, I count to ten before releasing it.

"Thank you for calling Andersen Law Firm. How may I direct your call?" a sweet voice asks on the other end of the connection.

"Mr. Andersen, please."

"May I tell him who's calling?"

"Isla MacLeod."

"Please hold, Ms. MacLeod."

My heart ratchets up a notch as the hold music nearly ruptures my eardrum. *Fucking breathe, Isla.*

"Andersen."

I jump at his curt voice but quickly recover, pulling myself together. "Mr. Andersen, this is Isla MacLeod. Before I begin, I want to offer my condolences for your father's death. He was a great man."

He grunts.

I clear my throat, plowing ahead with my spiel. "I've been working for your father for years. We had a verbal agreement that I would take over the pub. I'm not sure if he talked to you about it. Or me." I know full well he didn't. He never picked up when James called him.

"He didn't."

"I'd like to make an offer."

"How much?"

Fuck, this guy didn't mess around. "I looked at similar businesses in surrounding towns, and seventy-five thousand pounds seems more than fair."

He grunts again. "I'll have a real estate lawyer lock into it and get back to you."

"I'm open to negotiation," I say, unwilling to risk him selling it to someone else. He ignores me.

"Is the pub closed down now?"

"I was planning on opening it today and keeping it open through the sale–if that's amenable to you."

"As long as you're aware that you can't keep the money just because you're running the pub in the interim. All proceeds will be transferred into my father's estate."

"That's perfectly fine as long as we agree that you'll get back to me on my offer."

"Good. Anything else?"

"When are you planning on having your father's funeral? There are a lot of us here that would like to attend and pay our respects."

"I'm flying his body to London. His burial will be here."

"Oh." My heart breaks. James would hate that.

"If there's nothing else, I need to end our call."

"That's all, thank you." He hangs up before I can give him my information, so I call back and give it to his secretary.

Goddammit. I should have flown to London to talk to him face to face, where I could see his body language and get him to agree to the sale in person. I sigh, jerking my hands through the knots in my hair. There's no time for a pity party when I have so much work to do. With James gone, I'm the only one here besides the kitchen staff–who are now getting paid out of my pocket. Which means I'm the only one working front of house. It's a bloody nightmare.

Days pass by in a blur. I collapse into my bed at 1 a.m. every morning and head back to work at 10 a.m. to prepare the pub for lunch. As soon as I get word on the sale, I'll hire help, but until I have the signed contract in my hands, I'm not spending a single cent more than I need to. So, for now, it's just little old me. And little old me is fucking exhausted.

I STILL HAVEN'T HEARD from James' son two weeks into this hell. I've called and left messages with his secretary three times, but beyond going to London myself, I'm not sure what more I can do. If I haven't heard from him in two more days, I'm going to close the pub and make the drive down. I'm getting desperate.

A NOTIFICATION STARTLES me awake at four the following morning, telling me the house has just rented for the next three months. It's a fucking headache, but there's no way I can resist the influx of much-needed cash. I receive a monthly stipend from a trust fund my parents set up before their deaths, but I'm stretching that thin by paying the kitchen staff. Now I have to spend my entire Sunday–my only day off–cleaning a gigantic house for a stranger. Far from the day of rest I had been dreaming about all week.

The Manor House is technically the groundskeeper's house for Amhuinnsuidh Castle. Jack took over the maintenance of the castle when our parents died. I lived with him until I turned eighteen, when I realized I didn't want him breathing down my neck every time I brought a guy home. Lachlan joined me in the manor house a year later when he returned to help Jack with the estate. It was nice having him around—especially his cooking.

I'M SERIOUSLY REGRETTING my decision to rent out the house by the time I finish scrubbing the fifth and final bathroom. It's nearing nine o'clock when I wheel out the last of my odds and ends in an old, beaten-up suitcase. I pick my way down the treacherous path to the cottage with only the light of the moon to guide me. By the time I reach the door, it feels like my shoulder has been ripped from its socket. I jerk up on the door handle and jam my hip into the wooden planks, huffing in frustration. No matter how many times I've tried to fix it, the door insists on being a stubborn asshole. I have to throw my entire body against it before it finally opens. I leave my suitcase in the entry, set my alarm on the way to the bedroom, and throw myself onto the bed, passing out the second my head hits the pillow.

I JERK awake to my alarm blaring under my ear, my cheek sliding over a cold puddle of drool as I slide my hand around the bed, trying to find my phone.

"I'm bloody awake," I mumble, stabbing the off button. The cold morning air sends a shiver down my back as I throw my legs over the side of the bed and sit up. I haven't woken up this early on a Monday in ages. The only saving grace is that I'm headed to the café to pick out some pastries for the new tenant. I'll also be grabbing the largest coffee they offer. Maybe two. I stumble to the bathroom and step into a scalding shower. After scrubbing myself from head to toe, I dry off and pad into the bedroom, grimacing at the state of the clothes overflowing the drawers of the tiny dresser. I pull out the least wrinkled tank top and a pair of jeans. A leather jacket over the top hides most of the creases, and my boots complete the whole 'leave me alone, I'm a bad bitch' vibe I have going on. I stop by the bathroom once more to brush some mascara over my lashes and attempt to wrangle my hair into a braid. I snag my keys from the table by the door and walk up the path toward the garage. My fingertips are freezing as I key in the code to the garage door and watch my pride and joy come into view.

Years ago, Jack had imported a motorcycle. I jumped on the opportunity and upped it to a shipping container, importing the twin of Jack's bike and the car I've wanted since middle school. Her sleek lines give me goosebumps every single time. Nothing compares to the '67 GT500, my very own Eleanor. I sink into the seat and start her up, the sound of the engine roaring through my veins. I open the throttle as wide as I can for the two miles to the café. I pull into the parking lot slowly, trying my best not to disturb any of the customers. I love how the car sounds, but that doesn't mean everyone wants to hear it at seven o'clock in the morning.

This café is my favorite place in the entire world. It sits on the edge of a cliff, a gorgeous beach with turquoise blue water off in the distance. Besides the scenery, their food is fantastic. I come here almost daily, primarily because I can barely cook an egg, let alone an entire meal.

"You're up early, Isla," Jan says, greeting me with rosy cheeks and a huge smile.

"Right? It's a miracle," I laugh. "Someone's renting the Manor House, and I wanted some pastries to give them. Do you care to make me up a box?"

"Of course! Would you like anything to eat for yourself?"

"What kind of question is that?"

"Your usual, then? Morning bun and extra-large iced coffee to go?"

"Yes, please." I run my card through and thank her as she hands me a box, a bag, and my coffee.

"Give me the scoop as soon as you can, okay?" she whispers conspiratorially.

"You got it!" I whisper back, winking at her before I shoulder through the door and walk out into the brisk air. Jan is single, too. But unlike me, her biological clock is ticking. Loudly. It's been sad watching her wait for the right man to walk through the door year in and year out. I wouldn't be surprised if she takes matters into her own hands soon. Lord knows she has enough people in the community willing to help her care for a baby.

I place the box carefully in the car and sit at one a picnic table with a gorgeous view of the sea while devouring my morning bun and sipping on my coffee. I save the middle for last, licking the cinnamon sugar from my fingers before tossing my trash in the bin and heading home. I open the throttle, the wind whipping my hair free from its braid, enjoying my last moments of freedom before I have to worry about a tenant.

I notice three things as the house comes into view. The first is that the renter must be early because there's a car in the driveway. The second is the group of burly men standing on the front stoop, all staring at my car, their mouths hanging open. The third thing has my tires squealing to a stop in the driveway. I know them.

Glasses Guy, Henry, and Grumpy McGrumperson are standing in front of my house. The same three guys I *almost* considered entertaining last summer before I decided it would be way, *way* too much trouble. I fling open my car door, boots crunching in the gravel as I step out. I stare at them, hardly able to believe my eyes.

"Isla?" Henry asks, his voice cracking, eyes wide.

"The three of you rented my house? If I had known it was you, I wouldn't have spent the entire day yesterday spit-shining the fucking floors." I grab the box of pastries from the car and stalk toward them.

"This is *your* house?" Grumpy asks, incredulous.

"Yes, this is *my* house." I smirk. "But don't worry, you three will have it all to yourself. You can walk around naked and flex your muscles at each other all you want. I'll be staying in the cottage back there." I point with my chin.

"I got these for you." I shove the pastries into Grumpy's arms since he's the closest. "What are you guys doing here anyway?" I eye Henry. "Coming back to your favorite place for another holiday?"

Henry clears his throat. "Not quite a holiday. We bought the pub. The one where you work."

The blood drains from my face. "You what?" I whisper, needing to hear it again.

"We bought the pub," Grumpy repeats, annoyed.

"*I'm* buying the pub." My heart's in my throat, making it hard to breathe. I blink hard as tears start to sting the back of my eyes. I *will not* cry in front of them.

"*You?*" Grumpy laughs.

"Yes, me, you motherfucker. I talked with the owner's son. James and I had a verbal agreement for months."

Glasses Guy takes a step toward me. "He didn't tell us he had another offer. If we had known..." He trails off.

"I call bullshit." Grumpy snatches a croissant out of the box and tears into it.

"Is the fact that I've worked the front of house *alone* for the last two weeks bullshit? Maybe me paying the kitchen staff out of my own pocket is bullshit. OR MAYBE ME WORKING THERE SINCE I WAS SIXTEEN, POURING MY BODY AND SOUL INTO THAT PUB IS BULLSHIT!" I yell in his face. I knock the croissant out of his mouth and stomp on it.

None of the guys say anything.

"Sell it to me," I say finally, looking between them, holding their gazes until they look away.

"Never." Grumpy folds his arms over his chest.

I don't trust myself, so I throw the house keys at his head and return to my car, spraying gravel as I peel out of the driveway.

I SPEND the rest of the day on the tractor, readying the ground for my annual sunflower field between the Manor House and the castle. My mom used to plant one yearly, and I've kept it going in her memory. I usually would have already sown the seed, but with the chaos at the bar, I had let the rest of my life slip.

The sun is heading toward the horizon when I see Grumpy walking across my freshly plowed rows. Motherfucker. I turn the tractor off, climb down, and lean against the tire as I watch his shiny boots get swallowed up by the freshly turned dirt.

"Isla–"

"I don't want to talk to you."

"Will you just fucking listen?"

I sigh, tearing my eyes away from his full lips and picking at a rock stuck in the tire. "First, I don't even know your name. Second, why would I listen when you've been such an ornery asshole?"

He growls at me. "Theo. Nice to meet you. I'm sorry, okay? I know I was a jerk back there. At least let me explain."

"Explain why you're an asshole? Or why you think you can come in here with your daddy's money and buy up a piece of my town?" I die a little inside the second the words leave my lips. Why did I say that when I directly benefit from generational wealth? Fuck me.

"Stop." His countenance darkens. "You know nothing about me."

I sigh. "Fine. Tell me all about you, Theo the Asshole. Just help me while you do it."

He nods and follows me to the edge of the field. I push a bag of seeds into his arms and scoop out a handful, dropping them a few inches apart as we walk down the row.

"First of all," he says, his voice gruff, "every single penny my brothers and I have was earned by us."

"Got it," I say, grabbing another handful of seeds.

"Second, we're here because my brothers need a distraction. The last time they acted like themselves was when we were here in Harris. The day I saw the advertisement for the pub, I thought it was fate. If I had known you were planning to buy it, I wouldn't have pursued it."

"Now you know. You can sell it to me," I point out.

"I'm getting to that," he bites out, keeping a tight rein on his annoyance. "Like I said, we need a distraction–"

"From what?" I interrupt.

"Our parents were murdered a little less than a year ago."

"Oh my god." *Oh my god.* And here I am, acting like a total bitch.

"My brothers went downhill really quickly after it happened. The construction business we ran together started to struggle, so I decided to do something drastic to get us out of our funk. I drained our savings to buy the pub. They need this, Isla." The evening sun highlights the planes of his face, turning his dark brown eyes into caramel.

"I understand. I'm sorry I went off the deep end like that."

"Don't apologize. It must have been quite a shock."

I laugh, "You could say that." I grab another handful of seeds and turn away, but he shifts the bag to his hip and touches my wrist. I freeze.

"I have something to ask you."

I only raise an eyebrow at him, desperately trying to ignore how my skin is buzzing where his fingertips press into my flesh.

"Will you help us at the pub?" He squeezes me before dropping his hand. "We'll pay you, of course."

"I have a better idea."

"Let's hear it."

"I'll help you at the pub–for free–but you and your brothers have to help me renovate a building. Contractors are few and far between at the moment." I start on the next row.

"What building?"

"I'll show you tomorrow. I want to get this row done before the sun sets."

"It's a deal," he says, his lips curling into the smallest of smiles.

"Really? Even without seeing the building?"

"I don't know why, but I trust you. Even if you did try to bust my face open with a set of keys and ripped a croissant out of my mouth."

"I'd say I'm sorry, but I'm not." I shrug, biting my lip to keep myself from smiling back at him.

"No worries." He's silent for a few moments as I finish the row. "What are you planting?"

I drop the last seed in and stand up, smiling. "Sunflowers."

3

heo's POV
My heart stutters as Isla turns that mega-watt smile on me. Her hair glows like molten lava in the evening light, her skin golden, sun-kissed freckles beckoning me. My body's response to her annoys me to no end. She is the feistiest slip of a woman I've ever met. Watching her bend over repeatedly in those tiny little jean shorts and muck boots is not what I had envisioned when I stalked over here a few hours ago.

After that red-eye, I tell myself that I want to drink a beer, fill my belly, and go to sleep, but that's a gigantic goddamned lie, and I know it. The only thing I can think about is getting her to smile at me like that again. This move was supposed to be simple. Easy. A fucking walk in the park, for Christ's sake.

"Hey, Grumpy McGrumperson, are you coming?"

"What did you just call me?" She laughs, green eyes sparkling as she swings onto the tractor.

She pats the wheel well next to her. "Come on up. I'll park her in the barn and drive you back home."

I don't want to be that close to her. She's the exact kind of trouble I don't need right now. Or ever. I tell myself the only reason I'm taking her up on her offer is because it's almost dark, but I'm lying to myself. I grab hold and climb up, perching beside her like a goddamned parrot. She gazes up at me out of the corner of her eye, a grin pulling at the corner of those full lips.

"Drive," I snap, quickly turning my head away so she can't see the smile I can't seem to hold back. Isla puts the tractor in gear, her hand so tiny on the shifter it's almost startling. It can't be safe for her to be out here alone like this. "Where's the barn?" I ask, noticing that we're driving away from the house.

"On the other side of the castle grounds."

"The other side? Does that mean the field is part of the grounds?"

She nods. "The Manor House, too."

"Wait a damn minute." My mind races as I scramble to put the pieces together. "You own the castle, too?"

"Not just me—my brother, sister, and I each own a third."

"Then why the hell are you staying in that run-down shack? It looks like it could tumble off the cliff's edge at any moment."

Her shoulders stiffen. "It is *not* run down."

"Fine, why are you staying in the minuscule cottage instead of the castle?"

"Because my brother is a damn busybody, that's why. You're starting to remind me of him–sticking your nose places it doesn't belong."

I raise my hands in mock surrender. "Apologies. I didn't realize it was a sore subject."

She glares at me, her eyes dark in the dusky light. She pulls the tractor into the pitch-black barn like she's been doing it since childhood. Hell, maybe she has. God knows she's full of surprises. I jump to the ground, reaching my hand up to help her down, but she jumps off the other side and waits for me by the door instead.

"Come on," she says roughly, grabbing her jacket from a hay bale.

I follow her to her car, folding myself into the passenger seat with some difficulty. I look over at her as she gets in, amazed at how twilight has transformed her. Instead of a spicy ray of light, the night has turned her into a darkling sprite, complete with mahogany hair, leather, and the attitude of a honey badger. I hate tc admit it–even to myself–but I'm enamored. I can't wait to see what she's like when it rains. When it snows. At sunrise. Hell, I'm starting to think every day of every season will never be enough.

Those thoughts fly out of my head as she peels away from the barn, her hair billowing around her head as she shifts through the gears. Gravity presses me back into my seat, and I hang on for dear life. Thirty seconds later, she cranks the wheel, and we skid to a stop in the Manor House driveway, perpendicular to the road. She carefully backs into the garage and turns off the car, hopping out before I can say anything. I slowly unclench my fists, my knuckles aching. She's pulling her hair into a messy bun as I join her in the driveway, my knees trembling.

A glimmer of skin shows between her top and her shorts, and before I can stop myself, I'm toe-to-toe with her, breathing in the smell of her shampoo. She looks up at me, a doe in headlights. I jam my hands in my pockets to keep from wrapping :hem around her waist. Her tongue darts out to moisten her lips. Fuck me. I want to grab a handful of her hair and pull her mouth to mine. Find out what she tastes like.

"Fuck," I say under my breath, trying to rein myself in. Her pupils blow out at that one word, and I nearly lose contro.. I kiss her cheek, inhaling her as I slide my lips over her skin. "Goodnight, Sunflower," I whisper against her ear before turning around and heading to the house. I don't let myself look back.

I CLOSE the door behind me and sag against it. This was a mistake. Images flash on the back of my eyelids. The teasing smirk as I rode beside her on the tractor. The hard-ass that shrugged on her leather jacket and got behind the wheel of a vintage muscle car. The joy on her face as she whipped into the driveway and scared the ever-loving shit out of me. The surprise when I stepped close. The lust when I whispered that one word. Every expression, every laugh is burned into my mind forever. God, this is so fucking bad.

I stalk into the kitchen to find Henry at the stove and Dylan on his laptop. "We need to talk."

"What the hell took you so long?" Henry asks, slamming a spatula on the counter.

"It's a long story."

"Did you find out why she was so upset?" Dylan asks, worry lining his face.

Shit. "Not exactly."

"What the fuck, Theo? That's the whole reason you went. I knew Henry or I should have gone instead."

Henry turns toward me, anger hardening his mouth. "If you didn't find out why she was so upset, what exactly did you talk to her about?"

"I told her about us. Why we're here–"

Dylan cuts me off, "So you told her all about us and didn't think to ask her what the pub means to her? What we're *stealing* from her?"

Fuck. "We're not stealing anything. I'm sorry I'm not as good at this stuff as both of you." I rub the back of my neck, guilt creeping in. "We did come to a compromise, though."

"One she's happy with?" Henry asks, raising an eyebrow in disbelief.

"I think so. Isla will help us at the pub while we get everything figured out, and we'll help her renovate a building. She's had trouble finding contractors, so it works out for all of us."

The guys perk up, and I'm almost positive it's because they'll get to spend more time with her. It pisses me off. "I know I can't tell either of you what to do, but you shouldn't get involved with her. Remember what happened last time."

Dylan's only response is to slam his laptop shut and head upstairs. Henry motions for me to sit at the table and then places a skillet with a delicious-looking frittata in the middle. He grabs two plates and portions it out. "Asking us not to get involved with her is asking a lot, Theo. Dylan is already infatuated with her. I haven't been able to stop thinking about her since that night at the pub months ago. Maybe coming here was a horrible idea."

"Maybe so, but there's no going back now."

Henry sits across from me, raking his hand through his hair. "I know what happened with Katie has stuck with you, but it's in the past for us. We're all adults. We can handle ourselves." He shoves a bite of food into his mouth, his gaze on his plate.

"Fucking hell. You're both completely whipped, aren't you?"

Henry studies me, smirking. "She got under your skin tonight, didn't she?"

"You don't even understand," I groan, grabbing a beer from the fridge and taking a long drag.

"Then tell me."

I shake my head. I'm not ready to share. "Maybe tomorrow," I mumble, taking my plate to the sink. "Thanks for the food. See you in the morning." I take the stairs two at a time, not daring to look back at him. Scared of what he'll see in my eyes. I vow that I'll stay away from her as much as possible. Katie is still a barely healed scar across my heart, and there's no way I'll let another woman rip the three of us apart again.

I have difficulty falling asleep that night, but when I finally do, I dream of fiery hair and a freckled nose.

4

I wake exhausted, head foggy, muscles sore. I grab a towel, shove my feet in my sneakers, and head out the door like I do every morning. My attention is glued to the path as I carefully pick my way around the rocks, careful not to twist an ankle as I make my way to the beach. I don't see Henry until he's jogging across the sand toward me. His torso is gloriously bare, thick muscles shifting with every step, his skin burnished by the morning light.

"Morning, Isla." The baritone of his voice slides over me like whiskey, lodging deep in my core.

He stops several feet away, blue eyes sparkling, a shy smile pulling at his lips, dark hair falling in gentle waves over his forehead. I squeeze my hands into tight fists, resisting the urge to reach out and run my fingers through it.

"Morning," I mumble, realizing I didn't look in the mirror before leaving the house. I wipe underneath my eyes, hoping yesterday's mascara hasn't turned me into a raccoon.

"You came down here for a swim?" he asks, eyeing my towel. I nod. "It has to be freezing." He shivers at the thought, goosebumps racing over his skin.

"It is," I say, looking away from him so my eyes don't wander places they shouldn't.

"Why, then?"

"Try it every morning for a week. You'll never go back, trust me."

"Deal," he says, grinning.

"Wait–" That is *not* what I meant. I sigh and follow him toward the water. I should have kept my stupid mouth shut.

I drop my sweats in a heap on the sand, hesitating for a second.

"What are you waiting for?" Henry calls, testing the water with his toes.

I grimace. "I usually swim naked. I didn't bring a change of clothes, and it'll be freezing walking back up with wet clothes on."

Henry steps away from the water, turns his back on me, and drops his shorts to the sand. He looks over his shoulder, grinning from ear to ear. "Your turn. I won't look till you're all the way in the water." He keeps his back to me as he walks into the waves. I can't tear my eyes away as the rounded globes of his backside disappear below the surface. I swallow hard. Holy fuck. I drop my bra and underwear and jog into the water, dropping down once I reach my waist, so the water covers my breasts.

"You can turn around now." Henry turns toward me, powerful muscles bunching from the cold. I laugh as his teeth start chattering.

"Shut up," he chuckles, splashing me. "How are you not freezing?"

"I come from tough stock. My mom always said we're the type made for surviving long winters, not running."

"You sure about that? You look pretty damn fit to me."

I laugh. "Thanks to the hours I spend at the gym every day."

"Gym, huh?"

"Yeah, you don't look like you'd be familiar...they usually have weights you lift to build muscle," I say, somehow managing to keep a straight face.

He rolls his eyes at me. "There's a gym near here? I searched online yesterday but couldn't find anything close."

"It's a private gym only open to our community, so it's not listed. You and your brothers are welcome to work out anytime."

"If you'll tell me where it is, I'll check it out this morning," he says, dipping down so he's at eye level with me. "How much is it?"

"It's free. I'll take you there if you'd like. I'm going anyway."

"What do you mean free?"

"My brother, brothers-in-law, and I opened it years ago. We've expanded it over time to accommodate everyone. It's a way to give back to the community that has done so much for us."

He dunks his head under, blowing water from his lips as he comes back up. His eyelashes clump together, highlighting the depths of his ocean-blue eyes. "I have to admit that I'm envious of your way of life here. Time moves slower than it does in the States. Everyone is so incredibly kind. Back home, it seems like everyone is too busy struggling to survive to care about their neighbors."

"That can't be a healthy way to live." I can't imagine my life without the community that has supported me since I was a baby.

"It's not," he says, his teeth chattering.

"Fuck, you must be freezing!" My gaze hangs on his purple-tinged lips for a second too long. I pull my hair over my shoulders and stand. It plasters to my skin, shielding my breasts. Henry stays low in the water, his eyes hooded. "You ready to go?" I ask him, my heart pounding in my chest.

"I'll stay in if it means I get to spend more time with you."

I laugh, ignoring the butterflies fluttering in my stomach. "You'll freeze to death."

"It would be worth it, Isla." He pushes his hair out of his face, droplets cascading over his nose and cheeks. "I always wondered how sailors could be lured to their deaths by a siren's call. I understand it now." He pushes up, water lapping at the V of his abdominal muscles. Heat pools in my belly. He takes a step toward me and reaches out, running the back of his fingers over my cheek. His thumb sweeps down over my chin, catching on my bottom lip, pulling slightly. My knees buckle, and he catches me easily, one arm behind my back, drawing me onto my tiptoes, my nipples pebbling against his chest. I barely breathe, not sure if I want to break the spell or if I want to climb him like a motherfucking tree. He holds my gaze for a few more seconds before shaking his head like he's trying to wake up from a dream. His whole body trembles as he releases me, whether from desire or cold, I'll probably never know. He raises one eyebrow and then turns his back, waiting for me to leave the water and get dressed.

I try, but I can't get my feet to move anywhere but closer to him. I suck in a ragged breath, and he looks over his shoulder at me, his gaze dropping to my lips before bouncing back up. "Isla, I need you to go get dressed. This tension is testing my limits. You're supposed to hate me, remember?"

"You're really fucking hard to hate." My heart pounds in my chest as I press my hand to his shoulder, muscles rippling under my touch. Turning him toward me, I sweep my fingers over his throat, watching in fascination as his Adam's apple bobs. I run my hand over the ridge of his pecs, biting my lip when he jerks as I pass over his nipple.

"Isla," he growls, catching my hand in his before I can continue my exploration. A full-body shiver goes through him, and I notice he's clenching his jaw so his teeth don't chatter.

"God, I'm sorry. You're freezing. Come on." I pull his hand and walk toward the beach. "I won't look if you don't look."

"What if I want to look?" he asks, keeping his eyes on my face as we step out of the water.

I laugh. "Do you want *me* to look at *you* right now? You were just in freezing cold water."

He grimaces. "Good point. Don't you dare look at me." He runs toward his clothes, leaving me laughing in the arctic wind.

As much as I want to, I don't look until he gives the okay. I really shouldn't have encouraged him to swim. He only had his shorts and T-shirt, which are now stuck to his wet skin. He looks colder than he did before we got out of the water.

"Come on," I call, jogging toward the path. I make sure he's following me, worried about the blue tinge to his skin. When we get to the cottage, I grab his hand and lead him inside. "You're not getting out of my sight until I'm sure you're not going to die of hypothermia."

"I'm fine," he scuffs, a violent shiver wracking his body.

God, he looks big in here. His head almost hits the ceiling. I blow out a breath, trying to focus. I motion for him to follow me into the bathroom, cranking the shower handle and turning toward him. He dwarfs me in the tiny space, making me feel small. Delicate. Feminine. I drag my gaze up along the column of his throat, taking in the strong lines of his jaw, the dimple in his chin. We stare at each other, steam billowing between us, making it seem like a dream.

I turn to leave, but he grabs my hand and pulls me toward him. I stop myself from careening into him with a hand on his chest. "I will not have you dying of hypothermia because of a morning skinny dip. Get in the shower, Henry."

"Yes, ma'am," he whispers, his voice husky. Sexy. Sensual. I slam the bathroom door as I leave and head straight back outside, desperately needing the cold air to blow away the needy bitch that had taken over my body.

I almost trip over Dylan's feet as I rush out the door. "E-Everything okay?" He stammers, looking into the cottage like something will burst through the doorway and attack us.

"Fine," I bite out, fanning my shirt away from my body.

He points to the laptop cradled in his arms. "I thought we could go over numbers sometime today and maybe even procedure if you have the time."

"What time is it?" I ask, completely turned upside down. This morning could have been thirty minutes or eight hours.

Dylan pulls his phone from his pocket. "Almost 9:30."

Fuck. I normally finish up at the gym right about now. "Meet me at the pub in an hour?"

"Do you want to drive together?"

"Are you going to stay the whole night?" I ask, realizing I have no clue how this arrangement will work now that I'm not the one taking the bar over.

"Are *you*?"

I sigh. "I guess we probably have a lot more to talk about than numbers and procedure, don't we?" Henry chooses that very inopportune moment to appear in the doorway, a *very* small towel the only thing covering him. My gaze dips below the hem of his towel, taking in the perfection of his thighs. Fucking hell. I clear my throat. "This is NOT what it looks like," I tell Dylan, taking a step away from Henry.

"Of course not," Dylan says, pressing his lips into a hard line. I panic, thinking he's disappointed, but then I see the wink he throws Henry. What the hell?

"I'll meet you up at the house in an hour," I tell Dylan, watching him walk up the path until he's almost at the house before I spin around to give Henry a verbal lashing.

"I thought we were going to the gym," Henry asks before I can start my lecture. He's holding the towel loosely, and I'm having a tough time not focusing on how it dips–

"Isla?"

My gaze snaps up to his, and I clear my throat. "Can I get a rain check?"

"Sure. Speaking of the pub, what's the slowest time of the day?"

"Around three, usually."

"Perfect. I have a meeting at the visa office in an hour, but if I get done early, maybe the four of us can hammer out this agreement today. I want to make sure we're all happy with it."

"Fine. Now please go get dressed."

"Anything for you, my prickly pear." He turns and saunters into the cottage. I watch slack-jawed as his muscles shift with every step, and fuck if I don't want to trace them with my fingertips. With my tongue. With my teeth. This summer is going to kill me.

5

I shoo Henry out of the cottage the second he's dressed, not trusting myself with him for a moment longer. My body is in overdrive. These are three men I shouldn't be able to stand to be around. I should hate them, just like Henry said. But now I have a total infatuation with Henry. And I was *disappointed* when I thought Dylan was upset over Henry being naked in the cottage. Why should I even care what Dylan thinks? I barely know the man! And then there was last night. Planting the sunflowers with Theo was—well, it wasn't awful. I still don't like him, but I can't stop thinking about him. I give myself a pep talk in the mirror as I'm getting ready, reminding myself that these men *stole* the pub right out from under me and then refused to sell it back to me. Theo's explanation niggles at the back of my brain, but I ignore it. I need to stay emotionally detached. I need to become the Ice Bitch of Harris.

Smirking, I pull my hair into a ridiculously messy bun—I should be embarrassed, honestly. I wiggle into ripped black jeans, an old ripped band tee, and my jacket, running back to the bathroom at the last second to fasten my biggest pair of gold hoops to my ears. I sit on the couch and lace up my trusty boots. This pair has been with me for three years, but I've been wearing the same style for ages. They're my safety blanket. All I need to do is look down at them to feel like a bad bitch. Although anyone who knows me knows that if my shoes matched my personality, I'd be wearing Dorothy's red sparkly slippers. I snort at the thought. I debate between my car or the motorcycle on the way up to the house, but I don't think I have the guts to make Dylan sit behind me on the bike. Arms around my middle. Chin on my shoulder. Thighs—I pull myself out of my daydream when I see Dylan waiting for me by the garage.

I thought he was kind of dorky that first night in the pub, but that first impression was horribly wrong. He's dressed in all black, slim jeans and bomber jacket, making him look like he just stepped out of a cologne commercial. He's wearing his glasses, but whatever the opposite of nerdy is, they're that.

"Hey," he greets me softly, a huge smile on his face.

"We're twinsies," I laugh.

"I like it." His gaze sweeps down my body and back up, catching on my lips.

Sweet baby Jesus. I'm in so much trouble.

"Everything okay?" he asks, studying my face.

"Yeah, just having an existential crisis."

"Do you do that often?"

"Pretty much daily," I chuckle.

"We should start a club. The Existential Islanders."

I snort. "I'll have jackets made."

He grins. "I like you." There is no ulterior motive behind the words—just honesty.

"I think I like you, too." I key in the garage code. "Don't tell anyone. I have to keep up my bad girl image."

He pretends to lock his lips and then throws me the imaginary key. I motion for him to get in the car as I sink into the driver's seat. I turn her on, and Dylan's eyes roll back, his head dropping against the headrest. I shift in my seat, my visceral reaction to him burning through my body, turning my cheeks scarlet.

He looks at me, his glasses slightly askew, those big brown eyes wide open. "Holy shit, Isla."

"Right?" I grin and pull out of the garage, taking a left out of the driveway. I hold back on the gas, not sure if I can handle finding out if he likes a wild ride. If he does–Lord help me.

"You're not going to open her up?" he asks, confusion on his face. "Theo told me he thought he was going to die last night."

I laugh. "Do you have a death wish?"

He shrugs. "I think I'd be okay dying in this car."

"Yeah?" *Fuck me.* I don't dare look over at him. If I see the look that I *know* is on his face, I'm done for. Instead, I turn on the radio and stomp on the gas pedal, shifting through gears seconds apart. Dylan rolls his window down and sticks his arm out, riding the air current. The wind roars through the car, pulling my hair from its elastic. I blow past the pub, feeling too free to deal with what's waiting for me there. I sneak a look at Dylan and find him staring at me with a look I can't place. He blushes, throws his head back, and croons along with the song, using the dashboard as makeshift drums. I join in, singing at the top of my lungs. When we come to the roundabout, I do the responsible thing and head back toward the pub. I wish I could keep driving like this forever. Music up, good company, the sound of the engine drowning out the noise in my head. I pull into the parking lot and turn off the car. We both stare out the windshield in dead silence before bursting into laughter.

"God, I haven't had fun like that in so long," he wheezes, wiping tears from his eyes.

"That's kinda lame," I joke. "It was just a car ride."

"No, it wasn't. It was a ride in *this* car with *you*."

The grin slips from his face, and suddenly, the high-fashion model version of Dylan is looking back at me, oozing sex appeal. Heat roars through my veins, my fingers itching to slide off his glasses and pull his face to mine. I push the urge down and hop out of the car, slamming the door behind me. I look at Dylan before going inside. He's still sitting in the car with a slightly dazed look on his face. I raise my eyebrow at him when his gaze meets mine. He gives me a shit-eating grin and unfolds himself from his seat, pausing with a hand on the door, looking at me looking at him. He's fucking gorgeous. He closes the door gently, his eyes locked with mine.

"Say it."

"Say what?" I ask.

"What you're thinking. Life would be much easier if everyone were honest with each other."

He's right, it would be. But that's also terrifying. I clear my throat. "I was just thinking about how good you look in my car."

"Yeah?" The corner of his mouth tilts up.

"Yeah." My breath stutters as he stops in front of me, the toes of his shoes touching the toes of my boots. I crane my neck to look up at him, my heart in my throat. He dips his face closer, his thumb brushing my cheek.

"You have freckles in your eyes," he whispers in wonder.

"Are you two going to stand there forever, or are we going to get to work?" Theo asks roughly, poking his head outside, grumpy as ever.

Dylan blows out a loud sigh, pushing his glasses up his nose. "I guess we better get started." He holds the door open for me to pass.

The second my foot crosses the threshold, I'm struck by how different it feels inside. The hope I always carried with me, knowing that it would one day be mine, has disappeared. It's not a good feeling. Dylan sets his bag on the bar and pulls out his laptop. I round the bar and pour two glasses of water, making sure there's lots of ice. I watch as he pulls up the spreadsheets I sent him last night. We spend the next hour in accounting hell. Once we hash out all the numbers and I walk him through payroll, he closes his laptop and pulls out a notebook.

"What about marketing?"

I laugh. "What marketing?"

His eyebrows shoot up. "Really? So that's a completely untapped market. I know you must have some ideas–anything you're willing to share?"

I think for a second. "I've been wanting to go check out some of the pubs in Edinburgh. Not to copy," I clarify, "but to get inspiration."

"Great idea. Maybe you and I can go next weekend? I'm sure Henry and Theo could keep it running for one night."

"Can they, though?" I wince, thinking of everything that could go wrong.

"I'm sure it won't be as seamless as when you're here, but they're capable. We all took a bartending class before we came out, and lord knows we all know how to pour beer. Surely the two of them can keep up with you."

The dirtiest thoughts come to mind the second his sentence registers. My cheeks flame, and I gulp down my water, immediately choking on it. Dylan hits my back, trying to help. I look at him to tell him I'm okay, but there must be something in my expression. He sucks in a strangled breath. "I did *not* mean it like that."

Coughing turns to laughter. I wipe at the tears leaking from my eyes. I shrug an apology.

"You have a fucking filthy mind, don't you?"

"Guilty as charged," I admit. Why am I like this?

"Ready to talk about how this whole thing is going to work?"

I nod, shucking off my jacket and draping it over the barstool to my left. "I've been mulling it over, and I think we need to have two people here and two at the job site. Obviously, I'll be here every day, so maybe the three of you can rotate? That way, each of you learns how to run the pub from open to close, inside and out. Then the other two can work with my brother on the renovations. What do you think?"

"That seems fair. I'll tell the guys tonight and let you know if they have any issues with the arrangement." He pulls an envelope out of his bag and slides it over the bar to me.

"What's this?" There's a check inside for almost ten thousand dollars.

"The wages you're owed plus paying you back for the kitchen staff."

My heart softens the tiniest bit. "You don't need to do this. That was my decision."

He scoffs. "It was your decision when you thought the pub was yours. We owe you that money, Isla. It's only fair." He squares his body, facing me head-on. His teeth press into his bottom lip, making my heart jump. "I don't want us starting off with bad blood." He reaches out with one finger, brushing it over my knee in the lightest of touches. "You're sure we're good?"

"I can't promise I won't miss the dream I had for this place, but yes, you and I are good."

"And Henry? Theo?"

"Henry and I are good. Theo? That's to be determined."

"Understandable." He glances at his watch. "Ready to teach me some stuff?"

Before I can answer, Theo pushes through the door from the back, three plates in his arms, a kitchen towel slung over his shoulder. "Thought I'd experiment a little," he mumbles, setting the plates in front of Dylan and me. He puts his plate on my left, moving my jacket out of the way before sitting down. I wonder if he's met Greer yet or if she knows he's using her kitchen. I can't wait to see how that goes down.

"What's this?" I ask, breathing deep, my mouth watering.

"I found a recipe online for cottage pie. I tweaked it the tiniest bit to elevate the flavor." He looks at me, his eyes searching mine, "I'm not trying to change things. Just improve on what's already here. I want you to understand that."

I'm stunned. Is it possible this man is empathetic? "Thank you," I whisper. He nods, stretching his mouth into what I think is supposed to be a smile but looks more like a grimace.

6

Dylan's POV

The first customer walks through the door just as we're shoveling the last bites of Theo's cottage pie into our mouths. I don't get the chance to think about how this is the first time I've seen him in the kitchen since our parents died. Or how this is the first time he's cared about anything other than our survival since that day nine months ago.

"Ready?" Isla grins up at me, emerald eyes sparkling.

Her eyes meet mine, and I can't manage to speak around the boulder lodged in my throat. The best I can do is nod. She turns back toward the bar and fills a pint glass with beer before the customer even sits down.

"How are you doing today, Seamus?" She slaps down a cardboard coaster and plunks the beer in front of him.

"Just fine, Isla. Thank you for asking." He thanks her for the beer and hoists himself onto a bar stool. "I'll have the special today, please."

"You got it!" She motions me to the computer, shows me how to put the order in, and sends it back to the kitchen. I bend down a little to take the glare off the screen, mentally cataloging the steps. My cheek brushes her temple, and I swear she pushes back against me for a split second. I inhale sharply, the urge to wrap my arm around her almost unbearable. She steps away, blushing. I clear my throat and straighten my glasses. "What now?"

"Now we wait for the next person to come through the door. It stays pretty manageable until around 5:30."

"What happens after 5:30?"

"It's guns blazing until close."

"Sounds like fun."

She snorts. "You can't lie for shit."

I try not to stare at her as she leans over the bar to talk to Seamus. Her hair is up off her face, loose strands hanging down, brushing freckled skin. My fingers itch to bury themselves in it. Feel the heat from her scalp. I imagine the feel of her cheek against my palm. The way her gaze would dip to my lips. She looks over her shoulder at me, pulling at her bottom lip with her teeth. She laughs at something Seamus says, her eyes still on me. They widen, and she swings her head back toward Seamus and swats at his arm, her cheeks red.

"Do I need to break you two up?" I tease, stepping closer. I hold out my hand to him. "I'm Dylan. Nice to meet you."

"So you broke my girl's heart, did you, Dylan?"

"I–I did what?" I stammer, looking between him and Isla. She rolls her eyes.

"You stole this pub right out from under her."

My stomach sinks. "I assure you that was not my intention."

"Then what *is* your intention, lad?"

"Ignore him," Isla says, firmly pushing me to the other end of the bar. "I'm going to warn you now–there's going to be a lot of that. Almost everyone that comes here has known me since I was knee-high. They all knew I planned on making this into 'The Hebridean.'" She shrugs. "I hope you have thick skin."

"The Hebridean, huh? I like the sound of that."

"Yeah? Me, too." She sticks her tongue out at me.

"Fuck. Sorry." A couple comes through the door, saving my ass. Why can't I keep my foot out of my mouth for more than thirty minutes at a time?

The rest of the day goes by in a complete rush. People don't stop coming in until Isla hangs a sign on the door thirty minutes before closing. I watch her laugh with the people sitting at the bar as she pours their last drinks, an easy smile on her face, like she's entirely at home here.

God. What have we done? My heart physically aches. Fucking hell. I try to breathe, but I can't manage to get enough air into my lungs. Sinking to the floor, I drop my head between my knees, focusing on breathing in through my mouth and out through my nose.

"Hey!" Isla drops down next to me, her small hand cupping my jaw, angling my head so she can look me in the face. "Are you okay?"

"I will be." I close my eyes, focusing on the warmth of her hand against my skin before she pulls away.

I hear her saying goodnight to someone, then a bolt turning. Next thing I know, she's on her knees in front of me, her fingers brushing through my hair.

"What can I do to help?"

I give her a small smile. "Nothing. Truly. I feel better now."

She studies my face, making sure I'm telling the truth. "What was that?"

"That's what's known as a good ol' panic attack."

"Too many people?"

I shake my head. "People don't bother me. The thought that I ripped your dream right out from under your feet does, though. I promise I'll figure out how to make this right, Isla." My voice cracks, but I hold her gaze, hoping she can see the sincerity behind my words.

"God, Dylan. I'll be fine. You better not tell Theo, but I think this was good for me. I've been in a rut for years. It's exciting not to have everything planned out for once."

"Really? You're not just saying that?" I ask, my gaze resting on the freckle on the right side of her top lip that makes me want to–

"Really, really." She stands, holding out her hands so she can help me up. Pure instinct has me pulling her down into my arms. I tug gently, giving her the chance to step back. She doesn't. She folds herself into me, her knees on the floor between my legs, arms around my neck.

"Thank you for caring," I whisper into her neck, my lips moving against her skin.

She pulls back a little so she can look at me. "Thank *you* for caring. It means more than you know."

"Anytime, Freckles," I whisper, getting lost in her deep emerald eyes.

"You're growing on me, Dylan Walker." She stands, and I let her help me up this time. "What about me?" she asks, tidying up behind the bar.

"What about you?" I grab a rag and start wiping down the countertop.

"Am I growing on you?" She winks, teasing, but I'm not so dumb that I can't see that her question is genuine.

"No," I say, trying to keep a straight face.

"God, you're worse than Theo." She throws a slice of lime at me, laughing.

"I liked you from the moment I met you, Isla. You didn't need to grow on me."

She freezes for a split second, then continues with her work. "You didn't need to say that." She keeps her eyes down.

"Isla." I wait until she looks at me. "I'll always be honest with you. No, I didn't *need* to say it. I wasn't just returning a compliment. I said it because it's the truth."

"Do you say that to all the girls?"

"Isla."

"Sorry!" She throws her hands up. "I'm not used to nice guys. I don't know how to act, and I definitely don't know how to take a compliment."

We're going to have to work on that. "If it makes you feel any better, we haven't dated anyone in a couple of years."

She spins toward me. "We?"

Fuck. FUCK. My heart hammers in my chest. I nod, unsure what to say to get her to stop asking questions.

"You, Henry, and Theo haven't dated anyone in two years? All three of you?"

I nod dumbly.

She has the weirdest look on her face, and for a second, I'm terrified. Terrified she'll find out the truth and never look at me–us–the same way again.

"What was this last relationship like?" she asks, flipping off the lights. I follow her out the front door, waiting for her to lock up before saying anything.

"Her name was Katie. It ended badly."

She looks at me expectantly, waiting for the rest of the story.

"Short version is she tore the three of us apart. We barely talked with each other until nine months ago."

"When your parents died?"

I nod. "We won't ever let it happen again."

"She must have been something special."

"She was. In the beginning."

"Can I ask you something? It's kind of personal. Possibly offensive."

"Go for it."

Before she can ask, I hear gravel crunching behind me. "Did you losers forget about me?"

"Oh my god, Theo! I thought you left ages ago!" Isla turns toward him, her hand coming up to cover her mouth.

"Sorry, man." I hit him on the shoulder affectionately. "Need a ride?"

He eyes the Mustang. "Nah, I'll just sleep in the pub," he deadpans.

Isla rolls her eyes. "And you called *us* losers?"

"You haven't told her yet, have you?" I nudge Theo right in the ribs with my elbow.

"Told me what?"

"That I'm not scared of going fast; I'm just scared of your driving," Theo tells her, scowling at me over her head.

"You're such a jerk sometimes," she huffs. "Except when you make me cottage pie."

"He races. Cars. Motorcycles. Pretty much anything with an engine," I explain, spilling his secrets.

Isla turns to Theo. "Seriously? Do you work on them, too?"

Theo raises an eyebrow. "Something wrong with your car?"

"No, my motorcycle. I haven't had the time to get it looked at," she says, catching Theo by surprise. Isla tells him about it, her hands moving a mile a minute. By the time she's finished talking, he may as well be that cartoon wolf with hearts coming out of his eyes. It's that moment I realize that no matter how ornery he acts, he's just as smitten as me and Henry. This summer will be one hell of a ride.

7

The guys meet me at the castle bright and early the following morning. I'm not happy about giving up my gym time for the second day in a row, but mornings are the only time we can all meet, and I want them to get started on the renovations ASAP. I called Jack yesterday to give him a heads-up, and despite wanting to fight someone over the sale of the pub, he was pleased to finally have help.

We enter through the back service door, straight into the kitchen. Charlie and Cam are cozied up at the table, Jack is making coffee, and Lachlan is behind the stove in an apron. Charlie jumps up to hug me.

"Guys, this is Charlie. Charlie, this is Theo, Henry, and Dylan," I say, introducing them.

"Nice to meet you!" Charlie turns her back on them and wiggles her eyebrows at me. "Why don't you all sit down? Breakfast will be ready in just a couple of minutes."

"You're American," Theo says, studying her.

"You caught me!" Charlie laughs. "I came over for work, met these assholes, and never left."

My heart rate ticks up. I hadn't considered how the guys would react to Charlie's relationship with my brother, Lachlan, and Cam. It feels so normal–so right–that I didn't even think about the fact that they may not receive it well. I watch as Theo studies them, then glance over to see Dylan and Henry whispering to each other. Fuck. I should have said something before we came over.

Charlie and Cam help Jack and Lach plate up the food, then carry the platters to the table. As Charlie bends over to set her platter of eggs down, Jack slaps her on the ass. She squeaks in indignation.

Lach pulls her to him, rubbing her butt with his palm. "I'll make it better, Care Bear."

She pulls out of his grip and stumbles into Cam, who kisses her long and hard. "The three of you are insufferable," she says when she finally pulls away, her cheeks rosy, eyes sparkling.

Theo pushes away from the table, his chair grinding against the floor, and storms outside. Henry and Dylan look at each other and then scramble to follow him.

"Sorry, guys, give us a second," I apologize, running after them.

Theo is standing in the courtyard waiting for me, his anger palpable. "Is this some sort of fucking joke?"

"I'm sorry. I should have told you guys before we came over," I stammer, wracking my brain to figure out why he's so upset.

"How'd you find out?" Theo demands.

I pull my brows together in confusion. "Find out what?"

"Don't play dumb, Isla. They're obviously in there mocking us. Is this payback for the pub?" His eyes are murderous.

I turn toward Dylan and Henry. "Will one of you please explain what he's talking about?"

"He thinks they're making fun of our last relationship," Henry says quietly.

"What?" I'm so fucking confused.

Henry turns to Theo. "I think you're misreading the situation. I know it's a slap in the face, but it has nothing to do with us."

"What's a slap in the face?!" I ask, throwing my hands up in frustration.

"Their relationship," Henry says, motioning to the kitchen.

"What, it's against your morals or something?" I ask, grasping at straws.

Dylan barks out a laugh. "Not quite."

"Will one of you please fucking explain what's going on without speaking in code?" I snap, frustrated.

"The three of us were in a relationship with someone a few years ago. Theo thinks you found out about it and are using it to get under our skin," Dylan explains.

My heart thuds in my chest as I replay his words in my mind. "The three of you were in a relationship with one woman? Is that what you're saying?"

Dylan and Henry nod. Theo stands still as a statue, his predatory gaze locked on me.

"And you thought I would use that against you?" I ask Theo.

He finally drops his gaze and sighs. "Sorry. Being in there brought up some stuff I haven't thought about in a while. It seemed like too much of a coincidence."

"Maybe it's not a coincidence. Maybe it's fate," I say as I turn back toward the kitchen, leaving them before I do something stupid like blurting out what I'm really thinking.

Charlie raises her eyebrow at me as I walk back inside. "Everything is fine, just a misunderstanding," I say, looking over my shoulder as the guys follow me inside.

"I'm sorry if we made you uncomfortable," Charlie tells them. "I forget what a shock it must be when people first find out about us."

"It's not shocking to us," Theo mumbles, pulling out a chair for me to sit in.

"Oh," Charlie whispers, her lips forming a perfect O.

"What are the fucking chances?" Lachlan asks, slapping me on the back.

"What am I missing?" Cam asks, looking between all of us, totally lost.

Jack leans back in his chair, enjoying the show.

When Theo doesn't respond, Henry speaks up. "My brothers and

I are familiar with relationships like yours." His cheeks turn scarlet. He's adorable.

"No fucking way!" Cam exclaims. "We haven't ever met anyone like us. It's nice to know we're not alone. Not that we give a damn," he clarifies.

"You all need to eat," I butt in. "We have work to do."

"Yes, ma'am," the three boys echo each other, smirks on all three of their faces.

I STAND side by side with Jack, drying the dishes as he finishes washing them. "Do you want me to take them right to the outbuilding? Or should I show them the entire castle so they can better understand what you're looking for?"

"They need to be familiar with the castle. We want everything to flow and feel cohesive, so it's important for them to get the feel of the place," Jack says, drying his hands.

"That's what I was thinking. I'll show them around today, and then we can work on getting a supply list together tomorrow."

Jack looks down at me, pride in his eyes. "I don't know how you convinced them to do this, but it's brilliant. Thank you."

"Honestly, I'm still not quite sure why they agreed, but I'm running with it."

Jack looks over my head toward the table, then back down at me. "I think I know why they agreed." He smirks, his eyes sparkling.

My brows furrow. "Please share because I'm waiting for the other shoe to drop."

"Isla, all three of them look at you like Mr. Darcy looked at Elizabeth," Cam says, resting his arm across my shoulder.

"In the beginning or at the end?" I laugh, not taking him seriously. They have an entire life to go back to in the States. I haven't asked, but I bet they're planning on getting the pub to the point that it can run without them, and then they'll return to their real lives. I have no interest in getting involved in something that has a guaranteed chance of breaking my heart. Unlike Emily Brontë, I do not find that romantic at all.

We split off after breakfast—Charlie and Jack go to check on the sheep, Lachlan heads up to his office, and Cam has to go to work. That leaves me and the guys to tour the castle on our own.

"What exactly is the purpose of this?" Theo grumbles as we make our way up the original servants' staircase to the central part of the castle.

"I swear I think you're the only person who would complain about being given a tour of a castle by a descendent of the family that built it." I roll my eyes.

"Seriously?" Henry asks, eyes wide.

"Yep. Twelve generations ago." I push through the door at the top of the stairs, and we spill into a wide hallway.

"That's amazing. I can't believe it's stayed in your family so long."

"A lot of sacrifices were made–especially in the last few generations."

Theo butts in, "You still haven't told me why we're wasting time with a tour."

I spin toward him, poking him in the chest. "If you just shut up for one damn minute, I might get to it."

He matches me step for step until I have him backed against the wall with nowhere to go. "We want the renovation to look the same as the rest of the castle," I say, flattening my hand against his chest to keep him against the wall. He looks down at my hand, then back up at me. A muscle ticks in his jaw, nostrils flaring, eyes dark. He raises an eyebrow, challenging me. My heart races in my chest, my gaze bouncing between his eyes and lips. I'm so out of my league. This is bad. So fucking bad. I lick my lips nervously, watching as his pupils blow out in response.

"Um, we'll leave you two to figure this out," Dylan says, dragging Henry down the hall.

Theo steps forward, and I step back, instinct telling me to run. Fast. He keeps going until he has me pressed against the opposite wall.

"Why are you so annoying?" he asks, his face only inches from mine.

I snort. "I'm the annoying one? You're the one that has perpetual ornery disease."

He throws his head back and laughs—a real laugh. God, he's beautiful. I'm mesmerized by the strong column of his throat, the dark stubble sweeping over his jaw. He wipes his eyes and looks down at me. "I didn't plan for this."

"Plan for what?" I ask, focusing on how his tongue slides over his lower lip.

"You," he growls.

My gaze flies to his, and I suddenly feel like an apex predator has me cornered. He catches me by the chin before I can run. Turning my face up to his, he studies me, his gaze catching on my mouth. "

That's my favorite one," he says, sliding his thumb over the corner of my bottom lip.

"Your favorite what?" I rasp.

"Oh good! You're both still alive," Henry says, rounding the corner and stopping abruptly. Theo growls in warning, but Henry ignores it. "We better get a move on if we want to get to the bar in time."

8

The sun is barely peeking its sleepy head above the horizon as I step outside, pulling the cottage door closed behind me. It's unusually cold for this time of year–even my parka and scarf can't keep the chill away as I climb up the path to the house. I text Henry for the third time this morning. No answer. I knock softly on the front door, hoping he's pulling on his sneakers and ready to head to the gym. I'm about to knock again when Henry's arm snakes out and pulls me inside.

"I'm sorry, Isla. I didn't hear my alarm," he apologizes, pulling me up the stairs and into his room. "It'll only take me two seconds to get ready." My brain can't form a response, my gaze glued to the expanse of sleep-warmed skin only inches away from me. I clench my fists, resisting the urge to reach out.

"Isla. Look at me," he says, his voice rough with sleep. I don't dare, scared of what he'll see. "Isla." The command in his voice has me looking up, the raw desire in his eyes causing me to stumble back a step. "Good girl." He holds my gaze as he pulls on an old T-shirt. "Now that I'm safely clothed, what was that about?" he asks, stepping so close I have to strain my neck to keep eye contact.

I clear my throat. "I was thinking how you'll need another layer. It's cold out."

"No, you weren't."

Fuck. "I was thinking about crawling under those covers and warming up." He cocks an eyebrow, snagging my hands from where I have them crossed over my chest.

"God, you're freezing."

"I told you it was cold–" I shriek as he grabs me around the waist and tosses me onto the bed. "My boots!"

"It's laundry day, so I'm washing the sheets anyway," he says, the bed dipping as he lies down behind me, pulling the covers over us."Can I–?"

"Yes," I whisper, having no idea what he's asking me but cognizant of the fact that I would say yes to anything he asks me right now. His broad hand splays over my hip, and he pulls me tight against his body, wrapping me in his arms. I melt into his heat, wedging my frozen fingers between his forearm and bicep.

"Better?" he asks, his chin settling on the crown of my head.

"Now that I know you're the human form of a furnace, I may take advantage of you."

His chuckle slides through me like whiskey, setting my nerve endings on fire. "I'd like that."

Tension slithers around us like a snake, making it hard to breathe. "You're not as prickly today," he muses, the warmth of his breath feathering over my ear. "More like a thicket of blackberries. You know you'll get torn up, but it's worth it for that sweet burst of juice in your mouth."

I snort. "You could be a poet," I say, sarcasm dripping from my words.

"Isla, a lass in the Highlands so grand, with fiery red hair and a freckled hand. Her green eyes sparkled with mischief and glee, in a castle up high, she lived wild and free."

My jaw drops. I twist in his arms to face him. "That was actually good!"

"I'm feeling a little offended by your surprise," he chuckles, blue eyes sparkling.

"It's just that–" I stop before I say something offensive. "Do you write poetry often?"

"I've been writing since grade school. Mostly songs, but I suppose that counts as poetry."

"Will you write me a song?" I ask, sitting up, excited by the idea. Henry's eyebrows shoot up, his gaze softening. He folds his arm behind his head, his bicep bulging obscenely.

"Yes. I would love to write you a song."

I clap my hands. "Good. I can't wait." I glance at my watch. "We should probably get going. It may be too late for a swim, but we could hit the gym and then grab a coffee at the café afterward."

"That sounds good. Give me a minute to get ready." He sits up, kissing me on the cheek before disappearing into the bathroom. I cover my cheek with my hand after he closes the door, dumbfounded at the range of emotions ping-ponging inside my brain. I take a deep breath and reel myself back. When it all comes down to it, he's technically just another tourist who will end up leaving.

I can still feel his hand on my hip, the way his fingers brushed over my stomach. I know in my gut that he would absolutely rock my world and then break my heart when he returned to the States. I stuff my feelings into the deep recesses of my heart and climb off the bed, heading back downstairs before I do something stupid like join him in the bathroom.

"Want to drive?" I ask him, dangling the keys in the air as he jogs down the stairs in a navy-blue sweatsuit.

"Seriously?"

I shrug. "If you want to." What the fuck has gotten into me? I never let anyone drive her. Ever.

"You trust me?"

With my life, I want to say, but I clamp my mouth closed and toss him the keys. I mentally shake myself. *Get it together, MacLeod.*

It takes Henry a mile or two to get the feel of it. He looks so happy that I don't say a word when we fly past the gym. After about ten minutes, I show him where to turn to loop back.

"Why didn't you tell me we passed it?" he asks, catching on immediately.

"You were having too good of a time getting to know her to end it that quickly."

He slows and looks over at me, dark shaggy hair ruffling in the wind, a huge smile on his face. "Thank you, Isla. It's been a while since I've driven a car like this."

"Did you used to race with Theo?" I ask, trying to keep my breathing under control as he grabs my hand and pulls it into his lap.

"Another lifetime ago. I was eighteen and thought I could make it with the big boys." He moves our hands to the gear stick, shifting through the gears as we accelerate. Fucking hell.

"What happened?"

"Theo got in a wreck, and it scared the shit out of me. Seeing him in that hospital bed drove home the risks. I decided I wanted to be around to have a family one day. I never raced again."

I want to ask about what happened to Theo, but I know it will mean more when–if–he opens up and tells me himself. Henry follows my directions and pulls into the parking lot, ducking to get a full view of the building.

"I thought you said this was a small gym."

"It is. Well, at least it started that way." I key the code in the door, and Henry opens it for me, following me through, a chorus of hellos greeting us. "Henry, this is everyone." I raise my voice, "Everyone, this is Henry!" He waves at them, a shy, goofy smile on his face.

"You want to meet back here in an hour?" I ask, checking my watch.

"I thought we were working out together," he asks, his voice tinged with disappointment.

Oh. "That seems like a horrible idea," I blurt out.

"Am I really that bad? Do I smell?" he asks, looking horrified.

"No," I grumble, grabbing his hand and dragging him over to the squat racks so we're not making a scene. "I'll only work out with you if you show me how to get quads like yours." Henry sits on a bench, peeling off his hoodie to reveal a fitted athletic shirt. God. This is going to be absolute fucking torture. He slides off his sweatpants next, revealing shorts that perfectly show off the corded muscle of his thighs.

"Damn boi, he thicc!" Lach calls across the gym, wiggling his eyebrows when I look at him in mortification.

"That's a compliment coming from him," I say, my words muffled as I pull my sweater over my head.

He drops his face into his hands, peeking out at me through his fingers. "Damn it, Isla."

"What?" I look down at my sports bra, making sure everything's tucked in. His shoulder is warm beneath my palm as I use him to steady myself as I slip off my shoes and drop my yoga pants, folding everything up and stacking it neatly on the end of the bench, waiting for him to do the same. He stands without looking at me, setting his clothes beside mine.

"What's first?" I ask, trying to keep the smile off my face as he looks everywhere but directly at me.

"I usually start with split squats."

"Aren't those when you put your foot on a bench behind you and squat with one leg? Like this?"

He faces away from me and drops his head back, staring up at the ceiling.

"Are you not going to look at me the whole time?"

"What's that saying? Gouge your eye out if it causes you to sin?"

"If that's the case, we can gouge them out together because I've been sinning since you took your sweats off."

"You're not making this any easier."

"We're adults. I chose to wear this here. It's what I always work out in." He doesn't say anything. "I'm giving you explicit permission to look at me, Henry."

He turns finally. "Fuck," he says softly, his gaze like electricity crackling over my skin. "I think you were right. It would be better if we work out separately."

"Scared of a little tension?" I tease.

"A little?" He steps closer, backing me against the squat rack. "There's nothing little about this." He doesn't even have to touch me for my body to respond to him. My nipples harden under his gaze, the energy buzzing between us lodging in my core, burning like wildfire through my veins.

"Come back to the cottage with me," I blurt out, raging lust making every single line blur.

"Not yet." He grabs my wrist before I can duck away from him, my pride wounded. "This is more than that, Isla, and you know it." He nudges my chin with his finger, forcing me to meet his gaze.

"What if I don't want more than that?" I ask.

"Don't lie."

"Henry–"

"Look. It's too late." He holds his hands up in surrender. "That thorny personality of yours has dug its claws into my heart and isn't letting go. Look me in the eye and tell me you don't want this, and I'll leave you alone." He backs up a step as if to prove his point.

I can't do that because I want it more than anything. "I'll rip you to shreds," I whisper.

"And I'll love every second of it."

9

Henry's POV*

I try not to breathe as Isla shifts through the gears on the way back to the Manor House. Her scent is everywhere, ripping through the car on the wind, wrapping its fingers around my cock and tugging, forcing me to shift in my seat uncomfortably.

"You okay?" She looks over at me, those green eyes sparkling.

"No. No, I'm not." I clutch the handle on the door as she whips into the driveway, tires squealing.

"The offer still stands, you know," she says as she gets out and slams the door. I unfold myself from the seat, using the car to hide behind as I tuck my cock into the waistband of my sweatpants.

"I meant what I said, Isla. Not yet."

"You're right. It probably wouldn't be good anyway."

I walk around the car, chuckling when she juts her chin out stubbornly. I cage her between my arms, bending down to whisper in her ear. "You know it would be fucking amazing, Red."

She lifts an eyebrow at the nickname. "Prove it."

Fuck. I'm not a strong enough man to deny her, to deny that wildness that draws me like a moth to a flame. I step back, undressing her with my eyes. My cock twitches at the way her nipples harden under my gaze.

"Please," she whispers, her voice cracking. She crosses her legs, trying to ease the ache between them.

"How long has it been since you've been satisfied in bed?"

"A really fucking long time."

"When?"

"Probably never, if I'm being honest."

I growl my disapproval. "If we do this, we're not touching under our clothes until I know you're not going to rip my heart out of my chest and eat it for dinner. Understand?"

"Do what?" she asks, her rosebud lips dropping open in surprise.

I give in to the primal desire roaring through me, dropping to my knees and burying my face between her legs, breathing her in.

"Henry!" she shrieks, struggling in my grip.

"Do you want me to stop?" I ask, jerking down the front of her sweatpants and dragging my tongue along the seam of her shorts.

"Yes," she groans, angling her hips to give me better access.

I jerk back and look up at her. "You want me to stop?"

"No! God, please don't stop, Henry."

Fuck. Hearing her say my name like that makes me want to throw her over my shoulder, haul her up to my room, rip those shorts off, and show her what it means to be worshipped. Her fingers thread through my hair, pulling me closer. I slide my tongue along her slit, tasting her through the fabric. I hum my approval, teasing her clit with my teeth before fitting my lips over her and sucking hard.

"Henryyyy."

Her moan goes straight to my balls, drawing them up tight. I stand before I embarrass myself, pushing my thigh between her legs and maneuvering her hips until her heat is nestled against me. I hold her gaze as I tilt her hips, rocking her back and forth. She whimpers, taking over the movement, her thighs squeezing mine in a vise grip.

"Good girl," I whisper, pushing her hair back from her face. I want to kiss her so fucking badly, but it's a terrible idea. I'll never be able to think of anything else. Color high on her cheeks, teeth lodged in her bottom lip, she looks up at me, the emotion in her eyes punching me in the gut.

"Kiss me, Henry. I won't bite," she whispers, her eyes fluttering closed.

"I don't believe that for a second," I rasp, control slipping through my fingers like sand. I press my thumb against her bottom lip, tugging it down, wrestling with the feral need pulsing through my veins. What's the point in life if not for this feeling? For giving in to the moments that feel like fate crashing down on your head? She opens her eyes, shining emerald pools dragging me under, stealing the breath from my lungs and snapping the last frayed threads of restraint.

"I won't ask again," she whispers.

That's the only push I need. I don't want to live in a world where she's not asking me to kiss her. I cup her face, tracing the delicate sweep of her cheekbones before dipping down to press my lips against hers. Sparks bloom behind my eyelids as she strains up to meet me, her lips soft and sweet against mine. I growl, deepening the kiss as I slide my hands down her back to her ass, pulling her tighter against my leg. She whimpers, relaxing into my hands and letting me take over. She practically climbs my body, wrapping one arm around my neck to support her weight. I slick my tongue over her lips as I rock her against my upper thigh, her torso rubbing against my cock, with every tremor of her body.

She reaches her free hand between us, sliding her hand over the length of my cock. I can feel the heat of her palm through my sweat-pants. Jesus.

"Isla." I want to beg her to stop, but the lie refuses to leave my mouth.

"Come with me. Please, Henry."

"It'll get everywhere." I gasp as she wraps her fingers around me, dragging them up and down my length in the same rhythm I'm keeping with her hips. She twists and reaches into the car, snatching up her purse. I hold her steady as she rifles through it, the triumph in her eyes when she holds up a condom making me laugh. "Now you don't have to be worried about the mess." I almost die inside when she rips it open with her teeth. "I won't touch you. Only the condom," she promises, leaning back to make space between us. She pulls down on the waistband of my shorts and sweatpants, letting my cock swing free. "Holy fucking hell, Henry. You should be proud of that thing." I grunt as she unrolls the condom down my shaft, barely holding it together.

"I said over our clothes, Isla," I say, trying to regain control.

She looks down at my cock, desire blazing in her eyes. "A condom is kind of like clothes. A cock coat." I choke on my reply as she wraps her fingers around me again. "The offer still stands, you know. You can take me down to the cottage, strip me naked, and bury that magnificent cock of yours deep in my pussy. Feel my heat clench around you as we come."

Jesus save me. This woman is going to absolutely wreck me.

"Not fucking yet," I growl, pulling her up, massaging her ass as I drag her pussy up and down my thigh until her eyes glaze over. She jerks me off in the same rhythm, her small hand working overtime. I capture her lips with mine, our tongues tangling in a war neither one of us will win. Her body tenses, back bowing. She moans into my mouth, and that's all it takes to break me. I thrust into her hand, holding her pussy tight to my leg as we fracture into a million pieces, the world around us fading into nothingness. She starts shaking as she comes down, a body-wracking tremor that has her teeth knocking together. I pull up my pants and swing her into my arms, taking her inside and straight to my room. I don't dare let her go as I turn on the shower, keeping her warm while waiting for the water to warm up.

"What are you doing?" she asks, struggling against my grip.

"Let me take care of you, Isla."

"I can take care of myself."

"I know, but you can let someone else do it every once in a while."

She sighs. "Okay." Resting her head against my shoulder, she closes her eyes, a small smile on her lips. I marvel at the reddish-blond of her eyelashes and how they sweep over her cheek. "Why are you staring at me?" she asks, eyes still closed.

'Because my soul is telling me you're the one person I've been searching for my entire life, and I'm scared that if I blink you'll disappear,' I want to say, but instead I say, "You look like an extremely well-satisfied woodland fairy come to claw out my heart with hidden razor-sharp talons."

I startle when she opens her eyes, emotion roiling in their depths. "Why do you think you're not good enough for me?"

"I don't–"

"Don't lie to me, Henry. You're implying that I'll break your heart because you're not deserving of me sticking around to figure this out. It's not fucking true. If I dig my *claws* into you, it'll be because I think you're worth the incredible amount of fear and uncertainty that comes with it. Understand?"

I nod to appease her, but I'll never agree with her. I set her on her feet once the shower is billowing steam, making sure she's steady before loosening my grip.

"Do you need any help?"

"I've got it from here. Will you run down to the cottage and grab my boots and the outfit sitting on my bed?"

"Sure." I grip her waist, leaning in to kiss her cheek. She turns her head at the last second, her lips brushing against mine.

"Thank you, Henry."

"For what?"

"For making me feel alive again."

I close the door behind me, trying not to imagine her stripping off those skin-tight shorts as I walk down to the cottage. I duck through the doorway, and after a quick trip to the bathroom to clean up, I go straight to her bedroom, smiling at the outfit laid out on her bed– black leather shorts, an old cut-up band T-shirt, a black vest, and fishnets. The fact that I'm going to have to work with her for hours while she's wearing that has equal amounts of dread and excitement flooding my system. I fold everything into a neat pile, realizing she didn't lay out a bra or underwear. I open several drawers, rifling through them until I find what I'm looking for. My fingers brush something hard when I grab a pair of underwear, and I shuffle the pile aside to find a royal blue vibrator. I stare at it, images of her using it flashing through my mind like a movie. I act on my impulse and grab it along with the bra and underwear. I hide it in the pile of clothes and walk back to the house, pulling it out when I'm safely inside the bedroom. I'm cradling it in my hand when she walks out of the bathroom, causing her to stop dead in her tracks.

"I don't know if I feel like my privacy was seriously violated or if this turns me on," she admits, using a second towel to squeeze the water from her hair.

"I was looking for your underthings, and my fingers brushed against it. I could have just not said anything, but that seemed dishonest."

"So you brought it up here?" She laughs. "Why?"

"Because I want to watch the next time you use it," I say honestly.

"Fucking hell," she whispers, swallowing hard.

"If that's not something you're interested in, you can take it back to the cottage with you," I say, holding it out to her.

"Absolutely not. What's the fun in that? I don t want anything quite as much as I want you to watch me come."

I toss it into my nightstand drawer and scrub my hands over my face. I don't know how to do this. How to be this close to someone that burns hotter than the sun. I'll combust before I even enter her atmosphere.

"Breathe, big guy." She pats my shoulder, her eyes sparkling. "Go on and take a shower while I get dressed. We have just enough time to stop at the café before heading to the pub." I pull her hand off my shoulder and kiss her knuckles before disappearing into the bathroom. I turn the water as cold as it will go and spend the entire time thinking about what it would be like to wake up next to her every morning.

10

There's a charge in the car's atmosphere on the way to the pub, tension snapping like electricity between us. Once inside, I wait for Henry to disappear into the kitchen and then walk into the janitorial closet and close the door. I sag against it, slowly sliding down until my butt is against the cold concrete floor. What the hell was that? All three guys should be my sworn enemies. My arch nemeses. There must be a glitch in the space-time continuum—that's the only way to explain what happened this morning.

I stare out into the darkness as everything sinks in. I can't stop the grin that pulls at my lips or the giggle that strangles me as I try to hold it back. I know with one hundred percent certainty that he'll be phenomenal in bed. That man knows his way around a woman's body. If he can make me feel like that with his *thigh,* I can only imagine what he can do with his hands. His cock. Not to mention how selfless he is. He wasn't even thinking about getting there until I forced the issue. That turned me on more than how he manhandled me, dragging me up and down his leg until I exploded.

Fuck.

I need to think about something else. Anything else. A vision of the vibrator circling over my clit while Henry watches pops into my head without warning. I fly to my feet, jerking the door open and running straight into Henry's broad, incredibly muscled chest.

"Fuck me so I can get this out of my system," I demand, pushing him against the wall, my hand flat against his chest.

"Not a fucking chance, Red," he says, his voice husky, his gaze dropping to my lips.

"I don't have time for this, Henry."

"Yes, you do." He pushes off the wall, backing me against the closet door. "You have all the time in the world because of us, and I plan to make that up to you."

"With lust?"

"If that's what you want to call it," he says, looking down at me, his eyes dark.

"What does that mean?"

He shrugs, the corner of his mouth ticking up.

"I wish I hated you. It would make things so much easier," I say, not meaning a single word.

"Does that mean I have a chance?" He steps closer, caging me in with his arms, his biceps bracketing my ears. He slides his nose along mine, our lips a hairsbreadth apart. "I started writing a song about you. Do you want to hear it?"

I meet his big-eyed, ocean-blue gaze, my stomach flip-flopping. I nod.

"In the Highlands, where the mist embraces,
There lived a woman with tender graces,
In the pub's warm hum, a love did brew,
With every pour, her heart anew,
Slowly falling, like leaves in the fall,
In Scotland's arms, she found it all."

I swallow hard. I don't miss the ambiguity, how it could be about a man or about my love affair with my homeland. "Tender graces, eh?"

"Artist's prerogative," he says, winking.

"Okay, lover-boy. Time to get to work." I roll my eyes, pushing him toward the front of the pub, my cheeks hot.

. . .

THE PUB IS SLAMMED from open to close, and both of us are dragging by the time I lock up. We drive back to the house in silence, the bite in the air a sweet caress after the dank air of the pub. I need to figure out how to get more circulation in there. No. That's not my responsibility anymore. I haven't had the time to think about what I want to do now that the pub isn't part of my future, and the uncertainty keeps niggling at the back of my mind. I could always help Charlie and the guys with the castle, but I've never been one to do something because it's what's most convenient. I like taking the path of most resistance.

"What are you thinking about?" Henry asks, his gaze glinting in the moonlight as we pull into the driveway.

"I'm thinking about the fact that I have no idea what I'm going to do with my life now."

A look of regret flashes over his face, but he recovers quickly. "You would do well with anything you put your mind to."

"I agree, but I live on a tiny island in the middle of the ocean. There's only so much I can do here. There's already a café. No need for a restaurant since the pub already serves food." I sigh. "I'll figure it out eventually."

"That makes me feel like absolute shit, Isla."

"It should," I say honestly. "But I promise I *will* figure something out. I always do." Henry gets out of the car and stretches, a delicious sliver of his abdomen glowing in the moonlight. He walks around to my door, and I let him open it, taking the hand he holds out to me.

"I'll help in any way I can, Isla. Just say the word."

"Thank you, Henry." I glance down at the cottage, wondering how wise it is to invite him in and get more attached than I already am. I meet his midnight blue gaze, butterflies exploding in my stomach. Fuck it. "Do you want to come down with me? I'll make a fire and some hot cocoa. I think I may even have the stuff for s'mores."

"Sure. I'm going to shower first. Meet you down there in ten?"

"Okay." I pull my jacket tight around my shoulders, fighting back a shiver, and start walking toward the cottage.

"Isla, wait." Henry jogs toward me, slipping his jacket off his shoulders and carefully draping it over mine. "I can't stand to see you shiver like that."

"Thank you." I clench it around my body and hustle down to the cottage before I freeze to death. Once inside, I flop onto the couch, bringing the jacket up to my face and breathing him in. This is dangerous. Allowing myself to get caught up in my feelings is a really bad idea. I've kept the embers of my heart banked for years, and now Henry comes along and douses it with gasoline. Ugh.

I nearly have a heart attack when he bursts through the door, a guitar slung over his shoulder.

"Sorry! I didn't realize it wasn't closed all the way. Don't you want to change?" He asks, looking down at me snuggled deep in his coat.

"That's probably a good idea."

He holds his hands out and helps me up, wrapping his arms around me once I'm on my feet and giving me a long hug. I relax into his body, his sweater bumpy against my cheek. "Go on. I'll start the hot cocoa," he says, pushing me toward my bedroom with gentle hands.

I fully expect him to be floundering in the kitchen when I come out wearing a matching lounge set, but he's not. He's setting two cups of hot chocolate on a tray, along with the ingredients we'll need to make the s'mores. A man that doesn't need to be told where things are and what to do? I'm in so much trouble. I open the door to the deck, barely stopping myself from inhaling as he passes by. He sets the tray on the table between the chairs and begins building the fire with military precision.

"Impressive," I murmur, sitting down on the edge of the chair, leaning forward to watch him.

He looks up at me as he's striking a match, the fire reflecting in his eyes and highlighting the fullness of his lips. God, those lips.

"I used to go camping a lot back home. I've perfected my technique over the years."

"Are you going to camp while you're in Scotland? I've heard there are a ton of great spots."

"You've never been?"

I shake my head. "The pub took up too much of my time."

"Once Dylan and Theo can run the pub by themselves, I'll take you camping," he promises.

"That sounds nice. I'll ask Jack if we can borrow his stuff." Henry sits down, and we both take a steaming mug, sipping tentatively. It's rich, chocolatey, and divine. "I want you to make this for me every morning," I groan, taking another sip.

"Just say the word, and I'll be here every morning to make it for you," he rasps, winking.

I nearly choke on the intensity of his gaze. "That may be moving a little fast, lover-boy."

"Would it, though? Life is short, Red."

I've always hated being called Red, but somehow, when it comes from him, it's different.

"Don't like the nickname?" he asks, reading my mind.

I bite my lip. "The opposite, actually." The orange glow from the flames caresses the planes of his face, deepening the dimple in his chin, darkening his eyes to a bluish-black. My fingers itch to run through his hair at the nape of his neck where it curls against his skin.

He studies me back, stars in his eyes. Without saying a word, he pulls grabs his guitar and picks out a melody, humming under his breath.

"But this love is brave and wild. And I never saw you coming. And I'll never be the same," I sing softly, recognizing the tune.

He picks up when I stop. "This is a state of grace. This is the worthwhile fight." He pauses as tension sweeps us into its current. "These are the hands of fate," he sings acapella, setting his guitar on the deck, the baritone of his voice sliding over me like silk.

"You're my Achilles heel."

"This is the golden age of something good and right and real." He beckons to me, patting his thigh.

I straddle his lap, wrapping my arms around his neck. "And I'll never be the same," I whisper, laying my head against his shoulder and sinking into the safety of his embrace.

11

I wake up disoriented the following morning. I must have fallen asleep in Henry's arms at some point last night. The last thing I remember are his lips brushing my forehead as he tucked me in. I rub my eyes, trying to clear the fog. Yesterday seems like a dream. Better than any dream I've ever had, if I'm being honest. I turn over to look for my phone and see a note propped up to it on the nightstand.

THANK you for a day that will be the one I compare every other to. xoxo -H.

I SQUEAL, kicking my feet, grinning like I've lost my damn mind. This can't be real. Why does it feel like I've known him forever? Why am I acting like a fucking teenager in love for the first time? Whoa. Where did the L-word come from? I huff, annoyed with myself, and glance at my phone, then scramble out of bed. I'm half an hour late to meet Theo at the house to work on the bike. I dress in layers, puling on bike shorts, jeans, a tank top, a long-sleeve shirt, and a sweatshirt, finishing it off with my boots and some chapstick. I rush out the door only to run smack into Theo.

"Fuck!" he holds a mug away from me, steaming coffee sloshing over the edges and dripping down his hand.

"Oh my god. I'm so sorry." I try to take it from him, but he holds it out of my reach. He brushes past me, setting it on the coffee table along with something wrapped in foil. "Are you okay?" I ask, grabbing his hand to look for damage.

"Do you really care?" he asks, the muscle in his jaw working.

I drop his hand, his words scalding me. "Of course I care! Do you ever wake up on the right side of the bed? Because I don't know how much of this I can take."

"Are you always late?" he volleys back, his eyes dark.

"I had a late night," I say, the excuse sounding hollow to my ears.

"Yeah, I saw. Are you going to climb into my lap, too?"

"Why are you such a fucking asshole?" I ask, picking up the foil packet and throwing it at his chest. He catches it easily.

"Because I'm jealous, Isla."

And there it is. Out in the open. Plain as day.

"I'm jealous of your life here, I'm jealous of the passion you have for it. I'm jealous of Dylan and Henry and the bond the three of you seem to have." He stalks toward me, making me scramble backward until I'm pressed against the window, waves crashing against the rocks far below. "I'm jealous of the air you breathe. The floor under your feet." His breath stutters, his gaze dipping to my lips.

Thunder crashes through me, pulsing in my ears, between my legs.

"Why be jealous when you can have it, too?" I ask softly, trying to steady my breathing. "You have the pub. I'm sure you can figure out a visa that allows you to stay. Although you sure as hell don't act like you like being here."

"And what about you, Sunflower? Can I have you?"

"I think you may have to fight Henry for that one."

"We share."

God, the audacity. I duck under his arm before he can see how much his words turn me on. "Then you better stop being such a goddamned douche canoe!" I toss over my shoulder as I grab the coffee and head out the door. His laugh stops me in my tracks. I turn to look at him, almost dropping the mug. His smile has transformed his entire face, and suddenly he's not Theo the Asshole, he's Theo the Hottest Guy I've Ever Seen. Fuck me. I turn on my heel, ignoring the pounding in my chest, and continue up the path. He corners me while I'm keying in the code to the garage, pushing the foil packet into my hand.

"I made you breakfast."

I don't say anything. I can't. He hasn't shaved in a couple of days, and I desperately want to trace the dark shadow of his beard, the curve of his full lower lip.

"I'm sorry for being a jerk, Isla. Truly. That's been my default mode for a long time, and it's really fucking hard to turn off."

I blink. "I'll forgive you if you fix my bike."

"I'll make you an offer. If I fix it, I get to take you out to dinner."

"On the bike?"

He nods. "Preferably, but that's not a deal breaker."

"Deal." I peel the foil away as he wheels out the bike. "What is this, exactly?"

"Chicken and Waffles. A classic southern American delicacy."

"You made this?" I eye the fluffy waffles sandwiching a huge piece of mouth-watering fried chicken, and take a gigantic bite. Flavor explodes in my mouth. Holy mother of god. "Marry me," I say around my mouthful of food. I don't care how much of an asshole he is if he can cook like this.

He laughs, a blush creeping up his cheeks. "You're a fickle creature, Isla MacLeod." He heads back into the garage before I can respond and returns wheeling the toolbox Jack gave me the year I bought the motorcycle.

"What's the best restaurant near here?" he asks after a while, wiping his hands on a rag.

"We could go into Stornoway, but the drive back at night won't be fun." I have an internal debate about sharing one of my favorite spots. "I know a place we can get food. It's not a restaurant, though."

"As long as it's tasty and–" He stops abruptly.

"And what?" I ask, shielding the sun from my eyes so I can see his face.

"I was going to say 'as long as I get to spend time with you,' but that seems like a dangerous sentiment."

"Mmm." Should I lay my cards on the table? Tell him I want to spend time with him, too?

"Stop staring at me like that–it feels like you're looking into my soul," he grumbles, frowning.

"I am. It's pitch black."

"Pot meet kettle," he murmurs, squatting down to grab a wrench off the ground.

"Hey! My soul is not black."

He looks up at me with those dark eyes, pinning me in place. "You're right. It's fiery red."

I like that much better.

"Because it's sitting at the right hand of the devil."

"You son of a bitch." I throw the wad of foil at him, laughing when it pings off his forehead.

THREE HOURS LATER, he's still working on the bike, and I'm bored as hell. Dylan and Henry are helping at Jack's, and I refuse to leave Theo here alone while he's working on my bike for free. I scroll through all the gossip sites, catching up on the celebrity tea, and then move on to an e-book I've been trying to read for the past two months. After ten minutes of reading the same paragraph repeatedly, I decide to pull my car out of the garage and give her a good cleaning. I start on the inside, using the shop vac to clean out any stray debris, and then wipe down the seats and dashboard with a specialty cleaner. When I finish the inside, I unlace my boots and strip down to my bike shorts and tank top. I drag the hose out of the garage, hook it up to the spigot on the side of the house, and attach the sprayer. I resist the urge to drench Theo as I spray her down, then I dunk a sponge in soapy water and get to work cleaning off the grime. By the time I'm ready to rinse her off, Theo is starting up the bike and taking her for a test run. I forget the sprayer in my hand as he pulls back into the driveway, looking sexy as hell. Water pools around my feed as he parks and cuts the engine, silence enveloping us.

"Take a picture, it'll last longer."

Heat floods my cheeks, and I give in to my impulses, tilting the spray up until it's aimed squarely at his face. I realize my mistake when he launches himself at me instead of running away, tackling me around the middle and twisting underneath me as we fall. I shriek, losing my grip on the hose. I struggle against him as water rains down all around us, successfully pushing away from him until I'm straddling his stomach.

"Hey. Look up," he says softly. I follow his gaze to find a neon rainbow stretched over us, shimmering in the sunlight. "Beautiful," he murmurs, his eyes on me. My heart jumps to my throat as he threads his fingers through mine, the intimacy of the moment making it hard to breathe. I can't look away from how his eyelashes are sticking together in tiny points, the way his teeth sink into his bottom lip, the steady pulse in the hollow of his throat, the way I want to lick–

"Isla." My gaze collides with his, my heart galloping in my chest.

"You have a booger," he says, reaching for my face. I smack his hand away and roll off him, ducking down to look in one of the side mirrors. Nothing. "You're such a fucking ASSHOLE!" I scream, grabbing the bucket of soapy water and dumping it over him.

He pushes to his feet, water still pouring down his face, desire radiating in waves from his body. "Tell me you like to be tamed," he says, practically begging, his voice like sandpaper.

"Not by you, you goddamned twatwaffle," I lie. I turn on my heel, grabbing my belongings before heading down the path down to the cottage.

He grabs me from behind, his arms twining around my stomach.

"You're a terrible liar." I suck in a breath as he traces a wide arc around my nipple. "Your nipples ratted you out." His breath ruffles the tiny hairs on my neck, making a shiver race down my spine.

"Would you let me tie you up, control you, worship you?" I lock my knees, fighting the urge to sag against him as his fingers brush the waistband of my shorts. I break away from his hold, struggling not to look back at him as I walk down the path.

"I'll meet you back up there in twenty," I call. "You owe me dinner."

12

The butterflies in my stomach make my hands shake as I strip off my wet clothes and hop in the shower. I should text Theo and cancel dinner. This thing between us is too volatile. We're polar opposites hurtling toward each other, doomed to explode on impact. Instead of texting him, I take the shortest shower of my life and stand in front of my closet dripping wet, trying to decide what to wear for what suddenly feels like one of the most critical moments of my life. What do you wear to try to avoid a pre-destined collision? My gaze slides to the back right corner of my closet where a pile of giveaway clothes has been sitting for months. I pull on a pair of baggy sweatpants and a gigantic purple hoodie emblazoned with my high school mascot—a rearing unicorn—on the back. I look at myself in the full-length mirror hanging on the back of the bedroom door and start to doubt myself. I look ridiculous. Which is exactly what I'm going for, I remind myself. I pull on my tennis shoes and head outside before I chicken out.

I realize my colossal mistake when I see Theo pacing by the garage, hands in the pockets of tailored wool trousers, the collar of a quarter zip sweater framing his jaw, sleeves pushed up. I definitely don't pay any attention to the veins riding over his forearms. My cheeks flush as his gaze sweeps over me, one dark eyebrow slowly rising.

"I–I should go change," I stammer, plucking at my sweatshirt nervously.

"Don't." He bites his lip, the corner of his mouth twitching.

"Theo–"

"Are you comfortable? Warm?"

I nod.

"That's all that matters." He enters the code into the keypad, then steps back. "I know what you're doing." He glances at me over his shoulder.

"What's that?" I ask, crossing my arms over my chest. He heads into the garage and wheels the bike out, ignoring my question.

"Do you have a hair tie?" he asks, handing me a helmet. I nod, handing it over, utterly confused. I can feel the heat of his hands through my sweatshirt as he turns me away from him. I shiver as he rakes his fingers through my hair, gathering it into three sections and then braiding it.

"You decided on wearing the most hideous outfit possible because you think it'll stop whatever this is between us from happening. The only problem with that is I'm interested in what's up here." He taps the top of my head and then fastens the hair tie at the end of my braid, turning me to face him. "Everything else is just a bonus." He takes the helmet from me, holding my gaze as he slides it down over my head. "Did I finally figure out how to calm that razor-sharp tongue?" he asks, his smile widening when I can't think of what to say.

"Theo," I croak, my heart in my throat. Our eyes lock, the moment thick with inevitability. "We can't stand each other," I whisper, desperate to get us back on solid ground.

"Stop lying to yourself, Isla." He squeezes his hands into fists at his side, a muscle twitching in his jaw.

"Are you mad at me?" I ask, trying to decipher his body language.

His laugh is devoid of humor. "Mad?" He holds his palm up,

showing me the dark crescents in his skin. "Mad with desire, maybe. It's taking everything in me to keep from reaching for you."

"Why are you stopping yourself?"

"Because I don't want to ruin this shaky trust we've started building between us."

"Why do you care?" I push, desperate to fight this thing pulling us together.

"Why do I care? I was a goner the first day you walked up to me with those flashing green eyes and knocked that croissant out of my mouth, Isla."

Fuckity fuck fuck fuck. I turn away from him and pull off the helmet, looking out over the sea, trying to steady myself.

"I can't stop thinking about how badly we fucked up your life and how I'm powerless to do anything about it. I stay awake every night thinking about what I could have done differently, but then I can't help but be happy because it brought us to you."

The helmet drops from my fingers as I turn toward him. I close the distance between us, not stopping to think about anything other than how badly I want to touch him. He grabs a handful of my sweatshirt and pulls my body against his.

"Tell me to stop. Tell me you hate me," he begs.

"I can't." I slide my palm over the stubble on his jaw. He closes his eyes, pushing into my touch.

"I'm bad for you, Sunflower. You need sunshine to thrive. Henry has that covered. You don't need me."

"I need the clouds that bring rain, too, Theo."

"Thank fuck." He wraps me in his arms, pulling me onto my tiptoes, his face buried in my neck. My stomach grumbles loudly, and he pulls back, looking guilty. "Come on, let's go get you some food." He picks up my helmet and slides it back over my head, then grabs my hand, fingers interlocking with mine as he pulls me toward the bike. My entire body is buzzing with adrenaline, my heart beating steadily between my legs. He puts on the spare helmet and throws his leg over the bike, motioning for me to get on behind him. I climb on, keeping some space between us. He hooks his hands under my knees, pulling me forward until I'm snug against him. I realize how much trouble I'm in when we turn out of the driveway, and every bump has me rubbing against the edge of his belt. I shift away, but the next turn has me sliding back into place.

"You okay back there?" he asks.

"No, not at all."

He pulls to the shoulder, twisting to look at me. "What's wrong?"

I clear my throat, deciding to tell the truth. "Things are–ah–rubbing."

His eyebrows shoot up. "Do you want to drive?"

"Please," I practically beg, jumping off the bike so he can scoot back. I take his place, fitting my body against his, then start the bike, pulling back onto the road. He leans forward, wrapping his arms around my middle, and that's when I feel his cock pressing into my back. I push back against him, not able to control the raw, animalistic desire coursing through my veins. His groan is barely audible over the wind, but it sends goosebumps racing over my body. I make a last-minute decision and pull into the driveway of an old abandoned farmhouse, my heart pounding in my ears.

"What are we doing?" Theo asks, looking around at our surroundings.

"I'm about to jump you and we haven't even kissed yet. So I'm going on the other side of this house to get myself off before I do something stupid. You can join me if you want." My heart lodges in my throat. What the fuck am I doing? This is insane. I set my helmet on the bike and start walking through the thick weeds toward the back of the house, his footsteps heavy behind me. Once we're hidden from the road, I turn toward him, barely able to breathe.

"Are you real?" he asks, wonder in his eyes as he watches me lean against the side of the house, his gaze following my hand as I push it inside my sweatpants.

"Very." I close my eyes as my fingers brush my clit, a tsunami of need crashing through my system.

"Fuck, Isla."

I startle when Theo's hand slides over mine, adding pressure to my touch. I clench my thighs around our fingers, but instead of helping me, he pulls my hand up and licks my fingers clean.

"Theo," I beg, my chest heaving. His mouth crashes against mine, our tastes mingling as he slides his tongue over my lips, and I open for him. He doesn't pull back until we're both gasping for breath.

"There. We kissed. Can I get you there now?"

"Yes," I practically sob, my entire body shaking with desire. He hauls me into his arms and carries me over to the rock wall at the back edge of the yard.

"Use this to support your weight. I don't want you to fall," he says, pushing me down so my stomach is snug against it. I can barely breathe as his thighs bump against mine, gasping as his hand snakes across my hip, over my lower stomach and between my legs.

"You're sure?" he whispers, his voice husky with need.

"Yes, Theo." I moan as his fingers cradle my clit, sliding back and forth until I'm close. He moves his hand right before I come, sliding a finger inside me, anchoring the heel of his palm over my clit.

"You're so fucking tight," he groans, slowly pushing deeper, then adding a second finger. "This doesn't hurt, does it?"

"Don't stop," I beg, dropping my weight onto his fingers. He grabs my ass with his other hand, squeezing hard. I whimper, pushing back against him, letting my body speak for me. He runs his finger along my crack, testing the waters. A moan rips from the depths of my soul, my back arching, desperate for this. Wanting everything he's willing to give me.

"Turn around." The command in his voice has me facing him before I consciously decide to. The fingers that were just inside me slip easily between my cheeks to tease sensitive skin. I bite my lip, trying to keep in the ungodly sounds trying to escape. "Don't. I want to hear you."

"Theo, please." Our eyes lock as he pushes his finger against me, slowly breaching that tight ring of muscle.

"Fuck," I groan, reaching between my legs.

"That's it. Good girl," Theo breathes, sliding his hand past mine and pushing two fingers inside me, rubbing them slowly over my G-spot. He slides his finger farther into my ass as my body relaxes for him, both hands pushing and pulling in the same rhythm. I can feel the wet heat of his mouth through my sweatshirt as he sucks my nipple into his mouth.

"Fuck, my fingers are cramping," I gasp, shaking my hand.

"Have you been eating?" he asks, his expression thunderous.

"Can we talk about that later?" I beg, wanting to push his head between my thighs but too shy to do it. He squats down, using his teeth to drag down the waistband of my sweatpants. I help him, pushing them to my knees. He presses his nose just below my navel, sucking in a jagged breath.

He looks up at me, his eyes black. "Isla–" There's so much intimacy in how he says my name, and I know he's giving into whatever this is and asking me to do the same.

"Yes, Theo," I say, answering his unspoken question.

"You're all in?" he asks, his nostrils flaring.

"What about your brothers?"

"We'll figure it out. We always do."

"Then yes, I'm all in," I whisper, blinking back tears. What is happening to me? His hands continue their onslaught of my senses as he circles my clit with his tongue.

"Oh god, Theo." I thread my fingers through his hair, holding on for dear life as he breaks me down and builds me back up again. He fits his mouth over me, one long pull, and my vision goes black, my entire universe shrinking to this one moment.

"Come for me, Isla." The vibration of his voice has me bucking against him. He flattens his tongue over me, sliding it back and forth over my clit, increasing the pressure on my G-spot. It's too much.

"Theo, I–"

"You're doing so good. Lean into it. Don't hold back." One more thrust of his fingers and I'm dragging his mouth back to my pussy, grinding against him, the world exploding around us. My entire body clenches as my muscles spasm, ecstasy radiating through me in waves. He slows his movements as I come down, moving his lips to my lower stomach, nipping at my skin. He stands, pulls my face to his, and kisses me like he's been waiting for this his entire life. He breaks away to allow us to breathe, wiping the tears from my cheeks. "If I had known it would be like this, I never would have left last summer," he whispers, resting his forehead against mine. My stomach growls again, and he jumps back like I struck him. "Fuck, Isla. This was just supposed to be dinner." He pulls up my underwear and sweatpants, color leeching from his cheeks.

"I needed this more than I needed food," I assure him.

He swings me up into his arms, glowering down at me. I grin up at him like a fool. I never would have guessed there was so much heat under that stony exterior.

13

Theo POV*

*How can I ever go back to the man I was before her? Before her soft moans? Before she went limp in my arms and came on my hands? I'm absolutely fucking ruined.

"Here." Her cheeks are stained red as she flips the top on a bottle of hand sanitizer and squirts it into my waiting palm.

"Don't be embarrassed." I nudge her chin with my knuckle, my heart stuttering when those luminous green eyes meet mine. "That was fucking magical."

"Thank you," she whispers, her husky voice tugging at my balls.

"No. Thank *you*."

"For what?"

"For surrendering your body to me. For letting me peel away the layers to see the parts you keep hidden. And fuck is she magnificent." I can't stop myself from sampling her lips again, groaning when she angles her head and pulls me closer. It's my stomach that interrupts us this time.

"Come on, Grumpy. Let's go get some food."

My lips twitch at the nickname, liking it despite myself. Isla motions for me to get on first and then climbs on behind me, flattening herself to my back, her hands wrapping around my stomach. I follow her directions, pulling to the shoulder beside a roadside stand. It looks like a miniature Scottish house—white clapboard and a green roof.

"It's an honor system," she explains, pulling open the small door and disappearing inside. I follow her in, stooping through the doorway. The smell nearly brings me to my knees. Isla reads the roughly written chalk labels. Fish Pie. Vegetable Curry. Lamb Pasties. Cheese Scones. Frangipane Tarts. In the corner, there's a pot plugged in with langoustine soup.

"What kind of heaven did we just walk into?"

"Isn't it wonderful? Greer's parents took it over years ago. I suppose someday Greer will take the reins from them. At least, I hope she does."

"And leave the pub?" Anxiety draws my shoulders toward my ears.

She looks at me funny. "I know this amazing chef that could easily take her place."

"Who?" I pull out my phone and open the notes app, ready to write down the name.

"You, silly." Her words are soft and gentle. Reverent even.

"Me?"

"Yes, you! You're brilliant in the kitchen. I don't think I'll ever forget that cottage pie. I'm pretty sure that that was the day I–" She stops suddenly, her mouth snapping shut.

"You what?" I silently beg her to finish her sentence, desperate for her to admit that she shares this insatiable need inside me that's only happy when she's close. She shakes her head, turning back to the shelves. I can't take my eyes off her as she chooses a loaf of bread and ladles soup into a to-go container. She spins back toward me, licking her lips, her gaze focused on my mouth.

"Theo." Her voice is strangled, tension wrapping around us.

"Don't say my name like that," I beg, squeezing my hands into fists to keep myself from reaching for her. The light from the window caresses her hair, turning it into cherry red, a sliver of sunlight slicing over her eye, luminescent green looking up at me, stealing the breath from my lungs.

"Theo."

"Damn it, Isla." I take the bread and soup from her hands, carefully setting them down before walking her back against the wall, rucking up her sweatshirt, and molding her waist to my hands. So fucking soft. "If we keep doing this, I won't be able to let go. Won't want to share." I push a lock of hair away from her face, tracing the freckles over her cheeks, trying to ignore the panic blooming in my chest.

"We can worry about that later," she murmurs, her gaze roaming over my face. The slam of a car door has us jumping apart, Isla's face flushing crimson. I put several bills in the box, and we load up our arms, passing by a couple getting out of their car. I can't help the familiar stab of jealousy. I want that so badly, but a traditional relationship doesn't seem to be in the cards for me. It terrifies me even to be thinking of another poly relationship. I fucked it up so badly last time. I'd like to think I learned, but these feelings coursing through me are so fucking strong. It scares the hell out of me.

"What are you thinking?" she asks softly, stowing the food.

Is it too soon to tell her I'd like to buy one of these cottages and hide away with her? That I would give up everything if it meant I could take care of her for the rest of her life? Fucking hell.

"Me, too," she whispers, the same overwhelming emotion reflecting back at me. I give her a tight hug and then climb on the bike, pulling the vee of her thighs snug against me before taking off. She directs me to a small parking area for a local beach, and we trudge across the dunes, arms laden with food. I bump into her when she stops suddenly, nearly dropping everything in my attempt not to knock her over.

"Look."

I follow her gaze to the wide expanse of beach, turquoise water stretching toward the dark mountains in the distance.

"It takes my breath away every time," she whispers, looking up at me. I don't know how she does it, but she makes me feel like she's telling me a secret she's never told anyone else before. Like this is a sacred place meant only for us. Like I'm her end and her beginning. And god save me, that's exactly what I want.

"I don't know how to share you, Sunflower." The words tumble from my mouth before I can stop them. She holds my gaze, seeing the truth in my eyes.

"I wouldn't want to share you, either," she says simply, her eyes clouding. I follow her down the dune and onto the beach, the wind whipping fiery strands around her face. I never should have touched her. I never should have given in to this all-consuming need haunting my every thought. I'd rather have her as a friend than not at all, but there's no going back now. There will never be a day where I don't crave the softness of her skin beneath my fingertips, that teasing, husky brogue.

"So where does that leave us?" she asks, startling me with her bluntness. My jaw works as she settles herself on a rock, carefully taking the lid off the soup.

"Fuck if I know." I stare out at the horizon, realizing the pull to walk into the water and escape my life doesn't seem as strong with her by my side.

"Do we have to dissect what this is? Can we just go with the flow? Hope everything will work itself out?" she asks, pushing her hair out of her face.

"But what if it doesn't?"

"I won't choose just one of you, Theo. I would never get between the three of you like that. I understand you don't want to share, but that means not having a relationship with any of you."

"So you're in a relationship with the other two already?"

She shakes her head. "Dylan and I haven't had much time alone."

Fuck. A second ago I didn't want to share, but now I'm worried about what will happen if she and Dylan don't click. Would I be forced to give her up? "Why don't the two of you go check out those pubs you were talking about tomorrow?"

"Tomorrow?"

"Henry and I can hold the fort down."

"You sure you're ready for that?"

"Positive." I watch as she dips a spoon into the soup, carefully blowing before wrapping her lips around the utensil, her eyes rolling back. Fuck. I drag my gaze away from her, thinking about anything but how she'd look with something else in her mouth. Her groan has my cock twitching uncomfortably.

"You have to try this." She scoops up another spoonful and carefully steers it toward my mouth. The moment is incredibly intimate, the flush in her cheeks betraying exactly what she's thinking about. The flavor bursts over my tongue.

"Second best thing I've ever tasted."

"What's the first?" she asks, ripping off a chunk of bread, dipping it in the soup, and holding it to my mouth. I take it from her, licking the tips of her fingers.

"You."

"Jesus. You're smooth." Her eyes sparkle as she takes a bite of bread.

"If I were smooth, I would have put music on to set the mood a long time ago." I pull out my phone and press play to the song I've been listening to non-stop because it reminds me of her. The dulcet tones of "Sweet and Dark" float around us, adding even more tension to the atmosphere.

"It's never been like this before," she whispers, her eyes following the waves as they crash into the shore.

"Like what?" I need to hear her say it.

"Like you're a fresh mountain spring, and I haven't had a sip of water in years." No games. No cat and mouse. She's just telling it like it is, and it's so fucking refreshing. "Is it because I don't have experience, or is this normal?" she asks, looking up at me with wide eyes.

"There's not a single thing normal about this, Isla," I rasp, my voice breaking. I push to my feet, walking several steps away, running my hands through my hair, wondering what kind of hell I've gotten myself into. I turn back around, and she barrels into me, delicate hands gripping my collar, tipping my face down to hers, forcing me to meet her gaze.

"Don't close me out. I don't think I could bear it."

"I won't close you out, Isla."

"Promise me that no matter what happens, you'll always tell me how you're feeling." She's looking at me so earnestly, with so much hope, it almost hurts. "Promise me we'll figure this out."

I can't promise her that, so I pull her onto her toes and slick my tongue over her bottom lip instead. She kisses me hard and then breaks away, spinning with her arms out, her hair streaming around her like wildfire. I promised myself a long time ago that I would never again fall for the same girl as my brothers, but I never saw her coming.

14

"Ready to go, Freckles?" Dylan looks at me from the driver's seat, excitement radiating from him in waves, elegant hands flexing on the steering wheel. The guys are borrowing Cam's old Defender, and it suits Dylan well, highlighting his rough, rugged edges and reminding me he's not just a nice guy–he's an *incredibly attractive* nice guy. I fasten my seatbelt, trying not to stare at the chameleon beside me. This is the third time I've been reminded how horribly wrong my first impression of him was. Today, he's wearing a wool coat the same color as his eyes, dark jeans, and leather boots.

"You look really nice. Do you pick out your clothes yourself?" I ask, my cheeks heating the second the words are out of my mouth. What a stupid thing to say.

"Yes," he chuckles. "I've been interested in sustainable fashion for a few years now. I saw a video on wardrobe capsules and ran with it."

My eyebrows shoot up. "Really? I always wanted to do a capsule but never found the time. Maybe we can go shopping if we have extra time, and you can teach me your ways."

"I'd like that, but you don't need my help in the fashion department. I'm jealous of how effortlessly cool you look." His gaze slides over my body, making me shiver.

"Aw, shucks." I can't keep the smile from my face, and Dylan returns it tenfold, his dimples doing funny things to my stomach. I've never met someone quite like him. I could peel off layer after layer and still learn new things.

"Are you going to tell me where we're going?" Last night, when he texted me to ask if I was up for scoping out some pubs, he told me he'd plan the whole thing–all I needed to do was show up.

"We're going to Inverness. I originally wanted to stay on the islands, but I don't think we'll get the inspiration we need without going to a bigger city."

I nod my agreement. "As long as you have a coffee stop scheduled into this trip, it sounds perfect."

"Don't worry, I didn't forget about your caffeine addiction." We pull into the ferry terminal, park the car where the attendant instructs, and then Dylan jumps out, coming around to help open my door. "We have about twenty minutes. If we run, we'll make it."

"Dylan!"

"No time for arguing, come on."

"I can just get a coffee on the ferry!" I protest, trying to ignore the zing of awareness that plows through my body when he grabs my hand.

"You and I both know that's not good enough." He gives me a grin, and then we're off, dodging around cars and dashing up the street. I'm gasping for breath by the time we get to the café, mentally making a note to add more cardio to my gym routine. Dylan looks perfectly coifed, like we did nothing but take a leisurely walk.

"How are you not out of breath?" I pant, putting my hands on my knees as I struggle to suck air into my lungs.

"I'm an elite athlete, Isla. Didn't you know?"

I return his wink with a glare, wiping the sweat from my upper lip.

He holds up hands his hands in surrender. "Before we moved, I participated in triathlons. I'll have to start training again before I start losing progress."

"Triathlons? I've always wanted to do one, but the training alone is intimidating."

"They're not so bad after the first one."

"How many have you done?"

"My goal is three per year."

Holy shit. "What was the last one?" Our turn comes up before he can answer, but I get suspicious when he still doesn't respond after we step aside to wait. "Are you evading my question?"

"No," he laughs. "I just don't want to intimidate you." His dimple comes out, the sparkle in his eyes making my knees wobble.

"Intimidate me?"

"That's why we were in Scotland last summer."

I think back to last summer, and it dawns on me. "You're kidding. You were here for the Ironman?" He nods, a blush creeping up his cheeks. "I thought you were joking about your elite athlete comment. Holy shit, Dylan." I can see the relief in his eyes when the barista calls his name. He insists on holding my coffee as we head back to the car, not giving it up until I'm safely seated. "What made you decide to start doing triathlons?" I ask once he's joined me.

He thinks about the question, taking a minute before responding. "I was starting to believe people's perception of me—that I was just a nerd that liked numbers." He looks up at me. "I wanted to prove that I'm more than my IQ."

"I've never thought about it like that before. I know athletes are usually put in a box, but I guess I never realized it went the other way, too."

He shrugs. "It doesn't help that Henry and Theo were athletes in high school. I had a healthy dose of jealousy spurring my decision." I can't take my eyes off his hand as he shifts into drive and follows the line of cars onto the ferry. As soon as we're parked, he takes my hand, and we race inside to get the best seats.

"I'm glad we're doing this," I whisper, looking over at him, shyness creeping in.

"Me, too." He holds my gaze while he sips his coffee, licking the foam from his upper lip. "Now it's your turn to tell me your secrets."

"I don't really have any. What you see is what you get."

"I highly doubt that," he says, his eyes caressing every inch of my skin. I'm not sure if he realizes what he's doing, but my body's response is instantaneous. "Tell me something you're passionate about, then."

"I love planning the parties at the castle." God, that's such a ditsy thing to say. I cover my cheeks, hiding my embarrassment.

"What kind of parties?"

"There's the yearly masquerade ball coming up, then the Oidhche Shamhna ball."

"The what?"

"Halloween," I clarify, giggling at the look on his face.

"That's Gaelic, isn't it? Say something else. Please."

"Tha thu bòidheach."

"What does that mean?" he asks, stumbling over the syllables.

"You're beautiful."

He stills, his throat bobbing. "Do you mean that?"

"Have you seen yourself?" My gaze roams over him, appreciating the beauty of those big brown eyes, the dark fringe of his eyelashes, and those dimples I'm starting to love so much.

"Nobody has ever said that to me before."

"I'll make sure to say it more often then." On impulse, I lean toward him and brush my lips over his cheek. His scent punches me right in the gut. "God, you smell good." I bury my face against his neck, inhaling him. Spicy citrus with a hint of musk. He wraps his arm around me, and I rest my head on his shoulder, basking in the quiet intimacy of the moment.

THE FERRY RIDE and the drive to Inverness go by in the blink of an eye. Dylan puts on a playlist he made specifically for today, and we sing at the top of our lungs for the entire five hours. I've nearly lost my voice by the time we pull into a parking spot in the city center.

The first pub is lively despite it being barely past one in the afternoon. We opt for a booth so we can talk openly without the
bartender overhearing us. The ambiance is top-notch, and for the
first time since I accepted losing the pub, I'm nostalgic thinking about
what it could have been.

"I don't know why I thought this was a good idea," Dylan says,
reading me like an open book.

"It's fine."

"It's not fine. I'm asking you to participate in a dream-building
session for a dream we ripped right out of your hands, Isla. It's not
fucking fair."

"Hey." I grab his hand, squeezing gently. "I forgive you. I forgive
your brothers. You didn't do it on purpose, and that's what matters.
It's normal for people to look back at what could have been and feel a
little sad."

"You're too good for us, Isla. We're raw. Messy. Chaos follows us
everywhere we go."

"You're speaking my language, big guy." He starts to protest, but
I press a finger against his lips, lingering there longer than neces-
sary. "I'm happy to be here with you, still dreaming about what
the pub can be in the future. I may not own it, but it still means a
lot to me." He grips my wrist, turning my hand and kissing my
palm.

"I don't think I'll ever get used to how good of a person you are,"
he murmurs, the bottomless pools of his eyes drawing me in.

"If you could've heard my thoughts when the three of you showed
up, you wouldn't feel the same way," I laugh.

"Were you ready to murder us?"

"I would have just maimed you and Henry. I had already started
digging a hole for Theo." I sip my beer, closing my eyes as the flavors
burst over my tongue. It's phenomenal.

"Let me know next time. I'll help you."

"Dylan! He's your brother!"

"You underestimate how upset this whole thing made me. I
haven't been that angry with him in a long time."

"Let's make this the last time we talk about it, okay? I don't want to draw it out. What's done is done."

Dylan nods reluctantly, holding up his glass. "To the future."

I clink my glass against his, our eyes locked as we drink.

"Damn, this is good." He pulls out the menu, skimming his finger over it until he comes to the beer we ordered. "It's a local beer," he says, impressed. "Is there a brewery on Harris?"

"No, the closest one is in Stornoway."

"Have you ever thought about opening one?"

I rake my hands through my hair, pulling it over my shoulder. "Yes, actually. I took a summer course a couple of years ago."

"What happened?"

"Life." I shrug. It was a pipe dream, and I knew it.

"Do you still want to do it?"

I carefully unpack the old dream of starting a business from scratch—something I can call my own. I picture taking my creations to competitions and seeing how it stacks up against my colleagues, building a legacy for myself.

"Well, I'd say that's a yes," Dylan chuckles, reading my emotions.

"I'm sure it would be hard as hell, but having something of my own has always been appealing."

"Do you have somewhere to do it? We could help you get set up."

"Back when I was seriously considering it, Jack offered me the empty side of the barn."

"I think we should all sit down and talk when we get back," he says, absently tracing my hand with his fingertip.

"Who's we?"

"Charlie's guys and your guys."

"My guys?" I raise an eyebrow at him.

An alarm goes off, and Dylan glances at his phone. "Time to get to the next pub."

"You set an alarm?" I can't keep the smile off my lips.

"Multiple. How else will we stay on track and get back to the ferry on time?"

"God, I love you." He freezes, and I gulp down the last of my beer in absolute mortification. I push back from the table without looking at him and walk to the bar, pulling my card out of my back pocket.

He traps me against the bar, his chest warm against my back. "Don't you dare. You're here as a favor for us, you're not spending a single penny."

I can't help the shiver that slides down my spine, anticipation racing through my veins.

"Was that shiver for me?" The rasp of his voice stirs something low in my belly. His hand brushes my hip as he leans forward to hand the bartender his card, those long, elegant fingers resting on my waist. It takes everything in me not to turn around in his arms.

I need to get a grip. Take this slowly. He's the last hurdle before I launch myself headlong into a relationship with all three of them. I need to be one hundred percent sure that's what I want before I take this last step.

His other hand loosely circles the base of my throat, his thumb brushing my pulse. Oh god. My heart rate jumps, adrenaline surging. I twist and duck under his arm, murmuring something about meeting him outside. I slam through the door, pressing my back against the outside of the building, forcing myself to take deep breaths.

Dylan bursts through the door. "What's wrong?" He scans me from head to toe, his gaze settling back on my face when he's satisfied I'm not hurt.

"Are you sure this is what you want?" I ask, searching his gaze, desperate for the truth.

"What is 'this,' Isla?"

"Being stuck in a relationship with your brothers when it tore you apart last time. Being with someone not willing to choose between the three of you. How is it fair to any of you?"

He pulls my hands away from my face and links his fingers with mine. "First, I've never been more sure of anything in my life. Second, the reason I know this will work is *because* you're not willing to choose between us." He presses a kiss to my forehead, the intimacy bringing tears to my eyes. "Third, I don't want anyone other than you,

Isla. I've been dreaming of this moment since that day in the pub a year ago."

"This moment?" I ask, my lower lip trembling.

He hums his affirmation, bringing my hand up to hook around his neck and then cupping my face, his thumb sweeping over my bottom lip.

"Why this moment?" I ask, leaning into his touch.

"Because I knew if I ever got the chance to kiss you, it would be the first day of the rest of my life." He shifts closer, the sun slanting over him, deepening the angles of his face, sending a surge of red-hot desire through my body.

"What are you waiting for, then? Kiss me."

15

The moment right before a first kiss is one of my favorite parts of the human experience. Hearts racing. Held breath. Flushed cheeks. Anticipation buzzing in the air like electricity. Dylan draws the moment out in an exquisite form of torture. Fingers sliding into the hair at the base of my neck and tugging gently. His nose skimming along my jawline. The puff of breath against the shell of my ear. A trembling palm cupping my cheek. His thumb sweeping over my cheekbone, my eyebrow, my lips. He leans forward, his hips pressing me into the wall.

"Dylan, please."

"Let me enjoy my last first kiss, Isla."

I want to protest, insist that he can't possibly know I'm his last, but the fire burning for me in his eyes holds me captive, flames licking over my body, branding me. He tilts my face, brushing his lips over the corner of my mouth.

"Do you feel it?" He presses his forehead to mine.

"Like fate is holding her breath, waiting?" I whisper, my voice shaky.

"You two need to move it along," a deep voice says, pulling us back to reality. Dylan takes a step back, turning to face the police officer.

Heat rises like a tsunami, turning my cheeks crimson. The police officer winks at me, tipping his hat before continuing on his way.

"Oh my god. How embarrassing." I cover my cheeks with my hands, utterly mortified.

"We'll have a good story to tell our kids one day," he laughs, raking his hands through his hair.

"Dylan!"

"I'm teasing, Freckles." His eyes dance, the sun turning them amber. "Come on, we only have a couple of hours left."

My stomach twists. A couple of hours isn't nearly enough. "Why don't we stay in the city tonight? As long as we leave early, I'll be back in time to open tomorrow."

"You're sure?"

I study him, hearing the hesitation in his voice. "Are you trying to get rid of me that quickly?" I tease.

"I don't want to put you in a situation where you feel something more is expected of you."

"You're the sweetest, Dylan. Thank you." He smiles, his hand enveloping mine as we head to the next pub.

THE WORLD'S End is ancient and dark. The calendar hanging just inside the door is jam-packed with events—everything from live music to karaoke to board game nights. We sit in a private corner booth with a clear view of the stage, where a DJ is busy setting up.

"Are you familiar with any of the hotels around here?" Dylan asks, handing me the menu.

"My friend owns Dores Inn, which is right on the banks of Loch Ness. They rent out a couple of rooms on the side. I can text her and see if she has one available."

"One?"

Oh god. Now I'm the one that's making him feel like I expect something from *him*. "If–If that's okay with you?" I stammer.

"Sharing a hotel room with the girl of my dreams? How will I ever survive?" He rolls his eyes, a smirk playing on his lips.

Good beer and better conversation flow for hours until we find ourselves ending the night on stage singing "Islands in the Stream" at the top of our lungs. It's perfect.

THE ROOM at the inn is tiny, but perfect for one night. While I'm washing up, Dylan makes himself a spot on the floor at the foot of the bed.

"You don't have to sleep on the floor," I protest, weaving my hair into a loose braid.

"I can't control myself in my sleep, Isla. I won't take the chance that we wake up in a compromising position without meaning to."

I swear, I fall a little more every time he opens his mouth. I turn off the lamp and strip down to my bra and panties, shivering as I slide between the cool sheets. The only light in the room is a sliver of moonlight slicing across the ancient floorboards.

"How does it work exactly?" I ask, the darkness making me brave.

"How does what work?"

"Sharing a woman. Do you take turns?" I hold my breath while I wait for his answer.

"That depends on the woman and what she wants."

"Oh." I was hoping for more detail.

"What do *you* want, Isla?"

"What are my options?" I stare at the ceiling, my heart beating like a base drum.

"You could schedule us in. Each of us gets a different night."

"That sounds awful." I think I hear him sigh with relief, but I can't be sure.

"The other option is we share a bed."

"But how does it work, exactly? The three of you are brothers, which is vastly different from the relationship Charlie and the guys share."

"It just means that all of our attention is focused on you all of the time."

The idea of six hands and three tongues focused on me has delicious heat suffusing my body, settling between my legs.

"What goes where?" I croak, sliding my hand over my breast and squeezing, desperate to relieve the ache. "I'm not a prude, but I've never..." I trail off, not sure how to say what I mean.

"Fucked three guys at once?" Dylan finishes, his voice husky, the rasp tugging the thread of desire tethering us together.

"Yes, that," I whisper.

"It depends..."

"On what?"

"God, Isla, you're going to be the death of me."

I hear his zipper, and the butterflies in my stomach go wild. I force myself to stay still instead of crawling to the end of the bed to see what he's doing. Instead, I slide my hand down over my stomach, running my fingers lightly along my slit over my underwear.

Dylan clears his throat. "It depends on if you like to be fucked in the ass," he says, his voice strangled.

"That's still only two holes." I bite back a whimper as I press my fingers on either side of clit, rocking my hips.

"One of them stretches, Isla."

I push my underwear aside, sinking two fingers inside me, wondering how it would feel to be filled like that. For all three of them to be using my body to find release. I squeeze my eyes closed, too turned on to care about the moan that slips from my lips or the creak of the bedframe as I dig my heels into the mattress.

"Isla." Dylan whispers my name, his voice breaking. I open my eyes to see his shadow standing at the end of the bed.

"Dylan!" I shriek, pulling my hand away and clamping my legs closed. My gaze drops to the movement of his arm. I reach over and turn on the lamp, feeling like I may die if I can't see all of him. My breath catches in my throat as I watch him slide his hand up and down his cock, pre-cum glistening at the tip, begging for me to taste it. His gaze pins me in place, forcing me to make a choice. Shut this down or see it out. I hold our eye contact as I pull off my panties, barely able to breathe. I prop myself up against the headboard, my legs glued shut.

"Open them, Isla. Show me what you like."

Oh god. Is this really happening? I watch his hand twisting over his cock, his thumb sweeping over the head, then dragging down to pulse where the shaft and head meet. My knees fall open.

"Fuck, you're perfect," he groans, the muscles in his abdomen clenching. "Show me how you touch yourself."

My breath shudders out of me as I slide my fingertip down my slit, then back up, circling my clit. I push two fingers inside, feathering them over my G-spot, my vision going fuzzy.

"Good girl," he rasps, jaw clenching, nostrils flaring.

I hold my hand out to him, daring him to come closer.

"That's a bad idea, Isla," he pants, his gaze focused on the moisture dripping down my fingers.

"It's the best idea," I promise. I bring my hand toward my mouth, but he grabs my wrist first.

"Mine," he growls, sucking my fingers into his mouth, swirling his tongue over and between them until he's consumed every last drop. There's nothing quite like watching your man's eyes roll back when he tastes you for the first time–that visceral reaction with no pretense. His muscles ripple, control fracturing. "Isla." He falls to his knees beside the bed, looking up at me, only a sliver of his iris showing.

"We haven't even kissed yet," I whisper, my body moving without my permission until my ass is at the edge of the bed, not even a foot separating his face and the apex of my thighs.

"This will be the best first kiss of your life. I just need your permission first." He presses my knees wide, his moan ratcheting the tension higher. "You're so goddamned beautiful." His cheek scrapes along my inner thigh as he pulls my legs over his shoulders, a shaky breath puffing against my sex. "It's your call, Isla."

"Yes. Yes, Dylan. Kiss me." He doesn't waste a single moment, pushing my knees up toward my chest and licking me from asshole to clit in one long, velvety swipe.

"Fuck!" I bite the base of my thumb, my back bowing. "What is it with you guys and my ass?" I gasp, nearly melting off the bed as he feathers his tongue over the puckered skin.

"With three of us, every hole gets equal treatment." His lips vibrate against my skin, driving me wild. I push my fingers into his hair, pressing my hips into the bed until his tongue centers on my clit. Keeping my grip tight on his hair, I rock my hips against his mouth. Two fingers nudge at my pussy, slowly working their way in. The first brush of his fingers against my G-spot has me jerking in his arms. He presses harder, curling his fingers into my inner wall.

"Dylan, stop! That always makes me feel like I'm going to pee."

He stops immediately. "You just went pee, remember?"

"Then why does it feel like that?"

"Because the same muscles are involved. You need to stop thinking and just let yourself feel. It will be amazing."

"You promise I won't pee on you?"

"I promise. And even if you did, I'd be lying if I said that didn't turn me on." His wink has me melting back into the bed. I pull his head back between my legs, whimpering as he drives his tongue into me. He flattens one hand over my stomach, feeling every little jerk and gasp as I fall apart.

"I never want this to end," he whispers, slick lips moving against me, teeth scraping over tender flesh.

"Dylan, please," I beg, writhing against his mouth. He pushes two fingers into me, slowly sliding his tongue back and forth over my clit as he massages that spot inside me. It feels so fucking good. The urge to pee comes back, but I ignore it, focusing on the way his tongue is worshipping my clit, how his fingers stretch me, the way his hand holds me in place while he's eating me out like he's a lion and I'm his prey. Ecstasy batters me from all sides, stealing all of my other senses. My vision goes black. There's a high-pitched ringing in my ears as he drags me higher, forcing my body to do things it never has before.

"That's my girl. Let go. Feel," he urges, licking me once, twice, and then fitting his lips over me, sucking my clit into his mouth and increasing the pressure inside me.

"Come for me, Isla," he rasps, his voice like sandpaper. With the next pull of his mouth, I explode in his hands, waves of ecstasy wracking my body. I scream his name as my back bows, my thighs clenching around his head. He follows my lead, not letting up until I'm lying there boneless, my chest heaving.

Dylan stands, wiping his dripping face on his shirt, looking down at me with dark eyes. "God, your tits are fucking gorgeous. I'm sorry I didn't pay them any attention." He leans over me, his cock trapped between us as he pulls the cup of my bra down and drags his tongue over my nipple.

"Let me get you there." I rake my fingers through his hair, moaning as he draws me into his mouth.

"Tonight is all about you, Isla."

"Dylan, you'll be miserable."

"It's worth it." He moves to my other breast, palming and squeezing it, fluttering his tongue over my nipple until I'm pushing up for more. I make a split-second decision, hooking my heels around the back of his legs and pulling, his weight falling on me as his knees buckle. His grunt turns into a groan as I rub my clit against the underside of his cock.

"Kiss me, Dylan."

His lips crash against mine, his control splintering. He pushes his tongue into my mouth, moaning as I angle my head and deepen the kiss. He rocks his hips, his cock sliding in my moisture, riding up and down my slit.

"Fucking hell, Isla." He pulls away, chest heaving. "You must think I have the control of a saint." I wrap my legs around him, digging my heels into his ass, refusing to let him go. "Open your eyes, Isla. I want you looking at me when you come, know whose cock you're rubbing yourself on and how fucking crazy you make me."

The second our gazes lock, he drops his weight on me, his cock sliding between my lips, the ridge of his head catching on my clit. One wrong move and he'll be inside me. I sob his name as he pulses over that swollen bundle of nerves, fracturing me into a million pieces. Need flares in his eyes, desperation lining his face. His balls tighten against my pussy, his body trembling with restraint. The shadow of indecision disappears, our mouths meeting in a war of teeth and tongues. One more thrust and he surrenders, hips spasming against mine, hot cum spurting onto my stomach.

He peppers kisses along my collarbone as we come down from the high.

"That was so hot," I pant, trying to catch my breath.

"Just wait," he chuckles, tucking a stray piece of hair behind my ear. I prop myself up on my elbows, admiring his ass as he walks to the bathroom and returns with a warm washcloth.

"Sorry," he murmurs, gently wiping my stomach.

"Why are you sorry?"

"The mess."

"What if I told you I would rub it in like lotion if it were socially acceptable?"

He raises an eyebrow. "Then I would say that's hot as fuck." He tosses the washcloth into the bathroom sink and then hops in bed with me, shivering as he wraps his arms around me. "I'm glad that was my last first kiss because nothing will ever top that." He tucks his face into my shoulder, his breath tickling the nape of my neck.

Tears prick my eyes, the corners of my mouth pulling up into a tentative smile. Maybe–just maybe–this will actually work. Could this be it? My forever? I fall asleep to dreams of extra large beds, tangled limbs, and lazy mornings filled with coffee and laughter.

16

I t's been almost a week since I've seen the guys. Jack is making one final push before the baby is born and needs all hands on deck, which means I'm alone in the pub every night after spending my mornings planning Charlie's baby shower. Despite staying busy, I find myself constantly thinking of them.

When I arrive at the pub Saturday afternoon, a man who looks to be in his late forties introduces himself as Patrick and tells me he's taking over for me, and I have until opening to show him the ropes. My stomach roils and it feels like I'm going to be sick. I send a frantic group text to the guys, but they only assure me that he's competent and that the pub will be in good hands. I gape at the words on the screen. This isn't part of the deal. I'm training *them* to take over, not some random guy who will mess everything up. Why the fuck did they think this would be okay?

"You don't need to worry," Patrick says, his eyes crinkling at the corners when he smiles. "I promise I'll take good care of her."

"Where–How–When–" I groan, scrubbing my hands over my face. Why hadn't they asked me first? Because I don't fucking own the pub anymore, that's why.

"To answer your questions, I was a bartender at the Balmoral before I moved to Harris for some peace and quiet. I quickly found there's such a thing as too much downtime, so I put an ad online. Theo saw it and got in touch last week."

"The Balmoral?" I gape at him. "And now you want to work *here*?" That's the downgrade of the century. I look at him more closely. "Why do you look familiar?"

"I've been coming in every week for months, Isla. I have big shoes to fill."

I snort. "I guess I should be thankful I can finally move on. I just didn't think it would happen so fast."

The tears start the second I get in my car. I drive past the Manor House, parking by the barn, and enter the castle through the old servants' door. The stairs to the top of the west turret are brutal, but I welcome the pain in my lungs because it helps block out everything else. I throw my shoulder against the ancient wood door and squeeze through the opening. The battlement is rough against my shoulder as I sag against it, tears freely falling down my face, the wind ripping at my hair.

I feel so utterly lost. Like a plastic bag being whipped around in a storm—no direction, nowhere to go. I brace my hands on the blocks of stone, leaning into the space between them, screaming until my throat is raw. Screaming for the loss of a dream I held so close for so long. For the future I planned out so meticulously. For not having a plan for the first time in my life. My screams turn into sobs, and I fall to my knees, burying my face in my hands.

"Fuck, Isla." Theo's voice registers a second before his arms wrap around me, hauling me away from the ledge. He presses his lips to my hair as I sob into his shirt, smoothing his hand down my back. "Are you hurt?" he asks, a quiet urgency in his voice.

I can't do anything more than shake my head no, shuddering breaths wracking my body.

"I don't think I'm strong enough for this," I finally say, hiccupping.

"I don't know what you're talking about, but I'll lend you my strength as long as you need it."

I wipe my cheeks on his shirt, sniffling. "How do I walk away from what made me who I am? How do I start over?"

He swallows, his bottom lip trembling. "I'm so fucking sorry, Isla." He pulls me out of his lap and sets me on the ground, kissing my cheek. He turns in the doorway, "At least come inside so you don't tumble over." I blink up at him, confused. Emotion roils in his eyes like storm clouds, and then he's gone. I follow his advice and go inside, trying to ignore the pit in my stomach. I know I'm a lot sometimes, but out of everyone I've been with, he's the one I thought could handle it. Maybe I was wrong. Maybe this was all a gigantic fucking mistake. I wipe my cheeks and take several deep, shuddering breaths before heading back downstairs.

I find Charlie out on the terrace and distract myself by interrogating her on everything to do with babies so I can plan the shower she deserves. I desperately want to confide in her but don't want to cause stress, so I keep it in and paste a bright smile on my face. When Theo hasn't texted me after several hours, I turn my phone off and head back to the cottage, a mix of fury and sadness churning in my gut. What I need is a glass of wine, a hot shower, and a good night's sleep. Everything will be better in the morning.

I wake to sunlight streaming into my bedroom, thousands of gold specks floating around me like pixie dust. I yawn, stretching my arms above my head. As I reach for my phone, my fingers brush against a piece of paper. I jerk my hand back. That wasn't there last night. Heart pounding, I sit up and pick it up with my fingertips. *Warranty Deed* is written in bold letters across the top. My heart drops.

Oh no. No, no, no.

I skim the paper to the very end, where all three of them have signed it. I turn it over, looking for some sort of explanation, and find a Post-It note.

I'm so sorry, Isla. I'm going to do the right thing for once. I can't wait to come back someday and see your dreams come true. I'll never forget you. -T.
  P.S. Patrick is paid through the end of the month.

. . .

COME BACK? No. My fingers tremble as I power on my phone. Eleven missed texts and two missed calls. Henry sent all but two of the messages.

Isla

Isla answer me

You missed 2 calls from Henry

Is this what you want? Theo said he found you sobbing over the pub and that he couldn't stand it anymore. That he was going to do the right thing for once in his life.

He has us on the next flight out, Isla. Please answer me.

I don't want to leave. I don't remember the last time I was this happy.

God, that's selfish of me. I'm happy, but you're not, and that's what matters in the end.

Don't worry about us. We'll be fine. Can't wait to come back eventually and see what you've done with the place.

They just told us to put our phones in airplane mode. Our sim cards won't work in the states, so I guess this is goodbye.

See ya later, Red.

I wipe at the tears running down my cheeks, clicking over to the text thread with Dylan.

You have to do something, Isla. He's convinced he's doing the right thing.

Please.

Oh god. I grab my phone and the deed. When I can't find my keys, I lace up my tennis shoes and sprint all the way to the castle. I crash through the front door, calling for Charlie.

"Isla!" Charlie frames my face, her big blue eyes already filling with tears in response to mine. "What's wrong?"

"They left, Charlie." I sob into her neck, gasping for breath. My heart feels like it's shattering into a million pieces.

"Who left?"

I hold out the paper to her, my hand trembling.

She covers her mouth with her hand. "But I thought they sank everything they had into the pub."

"They did. The pub was all they had."

"Did you call them?"

I shake my head no. "Their sim cards won't work now that they're back in the States."

"What will you do?" she asks, tucking my hair behind my ear.

I take one steadying breath, then another, my mind racing.

"You should go after them," Charlie says, answering her own question.

"Go after who?" Jack enters the foyer, alarm flashing in his eyes. Charlie hands him the deed. He turns it over, scanning the note on the back. "They left just like that? Without saying anything?"

"Henry and Dylan tried, but I had my phone turned off."

"Why did you have your phone turned off?"

"Because Theo found me sobbing at the top of one of the towers. Said he was sorry and left me there without another word. I was annoyed."

"Why were you sobbing?" he asks, getting to the root of the issue.

My face heats. "They hired someone to work at the pub."

"And?" He's looking at me like I'm daft, and he has every right. I can't even count the number of times I've complained to him about having to work there when I don't own it. "I didn't take it well."

"Why, Isla?"

I turn away from him, unable to take the disappointment in his eyes any longer. "Because I'm scared. My entire future was planned out, and now it's...not."

"You're too smart to be this dumb." He smacks my shoulder with the deed, letting it flutter to the floor. "How do you feel now that everything you wanted has dropped into your lap? Are you looking forward to shouldering the responsibility of the pub on your own? What happened to the brewery you were just talking about opening?"

"Be nice, Jack," Charlie admonishes, taking my hand.

"No. She's a big girl. Answer me, Isla."

I suck in a breath through my nose. "You're right. The thought of going back to the way it used to be makes me sick to my stomach."

"There you go. And how do you feel when you think about starting a brewery?"

"Excited for the challenge." He pats me on the head like a puppy who finally learned a new trick. God, I really fucked this up. I let myself get pulled into the endless depths of what could have been instead of facing my fear of the unknown. "I'm going after them."

"No, you're not. You're staying right here and helping us get the roof back on the old groundskeeper's house before the floors get ruined."

"*The roof?*" Fucking hell.

"We had a three-day window, and they left after the first day. It will take all of us to get it done before it rains."

I want to be the petulant little sister. Ask him how that's my fault. But it *is* my fault. I shouldn't have let myself get in the way of the best thing that's ever happened to me.

"I think a bit of a cooling-off period will be good, anyway," Charlie says softly. "The four of you will have time to get your priorities straight."

I don't want to 'cool off,' but I nod anyway, knowing she's probably right, just like she always is.

"Meet me out back in ten. Charlie has some coveralls you can borrow," Jack says, leaving no room for protest. He wraps me in his arms, his beard scratching my temple. "You're the strongest person I know, Isla. You were wasting your potential by holing yourself up in that pub. Now's your chance to take your future by the horns and show it who's motherfucking boss." He turns me to face the mirror hanging on the wall. "Say it."

I meet his gaze, tears of gratitude nearly spilling over. "I'm Isla MacLeod and I'm a motherfucking bad bitch."

He grins. "Again."

"I'm Isla fucking MacLeod! And I'm a motherfucking bad bitch!" I yell, my words bouncing off the walls.

Jack kisses the crown of my head, pride shining in his eyes. "And don't you ever forget it."

17

The plane ride to this middle of nowhere, tiny Tennessee town takes entirely too long. My mind races the entire time, wondering if I did the right thing by not reaching out on social media. I want to confront Theo in person–where I can see his body language–but now that I'm stuck in this tin can for hours, I'm second-guessing my decision. What if he refuses to see me? Refuses to change his mind? I ask the flight attendant for a piece of paper and pen and start scribbling down my thoughts, eventually organizing them enough to turn them into a rough outline of what I want to say to him.

The pilot's voice blares through the speakers. *Welcome to Knoxville, Tennessee, where the current time is 11:54 am.*

Butterflies attack my stomach. This was a mistake. I should have told them I was coming first. Got an address. Why did I think I could drive around in a strange city and find them? Even if the town their PO box is in only has a population of 574, that doesn't mean they'll be there, or I'll be able to find them.

Fuck.

I take slow, measured breaths, closing my eyes and relaxing my muscles from the top of my head to the tips of my toes.

"Miss? Are you okay?" I open my eyes to the flight attendant leaning over me, worry creasing her face.

I plaster a smile on my face. "Yes. Yes, sorry." I grab my backpack and shuffle past her, my carry-on nearly breaking my nose when I pull it from the overhead bin. I turn away before she can see the tears in my eyes or the way my chin wobbles. I force myself to take slow, deep breaths as I walk past the empty seats and don't stop until I make it to the car rental counter.

Keys in hand, I walk through a pair of automatic doors into a solid wall of humidity. I knew it was going to be hot, but I didn't know it was going to be like *this*. I start shedding layers right there on the sidewalk, stripping down to my bike shorts and tank top before finding the car. I can't remember what they told me at the counter, so I press the lock button on the key fob several times, following the beeps until I locate the car. It's fucking huge. In my head, it had made sense to rent a bigger vehicle in hopes that we'd all be returning to the airport together, but now, seeing it in person, I think I made a gigantic mistake. It's the biggest car I've ever seen.

Doubt starts creeping in. I've always prided myself on being a strong, independent woman, but am I really? Jack has always been there if I needed anything. I've always had enough money to get by. Maybe I've just been faking it my whole life. I take a breath.

I can do this.

I start the car and crank the AC. Pulling my phone out of my backpack, I plug it in and power it on, a text from Charlie immediately popping up.

You're the most incredible person I know, Isla. You can do anything you put your mind to. You're a motherfucking bad bitch, and don't you ever forget it. You've got this.

I made you a playlist just in case you need to be reminded every once in a while.

I wipe away the tear that plops onto the screen with my thumb and press play. "Bad Bitch" by Bebe Rexha blares out of the speakers as I pull out of the parking garage. The GPS tells me I'm thirty minutes from the cabin I rented on the edge of Townsend—a tiny town that calls itself the peaceful side of the Smokies. The drive is beautiful. Wide highways eventually become two-lane roads with forested mountains rising on both sides. It reminds me of the high-lands. No wonder the guys felt so at home in Scotland. I turn onto a tiny one-lane road and follow a river for several miles before the cabin comes into view. I pull off the road and stare in disbelief. It sits on a rocky island in the middle of the river, a network of rope bridges connecting it to the mainland.

I clutch the suitcase to my chest as I navigate the bridges, juggling it to one arm in order to punch the code into the door. I drop every-thing on the floor and head back to the car, wanting to get to the post office as quickly as possible. It only takes me ten minutes to get there and have the postmaster confirm that privacy laws protect PO boxes. Several stops later, I start losing hope. Either the guys don't live here, or everybody's protecting them. And, hell, can you really blame them?

When I can't ignore the hunger pains any longer, I stop at the closest restaurant. The parking lot is packed with motorcycles, cars, and campers, most of them with out-of-state license plates. I do what the sign says and find a seat, opting for the outside patio to enjoy the views.

Thirty minutes later, I'm licking crumbs from my fingers as I flick through pictures on my phone when the waitress brings my check. Before I can give her my card, she stops me with a hand on my shoulder.

"I'm so sorry, but I couldn't help but notice the picture you have up on your phone. Do you know Theo?" She pulls a strand of thick chestnut hair over her shoulder, twisting it around her finger nervously.

My heart stops. "Yes. Do you know where he is?"

Sadness clouds her expression. "I don't. I was hoping you did."

"How do you know him?"

"I used to date him and–" She stops abruptly, her cheeks turning red. My gaze flicks down to her nametag. Katie. It takes everything in me not to show any reaction.

"I–I'm happily married now," she stammers, wiggling her ring so I can see. "I owe him an apology, but I haven't seen him in years."

My brows draw together. "Their construction company wasn't here?"

She shakes her head. "Their headquarters used to be in Knoxville. This is where their mama and daddy lived. They grew up here."

My stomach sinks. "Where would they go if they came back here?"

"Back to their parents' place," she says without hesitation.

"Their parents' place? I thought they sold everything."

"It's just a tiny cabin on the edge of the park where their parents lived right after getting married. The only value in it is sentimental, I'm afraid. There's not enough land for someone to build one of those monstrosities they're building nowadays," she says, her Southern twang drawing out the syllables.

"Can you tell me where it is?"

Her gaze turns suspicious, realizing she's already said too much. I hold my phone out to her, encouraging her to flip through pictures of me and the guys together.

"You're dating them."

I nod.

"Good. Don't screw it up like I did. I ruined all of our lives for a long time. And then their parents..." She looks off in the distance, pain in her eyes. "They deserve to be happy for the rest of their lives. I hope you can do that for them."

"I'm trying," I say, my voice cracking. "I need to find them first."

Katie tears a piece of paper from her notepad and scribbles down an address. "This is the closest house to the cabin. Park on the side of the road. There should be a path to the left of the house. Follow that until you come to a stone wall. Turn left there and follow it until you get to the cabin."

"Thank you," I whisper. "Is there anything–"

"No," she says, cutting me off. "It's enough to know they're doing well." She squats down, her gaze intense. "Treasure them. You'll never find anything that feels the same again. Trust me."

"I will. I promise." I let my instincts guide me and pull her into a hug. She hesitates at first and then wraps her arms around me, squeezing hard before pulling back.

"I *am* happy, you know," she sniffles, her eyes shining. "I just have so many regrets about that time in my life. Not a day goes by that I don't nearly drown in guilt."

"Don't do that to yourself, Katie. They have a great relationship with each other, and they were thriving before Theo ran halfway around the world to do what he thought was the right thing."

"Sounds about right," she chuckles. "Your meal is on the house. Go find your men."

"Won't you get in trouble?" I ask, trying to hand her my card.

"My husband owns the place. I'll tell him I was a bad girl when I go back to the kitchen." She winks, her eyes sparkling.

"Thank you. So much."

"I'm the one that should be thanking you. Knowing they have you makes me feel a million times better. I'm one step closer to forgiving myself. Now go!"

Paper in hand, I jog back to the car, feeling hopeful for the first time in days. I plug the address into my GPS with trembling fingers. My heart lurches in my chest when I see it's only five minutes away. I concentrate on my breathing as I navigate the narrow streets, parking on the side of the road across from the mailbox at the address she gave me. Wiping my sweaty palms on my shirt, I get out of the car and close the door softly. This is it. My only clue to go on.

I scan the trees, my gaze snagging on a partially concealed opening, newly broken branches littering the ground. I run down the path, choking back a sob, my heart pounding in my chest. Branches rip at my hair and skin, but I don't even feel them. I hold my breath as I pound over a rickety bridge, the river rushing below me, waiting for one misstep. I turn at the rock wall, dragging my fingers along it as I run. I stumble over a root, slamming into the wall, my shoulder and temple scraping along the rocks as I go down. Fuck. I pull up the hem of my shirt and dab at the blood, cursing under my breath.

I gingerly push myself up, brushing the dirt off my knees. I look up, and there it is. It's more of a shack than a cabin, but God, is it beautiful. The honeyed logs glow like amber in the afternoon light. I call Theo's name as I walk closer. Nothing. I rap my knuckles against the door, trying the handle when there's no answer. His scent envelops me the second I step inside. I sag against the doorframe, my eyes watering in relief.

Now what do I do? Do I wait for him to come back? Do I write a note and let him make the call? All I know is I don't want to be a sweaty, bloody mess when I see him, so I head back to the river to cool off and give myself time to think.

I clamber down the river bank, toe off my shoes and wade through ankle-deep water until I come to a pool deep enough to swim in. I peel off my tank top, tossing it onto a rock, and jump in. Crystal-clear water closes over my head, icy fingers sliding over my skin. It feels so fucking good. I stay in until my teeth chatter, draping myself over a sun-warmed rock on the river's edge, fanning my hair around my head. The sounds of bubbling water and chirping birds lulls me into a dream-like state.

"Isla?"

I startle, rolling off the rock into the water, spluttering as I stand and attempt to push my water-logged hair off my face. I hold my hand up to shield my eyes from the sun, the shadow in front of me taking the shape of a man—a man with full lips, chiseled abs, wearing nothing but swim trunks. I swallow hard. "Hi, Theo."

18

When Theo sees the blood dripping down my face, his knees give out, and he drags me down with him into the water. I don't even care that the river rock under my ass is the most uncomfortable thing I've ever experienced. He's here, right in front of me.

"Isla, what happened?" He reaches up with a shaking hand, wiping blood away from my eye.

"I tripped over a root. I'm fine. Are you okay?" I ask, alarmed by the color leeching from his face.

"You're not fine, you're bleeding." His jaw clenches, panic swirling in his eyes. "Come on, let's get back to the cabin. I'll find some antiseptic."

"Not until we talk."

"Isla."

"No. You left me, Theo. *You left*." My voice cracks.

He sighs. "You were up there at the top of that tower sobbing your heart out. Looking like you were going to fling yourself over the edge at any minute. Because of something *I* did, Isla. The only solution I could think of was to leave, having peace in the knowledge that you'd be living out your dream."

"What about you? Your brothers? What about *your* dreams, Theo?" I shiver as a cloud moves in front of the sun, the water instantly feeling colder.

"None of it matters if you aren't happy, Isla."

I shrug his hand off my shoulder, furious. "Do you hear yourself right now? Don't you think I care that *you're* happy? What did you think I was going to do when you left? Just go on with my life like I never met you guys?"

"Yes. No–I don't know, Isla. I didn't think that far ahead. I just knew I couldn't see you in pain like that again."

"I have big emotions, Theo. They're going to sneak out sometimes. If this is going to work, you'll have to accept that."

"If this works?" He meets my gaze, desperation in his eyes.

"Do you think I came all this way to tell you to go fuck yourself?"

"I wouldn't blame you."

Those four little words are all I need to finally understand where he's coming from. "You don't think you deserve to be happy, do you?"

He throws a rock into the river, storm clouds roiling in his eyes.

"Look, I don't know what happened with Katie and your brothers, but I know you blame yourself. How long are you going to play the martyr? You're only hurting your brothers all over again."

"You have no idea what you're talking about."

"I spent most of my life thinking I didn't deserve anything because so much was handed to me. So much so that I stayed in a job that worked me to the bone. I had one day off a week for years. No vacations. No fun. Until you and your brothers showed up and helped me understand that sometimes things need to be turned upside down. That I deserve to do something that makes me happy. Like opening a brewery."

He looks at me, his gaze piercing my soul, hope limning the edges of his doubt. "Do you really, truly mean that?" I nod, blinking back tears. "You'll be happy leaving the bar?"

I sniffle, choking out a laugh. "When you left, the thought of returning to the bar and shouldering that responsibility filled me with dread."

"Thank fuck." He leans forward and wraps his arms around me, pulling me into his lap. "I don't deserve you, Isla," he says, his voice muffled against my neck.

I pull back, framing his face with my hands. "Yes, you fucking do. You deserve the world, Theo. I don't know what I would have done if the three of you hadn't crashed into my life like that. I'm so thankful for you." I sweep a tear from under his eye, my heart aching. "Promise me you won't leave again."

"I don't think that will be a problem," he murmurs, his thumb tracing the freckles over my cheekbone. "The last three days have been absolute hell on earth. When I saw you sunbathing on that rock, like a vision out of a dream, I knew I never wanted to be separated from you again. Everything became crystal clear."

"What became clear?" I ask, leaning into his touch.

"I have no choice but to love you, Isla." His lips crash into mine, and I pour every fiber of my being into that kiss. I open for him, welcoming the warmth of his tongue, the saltiness of our tears. I straddle his hips, pressing my body against his. He squeezes me until I squeak, his low chuckle sending goosebumps skittering over my skin.

"It'll never be close enough, Sunflower." He pushes to his knees, palming my thighs to keep me in place. "Let's go up to the cabin and dry off. I need to call Henry and Dylan."

I grab my tank top and pull it over my head. "Where are they?" I ask, clinging to him like a koala as he picks his way over the rocks and climbs the bank.

"I have no idea. I've been dead to the world the last three days, wallowing in the misery I created." He kicks open the door to the cabin and goes straight back to the bathroom, turning on the shower.

"Theo," I rasp, my heart in my throat. His gaze collides with mine. "I love you, too."

A shiver wracks his body. "Thank fuck, Isla." He sets me on my feet, pulling me up on my toes to brush his lips over mine. "Will you let me take care of you?" he murmurs, his lips moving over mine.

"Yes, Theo." I won't admit it, but I'm exhausted. The adrenaline coursing through my system the last few days has finally crashed, and I feel like I could sleep for twenty-four hours straight. I lift my arms as he peels off my top and then shuffle from foot to foot as he shimmies off my shorts. The worry in his eyes when he studies the gash on my head leaches the sexual tension from the room, leaving something poignant and sweet. He walks me into the shower, guiding my head against his chest as he massages shampoo into my hair. Once rinsed, he runs conditioner through it and squirts body wash onto a washcloth, cleaning the river water from my skin. Tears prick my eyes, and my bottom lip quivers. I've never felt so pampered, so loved. Theo nudges my chin, tilting my tear-stained face up to his.

"You mean the world to me, Isla. I'm sorry I acted in a way that caused you to doubt that."

"You're forgiven," I whisper. I push onto my toes and press my lips to his, my body melting against him, safe and warm.

He pulls away after several seconds. "We can continue this after I get you dried off and patched up." He turns off the water, tucking a towel around his waist before wrapping me in a fluffy towel and carrying me into the bedroom. He folds a towel and lays it on the pillow, instructing me to lie down while he gathers the supplies to bandage my cuts. I must have fallen asleep because the next thing I remember is Theo and Henry whisper-shouting at each other.

"You better not ever pull that shit again, Theo. You can't fucking ask me to choose between the most important people in my life." Henry's voice is tight, angry.

"I thought I was doing the right thing. I'm sorry."

"Can we talk like adults next time?" Dylan asks. "Or are some of us incapable of that?" The sarcasm dripping from his words has my lips pulling up. Brothers till the end.

"Stop fighting over me," I say, poking my head out of the bedroom, my voice rusty from sleep.

Henry's face pales, Dylan's brows drawing together with concern.

"I'm fine! I had a run-in with a rock wall, that's all."

"You don't look fine," Dylan says, inspecting Theo's bandaging job. Satisfied, he meets my gaze, relief softening his eyes. "I'm so glad you're here. I missed you." He kisses me softly, sliding his hands over my back and giving me a tight hug.

"Don't hog her," Henry grumbles, not so patiently waiting his turn. Dylan releases me, our gazes locked until Henry's massive body blocks his view. "I fucking missed you, Isla." Those big arms wrap around me, and I melt into the safety of his chest. "Why didn't you answer our texts?"

I pull back so I can look him in the face. "I had my phone turned off. I'm so sorry."

"Never fucking again, I swear to God. I won't survive it." He buries his face in my neck, his grip tightening.

"I had a lot of time to think the last few days while I was helping Jack reconstruct the roof," I say, pulling away from Henry and facing all three of them. The look on Theo's face would have made me laugh if I wasn't nervous over what I'm about to say. "We need to all sit down and talk about how this is going to work."

"Isn't it fine how it's working now?" Theo asks.

I roll my eyes. "Obviously not. I just had to fly halfway around the world to find you. You're each your own person, and because of that, we need to be forming separate relationships. Each of them equally strong. It's the best way for us to ensure this is going to work. We also need to talk about what will happen if one of you chooses to leave again. I refuse to be in a relationship that will be torn apart because one of you has a tantrum."

Theo's mouth falls open, but he only snaps it shut, accepting the criticism.

"Also, I want to move back into the Manor House. The cottage is too freaking small to live in long-term."

"I have plenty of room in my bed," Henry says, smirking.

I cut him a glare. "I'll be moving into the fourth bedroom. I'll deduct a quarter of the rent to make it fair."

"Anything else, princess?" Theo drawls, looking like a goddamn supermodel leaning against the wall.

My mouth goes dry. "Yes, we need to talk about sex."

Dylan swallows hard, then coughs, his eyes watering. "Sex?" he wheezes, his cheeks coloring.

"You'd think you're a virgin with the way you're acting right now," Henry laughs, hitting him on the back.

"Yeah, because we're talking about having sex with *Isla,*" he fake whispers.

"You guys are making this so awkward," I groan, covering my face with my hands.

"Here's the plan," Theo says, pulling on a shirt. "I'm going to go into town and grab some groceries for dinner and a case of beer. We can get drunk, eat good food, and talk about sex all night long. Deal?"

"Deal."

19

By the time Theo gets back with the groceries, Dylan and Henry have built a fire, and I'm sitting there feeling like I'm going to throw up. My earlier bravery has worn off, making me wonder what I was thinking when I suggested this talk. It would have been a hell of a lot easier to type out a text or email. I could have taken my time and said everything I needed to without all this tension clogging my throat. If it were up to my body, I would just fuck all three of them right here in the woods and be done with this nonsense.

"You're awfully quiet," Henry says, sitting in the Adirondack chair beside me.

I glance over at him, my response evaporating from my tongue. He's wearing shorts and a tank top that show off his incredible muscles. Smooth skin for days. God I want to touch him. Lick him. I lick my lips instead, desire coursing through my bloodstream. I slide my gaze along the veins on the back of his hand, up his forearm to his bicep. I want him to manhandle me. Hold me down. Fu–

"Isla."

I drag my gaze to his face, to the color rising up his cheeks, his hooded eyes. Fuck. "Yes?" His tongue slides along his bottom lip, and I nearly combust.

"If you keep looking at me like that..."

"You'll what, Henry?" Kiss me? Touch me? Fuck me? God, I wish I had the guts to just say it.

"What I *would* do or what I *want* to do?" he asks, eyes dark.

"Both."

"I would pull my cock out and fuck my hand while you watch. Relieve some of the goddamn tension that's eating me alive."

Oh fuck. I wasn't ready for that. "And what do you *want* to do?" I ask, needing to know like I need air to breathe.

"I want to pull you out of the chair, spread you out on the forest floor, and feast like a king. Worship you like the goddess you are. Does that answer your question?"

God damn. I cross my legs, trying to ease the ache.

"What are you two whispering about?" Dylan asks, setting down a cooler and sitting on my other side. One look at me, and he's pulling at the neck of his T-shirt, shifting in his chair. "Oh," he croaks, understanding dawning in his eyes. He grabs three beers, handing us both one and then cracking his own. "I'm not going to be able to get through this unless I have a little liquid courage."

The door to the cabin crashes closed, and I look over my shoulder to see Theo pounding down the steps, his arms full. His eyes don't leave me as he sets everything down, the warmth of the fire pulling out tiny drops of perspiration on his skin, making him look like he's sparkling in the evening light.

"The skin of a killer," I call out, biting my lip to keep in a laugh. He stalks toward me, not even a flicker of a smile.

He pulls me out of my chair, bands his arm around my ass, and lifts me up, wrapping my legs around his torso. "You'd better hold on tight, spider monkey," he whispers in my ear, walking away from the fire.

I crack up. "I thought it went over your head!" My smile falls from my face when he traps me against the side of the cabin, his cock pressing against my stomach.

"I should have kissed you earlier, and now it's all I can think about," he breathes, skimming his nose along my jaw.

My body is on fire, need racing like electricity over my skin, puckering my nipples before settling into a steady pulse at the apex of my thighs. "Theo," I groan, tilting my neck to the side to give him access to my neck.

"When you say my name like that, fuck, Isla. It makes me want to bury my cock in your pussy and make you feel things you've never felt before."

God. I whimper, using his shoulders to pull myself up until his cock nestles between my legs. He rolls his hips, making direct contact with my clit. "Theo, we need to talk first," I moan, rocking against him.

He grumbles, hauling me away from the cabin and depositing me back in my chair, not bothering to hide the way his shorts tent in the front. "We need to get this talk out of the way. Now," he says, popping the top on a beer and taking several long pulls.

I sit up tall in my chair, squeezing my thighs together, desperately trying to come back down to earth.

"Go on, Isla," Dylan says, giving me an encouraging smile.

"If we do this, I want to do it right. I need to build individual relationships with each of you first. Strong ones. So that what happened earlier this week doesn't happen again."

"It won't happen again," Theo says, squatting beside me. "I promise."

"I know, but that doesn't change anything. Charlie and the guys did the same and have a rock-solid relationship because of it. This needs to be done the right way or not at all."

"You're in charge, Isla," Dylan says.

"For now," Theo mutters under his breath.

Images of him controlling me flash through my mind. God. Why can't I let my body call the shots like I always used to do? I could be having the best fuck of my life right now. But that little voice in the back of my head reminds me I don't want this to be like the other times. I want them to be my endgame. And that means taking it slowly. Going out on dates. Really getting to know each other.

"Should we set up some sort of timeline? Maybe a schedule?" Dylan asks, taking out his phone and opening the notes app.

"God, I love you," I laugh, snorting when his face turns the color of a strawberry. "The masquerade party is a month away. Why don't we make everything fair game starting the night of the party?" Dylan nods, typing away. "I think we should make a point to actually date each other—so maybe one date with each of you a week? And one group date a week?"

"What are the ground rules for when we're alone versus when we're all together?" Henry asks, his gaze dipping to my mouth, sex practically radiating from him.

"Anything goes on our one-on-one dates. No group sex until after the party."

Henry runs his hand through his hair. "You'll have to be more specific about what you mean by group sex, babe."

I always thought couples calling each other babe was so cliché, but hearing it come from his lips has me feeling some kind of way. "Um–" I clear my throat, my mind clouded. I close my eyes, blocking out the absolutely overwhelming eye candy surrounding me. "Nothing going in anywhere. Except fingers." Dylan's groan has me shooting to my feet and stepping away from them before I do something stupid. "Do we have a deal?"

They all stand simultaneously, walking toward me like I'm their prey. Oh god. "Do we have a deal?" I ask again, my voice cracking.

"Yes, we have a deal, Sunflower," Theo rasps, reaching out for me. I shriek and pull back, my heart hammering in my throat.

"Dylan, Henry?"

"Deal," they echo each other, coming closer until I'm surrounded. I suck in a shaky breath as I turn in a circle. "What're you doing?"

"Showing you what you're missing," Henry says, his big hands wrapping around my waist.

"But–"

"We'll follow your rules, Isla," Dylan murmurs, pushing my hair behind my shoulder and kissing my neck. Theo grabs me from behind, pulling me against his chest, kissing the crown of my head.

Henry slides his fingers along my jaw, pushing my chin up so I'm looking at him. My knees turn to Jell-O. Theo's arm the only thing preventing me from melting into a puddle.

Henry's eyes are midnight blue in the waning light, the sparks of desire in their depths burning me alive. He dips his head and pulls at my bottom lip with his teeth before tilting my chin and pressing his lips to mine. He sweeps his tongue along the seam of my mouth, and I open for him, sliding my tongue along his. This kiss isn't soft or gentle, it's rough and punishing. Lust incarnate. His groan feeds the part of me that's desperate to strip their clothes off and fuck them like my life depends on it. The part that doesn't want to think, just feel. And god, it would feel so fucking good. I push my hands under Henry's T-shirt, dragging my fingers over his abs, over the V of his abdomen to his lower back. I pull him closer, moaning as he rolls his hips against me, his cock pressing into my stomach. He breaks our kiss, peppering kisses down my throat. Dylan closes in, gripping my chin, pulling my mouth open. His eyes are dark with desire, something dangerous in their depths that has my nerve endings pricking with excitement.

"Such a filthy girl," he murmurs, dragging my bottom lip down with his thumb. "I can't stop thinking about how your perfect lips will feel wrapped around my cock." He captures my mouth, his tongue meeting mine with rough, desperate strokes. Theo's hands skim over my ribs, coming up to cup my breasts, testing the weight of them before tracing his thumbs in a wide arc around my nipples. I moan against Dylan's lips, pushing into Theo's hands as Henry licks a path over my collarbone. Theo pulls my top down, giving Henry full access. He drags his teeth over my nipple, then pulls me into his mouth, sucking hard and deep. My lips break away from Dylan's as my knees buckle. Theo scrambles to catch me, going down with me, cushioning my fall. He hauls me into his lap, his cock pressing against my ass.

"Arms up," Dylan commands, his gaze heated. He strips off my top, the campfire bathing my tits in flickering orange light.

"You're so fucking gorgeous," Henry breathes, falling to his knees, crouching to trace my nipple with his tongue.

Theo lies back, pulling me on top of him, sliding his hand over my stomach, over my shorts, and between my legs. I buck against his fingers, my body strung tight as a bow. "Tell me," he whispers in my ear, sliding his finger along my slit.

"Please," I gasp, my back arching as Henry's hot mouth closes over my nipple and pulls.

"Tell him what you want," Dylan says, palming my other breast.

"Harder," I demand, covering Theo's hand with mine, adding pressure. I close my eyes and relax against him, floating on a cloud of sensation. Henry's scruff scratches my inner thigh as he kisses his way to my center. Dylan rolls my nipples between his fingers, forcing me to ride the line between pain and pleasure. Henry pushes Theo's hand away and nuzzles his face between my legs, nipping at my clit before hooking his fingers into my waistband and stripping off my shorts.

"Forget what I said," I pant, mewling as Theo runs his middle finger along my slit. "No deal. I want to fuck. Now."

Theo's chuckle has me bucking against his hand, so fucking desperate. "We're not reneging, Isla. Fingers only." He pushes two fingers into me, the heel of his palm putting pressure on my clit as fucks me.

"I want the three of you naked. Let me touch you," I beg, my eyes rolling back as Theo hits my G-spot. Dylan and Henry stand, shedding their clothes. Theo lifts his hips, and they each grab one side of his waistband and pull his shorts off. I settle my weight against him, the shaft of his cock pressing against my ass cheeks. Fuck. I squirm until he curses, his hips jerking on their own, thrusting between my cheeks.

"God, Isla," he groans, matching the rhythm of his fingers.

Henry drops between my legs, pushing Theo's hand away again. The first swipe of his tongue brings me right to the edge.

"Henry, holy fuck," I pant, tugging his head away to give myself a second. He looks up at me with an evil grin, his eyes sparkling. Move-ment catches my eye, and I look up, the sight of Dylan fucking his hand nearly doing me in. "If you guys won't break the rules, I'm going to push the boundaries as far as I can go. We're all getting there together. Theo, are you good where you are?" His grunt of affirmation turns into a moan as he flexes his hips against me, his cock riding up my ass crack. Holy fucking god. I don't know if I'm strong enough for this. I clear my throat, desperately trying to rein myself in. "Henry, I want your cock against my pussy," I demand. He shuffles forward, wrapping his fist around his cock and sliding the head along my slit. He notches himself at my entrance, bearing down with his hips, pulling back right before he goes in. I sob in frustration, desperately needing to be filled.

"Dylan, straddle my stomach. Fuck my tits." The change in his face as he steps over me has adrenaline pounding through my veins, my body responding to his animalistic need. He holds my gaze as he spits in his hand and slides it over his shaft. I push my breasts together, only breaking eye contact to watch his cock slide between them, the head poking out at the top, red and angry. I want him in my mouth so fucking badly. I want to suck him until he's on his knees begging for mercy. My eyes flutter closed as they all move at once, the head of Theo's cock sliding over my asshole as the ridge on Henry's cock catches on my clit.

"Yes," I moan, moving my hips to meet their thrusts, the danger of them ramming inside any second driving me mad. Two more thrusts and I lose control of my body, my muscles spasming. Dylan isn't far behind, but Henry, god bless him, pulls away, his mouth between my legs before I can protest. Two fingers massage my G-spot while he flays me alive with his tongue. My nails dig into Dylan's thighs, and I cry out, our gazes connecting, his jaw clenching as he comes with me. Theo's moan blends with Dylan's as his hands flex on my hips, pulling me down tight against his cock, his body trembling as he tries to hold back. Dylan climbs off me, and Henry takes his place, pulling me into a demanding kiss as he slides his cock back and over my clit.

He breaks the kiss, breathing hard. "Again, Isla. Come with me."

I've never come twice back-to-back, but the way he looks at me, the way he charts every movement of my body like he's a sailor and I'm the sea has me diving deep in search of another.

"The second that fucking party is over, I'm burying myself so deep inside, you won't know where I end and you begin," Theo says roughly, his lips hot on my neck. I moan into Henry's shoulder, my teeth grazing his skin. I dig my nails into his ass, the three of us finding a rhythm that has me clawing myself back to the precipice. Dylan slips his hand between Henry and me, scooping up the cum dripping over my chest and rubbing it into my tits, tweaking my nipples.

"Fuck, you like that, don't you?" Henry growls, his pupils dilating. "When we're finished, I'm going to write my name on you with my cum so everyone knows you're fucking mine." He holds my gaze as I splinter apart beneath him. He lowers his weight, increasing the friction. One more thrust, and he drops his head to my shoulder, his groan so erotic I know I'll remember it forever. Theo's holding out, his moan broken as he slows down his thrusts, making the moment last.

"Fuck, Isla," he chokes out, his hips stuttering, cum warm and sticky on my lower back. Henry sits back on his haunches, looking at me like a lion looks at a rabbit. He slides his fingers through the cum pooled on my stomach and writes his name along my inner thigh, branding me. He extends his hand toward my mouth, giving me a choice. I lick off every drop, greedy for him.

"Let's wash you up while Theo cooks us some dinner." He scoops me into his arms and starts walking toward the cabin. I snuggle into his warmth, sighing contentedly. "You're not so prickly when you're satisfied," he chuckles, kissing my forehead.

"Looks like you have your job cut out for you then, doesn't it?" I say, hiding my smile against his chest.

20

W e don't waste any time hauling our asses back to the airport for the first flight home. Now that I've finally let go of the pub and embraced opening a brewery, I'm chomping at the bit to get started. It's the wee hours of the morning by the time we pull into the driveway of the Manor House, and after the trauma of the last few days, all I want to do is go down to the cottage and sleep.

"You said you were going to move back into the house," Henry says, snagging my arm as I turn toward the path.

"It's late. I'm exhausted. All my stuff is in the cottage."

He tips my chin up to him, studying my face. "Are you saying you need alone time or that you're too tired to move your things?"

"The latter." I cover my mouth to hide a yawn.

"Go in the house and get comfortable. We'll take care of it." I'm too tired to argue, so I just kiss his cheek and head inside, collapsing on the couch. I wake hours later, sunlight streaming through the window, the smell of bacon making my stomach grumble. I yawn and stretch, untwisting the blanket from my legs as I sit up.

"Morning, Freckles."

Dylan is sitting in a chair opposite me, bathed in a golden glow, wearing sweats and a worn T-shirt. "Were you watching me sleep?"

"How could I not?" he asks, like there's nowhere in the world he'd rather be.

I cover my face with my hands, hiding my smile under the guise of rubbing my eyes. Is this real? A real full-blown committed relationship? Times three? The girl inside me wants to squeal and kick her feet.

"Don't hide." Dylan peels my hands away from my face, framing my face, those expressive brown eyes drawing me in. He traces the edge of my lower lip with his thumb. "Jack came over this morning and talked with us."

I pull back, studying his face. "He what?"

Dylan grimaces. "First, he told us to 'never fucking do that to you again.' Then he told us we better run the pub to the same standards you did, that he wasn't going to watch all of your hard work go down the drain. And third, since we're not bartering labor anymore, he said he'll pay us if we agree to continue working on the castle."

"And what did the three of you say?"

"We agreed. Jack said that with the baby coming soon, he'll be stepping back and letting us finish. Which gives us a little more flexibility in scheduling."

"Well, that works out perfectly, doesn't it?" It feels so good to have all the pieces falling into place.

"It does, and it also gives us time to help you build out your brewery."

My heart jumps in my chest, something in me stirring, ready to create something new. "You guys would do that?"

"Of course we would, Isla."

"Breakfast is ready," Theo calls from the kitchen. "Someone go wake Henry up."

"I'll get him." I jump up, wrapping the blanket around my shoulders, and head to his room. I stop in the doorway, completely enamored with the dark curls falling over his forehead, the dark crescent of lashes against his cheek, the cleft in his chin. He reaches out the second my knee sinks into the bed, pulling me down against his body and burying his face in my hair.

"We should have moved your things into my room," he murmurs, sleep making his voice deliciously raspy. "We could wake up like this every morning."

A steady throb takes up residence between my legs as his hand sweeps over my stomach. There's just something about him. Raw need bound in flesh and bone. A real-life incubus that's impossible to resist. I bite back a gasp as he slides his hand over my breast, his groan like the burn of pure-grain alcohol, licking at my nerve endings.

"Breakfast is ready," I stammer.

"Give me thirty seconds to get you there, and then we can go down to eat."

"What?" I squeak, trying to turn in his arms. He holds me in place, tracing along my waistband with his fingers.

"Please, Isla." The growl of his voice has my legs opening. "That's my girl," he breathes, slipping his hand into my shorts and dragging his middle finger along my slit. I push my hips into his hand, need rising like a tsunami. He centers his fingers over my clit, rolling it under his fingertips.

"Oh god," I moan, arching my back, as he slides his other hand up to my tits.

"If it's my hands on you, you better be calling my name, Isla," he growls. He slides two fingers into me, pushing deep. "This has nothing to do with any god. It's me your pussy's weeping for."

I choke back a sob as he works his fingers in me, the heel of his palm rocking back and forth over my clit. "Fuck, Henry," I moan, writhing against him, needing more. Needing all of him. I press my ass against his cock, desperate for him to be in me. I reach back, sliding my hand over him and squeezing.

"You're playing with fire, Red."

I twist in his arms and push him onto his back, scrambling up, sitting on his thighs, and pinning him to the bed. "What makes you think I don't like dancing in the flames?" I ask, flipping my hair to one side, holding his gaze as I plant my hands on either side of his hips and slowly lower my upper body. He pushes up on his elbows, watching me through hooded eyes. His muscles tense when there's only several inches between my mouth and his cock.

"You okay?" I ask.

"The second you take my cock in your mouth there's no going back, Isla," he warns. "You'll be mine. Forever."

"I'm already yours," I murmur, sweeping my tongue over him, salt and musk and *him* bursting in my mouth. I feather my tongue over his frenulum, greedy for those small twitches, the way his hand clenches in the bedsheets. I open wide, taking him in as far as I can, my hand still wrapped around the base of his shaft, the head of his cock hitting the back of my throat. He's so fucking big. God. I hum my appreciation as I hollow my cheeks, sliding my lips up and down his shaft.

"Isla," he groans, his abs trembling. He wraps his hand in my hair, pulling me off his cock. "It's too much," he pants. "Seeing those green eyes sparkle while they bob over my cock—fuck, Isla."

"Breakfast. Now!" Theo yells from downstairs.

"Henry, please." I lick my lips, and he jerks me up his body, crushing his mouth to mine. I melt into him, rolling my hips over his cock, my body buzzing like a live wire. He drags his teeth over my bottom lips, sucking it into his mouth, sending pure unadultered lust coursing through my system.

The sound of someone clearing their throat at the doorway has both of us freezing.

"If you two don't come down and get your breakfast while it's hot, I'm never going to cook for you again," Theo says, crossing his arms over his chest.

Henry throws me to the end of the bed, hopping on one leg, then the other as he pulls on sweatpants. "I'm not taking a chance that he's being serious," he says, kissing my cheek before jogging past Theo and pounding down the stairs.

"I take it your cooking is important to him," I laugh, climbing off the bed and straightening myself. Theo walks toward me, smoothing my hair and tucking it behind my ear.

"I really just wanted a second alone with you," he says, smiling. "Good morning, Sunflower."

"Good morning," I whisper, the intensity of his gaze causing shyness to creep in. He tugs me closer, angling my head, but I press my hand to his chest to stop him. "I was just–"

He backs me against the doorframe, pushing my chin up, forcing me to look him in the eyes. "I don't care what the fuck you were just doing, Isla." He gently circles my throat with his hand, holding me still while pressing his lips to mine. I scrape my nails over his scalp, pulling him closer, pushing my tongue into his mouth, meeting him stroke for stroke. He releases me a moment later, breathing hard, his gaze dark. "I can't wait for the day when I can wake up beside you and eat *you* for breakfast. But for now, we need to go eat before the food gets cold."

BREAKFAST IS STUFFED FRENCH TOAST, sausage links, and fresh fruit. The guys gobble it down without even thinking about it, but I eat slowly, savoring every bite, slightly in awe of the fact that I have a man who wants to cook for me. I look around at all of them, realizing this may be the first day of the rest of our lives. If this goes well, if they stay, will they live here? Will we be sitting here sharing breakfast fifty years from now? Old and gray, a lifetime of memories between us?

"I'm claiming the first date," Henry says, gulping down the last of his orange juice. "If that's okay with you, sweetheart," he drawls, his wink doing unspeakable things to my body.

"But–" Dylan begins, blinking those big brown eyes.

"No buts. Isla and I haven't had any real time alone in a while."

Theo nods. "Henry's right. Dylan, you can go next. I'll go last. Then our group dates can be over the weekends." He turns to me. "How does that sound to you?"

"Ah–" The sun cuts across his face, highlighting the slash of his cheekbones, the sharpness of his jaw. He arches an eyebrow, his gaze dropping to my lips. I sit up straight, clearing my throat. "Yes, that's fine." Logically, I know why I told them I wanted to wait a month until all four of us sleep together, but fuck is it going to be absolute torture. "So, what are we doing?" I ask Henry.

"I'd like to take you camping. Tomorrow night, if that works for you. It'll give us one more night to catch up on sleep."

"Speaking of sleep," Dylan says, leaning back in his chair, a glint of mischief in his eyes. "Do you really want to sleep by yourself the nights you don't have dates?"

"I mean—maybe? I don't know yet. This is a first for me. Before you guys moved into the house, I had been living by myself for almost a year, and before that, Lach lived here, but he was only here in the evenings. What if I don't like sharing my space? What if it's too much?"

"Fair enough. We'll revisit the conversation after the masquerade party."

"About this party," Theo butts in. "Do we have to dress up?"

"You can, or if you'd rather, a tux and mask would be fine."

"A tux?" Henry asks, doubt flashing in his eyes.

I reach across the table and squeeze his hand. "It'll be fun, I prom- ise. It's usually the highlight of my year." I push back from the table, gathering empty dishes. "Thank you for breakfast, Theo. I need to go shopping for the baby shower. Anyone want to come with me?" Dylan and Henry both look at Theo. I follow their gazes, my eyes connecting with Theo's, my toes curling against the flagstones of the patio. "How about it, Theo? I know how much you absolutely love shopping," I tease.

"I'll be happy if I'm with you, Sunflower." The simple sweetness of his words has a lump forming in my throat. I could get used to this.

21

By the following afternoon, I have everything for the baby shower set up and ready to go, and I'm sitting in my room, my heart racing as I pack a bag for my date with Henry. The anticipation is killing me. I rifle through my drawers, trying to find something to wear, finally deciding on a T-shirt and cutoffs.

"Ready?" Henry asks, sticking his head in my door. I turn toward him, trying to breathe normally even though it feels like all the oxygen has been sucked from the room. He's wearing a worn-in baseball cap, dark hair curling around his ears and the nape of his neck. He smiles shyly, his dimple nearly doing me in.

"Almost," I finally answer, my pulse thrumming as I shove the last of my things in my duffel bag and zip it up.

"Make sure you bring a swimsuit," he says, stretching his arm over his head and leaning against the doorframe. "Actually, on second thought, don't."

"Don't?" I echo, trying not to stare at his bicep and the way it flexes when he moves. The moisture in my mouth evaporates as I wrestle with the desire snaking through me. I clear my throat, dropping my gaze only for it to land on the sliver of skin above his waistband. "You have got to stop doing that," I rasp, licking my lips.

"Why?" he challenges, the corner of his mouth ticking up.

"You know why," I say, taking a step toward him.

"Tell me, Isla," he murmurs, leaning farther into the room, nudging my chin up until our eyes meet.

Fuck he's mesmerizing. Eyes so blue they're almost purple, looking at me like I'm the one thing that'll solve all his problems. And god, I know just one touch will solve all of mine. "Because we won't make it out of my bedroom if you don't," I finally answer, pushing up on my tiptoes to press my lips to his. He growls against my mouth, turning his hat backward and pulling me close, walking us toward the bed.

"Do you know why I picked camping?" he asks, kissing his way along my jaw, pulling at my earlobe with his teeth.

"Why?" I ask, wrapping my legs around his waist as we sink onto the mattress.

"So nobody will be able to hear you scream when I make you come." He bites my nipple through my shirt, and I arch my back, wanting more.

"You can do that here. Now," I say. "I promise I'll be quiet." His chuckle skitters over my skin, pebbling my nipples.

"I don't want you to be quiet, Red." I thread my fingers through his hair, pulling his mouth back to mine, reminding him what he could have right now if he would just take it. He pulls away, breathing hard, eyes hooded. "I'm going to blow your mind tonight."

"Is that so?" I tease, letting him help me to my feet.

"You have no fucking idea," he says, completely serious. "I need to go pack the cooler. Come down when you're ready."

"Okay," I whisper, biting my lip as I watch him walk from the room. God, I love a confident man. I blow out a long breath, completely frazzled. I go into the bathroom and stare at my reflection like she's a stranger. Rosy cheeks, sparkling eyes, swollen lips. I think I like this version better. I bite back a smile, pulling my hair into a bun and swiping on some mascara. I grab my bag and head downstairs before my nerves get the best of me. Henry is outside loading the cooler into the back of the farm truck.

"You know Jack has a truck set up for camping?" I ask, swinging my bag into the back.

"I know, but I've been thinking about this for a while, and I've always envisioned us cooking our food over a fire and sleeping in a tent. If you'd rather–"

"No," I assure him. "This will be perfect." The fact that he's put so much thought into it has me feeling some kind of way. I can't wait to see Charlie's face when I tell her.

"I made a playlist for our date," Henry says, plugging the aux cord into his phone. "I hope that's okay."

"More than okay," I laugh, side-eyeing him, wondering how he's real. Hozier's voice fills the cab as Henry cranks the truck. Goosebumps race over my arms as life takes on an other-worldly quality. Like a movie or a book. Almost too perfect.

Thirty minutes later, Henry pulls off the side of the road, large dunes blocking what would be a spectacular view of the ocean. We scout for a spot and decide on a high rocky outcropping overlooking the beach. I gather driftwood while Henry sets up camp.

"This should last a while," I say, dropping a pile of sticks beside the makeshift firepit.

"I would say so," Henry laughs, wrapping his arms around me. "Ready to catch our dinner?"

"To what?" I ask, eyes wide.

"Don't tell me you've never been fishing, either."

"I never had a reason." I shrug. Until now. Now I want nothing more than to do exactly what Henry wants to do.

"Let me teach you. If you don't like it, we can stop. I brought extra food just in case." I follow him back to the truck, taking a fishing pole from him. "There should be a path," he says, scanning the pasture on the other side of the road. "Yes, there it is. We just have to follow that until we get to the river." We walk side-by-side, fishing poles slung over our shoulders, a tackle box under Henry's arm. "Secret for a secret?" he asks after a few minutes, breaking the silence.

"What kind of secret?"

He shrugs. "Anything."

"You know that night you and your brothers came to the pub?"

"Last summer?"

I nod. "I couldn't get you out of my head, and when I got home–" I stop, swallowing hard, suddenly unsure if I should share this.

"You better finish that sentence, Isla," Henry says, dropping the tackle box and stopping me with a hand around my wrist, his fingers brushing over my racing pulse.

"I got myself there thinking about your hands on me. Your mouth." I look up at him, biting my lip.

"Fucking hell, Isla," he growls. "I would have gladly tongue-fucked you that night and then thanked you for the opportunity."

Heat pools between my legs, the ache almost unbearable. I pull my hand away and keep walking before I do something stupid like push him down right here in the open. "Your turn."

"When Theo told us the sale of the pub went through, I had a dream about you." He pauses, licking his lips. "In that dream, I proposed to you with a ring I carved from a piece of wood. It stuck with me ever since."

"Go on," I say when he doesn't continue.

"I brought a piece of driftwood back to the house the day we met on the beach."

"And?" I ask when he pauses, my heart pounding in my ears.

"I finished it this morning." He fishes in his pocket, depositing a delicate band gingerly in his palm.

My mouth drops open.

"I'm not proposing," he says as he drops to one knee.

"Then why are you on one knee?" I ask, my voice cracking. This feels like a dream. The colors are too bright, the air too crisp, the distant sound of burbling water too loud.

"God, I don't know. This was a horrible idea." He starts to get up, but I put my hands on his shoulders, stopping him.

"Say what you were going to say."

He takes off his hat, running his hand through his hair nervously. "I just want you to have something that reminds you of how much you mean to me. When you're having a shitty day, you can look down at it and remember that you mean the absolute world to me."

"Fuck," I whisper, blinking back tears. "I think that's the sweetest thing anyone has ever done for me."

He slides the ring onto the middle finger of my left hand, then stands and pulls me against him, squeezing tight. I look up at him, registering the heat in those impossibly blue eyes. He holds my gaze as he lowers his mouth to mine, humming his approval as I bite his lower lip, his eyes fluttering closed. It only takes one slow, languid slide of my tongue against his, and his hands are in my hair, angling my head, dragging me deeper. When we finally break apart for air, we're both breathing hard, hair disheveled, pulses pounding. "I don't know what I was thinking bringing us out here," he groans, palming my ass and pulling my hips flush to his. "I should have booked a hotel room and had my way with you."

"This is perfect," I promise, giving him one last peck on the cheek before picking up the tackle box and heading down the path. If I don't put some distance between us, distract myself by attempting to catch some fish, I'm going to do things I'll regret. Like having our first time be on a gravel path in the middle of a field with all of God's creatures as witnesses. Henry catches up with me, winking one of those big blue eyes, sporting a smirk I'd like to ride right off his face. Jesus. I clear my throat, my cheeks heating as images of us in all sorts of compromising positions flash through my head.

"You okay?" he asks, dimple flashing.

"No." The river comes into view, and I start running, dropping the tackle box and rod into the grass, pulling the elastic out of my hair, and stripping clothes off as I go. I hop on one foot, then the other, pulling off my sneakers and then wiggling out of my cutoffs. I don't look back to see Henry's reaction to me standing here in my skivvies before I jump. Freezing cold water envelops my body, closing over my head. I push up just in time to watch Henry strip his T-shirt over his head, those 8-pack abs shifting as he tosses it aside.

"Did you think you could get away from me that easily?" he asks, raising one dark eyebrow. I don't say anything–I can't– as he toes off his shoes and drops his shorts.

Holy fuck. I don't think I'll ever get used to the amount of muscle this man has. His thighs...god. He takes two running steps and leaps through the air, tucking his legs up for a perfect cannonball. I shriek, laughing as I shield my face from the wave of water. He grabs me around the waist and hauls me up as he stands, wrapping my legs around his waist.

"You're so beautiful," he murmurs, tracing my lower lip with his thumb. "My tiny water sprite, a flame-haired delight, with eyes so green, and a magical bean."

"Henry!" I flick water into his face, laughing. "I don't know what to do with you." I bite my lip, trying not to smile like a fool.

"Love me," he says without hesitation, crushing his mouth to mine.

22

I pull my sweatshirt up to cover the ridiculous grin I can't seem to wipe off my face. As I watch Henry feed sticks into the fire, his words bounce around in my head. *Love me*. God. If only he knew that I'm tumbling head over heels for him. It feels like I jumped out of an airplane without a parachute. Henry looks up at me, flames reflecting in his eyes, the fire casting a red glow over his skin, highlighting the veins riding over his hands and up his arms. I suck in a shaky breath, my heart pounding in my ears.

"Tell me what you're thinking," he says finally, his gaze sweeping over my body.

I swallow hard, scared of admitting how badly I want this. How badly I want him. "I'm thinking that you look like Lucifer come to lure me away using one of the seven deadly sins as bait," I rasp.

The corner of his mouth kicks up, and he licks his lips, his gaze dipping to my mouth. "And what deadly sin would that be, Isla?" His voice is like velvet sliding over my body and between my legs.

"I think you know."

He walks closer, towering over me, nudging my chin with his finger until I'm looking up at him, fire and ice warring against each other. "Tell me, Isla."

"Lust," I answer, my voice cracking. With him this close, all I can think about is pulling down his pants and burying his cock in my throat. I clench my hands at my sides, digging my nails into my palm, resisting.

"Good girl," he murmurs. Those two words hang heavy between us until my stomach growls, ruining the moment. "We better get you fed before we continue this conversation," Henry laughs, kissing my cheek before heading back to the car and returning with the cooler. He pulls out container after container of ingredients, everything chopped, sliced, and ready to cook.

"I'm impressed," I admit as he lays a grate over the fire.

He chuckles. "Why is that?"

I shrug, not sure if I want to put it into words. "You went through a lot of effort is all."

"You're worth the effort, Isla. You shouldn't be impressed by the bare minimum. It makes me want to find every other guy you've dated and wring their fucking necks."

"I'll make you a list when we get back," I laugh, the possessiveness of his words doing unmentionable things between my legs. "What can I help with?" I ask as he places three cast iron pans on the grate.

"You can pour us both a glass of wine and then talk to me while I cook for you."

I pour two glasses as he tosses chunks of butter into the pans, pulling my chair closer to where he's working. "What do you want to talk about?" I ask, savoring the first sip of wine.

"I want you to tell me how you really feel about being in a nontraditional relationship," he says, dumping a bowl of fingerling potatoes into one of the skillets. "I worry we're being selfish by dragging you into this."

"Nobody drags me anywhere I don't want to go "

He looks at me, a grin pulling at his lips. "Good. Now that we have that covered, I want you to tell me one of your fantasies."

"You first," I insist, my self-preservation instincts kicking in.

He cocks an eyebrow as he dumps a container of green beans into the second pan. "The number one thing I jerk off to is imagining your face when I sink my cock into your pussy for the first time," he says, his eyes meeting mine.

Fucking hell. Desire slides through my body, igniting my nerve endings, leaving insatiable need in its wake. I squeeze my thighs together, wondering how much of this I can take before I cave and make the first move.

"Your turn," he says, carefully placing two filets in a screaming hot pan.

I don't have to take time to think about it. I know exactly what I want. "I want to be worshipped, ravished, fucked, and filled until it's the only thing I can think about. I want to be so immersed in it that everything else disappears. I've never had that before, and I crave it so badly. I need a true release."

"Jesus." He clears his throat, his cheeks scarlet, eyes dark in the waning light. "It's like you were made for us," he whispers. "We will gladly make that come true for you, Isla. And I'll go so far as to say it will happen *every* time." He picks up my hand from my knee and kisses my knuckles before pulling the food off the fire and plating it. He moves our chairs so our backs are to the fire and motions for me to sit.

"Why are we facing away from the fire?" I ask, taking a plate from him.

"Because the show is about to start," he says, winking.

"The show?" I ask, confused.

"You'll see. Eat before it gets cold."

I cut a bite of steak, trying to ignore how closely he's watching me. The flavors burst over my tongue, and I can't help the moan that slips from my lips. "I didn't realize you could cook like this. It's amazing. Why didn't you guys open a restaurant?"

"None of us are classically trained."

"Why does that matter?" I ask, eating a potato coated in garlic butter. So fucking good.

Henry shrugs. "Maybe it doesn't. We always thought we could dabble with cooking for the pub, but Greer is such an amazing chef, we wouldn't want to cramp her style."

"I have a feeling Greer will want to step back soon. Maybe not completely, but she has responsibilities outside of the pub that she'll have to take care of. It could be the perfect time to stretch your wings."

"That's terrifying," he admits.

"If I can start completely over, you can cook a couple nights a week for strangers."

"I've never had to cook for more than a handful of people before."

"This won't be any different; it's just a little more fast-paced. Plus, everyone will be so excited for something new that they won't care how long they have to wait."

"The community here really is something special," Henry says, setting his empty plate down and picking up his glass of wine. "I already feel more at home than I ever did in my hometown."

"Really?"

"Really. It makes me never want to leave."

"Leave?" My heart stutters in my chest.

"We're here on a tourist visa, Isla. There may be a day when we have to leave if the government won't grant us a start-up visa."

Why hadn't I thought to ask them about this before? "But you can't work on a visitor visa," I protest, confused.

"We're not taking any income from the pub, so technically, we're not doing anything illegal."

"You only have six months?" He nods. Fuck. "I wish I could go back to a minute ago when I was blissfully unaware."

"Hey." He angles his body toward me, sliding his hand over my jaw and turning my head to meet his gaze. "We'll figure it out. It's not your responsibility to worry about."

"But what if—"

"No. No what ifs." He looks up suddenly. "Look!" I follow his gaze, catching the tail end of a meteor streaking through the sky. "Come here, Isla." He pulls me into his lap, wrapping his arms around me. We sit like that for a long time, watching stars shooting across the sky. When our necks start hurting, he takes out his phone and pulls up the playlist he made. He presses play and sets it in the cupholder, pushing me from his lap as he stands. He grabs my hand and spins me under his arm, pulling me in and holding me close as we dance beneath the shooting stars. It's impossibly romantic.

"Thank you," I whisper, laying my cheek against the soft cotton of his T-shirt.

"For what?" he asks, his lips moving against my hair.

"For planning this." I look up at him, not bothering to hide the emotion in my eyes. "For making me feel worthy of something as romantic as this."

"You're worthy of everything your heart desires, Isla. I'll spend my entire life trying to prove it to you if I have to. I've never met someone that works as hard as you do. That has a bigger heart. You put everyone's needs above your own, so I'm making it my personal mission that *all* of your needs are met.

Emotion swells in my chest with every word that comes out of his mouth, eventually spilling out of my eyes in an uncontrollable stream of tears. I don't hide them. I don't need to. Tears leak out from under my eyelids as he turns my face up to his, swiping his thumbs across my cheeks, catching the tears as they fall. "You're so beautiful, Isla," he murmurs, licking a teardrop from my lips. "So fucking sweet under that prickly exterior." I push up on my tiptoes and press my mouth to his, needing to lose myself in him. He growls against my lips, banding his arm around my waist and pulling me up. I wrap my legs around him, his cock settling between my legs, stoking the flames until I'm sure I'm being burned alive.

"I need you," I say against his lips, my voice desperate and unfamiliar to my ears.

"You have me," he murmurs, peppering kisses along my jaw.

"I need your cock. In me," I say, rocking my hips against him.

"I don't have sex on the first date," he says, his lips moving against my neck, licking a path down to my collarbone.

"Fuck you," I groan, dropping my head to the side to give him easier access.

"Yes, please. But not until date three."

"Henry." I straighten, my eyes meeting his. "Are you serious?"

"Yes. I'm not rushing this, Isla."

"I think my pussy may shrivel and die by our third date," I pout, untangling myself from his body and taking a step away from him.

"I'll take good care of her in the meantime," Henry rasps, his gaze sliding down my body. "Sit," he demands, pointing to the chair.

"No."

"Sit, Isla." The tone of his voice has my knees bending against my will and my ass plops into the chair.

"Good girl," he growls, pushing my legs apart and dropping to his knees between them.

"What are you doing?" I gasp, leaning back as he drags his lips up my thigh.

"Reminding you of the other ways I can take care of that sweet pussy of yours." I lift my hips for him as he peels off my shorts and underwear, my heart pounding in my chest. "Do you know how many times I've dreamed of this moment?" he asks, resting his cheek against my inner thigh and inhaling deeply.

"How many?" I rasp, barely able to breathe,

"I can't count that high," he answers, biting, nipping, and licking his way to my core, pausing a hairsbreadth away.

"Henry, please," I beg. His gaze lifts, holding mine as he presses my legs wider, sliding his tongue up my slit. His eyes roll back in utter ecstasy as my body jerks against his mouth. He feathers his tongue over my clit and then drags it down, tongue-fucking me before pulling back, breathing hard.

"Will you come to bed with me, Isla? I need to do this properly."

23

I glance back as I walk to the tent, watching Henry, appreciating him. The planes of his face glow orange as he banks the fire, the hair curling over his forehead, blue-black in the dim light. A star shoots across the sky as he straightens. A sign. It has to be.

"We'll miss the meteor shower," I point out as he joins me, threading his fingers through mine.

"The only stars I want to see right now are the ones on the back of my eyelids when I have my face buried between your legs," he says roughly. "Give me a second to get things situated." He toes off his shoes and ducks into the tent. A second later, a thin camping mattress lands at my feet, halfway outside the tent. "There," he says, returning, "Now you can watch the stars while I eat you out."

Jesus. He raises an eyebrow, pointing to the mattress. My heart-beat pounds in my ears as I lie down, looking up at him, starlight limning his shadowed features. This feels impossibly special. Magical. Otherworldly. I reach for him, pulling him down until his weight settles over me, his very essence sinking into my bones, becoming part of me. It's that moment I know that if I kiss him here, like this, that I'll be sharing the deepest parts of myself, parts of me I've never shown anyone else. But it doesn't scare me. I don't push him away.

Don't warn him. For once, I trust that everything he's told me is true. Basking in his gaze, I frame his face, his stubble soft under my fingers.

"This can't be real," I whisper, sliding my thumb along the bottom edge of his lip.

"It's fucking real, Red. I've been waiting my entire life for this. For you." He dips his head, nipping at my bottom lip. I surge up as he pulls away, catching his mouth with mine, pulling him back down, tumbling head over heels, dizzy with desire. He tastes like wine, smoke, and sin. I could kiss him forever and never get tired of the way his lips feel against mine, the scratch of his scruff against my chin, the caress of his fingers, the perfect weight of him between my legs. I catch his lip between my teeth, and he groans into my mouth, breaking away from me, his mouth coasting over my jaw and down my neck. He sits back on his haunches, pushing my hands above my head, and carefully tugs off my shirt. His touch is reverent. Holy. He reaches around my back and unhooks my bra, laying me back down before sliding the straps off my shoulders and down my arms.

"Fuck, Isla," he breathes, sliding his hands over the dip in my waist, skimming my ribs and cupping my breasts. I arch my back, pushing into his touch. He licks one thumb, dragging it around my nipple, blowing until it's drawn into a hard point. His growl muffles as he presses his open mouth against me, sucking my nipple deep. A lightning bolt of desire shoots straight between my legs, electricity buzzing along my nerve endings, lighting me up. I squirm against him, trying to pull him back down on top of me, but he only chuckles as his focus switches to my other breast. I push my hands beneath his shirt, tracing every dip and divot with my fingers, memorizing how his muscles feel. I have the ridiculous urge to rub myself all over his body, to mark him as mine. Tattoo my name across the smooth skin of his abdomen.

My breath catches in my throat as his lips graze my sternum, licking his way down to my navel, biting the swell of my lower stomach. "Tell me what you want," he murmurs, resting his chin on my pubic bone, looking up my body at me.

I push myself onto my elbows, holding his gaze. "I want you to fuck me with your fingers while you're sucking my clit, and I don't want you to stop until I'm screaming."

"My pleasure." He keeps my legs trapped between his, burying his face in the vee of my thighs, breathing deeply. He slides his tongue along the crease, making my back bow, desperate to open for him. He sits up and leans to one side, pulling my leg from beneath him, then does the same for the other. He drags me farther into the tent until only my head and shoulders are outside and then starts zipping the opening closed.

"What are you doing?" I ask, confused.

"I don't want you worrying about me and what I'm doing. I want you to have the best orgasm of your life while you watch the stars falling above you."

Oh, god. This man. I flop down on my back, staring at the sky, wondering how the hell I got so lucky. A thrill pulses through me as Henry palms the back of my thighs, sliding his hands toward my center, his thumbs barely grazing me. I wriggle in his grip, trying to get closer to where I can feel his breath puffing against me. He holds me still, and I feel his lips curve against my inner thigh.

"You're enjoying this, aren't you?" I pout, crossing my arms over my chest.

"Yes, very much so." He drags his tongue up the crease of my thigh, biting me when I try to maneuver closer.

"Henry!" I protest, going limp in his hands as he licks away the pain.

"Be a good girl and stop moving," he chuckles.

I gasp as he runs his tongue down the other side, my nails digging into my palm in an effort to stay still. I tense when I realize I probably smell like nasty river water. What if I taste like it, too?

"Stop thinking and just feel, Isla. You're getting eaten out under a meteor shower. You'll probably never have this experience again in your entire life."

I take a deep breath, forcing myself to relax. I stare up at the blanket of stars stretched across the velvety night sky. A star shoots across the expanse of midnight blue sky just as his lips brush against my clit. Fuck. I bring my hand up to my mouth, biting the base of my thumb as his tongue explores the most intimate part of me. His hum of appreciation rolls over me, the tiny hairs on my body rising as if to say thank you. Resting his cheek against my thigh, he traces my opening with one finger, a gentle caress, teasing, promising. I dig my heels into the floor of the tent, lifting my hips, using my body to tell him I'm ready. He dips one finger in, testing the waters. The finger retreats, but before I can voice my disappointment, he groans, and I imagine him sucking me off his finger, eyes hooded, nostrils flared. A fresh wave of desire floods my system, and he expertly rides it, pushing two fingers into me with perfect timing. I squeeze around him, pulsing my muscles, desperate for him to start moving.

"I can't wait to slam into you and feel you squeeze around my cock," he says, his lips moving against my inner thigh.

I moan as he curls his fingers, massaging my G-spot with slow, even strokes. Just the right amount of pressure to have me on the edge.

"I can't see your face, Isla. I need to hear you." He stops moving his fingers when I don't respond. "Understand?"

"Yes," I groan, dropping my hand to my side.

"Good girl," he murmurs, kissing the apex of my thighs, teasing me with the tip of his tongue.

"Henry, please," I beg. He flattens his tongue, feathering it over my clit, fucking me with his fingers until I'm sobbing his name.

"The way you move. Fucking hell, Isla." I whimper as he seals his lips over me, sucking hard. He pulls back, ragged breaths heating my skin. "Isla, you're going to have to come for me before I embarrass myself."

"But I want you–"

"Not tonight. Tonight is about you," he says, cutting me off. "I was planning on edging you longer, but I'm about to nut in my pants, and I don't want that to be the memory you have of our first date."

My grin melts off my face as he adjusts his hand, his pinky sliding up my ass crack, teasing sensitive skin as he kneads the inner wall of my pussy with his fingertips. My jaw clenches, my abs contracting, my entire body poised on the edge of something life-changing. I stare up at the sky, the stars melding into one guiding light as he drags his tongue up my slit before pulling me into his mouth, syncing the rhythm of tongue with his hand. Lightning crashes through me, brighter than any shooting star, lighting up parts of me that I didn't even know existed. I moan as ecstasy crackles along my synapses, making me a prisoner to my own body. I scream his name as I lose control, my orgasm launching me into another dimension. Henry hooks a hand around my thigh, holding me tight as I buck against him, not easing up until the tension melts from my body and all that's left are the aftereffects of the best orgasm of my life. I push up on a trembling arm, unzipping the tent, desperate to see his face.

"Come here." I pull him on top of me, licking his lips before sliding my tongue against his, showing him exactly what I would do if he would only let me.

"Enough," he says roughly, rolling so his back is on the mattress, cuddling me in the crook of his arm. He reaches into the tent and pulls out a pillow and blanket, tucking it around me before putting the pillow under his head. "Perfect," he murmurs, kissing my forehead. We fall asleep as the stars paint streaks across the canvas of the night sky.

24

I spend the next two days cleaning out the space for the brewery. It's tedious, back-breaking work. Over the years, this part of the barn has turned into storage for everything from broken farm tools to extra sets of china and silverware.

"Mind if I join you?" Charlie asks from the doorway, a pitcher of icy lemonade in one hand and two glasses in the other.

"Thank god. I feel like my mind is atrophying from boredom." I drag an armchair near the doorway and brush the dust away. "I'm hoping you'll get a bit of a breeze being close to the door. If not, I can run an extension cord and grab a fan."

"I'll be fine, Isla, I promise." Charlie hands me a glass and fills it up before sitting and pouring her own. She winces as she places the pitcher on the ground.

"How are you feeling?" I ask, wondering how she can possibly carry this baby for one more day.

"Everything hurts. I'm ready for our little surprise to be born."

" Are you excited for the baby shower this weekend?" I wipe the sweat off my brow with my forearm, wincing at the streak of dirt it creates on my arm. I'm filthy.

"So excited! Are you sure you don't need help with anything?" she asks, leaning back in the chair and sipping her lemonade.

"I don't want you to lift a finger. You only have a month of peace and quiet left. Enjoy it."

"Oh, I am. Don't you worry about that. The guys are waiting on me hand and foot."

"As they should."

"Speaking of guys... You've been awfully quiet. Is everything okay?"

"More than okay. So okay I'm scared that if I talk about it, I'll jinx it."

"That's not how it works, Isla."

"I know, but sometimes it doesn't even feel real. Like if I pinch myself I'll wake up from a dream."

Charlie's gaze softens, losing focus as memories rush back. "I remember feeling the same way. I still do sometimes, if I'm being honest. Just don't let that get in the way of enjoying it, Isla. Don't be so worried that it won't last that you forget to have fun."

"I remember having a very similar conversation with you when you started getting serious with–"

"Was that the same conversation you swore you'd only ever date one guy?" she asks, cutting me off, eyes twinkling.

"Maybeee," I hedge, biting my lip to keep from grinning.

CHARLIE STAYS with me for the rest of the day, barring her frequent bathroom breaks. It's so good to catch up with her. I missed our gossiping and girl talk. I'm mad at myself for not making more time for her. When James died, it felt like my world turned upside down, and I tried to shoulder that weight alone instead of leaning on the people who love me. I won't make that mistake again.

As I'm locking up, the farm truck pulls up to the barn. The windows are down, Dylan's tan arm hanging out. It's such a casual thing. I shouldn't find it sexy, but god, do I ever. "Hey, good lookin'," he drawls. "Ready for our date?"

I look down at myself and the literal coating of dust covering my skin, then back up at him, arching an eyebrow.

"Fine, we can go shower first." He rolls his eyes, holding back a smile.

"We?" I ask as I climb in and slam the door shut. "I like that sound of that."

"We'll have to be quiet. Theo and Henry are already back at the house."

"Good thing there's an empty cottage far enough away where nobody will hear us," I say, wiggling my eyebrows suggestively.

Dylan parks the car in the driveway and looks over at me, so much heat in the depths of those brown eyes. I forget about everything but my need to touch him. It doesn't matter that we've both been working all day, that I'm grimy and covered in dust. I straddle his lap, swallowing his groan as our mouths meet. This. This is what matters. The caress of his thumb against my cheek, the heat of his palm on my lower back, the small sound he makes in the back of his throat when I bite his lip and suck on his tongue. He leans his head back, breathing hard, eyelids heavy with desire. "Do you want to stay in tonight? Watch a movie?" he asks, his voice rough. I lean into his touch as he sweeps my hair away from my face.

I know exactly where this is going if I say yes. "Yes. But I have to eat soon before I turn into somebody you don't want to know."

"I don't think that's possible."

"You're underestimating me."

He grins. "I'll run to the pub to pick up some food. Why don't you grab what you need from the house, and I'll meet you down at the cottage?"

I push open his door and slide off his lap. "Do you need anything?"

"Will you grab me some comfortable clothes?"

"Sure. Don't take too long." I press my lips to his, lingering. He pushes me away when my stomach growls, slamming the door and peeling out of the driveway, blowing me a kiss as he races down the road toward the pub. I can't help but grin as I push through the front door of the house, and run smack into Theo.

"Easy there, Sunflower." He reaches over my head and presses his palm against the door, closing it as he cages me in. One finger tilts my chin, our gazes colliding, awareness buzzing between us. "This week is going so slowly. You have no idea how close I was to begging Dylan to switch days with me," he murmurs, tracing my lower lip with his thumb.

"Two more days, then it's your turn," I say gently, pushing up on my tiptoes to kiss his cheek. He turns his head at the last second, catching my mouth with his, his passion consuming me. I pull away after a couple of seconds, breathing hard. "If you kiss me like this on Dylan's day, then he can kiss me on yours."

"Not a goddamn chance," Theo growls, his face dark.

"That's exactly what I thought." I laugh, ducking under his arm and running up to my room to grab pajamas before heading back downstairs.

"Red, is that you?" Henry calls from the kitchen, coming out in shorts and an apron. No shirt in sight. Jesus Christ.

"Hey, big guy." I smile, suddenly feeling shy. He stops two steps down from me and pulls me into his arms, hugging me tightly.

"I missed you."

"I just saw you at breakfast, Henry," I say, breathing him in. I missed him, too.

"I know, but I miss having *time* with you. A meal here and there doesn't count, especially when we're all rushing around."

"Three more weeks," I whisper against his shoulder. Three more weeks and we get as much quality time as we want together. Which means sleeping together. All four of us. A shiver wracks my body, desire sliding down my spine, goosebumps following in its wake.

"What was that?" Henry asks, looking down at me.

"Oh, just imagining what it'll be like."

"What *what* will be like, Isla?" he asks, a sinful edge to his voice.

I give him an exaggerated wink and a quick kiss, pulling away to continue up the stairs. "I have to grab a change of clothes before Dylan gets back."

"Where'd he go?" Henry asks, looking up at me.

"To go get us dinner. We decided to stay in tonight."

"In? Like here?"

"Down at the cottage," I explain, ducking into my room to grab some clothes. When I return, Henry is in the same spot, his hair standing on end like he ran both hands through it.

"You okay?" I ask.

"Fine," he grumbles, turning to head back down the stairs. "This is going to be the longest three weeks of my life," I hear him say as he disappears into the kitchen.

I bite the inside of my cheek to keep from laughing. He's adorable. Like a lost puppy dog. A few months ago, I would have thought it ridiculous to have a man pouting over being unable to spend time with me. But when it's Henry, how can I resist? The sweetness. Those muscles. That tongue. My core spasms just thinking about what he did to me the other night. *Pull it together, Isla.* I take a steadying breath and head to Dylan's room, grabbing some sweatpants and a T-shirt, and then pound back down the stairs, yelling goodbye as I head back outside. I peel my dirty clothes off before going inside the cottage, and head straight to the bathroom, turning the water on as hot as it'll go before pulling out my hair elastic and combing through the knots with my fingers. I moan in absolute ecstasy as I step into the shower, turning my back to the spray, steam filling the small space. Once my hair is wet all the way through, I turn around, washing the day's dirt away from my face.

"Honey, I'm home!" Dylan calls from the front door. I hear the sound of rapid footfalls over the water, and then he's practically falling into the bathroom, shirtless, hopping with one foot still in his pants. "Fucking hell. Leave it to me to have the most difficulty getting undressed."

"Come here," I say, opening the shower door and dropping to my knees.

"Isla—"

"Come here, Dylan."

"Fuck." He rubs his hand through his hair a couple times, finally making up his mind and approaching me. I jerk his pants over his foot, throwing them behind him. Sitting back on my heels, I look up at him. Steam caresses his chiseled muscles, making his skin glow. Big brown eyes capture mine, molten desire swirling in their depths. I drag my hands up his legs, ever so slowly, squeezing his ass before sliding my fingertips into his waistband and tugging his boxers down. I go an inch at a time, teasing myself just as much as I'm teasing him. His cock is heavy against his thigh, rising little by little as I uncover him until he springs away from the material, perfectly in line with my mouth. And fuck if I'm not drooling.

He runs the back of his finger over my cheekbone, his touch tender. "Do your worst, Freckles."

25

I take my time, drawing out the seconds, holding Dylan's gaze as anticipation rises to dizzying heights. I drag my fingernails up his lean, muscled thighs, then sweep my palms over his hips, pulling him closer. He groans, his cock jumping, desire leaking from the tip. It takes everything in me not to lean forward and bury him in my throat. I wrap my fingers around the base of his shaft, squeezing gently.

"Fuck, Isla." His knees tremble, and he reaches up, holding onto the shower frame for support. My gaze slides up the line of dark hair, over his taut abs, to the ridges of his pecs. Unbridled lust takes control, burning through my veins. I lick him like an ice cream cone, sliding my tongue from base to tip, moaning as his taste permeates my senses. I drag my tongue around the head of his cock, then feather it against that spot underneath. One strong hand slides into my hair, and he flexes his hips, pushing into my mouth. I take him deep, hollowing my cheeks, focusing on breathing through my nose as I bob my head, fucking him with my mouth. I look up at him, holding his gaze as I pull him toward me, not stopping until I feel him at the back of my throat. I swirl my tongue around him as I pull back, repeating the motion with my hand, twisting my hand over his slick shaft. His moan raises the hairs on my arms.

"If you keep going, I'm going to embarrass myself," he rasps, dropping to his knees, tossing his glasses onto the countertop before framing my face with his hands. He traces my lips with his thumb, gasping when I sink my teeth into soft flesh, leaving a mark. Fingers gripping my chin, he pulls me into his lap, plundering my mouth. I support myself with my elbow as he leans over me, adjusting my legs so I'm gripping his torso with my knees. I slowly melt back onto the shower floor as he makes his way down my body, teeth scraping before he soothes with his tongue, kissing it better. He slides me across the floor, making sure the water isn't in my face before lowering his head to my breast, flicking his tongue over my nipple, then sucking it hard and deep. My body bows, begging for more.

"Fuck, we're flooding the bathroom floor," he mutters, grabbing a towel and throwing it over the water before pulling me to my feet and closing the shower door. "There wasn't enough room for me to do what I wanted to, anyway," he murmurs, pressing me to the glass, his cock digging into my ass.

"What did you want to do?" I rasp, pushing back on him, need pulsing through my veins.

"I'll show you after dinner." He slides his hand around my hip and down my stomach, not stopping until his fingers are diving between my legs. I moan, rocking against him. He slips a finger into me, slowly sliding it in and out. "God, you're wet," he groans, expertly circling my clit.

"Dylan, please." I whimper in disappointment as he takes a step back, but it turns into a groan as he slides his cock down my ass and between my thighs, nestled along my slit, the head of his cock riding over my clit as he thrusts his hips.

He pushes my chin up with two fingers, our gazes colliding in the mirror. Fuck. My muscles tremble as I struggle to keep myself upright. He notices immediately, turning me around, capturing my mouth with his, hauling one of my legs up on his hip, his other hand going back between my legs. I moan into his mouth as he pushes two fingers into me, the heel of his palm rocking back and forth over my clit with every thrust of his hand.

"Come for me, Isla," he whispers, biting and sucking on my lower lip, breathing hard. I come alive beneath his capable hands, my body his instrument, and god, does he know how to play. I drop my forehead against his shoulder as I come, waves of ecstasy wracking my body. "You're so fucking sexy," he rasps, tilting my face up to his, licking his lips. "I can't wait to see what you look like when you're coming on my cock."

"Why do we have to wait?" I ask, my voice shaking as I try to catch my breath.

"Let me at least wine and dine you first, love," he chuckles, those big brown eyes sparkling.

My heart stutters at his casual use of that four-letter word as he turns me toward the spray, grabbing a bar of soap and running his sudsy hands all over my body. I would stay with him like this forever if I could. Our own, personal real-life wet dream. Turning toward him, I soap up my hands and tease his nipples before I wrap my fingers around his cock, sliding up and down his length with firm, measured strokes. He covers my fingers with his, squeezing, hips thrusting, fucking my hand.

Fucking hell.

All I can think about is getting him out of this damn shower and riding him until we're both a melted puddle of goo.

"What are you thinking about?" he rasps, eyes hooded, cheeks ruddy.

"Climbing you like a tree and fucking you until we forget our names," I say, picking up the pace with my hand, watching the head of his cock slide past my pinky, thick and red and utterly perfect. It'll feel so goddamned good inside me. His abs clench, his thrusts becoming uncoordinated.

"Isla," he moans, his jaw clenching. I pull my hand away, letting the water wash away the soap, and then I'm on my knees, gobbling him down. He stops moving, breathing hard, looking down at me, his eyes roiling with indecision.

"Use me, Dylan. Please."

He makes a broken sound, his hands diving into my hair, holding my head still as he thrusts past my open lips. I pull him closer, encouraging him to take what he needs, concentrating on breathing through my nose as he fucks my mouth. I palm his balls, rolling them in my hand, tugging gently. He groans my name, thrusting once, twice, before I feel the heat of him hitting the back of my throat. I swallow him down, keeping the suction until he's completely spent. I don't stop until I've licked him clean, giving his cock the attention it deserves. He pulls me up, pushing my hair away from my face before lifting me, wrapping my legs around his waist, and pressing me to the glass.

"You're a fucking minx. That mouth of yours will be the death of me."

"Would you be happy dying with your cock in my mouth?" I murmur, sluicing the water droplets off his eyebrow with my thumb and watching them drip down the angles of his face.

"I'd want it engraved on my tombstone," he says, catching my lower lip with his teeth.

"Death by blow job?" I ask, chuckling. "Was it that good?" I slide the tip of my nose along his.

"The fucking best I've ever had."

His praise makes me blush. I bite my lip to keep from grinning. I'm beginning to think I may have a new kink.

"Let's dry off and eat while we watch a movie. Then we can move on to round two."

"Round two?" I ask, arching an eyebrow.

"And three and four, if I get my way. Maybe even five if we're lucky."

Fuck. Me.

I've been waiting my entire life for this.

26

Dylan holds the towel open for me as I step out of the shower, wrapping it around my shoulders and using another to squeeze the water from my hair. The tenderness in his touch has tears pricking my eyes. I had his cock between my lips less than two minutes ago, and here he is, gently drying me off, taking care of me. It makes what we did–what we're going to do–seem so sacred. Religious, almost.

"I'll heat up dinner while you get dressed," he says, pulling on his sweatpants, leaving them slung low around his waist.

"Okay," I whisper, looking up at him, knowing there are stars in my eyes and not giving a single fuck. This man has me wrapped around his little finger, and I'm here for it. He gives me a crooked grin and kisses me soundly before leaving the bathroom. I press my fingers to my swollen lips, turning toward the mirror. The woman looking back at me can't hide the blush creeping up her cheeks. There's an extra sparkle in those green eyes. A secret behind that smile. Holy hell. I'm in so much trouble. I pull on my pajamas and run a comb through my hair, leaving it loose to air-dry. Walking down the short hallway to the kitchen, I peek around the corner. Dylan is standing at the stove, stirring something in a large pot, two bowls next to him on the counter.

"What can I help with?" I ask, watching as the muscles in his back shift with every rotation of the spoon. He glances over at me and then does a double-take.

"Are those guinea pigs?" he asks, his gaze sliding over my body, his eyebrows almost touching his hairline.

I look down at my favorite pair of pajamas, not realizing how ridiculous they must look until right this moment. "Not exactly sexy, are they?" I laugh, shrugging my shoulders.

"You could be wearing a floor-length Victorian nightgown and you'd still be sexy," he says, spooning the contents of the pot into the bowls. "But I have to ask–why guinea pigs?"

"I had one when I was little. Her name was Little Bit. She was my best friend, really. I was beside myself when she died." I take the bowl of stew he hands me.

"You never got another one?" He grabs two spoons and leads the way to the family room.

"No. And then I grew up and didn't have time to care for myself, let alone a pet."

"And now?" Dylan sits, looking up at me with those chocolate-brown eyes.

"Now?" I ask, raising an eyebrow. "I guess I haven't really thought about it."

"You should." He motions for me to sit and points out the two glasses of wine on the coffee table. "I took the liberty of opening a bottle of wine I found. I hope that's okay."

"It's perfect. Thank you, Dylan."

"You're welcome, Freckles. What should we watch?" He picks up the remote and turns on the TV, scrolling through the apps.

"I've been wanting to watch this new show on Netflix called *Fool Me Once.* Have you seen it?"

"No, not yet." He navigates to the series, starting the first episode before taking a bite of his food. "God, this is good," he groans, his eyes rolling back as he chews.

"Do you cook, too?" I ask, realizing I've never seen him cook anything before.

"Only if it's something simple like a fried egg or grilled cheese. I do love to bake, though. I had a job at a bakery when I was seventeen."

"What's your favorite thing to make?" I ask, trying to imagine a younger version of him covered in flour, kneading a loaf of bread.

"Bagels, probably."

"It's been forever since I've had a bagel," I groan, practically drooling.

"We'll have to fix that, won't we?"

We both finish our food at the same time, falling into companionable silence as we watch the show. It's a murder mystery that sucks us in quickly, and before we know it, we're on the third episode, and I'm cuddled in Dylan's arms while we're spooning on the couch. It's nice. More than nice.

As the evening passes, the tension between us grows, ratcheting up my heartbeat, butterflies going haywire in my stomach. When I can't stand it any longer, I act like I'm adjusting my body to get more comfortable, but it's really so I can get my ass closer to his lap. He splays his hand over my stomach, pulling my body flush to his, his cock already standing at attention.

"Why didn't you say something?" I ask, looking back at him and biting my lip.

"Because I didn't want you to think that's the only reason I want to be with you."

"You know, there's such a thing as being too nice," I say, laying my head back down on his arm.

"You don't want me to be nice?"

"Not right now." My whisper turns into a groan as he slides his hand underneath my shirt and cups my breast. I arch my back, pushing into his hand. He growls deep in his throat, the sound making goosebumps erupt over my entire body. I turn to face him, and he caresses my cheek, sweeping his hand over my shoulder, down my back, and over my ass, cupping the back of one thigh to pull my leg over his hip. In one smooth movement, he maneuvers us so his back is flat on the couch and I'm straddling his hips.

"You're so fucking beautiful," he breathes, tugging on a strand of my hair, the back of his fingers grazing my nipple.

"Even with my guinea pig pajamas on?" I tease, leaning over him, my hair creating a curtain around our heads.

"Especially with your guinea pig pajamas on," he says, his voice dropping as he drags his thumb over my lips. I lower myself as he surges up, our mouths colliding in a war of teeth and tongues. I lose myself in the feel of his body against mine, the way he holds my face like I'm a precious, fleeting thing that may disappear at any moment. It makes me feel cherished and wanted and–and *loved*. My heart jumps as that thought registers. I break away from him, trying to catch my breath.

"Are you okay?" he asks, studying me with concern in his eyes.

"More than okay," I say honestly, unable to hold back my grin.

"Good," he says, returning my smile. "Should we take this to the bedroom?"

"Why would we do that?" I ask, rocking my hips against him.

"Fuck, Isla," he groans, reaching up to squeeze my breasts, rolling my nipples between his fingers. A bolt of lust streaks down my spine, desire crackling through my veins like electricity before settling low in my stomach, a ball of raw, aching need. Nimble fingers undo the buttons on my top, and he slides it off my shoulders. Swinging his legs over the side, he sits up, leaning against the back of the couch, pulling me close. He buries his face between my breasts, breathing me in before catching a nipple in his mouth and swirling his tongue around it.

"I'll never look at your tits the same way again. You know that, right? That night was fucking amazing." He switches his attention to the other side, worshipping my body. Worshipping *me*. Making me feel like the most desirable woman on planet Earth. He looks at me the way people gaze at a once-in-a-lifetime sunset. Bathing in me, drinking me in like I'm the elixir of life, and he's on death's doorstep.

The reverence in his touch topples my already crumbling wall of doubt, paving a new path to something I've only dreamed about.

"Take me to the bedroom, Dylan," I murmur, emotion clogging my throat. "Make love to me."

"Do you mean that, Isla?" he asks, pressing his forehead to mine, hope bubbling up. "The love part, I mean," he clarifies, running a finger over my cheek.

"Yes. I don't think I've ever meant anything more in my entire life."

"Thank fuck," he sighs. Pulling me closer, he pushes his hand into my hair, tilting my head to get the perfect angle. His lips are soft, his tongue like velvet. He stands suddenly, wrapping my legs around his waist and carrying me to the bedroom. "This bed isn't nearly big enough for what I want to do to you," he grumbles, glaring at the tiny twin mattress.

"It's this or going back to the house with your brothers. Your call."

"Hell no. I don't want to be anywhere near them tonight. This is you and me, Isla."

"You and me," I echo, tracing his jawline with my fingers. He walks to the end of the bed and sets me in the middle, pushing me back onto the pillows. I take a shuddering breath as he hooks his fingers into the waistband of my pajama pants and pulls them off, dropping them on the floor.

"Now you," I whisper, my voice trembling. He takes a step back and pushes his sweatpants down, stepping out of them and then standing there, both of us staring at each other in complete and utter awe.

"Are you real?" he asks, his voice cracking. "Is *this* real?"

I climb off the bed and take his hand, pressing his palm against my heart. I lift my hand and do the same to him, and we stand there, our hearts racing, barely breathing.

"God, I love you," he chokes out, cupping my face between his hands, kissing me like he's been waiting for this moment his entire life.

27

Dylan POV*

"I love you, too, Dylan," Isla whispers, her voice cracking.

Her heart is galloping like a wild mustang beneath my fingers. She looks up at me, wonder rippling through pools of deep emerald green. My breath catches in my throat, the beauty of this moment tearing me wide open. I cup her face, tracing her freckles with my thumb. How can any of this be real? She blinks, a solitary tear running down her cheek. I catch the salty drop with my tongue, palming the back of her neck and pulling her to me, crushing my mouth to hers. She pushes up onto her toes, her kiss echoing my desperate hunger. I walk her backward toward the bed, gently laying her down. Her shy smile is a balm for my soul, nourishing parts of me I didn't know existed until I met her. Reaching up, she pulls me down on top of her, our bodies fitting together like we were molded by the same hands. Created for each other. She feels so soft and delicate beneath me that I'm scared I'm going to crush her. I try to move my weight onto my knees, but she wraps her legs around my waist, holding me in place.

"I'm going to hurt you, Isla," I protest, planting my elbows on either side of her head.

"You're not. I promise," she murmurs, rocking her hips against me.

I look down at this creature that has captured my heart. Flaming hair. Ruddy cheeks. Swollen lips. Heavy lids concealing the most beautiful eyes I've ever seen. "I don't know what I did in a past life to get to this moment, but it must have been something fucking amazing."

"Maybe we find each other in every life," she muses, running her fingertips over my cheek.

"I hope so," I whisper, emotion choking me. Sliding her hand into my hair, she pulls my head down, our lips locking together, her tongue sliding slowly over mine. I realize in that moment that even if we spend every day of the rest of our lives in each other's arms, it will never be enough. I kiss the freckle on the right side of her top lip, connecting the dots over her jaw and down her neck.

"My last test came back clear and I'm on the pill," she breathes, her back bowing as I drag my tongue down her sternum.

"Mine as well, but it's your body, Isla. It's your call to make."

"I want you in me. Now." Our gazes lock, something words could never express passing between us. I kiss both of her nipples before pushing back onto my knees, her legs falling open on either side of me. She's so fucking gorgeous. Milky white breasts with a smattering of freckles that lead the way to the dusky rose of her nipples. I follow the curve of her waist with my hands, the outward sweep of her hips. I pull her toward me so her ass is on my lap, my cock millimeters from her core. I want to bury myself inside her, lose myself in her warmth, but at the same time, I never want this moment to end. I slide my hands up her thighs, her skin velvety soft beneath the roughness of my palms. Goosebumps race over her skin, drawing her nipples tight.

"You're so goddamned beautiful it hurts to look at you," I rasp, my heart thudding in my chest as I sweep my thumbs over her inner thighs.

"Dylan," she groans, digging her heels into the bed, lifting her pelvis toward me. I massage her thighs, coming closer to her center with every pass. I don't stop until her pussy is weeping for me. I press my thumb against her clit, my cock jumping at the sound she makes. I drag my finger down through her desire, pushing into her, fucking her. Her eyes flutter closed, and she squeezes around me like a vise, rocking her hips.

"Fucking hell, Isla," I groan, wiping my finger on my cock before taking it in my fist and dragging it down her slit, getting it wet before sliding it back and forth over the bundle of nerves at the apex of her thighs.

"Now, Dylan." She opens her eyes, trapping me in her gaze. I can't resist the call of her body any longer. I keep eye contact as I lean over her, my cock naturally lining up with her body, nudging at her entrance as she locks her legs around me. Time slows, every heartbeat feeling like an eternity, but even that isn't long enough.

"Don't look away, love," I whisper, holding her gaze as I sink into her, not stopping until our bodies are flush, watching the ecstasy ignite behind her eyes. It's a perfect fit, so perfect I have to distract myself from it. I drop my head to her shoulder, breathing hard.

"What are you thinking about?" she asks, immediately picking up on my predicament.

"The steps to making bagels," I confess, chuckling. She laughs, her pussy squeezing my cock, and I groan, clenching my jaw, refusing to ruin this.

"Sorry," she gasps, snorting as she tries to hide her laughter. She wipes tears from those sparkling eyes, her entire face lit up. "What's the first step?" she asks, biting her lip to try to stop herself from smiling.

"First, you stir sugar and yeast into warm water to encourage the yeast to bloom," I murmur, slowly sliding in and out of her.

"Fuck, you feel good," she moans, her body soft and pliant beneath me. "Then what?" she asks, her gaze slightly unfocused. It dawns on me that she's trying to hold off, too. Draw this moment out as long as possible.

"You stir in flour, oil, and salt. Then you knead the dough." My voice is rough around the edges as I struggle for control. I slam into her several times, my cock screaming in protest as I pull out before I come.

"Dylan, no, I'm so close. Get there with me."

"I want this to last forever, Isla." I trace the curve of her jaw with my finger, trying to memorize every little detail.

"We have all night." She pulls my lips to hers, kissing me tenderly as she rakes her nails down my back. I push my tongue into her mouth as I impale her, fitting my pubic bone against her and rocking back and forth, her clit rolling between us as I thrust into her. "Oh god, Dylan. Don't stop," she gasps, breaking our kiss, her face crumpling as her body finally gives in.

"Yes, Isla. Come for me. That's my girl," I rasp, coaxing her through it, hanging onto my control until her body relaxes beneath me. Only then do I give myself permission to let go.

"Look at me," she whispers, soft hands framing my face as I slam into her, my entire existence narrowing to this moment. I hold her gaze as I fall apart, ramming into her, surrendering my soul to her, giving her a part of me I've never given to anyone else. She draws me into a kiss so sweet, so poignant, it brings tears to my eyes.

"Thank you, Isla," I rasp, rolling off of her and gathering her in my arms, pulling her tight to my body.

"For what?" she asks, looking up at me.

"For being you." I kiss the tip of her nose, wishing we could stay like this forever. "Let's get you washed up and then we can come back and cuddle." I untangle myself from her arms and scoop her out of the bed, carrying her to the bathroom.

"What if I don't want to cuddle?" she asks, raising an eyebrow as I set her down next to the toilet. My heart rises to my throat.

"Do you want me to leave?" I ask, my voice cracking.

"Yes, get," she says, shooing me away.

I close the door softly behind me. Did she really just tell me to leave? Swallowing hard, I pick up my sweatpants from the floor, stepping into them as she comes back out of the bathroom.

"What are you doing?"

"You asked me to leave."

"Leave the bathroom so I could pee, you dummy."

"You said you didn't want to cuddle!" I protest, standing there with my pants half on like an idiot.

"Because I want to do *other* things, Dylan." She plants her hand on my chest, pushing me back onto the bed, sinking to her knees.

"Isla–"

She presses her finger to my lips, silencing me. "You promised me five rounds, remember?"

"I said if we're lucky."

"Oh, we're going to be lucky. Don't you worry about that," she says, mischief sparkling in her eyes.

I WAKE up early the next morning, my body already reacting to the feel of her skin against mine, the smell of her shampoo, the soft puffs of breath against my chest. I extricate myself from her limbs, rolling out of the bed and pulling the blankets over her. I can't help but stand there and stare. The glow of the sunrise lends a rosy hue to her skin, her hair dark in the dim light. She opens her eyes, startling me. One slow blink and then she rolls over and falls back asleep. I grab my sweatpants and tiptoe out of the room, closing the door carefully behind me. I start a pot of coffee and leave a note in case she wakes up while I'm gone, and then wrestle with the front door, wincing at how loud it creaks as I open it.

Two hours later, I'm heading back down to the cottage with a plate of hot bagels, some cream cheese, and orange juice. I peek through the side window and nearly fall flat on my face. Isla is standing in front of the picture window, completely naked, sipping on a steaming cup of coffee.

"Morning, beautiful," I say as I push through the door, setting everything down on the coffee table and carefully taking her mug from her before pulling her into my arms.

Her face lights up like a Christmas tree. "Did you make me bagels?"

"I did. Would you like one now?" I ask, curling a lock of her hair around my finger.

"Later," she whispers, winding her arms around my neck and pulling my lips to hers.

28

I set down my paintbrush and shake my arm out, looking over my shoulder at Theo to see how he's faring. When I started complaining about having to paint the walls last night at dinner, he immediately offered to help me. Despite my protests, here he is, slapping a deep sage green over ancient plaster walls. He pauses, feeling the heat of my gaze, and looks over at me.

"Are you ready for our date later?" he asks, dipping his brush back into the paint.

"Once I scrub this paint off, I will be." He sets his brush down and walks toward me, stalking me like I'm his prey and he's an apex predator. I step backward, bumping into the wall.

"This paint?" Before I can protest, he dips his finger into my paint can and draws a line down my forehead and over my nose.

"Theo!"

"Isla!" he whines, mimicking me.

Red bleeds over my vision as I dunk my hands into the paint, planting them on his cheeks and dragging them down over his jaw. The shocked 'o' of his mouth makes me giggle. "No, this paint," I say, my voice as sweet as sugar as I blink up at him innocently.

"You're going to regret that," he growls, grabbing the waistband of my bike shorts and holding me still, reaching over to pick up the can of paint. My heart crashes in my chest as he manhandles me onto the drop cloth, lifting the bucket over my head. I hear the threads in my shorts pop as I wrench out of his grip, bolting out the door and across the driveway toward the castle. The crunch of his shoes on the gravel behind me has me changing course. Jack would kill me if I ran through the foyer covered in paint. I run around the side of the building and over the lawn, aiming for the shore of the loch. I kick off my flip-flops as I run, peeling off my T-shirt and diving into the water in my shorts and bra. Re-surfacing fifty feet away, I gasp for breath as I raise my head above the water, scanning the shore for Theo. I spy the paint can sitting on the edge of the firepit, but there's no sign of life anywhere. Did he come in after me? My gaze skims over the water, looking for bubbles. Nothing. Surely he can swim, right? Panic grips my chest as I turn in a circle, desperately searching for him. My heart rises to my throat as fingers wrap around my ankle and tug me beneath the surface. I kick out, connecting with something solid. I breach the surface at the same time as Theo.

"Fucking hell, Isla!" He presses his fingers to a red mark on his cheekbone.

"That's your fault. I thought you drowned!" I splash him before turning and swimming back toward shore, furious.

"Isla!"

I ignore him, not looking back until my feet can touch the bottom.

"Does that mean you were worried about me?" he asks, exploding out of the water next to me, shaking droplets from his hair. I turn away from him, but he circles my wrists with his hands, forcing me to look at him. "That you care?" he whispers, holding my gaze, pulling me closer until we're toe-to-toe.

"I'm going to stop caring if you keep being so goddamned infuriating," I spit out, trying not to notice the way his eyelashes are stuck together or the bead of water sitting in the hollow of his throat or the way his tongue slides over his lips. Goddammit.

"Don't lie. You love it."

"Theo–" he cuts me off by pressing his lips to mine, and every single thought in my brain is replaced by red-hot need. I climb him like a tree, wrapping my legs around his waist, capturing those broody features between my palms. "Why are you so fucking annoying all the time?" I breathe against his lips.

"Because I want you to have an outlet for all that emotion you keep bottled up inside," he rasps, dragging his lips down my throat.

"You want me to use you as an emotional outlet?" I ask, lifting one eyebrow. I don't think I ever expected those words to come from a man's mouth.

"Mmhmm." He bites my earlobe, making me shiver. "Tell me what you're feeling right now."

It's hard to think with his lips roaming over me like this. "Bewilderment. Annoyance. Lust."

"Use me, Isla." He captures my face between his hands, a seriousness in his eyes that isn't usually there. "I can take it, I promise."

I shake my head. "You deserve better than that."

"Do I, though?" he asks, tilting his head back, a bitter edge to his laugh.

I pull away from him, wondering how I missed this part of him. Was it hiding beneath the hard exterior, behind the jokes and teasing? "Of course you do, Theo. Everyone deserves to be cherished. To be loved."

"And what about you, Sunflower? Do you love me?"

"It's hard when you won't let me."

"Fair enough."

"So what about this date?"

"Shit. We're going to be late." He scoops me into his arms and carries me toward shore, pushing through the water like it's nothing.

"Where are we going?"

"You'll see when we get there," he says, keeping me in his arms all the way up to the car.

"What should I wear?"

"We need to look like we're loaded."

"I *am* loaded."

He stares at me, the corner of his mouth pulling up. "You're so normal that I forget sometimes."

"*Normal?*" I ask, shuddering.

"Stop. You know what I mean," he laughs.

"I'm going to make you pay for that." I grin as I crank the keys in the Mustang, revving the engine.

I WALK OUT of my bedroom in a sundress and cardigan fifteen minutes later, my hair hanging in damp waves around my shoulders. Theo is waiting at the bottom of the stairs, wearing crisp khaki pants and a button-down shirt. The top two buttons are open, exposing a sliver of tanned skin. He looks good enough to eat. Good enough to—

"If you keep looking at me like that, our date will be in my bedroom," he says roughly.

"You look nice," I say, holding his gaze as I walk down the stairs.

"You're not so bad yourself, Sunflower." He tugs at the strap of my sundress playfully, bending to press his lips to my cheek, his hand warm on my shoulder.

"Do you want to drive or should I change shoes?" I ask, glancing down at my four-inch heels.

"I want to end the night with those shoes over my shoulders, so I'll drive." His gaze sweeps over me, appreciation gleaming in the depths of his eyes.

I cough, choking on my own saliva.

"You could at least wait to choke until later."

"Yeah?" I make a face. "Are you going to give me something to choke on?"

His fingers close around my wrist, jerking me to a stop, his other hand wrapping in my hair, tugging until my gaze locks with his. "Yes, and when I do, you will be begging for it."

"Is that a promise?"

"Don't tempt me, Isla."

"Or what?"

"I'll punish you later."

"Looking forward to it."

Heat flares in his eyes before he turns and drags me outside, depositing me in the passenger seat of my car before carefully closing the door and rounding the hood.

"You look so fucking good in this car," he says, swallowing hard. "Not that I'm telling you something you don't already know."

"No, but it's nice to hear it. Especially from you." I angle my head, looking out the window as we pull onto the road, hiding the smile I can't seem to wipe off my face. He's probably the most annoying person I've ever met, but it's invigorating. Fun. I never know what he's going to say next, and I kind of love it.

After ten minutes of trying not to drool all over myself while I watch him shift gears, I pull his hand into my lap. He slides his palm down past the hem of my dress, pushing it up, his calluses scraping over my skin in the most delicious way. He squeezes my thigh, his pinky creeping up higher and higher. I blow out a shaky breath, trying to calm my nerves, but the heartbeat between my legs only grows stronger. I drop my head against the headrest as his fingers brush over my panties.

"Are you wet for me, Sunflower?" he murmurs, the wind wrapping his words around me. I whimper when he pulls his hand away to shift gears, my body strung tighter than a tightrope.

"Please tell me you're taking me somewhere you can fuck me and nobody can hear us."

"Not quite."

I mentally curse the curvy roads that keep Theo's hand on the gear shift as we make our way from Harris to Lewis. He looks at me as we pull off the road, turning through a large iron gate guarded by concrete lions set high on stone pillars. "We've been married two years, and we're looking for a place to raise our future children and possibly open a small boutique hotel."

"We what–?" Words evaporate from my tongue as a beautiful castle comes into view, spires reaching toward the sky.

"There used to be a five-star resort here. The owners retired and are selling the estate. I figured it would be the perfect place to come for ideas on what we can do to improve what we're working on over at Jack's, especially now that you're starting a brewery. It could be amazing, Isla."

"But we have to pretend to be somebody else?" I ask, my heart jumping to my throat when I see a man walking toward us.

"The only way we could get a tour is by acting like buyers. Just play along, wifey." His demeanor changes as he gets out of the car and greets who I assume is the realtor. He shakes the man's hand, then comes to my door and opens it for me. I take his hand, steeling my shoulders.

"Matthew, this is my wife, Isla," Theo says, introducing us.

Oh, this is going to be fun.

29

T heo is on his best behavior for the next hour. I play the dutiful wife, quiet and demure, even while taking copious mental notes. The estate is gorgeous. Matthew told us about how the previous owners renovated their home, keeping true to the castle's time period while also adding their own touches. The result is a beautiful and eclectic masterpiece that has me itching to get back home and get to work. Matthew leaves us after a while, encouraging us to explore while he gives the tour to another client.

"You're a genius!" I whisper, giving Theo a loud kiss on the cheek once Matthew is out of sight. "I have so many ideas." He doesn't say anything, only stares at me, the corner of his mouth pulling up. "What?" I ask, a blush creeping over my cheeks.

"I'm memorizing the way you look right now. Brimming with inspiration. Excited about the future." He grabs my hand, threading his fingers through mine. "Do you want to go outside and look at the grounds?"

"I'd love to. We have so much untapped potential just sitting there. Jack and I talk about what we could do every spring, but then life happens."

"Maybe now that we're here, we can help," he says. I bump into him when he stops suddenly. He turns in a slow circle, studying the maze of hallways fanning away from us. "Any idea *how* we get outside?"

"Nope, but it'll be fun figuring it out." I hold onto his shoulder as I take off my heels, snatching them up and skipping down one of the hallways. I turn to look back at Theo, and my heart skips a beat, awareness crackling between us. He walks closer, reaching out and grabbing my wrist, pulling me in for a kiss. I twist away from him, my cardigan sliding off in his grip. I walk backward, watching as he lifts my sweater to his nose, his eyes never leaving mine.

Goosebumps race over my body as he starts toward me. I turn and run, blindly darting down hallways and through doors. I see a sliver of sunlight and run toward it, praying it's a door. I pull floor-length curtains aside, revealing a floor-to-ceiling window. I crank the handle, glancing over my shoulder to make sure Theo hasn't found me yet. I'm leaning through the casement when I hear him behind me. I step out onto a rooftop terrace, gravel digging into my feet, the sky spitting a mist so fine it's sticking to my skin in tiny droplets. I hobble as fast as I can around the corner, stopping dead in my tracks as a sprawling two-story greenhouse comes into view. I run to the door, humid, fragrant air enveloping me as I step inside. I turn in a slow circle, taking in the tropical paradise, awestruck. Butterflies flit around me as I pad over a bridge, brightly colored koi following my every movement. If I were in the market for a new place to live, I would buy this castle just for the greenhouse. I've never seen anything so beautiful.

"Do you have any idea how gorgeous you are?" Theo asks, leaning casually against the doorframe, watching me.

"Isn't this magical?" I ask, closing my eyes and breathing deeply.

"Yes, yes it is," he rasps, walking closer, that rich mahogany gaze tracking me. He picks me up by the waist, holding me high as he spins me in a circle. He lowers me, my stomach sliding over the hard planes of his chest, my breasts tantalizingly close to his face. He drags his tongue over the fabric of my dress, finding my nipple, then closes his teeth over it. It's the most exquisite form of torture.

"Theo," I breathe, trying to wrestle my body under control. I should pull away from him. Put some distance between us. Douse the flames burning me from the inside out. But I don't. I groan as he palms the back of my thighs, pulling my legs around his waist. I meet the crush of his mouth with a throaty groan, giving in to the desire coursing between us. He rucks up my dress, squeezing my ass, brushing his fingers over the fabric between my legs.

"Someone will see us," I pant, taking deep gulps of air.

"This wasn't part of the tour, Sunflower. Nobody knows we're out here. Let me have one taste." He holds me tightly as he walks through the foliage, hiding us from view. He sits me on a potting bench littered with pots and trowels, pressing my knees open as he slides his hands up my thighs. I drop my head back with a low moan, my lust-addled brain incapable of making responsible decisions. He buries his face between my legs, licking me through the fabric, sucking my clit into his mouth. I moan, straining toward him. He pulls my underwear to the side with one hand, reaching up and covering my mouth with the other. I suck in a breath through my nose, whimpering as he drags his tongue along my slit, dipping inside before focusing on my clit, feathering his tongue over me in a maddening rhythm. I grab a handful of his hair, keeping his head still, riding his face as instinct takes over. He pushes two fingers into me, fucking me, pushing me over the edge. His hand muffling the cries his mouth draws out of me.

"Fuck, Theo," I pant, pulling him up, winding my arms around his neck, kissing him, reveling in my taste on his tongue. Something in him calls to that a part of me I've always kept hidden. The part of me that wants to buck the system, tear up the rules, do whatever the hell I want. Like dropping to my knees and sucking him off until he's moaning my name, begging for release. My knees hit the dirt before he can protest, my fingers nimbly pulling at his belt, rushing to unbutton and unzip before he comes to his senses and tells me to stop. I pull him out and stuff him in my mouth, my eyes rolling back as he permeates my senses. I palm his ass, squeezing, pulling him closer, not stopping until he's touching the back of my throat.

"God, Isla," he chokes out, his hips jerking.

I pull away from him with a pop, looking up at him innocently. "Your turn to use *me*."

Resistance melts from his features, and he cups the back of my head, his thumbs sweeping over my cheeks tenderly. "You're sure?"

"Fuck my mouth, Theo." I drag my tongue on the underside of his cock, teasing that spot where the head meets the shaft. His grip on my hair tightens as he fights with himself. He looks down at me, dragging the head of his cock over my lips. I can see it in his eyes when he finally gives in, control slowly replaced by something wild and feral. I take a deep breath, welcoming his thrust with an eager mouth. He flexes his hips, pushing deep. I groan around him, my body thrumming, the feel of him sliding over my tongue turning me on just as much as when his fingers were inside me. I cup his balls, rolling them in my palm, reaching behind them to press two fingers to his taint, massaging until he can't help but slam into my mouth, taking what he needs. I let him use me, tugging and teasing as he falls apart, greedily swallowing as he empties himself into my throat. I pull back slowly, licking him clean as he sags back against the bench, his legs trembling as he comes down from the high.

"Your mouth–God, Isla. I've never felt anything like it," he says, his voice hoarse. I look down, hiding my smile behind a curtain of hair as I fasten his pants and buckle his belt.

"Thank you for letting me make you feel good, Theo." I turn my face up to his, tracing his lips with the tip of my finger. I would let this man do very, very bad things to me. Those eyes. Those lips. A lifetime wouldn't be enough.

"I'd say thank you back, but that doesn't adequately express what I'm feeling right now." He cradles my face between his hands, holding me like I'm the most precious thing in the world. Three words are on the tip of my tongue, but I hold them in, waiting for the perfect moment. "Should we continue the tour?" he asks, sweeping my hair behind my shoulder.

"Yes." I pull out my phone and open up my notes app. "I'm going to write down our ideas so they don't get lost in a haze of lust."

"Good idea," he chuckles, drawing me in for one last kiss before grabbing my hand and leading me back inside.

WHAT'S NEXT?" I ask as Theo helps me into the car. "Please don't say another surprise." I laugh at his stricken expression, realizing that's exactly what he was going to say.

"You're no fun," he grumbles, closing my door and walking around the front of the car.

"That's not what you thought earlier," I tease as he gets in, sliding my hand up his thigh and squeezing.

He blesses me with a wide smile, and I swear it's like the sun shining down on me, like everything is finally right with the world. "I'm going to have to tell you anyway, or you're liable to choke someone out." He starts the car, the roar of the engine making it impossible to talk until we're on a straight stretch of road.

"What do you mean 'choke someone out'?" I ask, gathering my hair into one hand to keep the wind from whipping it around our faces.

"I booked us on a murder mystery cruise, Sunflower."

My heart jumps. "Really?"

"Really, really."

I bounce up and down in my seat, excitement making it impossible to keep still. "How long is it? Just dinner?"

"If I had known you'd be so excited about murder, I maybe would have reconsidered," he chuckles, eyes sparkling. "It's overnight," he says, answering my question.

"But I didn't pack a bag!"

"Look behind you."

I look in the back, noticing a small duffel bag for the first time. "You're the best, Theo. Even if you're grumpy most of the time."

"Thanks, Isla," he deadpans, surprising me with a wink.

I turn away from him, blushing. I've had his head between my legs, but lord, when he winks at me, I fucking melt. I cover my face with my hands, peeking at him through my fingers, hoping he didn't see my reaction. His goofy grin tells me all I need to know. I bite my lip and look out the window, focusing on the scenery before I find myself sitting in a puddle of my own making.

30

I'm a hussy. That's all there is to it.

We're sitting in the parking lot killing time and I can't seem to tear my gaze away from Theo's hand. The tan roughness of his work-hardened palm against the soft, milky-white skin of my thigh. The sight of it is erotic. But the feel? God. I want to drag his hand between my legs and trap it there. Ride his fingers until the world disappears around me.

"What are you thinking about?" Theo asks, his voice low and husky.

I bite my lip, unsure how much of my hand I want to give away.

"Tell me, Isla."

Fuck. I clear my throat, but the words don't come, so I show him instead. I cover his hand with mine, sliding it up my thigh and opening my legs. I stop just before his hand brushes against my panties, body thrumming, chest heaving. Theo's gaze flits between my face, my panties, and the road, swallowing hard.

"That's all you were thinking of?" he asks roughly. "My hand on your thigh?"

I blow out an unsteady breath, guiding his hand over my lower stomach, the tips of his fingers sliding beneath my underwear. When

I pause again, he growls, pushing his hand between my legs, his fingers easily sliding along my slit.

"You're so wet for me, Sunflower." He groans as my back arches, desperate for more contact. The ship's horn makes us both jump. Theo glances at his watch and mutters a curse under his breath. "I promise we'll finish this later, Isla, but if we don't go now, we'll miss the boat."

I don't want to go anywhere. I want to stay in the car and fuck him within an inch of my life. Until we can barely breathe and can't remember our names. But I don't say that; I just watch as he pulls his hand away, licking me from his fingers like I'm the nectar of life. Making love to this man is going to be life-changing. I crave his need for control and my desire to give it up for once in my life.

"Theo—" I groan, breathing hard.

"I know. Believe me, I know." He takes my hand and pulls it to his lips, pressing a kiss to my palm. Grabbing the bag from the backseat, he walks around the car to open my door. I step out on shaky legs, clutching his arm for support.

"If my fingers on your pussy makes your knees weak, I'm going to be carrying you off the boat tomorrow," he says, his eyes dark.

"I can't wait," I manage to say, trying to get my feet to cooperate.

By the time we make it up the gangplank, I have my legs back under me, and I'm practically running, dragging him toward the boat. The ship is sleek. Navy, cream, and chrome everywhere you look. We're greeted by a waiter in a tuxedo holding a tray of champagne.

"Welcome to *The Tide Runner*. Please enjoy a glass of champagne, compliments of the captain. Please look for your names on the board behind me. There you will find your key. Further instructions await you in your room."

I bite my lip to keep in my grin. This is so fucking cool. Theo hands me a glass, clinking his against mine. "To a future better than anything we've ever imagined," he whispers, his gaze caressing my face as we take a sip. He grabs our room key from the hook below our names and picks up a printed diagram of the boat before guiding me toward the elevator. Crystal chandeliers shine a warm light on every surface, giving the perfect magical ambiance. It feels like we're in a movie.

"This is incredible," I say, looking at what a cute couple we make in the mirrored elevator doors.

"Yes, you are," he murmurs, his lips moving against my hair. He pulls me into the elevator the second it opens, slamming his palm on the button to close the doors before trapping me against the wall, his elbows boxing me in. His lips are on mine before the doors close.

"What is it about you?" he growls, dragging his lips along the sweep of my jaw. "I can't keep my hands off of you. All I can think about is how your skin feels beneath my fingers. We're on a beautiful yacht, and all I want to do is lock you in the bedroom and ravish you."

"I'm not opposed to that." I shiver as he rakes his teeth over my collarbone.

"We're going to have to continue these single dates forever, you know."

"Why's that?"

"Because I'm a selfish motherfucker, Isla."

The door to the elevator opens before I can respond, another couple waiting to get on. I follow Theo down the plushly carpeted hallway, running my fingertips over the textured wallpaper. Theo bites his lip as he wiggles the key in the lock, pushing the door open and scooping me into his arms before crossing the threshold. He stops just inside the door, and both of our jaws drop.

"What is this place?" I whisper, not knowing where to look as he spins us around in a circle. The room is straight out of the 1920s. Opulence and extravagance everywhere you look. He sets me down, pointing to an envelope waiting for us on a table just inside the door, our names written in elegant calligraphy on the outside. I slide my nail under the flap and pull out the card inside, angling it so Theo can read it, too.

WELCOME, *Theo & Isla. This evening, you are John and Anna DuPont, newlyweds here on holiday. Anna is an heiress to an oil fortune, and John is the groundskeeper she fell in love with and begged her daddy to marry. You are both tasked with finding out who committed the murder.*

Please look inside your wardrobe to find your costume for dinner. You must always remain in character in public spaces until you leave the ship after lunch tomorrow.

I JUMP UP AND DOWN, clapping my hands. "This is so much fun! Do we get anything if we guess correctly?" I ask, walking over to the built-in wardrobe and pulling it open.

"The satisfaction of knowing we're smarter than everyone else." Theo smirks, joining me. I forget what we were talking about the second my gaze lands on our outfits for the night. Theo has a tux with emerald green accents that perfectly matches the sleek, shimmery dress hanging next to it.

"Damn, they really went all out, didn't they?" I ask, pulling the dress out and admiring it. "Thank you for setting this up, Theo. I can already tell it's going to be amazing."

"Only the best for my baby," he murmurs, kissing my cheek. I can't describe what those simple words do to me. What they mean to me. I feel like my brain is melting. Every wall is crumbling down. Defenses breached.

"Look at us. How far we've come," I whisper, smiling up at him. "Who would've thought?"

"I did." His lips cover mine, and I surrender to him, softening in his arms, molding to his body, greedily soaking up every touch. This. This is what I've been waiting for my entire life. Someone who makes the world around me disappear when I'm in his arms.

"We only have thirty minutes until cocktail hour starts," Theo says once we've finally managed to break away from each other.

"So what exactly do we do?" I ask, pulling my dress from the hanger and laying it on the bed.

"Work together to figure out who the murderer is."

"But who was murdered?" I ask, unzipping my sundress and watching as it puddles at my feet.

"I guess we're going to find out." He walks up behind me, winding his arms around my torso and pulling me against his chest.

"Or we can stay in the room and try to murder each other with sex?" I suggest, turning to face him, biting my lip and blinking up at him innocently.

"We'll have plenty of time for that later, Sunflower."

He gathers the dinner dress in his arms, unfastening it and crouching, holding it open so I can step into it easily. I shimmy as he slides it up my body, slipping my arms through the straps. I turn to look at myself in the mirror, not able to stop myself from watching Theo instead of myself as he fastens the back, fingertips skimming my shoulder, his gaze caressing every inch of bare skin.

"Your turn," I rasp, grasping the hem of his shirt and pulling it over his head. I can't stop myself from flattening my palms against his abdomen, reveling in the way his muscles jump under my touch. If I were him, I would never be able to stop looking at myself in the mirror. "You're so goddamned sexy." I drag my palms up his chest, his heartbeat strong under my hand.

"Isla, this is dangerous territory," he warns, his eyes dark, the tip of his tongue sliding over his lips.

I bite my lip to keep in a whimper, making quick work of his belt and pants, pushing them down past his ass and letting them fall to the floor. I skim my pinky along the waistband of his boxers, and he locks his fingers around my wrists, forcing my hands above my head.

"Good things come to those that wait, Sunflower."

"Is that a promise?"

"You know the answer to that," he chastises. "As long as my heart is beating, I promise I will want to ravish you until you don't remember your own name. Even when we're both ninety and can barely walk."

"Oh, God. That's terrifying."

"We'll be the luckiest men alive to grow old with you, Isla."

"Even when I'm tucking my tits into my pants?"

"Especially then." He winks, chuckling as he releases me and pulls on the dress pants.

"Even when my freckles have turned to age spots?"

"Nothing could make me love you less, Isla." His voice is confident, sure. Like this is something that he's considered before.

My heartbeat thunders in my ears. Love. He loves me.

"Do you mean that?"

"I've never meant anything more in my entire life."

I close the distance between us, rushing into his arms. He catches me easily, spinning me around, our lips meeting like waves crashing against the shore. Rough. Electric. Inevitable.

I cradle his face in my hands, pulling back, losing myself in his eyes. "I love you too, Theo."

"Thank fuck," he breathes, the relief in his eyes making me giggle.

"Were you that worried?"

"You would be too if you were in my position, Sunflower."

I push out my bottom lip, stepping back to give him room to shrug on his shirt, sad that he's covering those glorious muscles.

"I'll do better," I promise.

"I like you just the way you are, Isla. Never change for anybody. I like the challenge." He flips up his collar, sliding a tie around his neck. "Will you tie this for me?"

I take my time tying the knot, enjoying the intimacy, my body humming. I glance up at him, my gaze narrowing on how his teeth are sunk into his bottom lip. God, those lips. Heat flares between my legs when I think about all the places those lips have been.

"If we don't leave the room now, I'm going to lock you in here and take advantage of you for the next 36 hours." I whisper, straightening his tie and stepping away from him, fanning myself with the schedule.

"I thought our escapades in the greenhouse would take the edge off a little."

"It did the opposite of that. All I can think about is how badly I want you inside me."

"God, Isla. You can't say stuff like that." He adjusts himself, trying to hide his desire.

"Theo—"

"I want this experience with you, Isla. I want to look back on this day and remember how perfect it was. I won't waste this opportunity by staying in the bedroom the whole time."

"You think that would be a waste?" I ask, slightly offended. I turn and look out the window as he puts on his shoes.

"Hey," he whispers, winding his arms around my stomach, tucking his chin against my temple. "I'm not just interested in what we can do in bed, Isla. I love being around you. You make everything light up. My life used to be black and white, and when I met you, everything turned to color. I want to experience new things with you by my side. And that includes solving murders and then coming back to the room and making love."

How does he say the perfect thing every time? Like he knows exactly what I need to hear to assuage my fears. I never would have guessed this man was inside that rock-hard, gruff exterior.

"Do you understand?" he asks, turning me toward him and tilting my chin up until my eyes meet his.

"I understand, Theo," I say, blinking back tears.

"Are you ready to solve a murder?"

"Let's do it." I don't bother to tell him that I'm going to try to solve it as fast as possible so I can drag him back up here and rip every stitch of clothing off his incredible body.

31

Theo and I study our information cards before heading downstairs, attempting to memorize all of the details. Theo sticks them in his pocket in case we need a refresher, gives me a sound kiss on my lips, and then escorts me out the door. We don't even make it to the elevator before he has me pressed against the wall, his hand cradling my head, his lips devouring mine. The only thing that pulls us out of our embrace are the lights lowering twice, telling us it's time to make our way to the dining room.

I don't think I'll ever forget this night. I feel like we're in a dream as we step off the elevator and into the dining room—it's like a scene straight out of the *Titanic*. Theo's hand is warm in mine, the steady sweep of his thumb over my wrist tethering me to him. An enormous mahogany oval table is set in the middle of the room, crystal chandeliers dripping light over the opulent place settings.

"Welcome, Mr. and Mrs. DuPont. Please follow me to your seats." I glance at the waiter then up at Theo, unable to hide my nervous smile.

"Chin up, baby girl. We've got this," he murmurs, squeezing my hand. He pulls out my chair for me, and I sit, the chairs on either side of us still empty.

"Champagne, madame?" another waiter asks, the bottle poised over my glass as he waits for my answer.

"Please." I drink half the glass immediately, hoping to calm my nerves. Someone brushes against my shoulder, and I look behind me to see an older gentleman pulling out the chair next to me and settling into his seat.

"Good evening," he says, smiling at me, his face creasing into good-natured lines, blue eyes sparkling.

"Hello. I'm Anna Dupont, nice to meet you."

"Franklin Astor. Pleasure is mine." His smile is warm and friendly.

"Tell me about yourself, Mr. Astor." I already know from my information sheet that he's my father, and the woman sitting next to him is his new wife.

Just as he starts to answer my question, someone taps on a glass with a knife, the stragglers slipping into their seats and quieting down.

A well-dressed woman greets us with a tight smile. "Welcome to the *Tide Runner*. We are so happy to have you on board. Please spend the next hour enjoying your meal and getting to know the other guests. The information you learn now will be vitally important in the coming hours."

"I believe you're my father," I whisper conspiratorially, leaning closer to Franklin.

His mouth drops open in surprise before he remembers the part he's playing, making me giggle. "I think I just watched your life flash before your eyes," I say, grinning.

"I nearly had a heart attack. This is the first time I've ever done anything like this. It's going to take me a bit to get used to playing a part."

"Did you come with anyone?" I ask, glancing curiously at the beautiful woman at his side. "My mother, perhaps?"

"Your mother died six months ago. This gorgeous woman beside me is your new stepmother, Camila DuPont." He winces an apology.

This is so bizarre. I love it.

"So soon, dear Father?"

"When you know, you know," he says, paling a bit at the callousness of his words.

Conversation dies down as our meal is served. Duck breast with a tart cherry sauce, roasted potatoes, and sauteed broccolini. It's delicious.

"How did my mother die?" I ask, trying to glean as much information as I can before dinner ends.

"It happened very suddenly. The doctor said it was a heart attack."

"And Camila? Where did you meet her?"

"She's been my secretary for the past year."

Hmmm. Suspicious. I turn back to Theo, sliding my hand over his arm to get his attention.

"What have you found out so far?" I ask.

"The man beside me is Peter Hyland, Franklin Astor's business partner. His wife, Emily, is sitting to his right, hanging on every word he says."

"Should we get up and mingle?" I ask, setting my napkin on my empty dessert plate and pushing away from the table.

"That's a good idea. I want to find out as much as we can about the people we haven't had a chance to talk to before the murder happens."

Theo takes my hand as I stand, pushing to his feet next to me. That's when everything goes black.

"Too late," I whisper, my heart in my throat. "I think it's happening now." Will it be one of us? I hadn't even considered that. Oh god. I nearly jump out of my skin at the scream that erupts to my left.

I grip Theo's arm, my heart racing. Something hits the floor hard, and Theo draws me against his body, holding still as we both listen to the commotion going on around us. The lights flicker, and I spin to my left, getting a glimpse of Franklin sprawled on the ground, a knife sunk into his abdomen, his wife sobbing beside him before the lights go out again.

Fuck. This is legitimately terrifying.

"Folks, we have a temporary power outage," The same woman from earlier announces, walking into the room with a candle, setting it in the middle of the table. "Please enjoy drinks on us while we get it fixed." She pulls a flashlight out of her pocket, shining it around the table to ensure everyone is okay.

"Theo!" I tug on his arm until he turns toward me, and I point to Camila, sitting in her chair, her body trembling, a bright red slash on her arm, her hands covered in blood.

Jesus.

"What's this?" the woman asks, the beam of her flashlight traveling along Franklin's body. Her shrill scream startles me. She drops the flashlight, the beam cartwheeling. I catch a glimpse of an arm reaching out to the candle, setting a scrap of paper on fire. I don't get a chance to see the face, I only know that it was someone close, on our side of the table. I set a glass upside down over the curl of black paper, snuffing out the flame. Someone brushes my arm, sneaking behind us.

"Where were you?" I hear someone rage-whisper before the words are cut off abruptly. My mind is spinning, trying to put together puzzle pieces that don't fit. A gong sounds, and a man holding a lantern stands on a chair, towering over all of us.

"Good evening. I'm Detective Randall Evans. There has been a murder. Nobody is allowed to leave this level of the ship until everyone has been questioned. You may talk to each other, ask each other questions, and ask me questions when we have our one-on-one interviews. If you have the information requested, you are obligated to answer the question truthfully. Take your time. The person who solves this murder will be the person who asks the right questions. Ms. Johnson, you're first. Please follow me."

Ms. Johnson–the governor, if my memory of the information card serves me right–huffs. "I was on the opposite side of the table, it very obviously wasn't me." Mr. Evans gives her a stern look, and she snaps her mouth shut, following him out of the room.

"I didn't realize this was going to feel so real," I whisper, my heart pounding from the adrenaline roaring through my system. I grab the candle from the table and hold it over Franklin's body, looking dubiously at the pool of red forming beneath him. I bend down and hold my fingers to his neck to satisfy my worry. I gasp when he opens his eyes, giving me a quick wink before resuming his position. Thank fuck. This was all getting a little too real for comfort. The lights come back on suddenly, and I take a deep breath, steadying myself.

"Come on, let's get away from everyone and talk about what we know." I grab Theo's sleeve and tug him out of the room, winding our way around the odd staff member until we reach the mostly empty salon. I sit at the piano, needing to do something with my fingers while I think. I pick out "Twinkle, twinkle little star" while the details of the night spin through my head. "It seems like almost everyone in that room could have had a motive to murder Franklin," I muse, adding some simple chords with my left hand.

"Really?" he asks, leaning against the piano and watching me closely, his eyebrow lifting. "The only people with any motive would be you or Camila, depending on Franklin's will."

"Me?"

He shrugs. "You're his daughter and probably stand to inherit his half of the business."

"Yes, but why would I murder him?"

"Perhaps he said he was going to change his will. Take you out and add his wife."

"Damn. You're good at this. Except it wasn't me."

He narrows his eyes, studying my face, trying to sniff out a lie. I purse my lips, keeping my cards close to my chest.

"I think we should split up, find out as much as we can from everyone, and then come back together and compare notes," I say, standing.

"Smart. Meet me back here in thirty minutes?"

I nod, walking out of the room without looking back. I stop around the corner, peeking back into the room, watching Theo pick something out from underneath his nails, wipe a smudge from the back of his hand, and then head into the bathroom, annoyance written in the lines of his face. I shake my head. It can't be Theo. Can it? He was right next to me the whole time. I return to the dining room, studying everyone, letting their body language speak to me. The only problem is that everyone here is pretending to be someone they aren't, so how can I rely on body language? Ugh. I pull out a pad of paper and the pen I took from the room, jotting down a list of questions along with everyone's names. That will at least help me to stay organized. Perhaps I'll have a fighting chance of figuring this out quickly so I can drag Theo back to the room and have my way with him.

"Do you have a second to chat?" I ask Ms. Johnson, smiling.

"Of course, as long as I can ask you questions, too."

I nod and smile, leading her into the hallway where we can have a bit of privacy.

"Did you know everyone at this party before today?"

"No."

"Who did you know?"

"You, your husband, your father, and his wife," she says softly.

"How did you know my father?" I ask, curious.

"We have had ties up until last year. He would donate to my campaign."

"What happened last year?"

"He decided to run for my position."

Ah. "And how did that affect your relationship with him?" I ask, becoming increasingly suspicious.

"Negatively."

"How so?"

"I haven't talked to him since he told me."

"Did he have a chance of taking your position? Had any polls been done?"

She winces. "A poll last week showed him ahead by 9 points."

I suck air through my teeth. Well, if that's not damning, I don't know what is. "Those are all the questions I have," I say, writing the details down. Could she have crawled under the table when the power went out?

"You were sitting next to Mr. Astor, correct?" Ms. Johnson asks.

"Correct."

"And you're his daughter?"

"Correct."

"Were you happy when he remarried?"

"No," I admit.

"Why not?"

"I felt like Camila was marrying him for his money."

"There was no prenup?" she asks, her eyebrows jumping up her forehead.

"Not that I'm aware of."

"What about a will?"

"Yes, I was with my father when he made his will," I say, shifting on my feet. She sure has a lot of questions.

"And what did he leave to you?"

"His half of the business."

She makes a choking sound, backing up a step, like she forgot for a second that this isn't real. I have to admit, she already has a solid case against me. The disgruntled daughter who doesn't want to lose her inheritance, so she murders her father before he can change his will.

"Did his new wife know about the will?"

"Not that I'm aware of." I look over at Camila. She meets my gaze, her eyes darkening with suspicion. Is she a good actress, or does she really suspect me?

"That's all for now, Mrs. Dupont. Thank you."

I seek out Peter next, feeling like perhaps he'll have an idea who would have it out for his business partner.

"Mind if I ask you some questions?" I ask Peter, studying his face for clues.

"Of course." He smiles, his gaze traveling around the room before landing on me.

"How is your relationship with your wife?"

"It's been better," he admits.

"Why's that?"

"She filed for divorce last week."

"Why?"

He clears his throat. "She found something out that I've been hiding."

"And what is that something?"

"An affair."

"With whom?"

"I'm not sharing that information." His gaze betrays him, though. I follow it as it crosses the room, stopping on Camila.

Shit. Did he kill Franklin so he could be with Camila? Seems like a solid motive. He nods his head and leaves, not asking me any questions, which seems suspicious.

"Mrs. DuPont?"

I spin on my heel to see the detective. Shit. I was hoping to have some more time before I was called in for questioning. I follow him into a small office, sitting in a comfortable leather chair on the opposite side of a large wooden desk.

"Tell me about your relationship with your father, Mrs. DuPont."

"We've always had a great relationship. I've been working for him since I was seven or eight. Answering phones, taking orders, helping out wherever I could."

"And now?"

"Now I'm the vice president."

"And your relationship with him was stable up until his death?"

"Yes, he and I were very close."

"Even after he married Camila?"

I lean back in my chair. "I'll admit that that wasn't the best decision he's ever made, but I don't fault him for it."

"Do you fault her for it?"

"Yes."

"You feel she's a gold-digger?"

I start to protest, then remembered I have to answer based on what's on my card. "Yes," I admit, looking down at my lap.

"I believe those are the only questions I have right now, Mrs. DuPont. Do you have any questions for me?"

"Do you know who Peter is having an affair with?"

"Yes, but I'm not at liberty to share."

"Can you tell me if it's someone on this boat?"

"Yes, it's someone on this boat."

Bingo.

"Was anybody else injured in the attack?"

"Yes, the blade grazed Camila before Franklin was stabbed."

Could she have been the intended target all along?

"Did Camila know that my father willed his half of the business to me?" I ask, finally coming to what may be the most important question.

"No."

Fucking hell. They've made it so absolutely everyone is a potential suspect. *Think, Isla.* The image of the hand holding that scrap of paper comes back to me. Could that have been Theo? Peter? Emily? I say my goodbyes to the detective and make my way back to the dinner table. Franklin's body is covered, and I rein back my curiosity to pull the sheet back and see if he's actually still under there or if there's a mannequin in his place. I make sure nobody is watching and remove the cup over a scrap of paper and fold it into my palm, walking to the women's restroom and closing myself in a stall before examining it.

Keep he–

out of th–

I stare at it, tilting it back and forth under the dim lighting, trying to decipher the missing words. I glance at my phone. Only five minutes until I meet back up with Theo. I head back into the salon to go back over my notes, coming up with several hypotheses to run by him.

"Ready, wifey?" Theo comes up behind me, his breath tickling my ear as he rests his chin on my shoulder, his arms wrapping around my middle.

"Did you get any good information?" I ask, turning in his arms and looking up into those mesmerizing eyes.

"I did. You?"

I nod, letting him lead me into the corner where we can talk in private.

"Was it you that burned the scrap of paper?" I ask, pulling it from my pocket.

"Yes, it was slipped in front of me right before the lights went out. It said *Keep her out of the way*. That's why I grabbed you."

"Any idea who put the paper there?"

"No, I didn't see."

Bummer. We compare notes, and after about ten minutes, we have a solid theory just in time for the lights to lower twice, calling us back to the dining room. I'm relieved to see that the sheet-covered body is gone as I slip back into my seat. The detective stands at the head of the table, and the room falls into a pregnant hush.

"Has anyone deduced who murdered Franklin Astor?" he asks, his gaze sliding to each of us.

Emily stands. "I believe Camila murdered her husband in order to inherit his fortune."

The detective raises an eyebrow. "You only get one guess. Is that your final answer?"

"Yes."

"Incorrect. Next?"

Ms. Johnson stands, pointing at me. "Anna DuPont murdered him so her fortune wouldn't be willed to her new stepmother, Camila."

"Anna, what do you have to say about that?"

"You're wrong," I say simply, giving her a sympathetic smile. "It was Emily."

A collective gasp goes up, every gaze in the room swiveling to Emily.

"She meant to kill Camila but tripped, slicing open Camila's arm, before the blade found a home in Franklin Astor's abdomen instead of her husband's mistress," Theo finishes, revealing our theory.

The detective claps slowly, the staff joining in. "Congratulations to the DuPonts. You solved the mystery. This concludes that portion of our evening, ladies and gentlemen. Our guests are welcome to enjoy the amenities for the rest of this evening. Brunch will be between nine and eleven in the morning. We hope you enjoyed your dinner."

I take Theo's hand and start dragging him toward the elevators, determined to get him back to the room as quickly as possible.

"Isla, Theo?" The detective stops us, holding out a bottle of champagne. "Your prize. Enjoy your evening."

"Thank you so much, that was thrilling."

"I'm impressed you figured it out so easily."

"I had some extra motivation," I say, looking up at Theo.

"And she's the most competitive woman you will ever meet. I'm sure that had nothing to do with it." Theo winks, taking the bottle of champagne from his hand. "Should we go out on the deck and enjoy the champagne under the stars?" he asks once the detective leaves to mingle with the other guests.

"Or, we can go back to the room, and you can lick it off my body. Your choice."

"Fuck. Me. Isla."

His voice is deliciously husky, and I desperately want to hear him call me a good girl as he slides inside me. "Gladly. Room. Now."

"Yes, ma'am," he growls, swinging me into his arms and kissing me hard.

32

We can't take more than two steps without touching each other. The brush of our shoulders, his fingers sliding over my wrist, my hand trailing down his chest. It's like the world is holding its breath, waiting for this cataclysmic collision to finally happen; like fate has been leading me here since I took my first breath.

"In order to set the proper expectations for tonight, I have to ask you a question," Theo rasps, his breath warm on my ear.

I look up at him, running my thumb along the edge of his bottom lip, thinking about how those lips feel in *other* places.

"Do you want to have sex tonight?"

"Are you really asking me that question?"

"Answer me, Isla."

"Yes. Lots of it." I answer, enunciating every word. "Is that clear enough for you?"

"Crystal." His hand brushes over the side of my breast as he takes hold of my upper arm, pulling me from the elevator. My back arches, a lightning bolt of desire streaking down my spine, igniting a fire deep in my core.

"Theo," I moan, my knees threatening to give out as my body tries to recalibrate.

"God, Isla. I'm not sure we'll survive the night." He sweeps me into his arms, carrying me down the hallway. I pull the room key from his pocket and unlock the door, twisting the handle so he can kick it open. He sets me down, slams the door closed and pushes me against it, hauling my legs around his waist.

"Do you know how long I've been waiting for this?" he asks, pushing a lock of hair behind my ear, his touch tender.

"Probably not as long as me," I tease, the corner of my mouth pulling up.

"Bullshit. I couldn't figure out why I only seemed to be able to think with my dick until I realized."

"Until you realized what?" I ask, tracing his cheekbone with my thumb before skimming my fingertips over the short hair at the nape of his neck.

"That it's not lust."

I raise an eyebrow.

"Not *just* lust," he corrects, chuckling.

"What is it then?"

"I am so fucking in love with you, Isla."

My soul breathes a sigh of relief. Everything is finally right with the world.

"Tell me you love me, too, Sunflower. That you can't imagine life without me."

I look up at the man before me, at the thorny exterior that hides the gooey center I never would have guessed was there if I hadn't given him a chance.

"Tell me you're all in," he begs, his voice husky. "I know we're a lot, I swear to god we'll make it worth it. I need you to tell me before we make love because I know the second my cock slides into you, it's over for me."

A pulse starts between my legs, desperate for him. "I love you, Theo. And I love your brothers. I'm all in. For as long as you'll have me."

"Forever," he growls, crushing his lips to mine. His touch is wild, desperate. I meet his energy, pouring all of my feelings into this kiss, wanting to show him that I'm his until the end of time. That I'd surely die without him. My legs start slipping down his hips, my dress making it impossible to keep my grip. I kick off my shoes the second my feet are on the floor, pushing up on my tiptoes to keep his lips on mine.

"This dress has to go," he says roughly, turning me and slowly tugging down the zipper, his breathing jagged and uneven as he slides his palms up my back, nudging the dress from my shoulders. It slips over my body and puddles at my feet on the floor in a pool of emerald green. Theo's gaze trails slowly over my bare skin, blazing a trail of hunger in its wake. He reaches to unhook my bra, but I take a step back.

"Your turn," I insist, desperate to be able to run my hands over every inch of his skin, to brand him with my touch and claim him as mine. My eyes follow his hands as he moves from button to button, slowly exposing more and more of his chest until I feel like I can barely breathe. He slows once he gets to the fourth button, and I lose my patience, wrenching his shirt open, buttons popping off and rolling away across the floor as I push the fabric off his shoulders. This is what I've been waiting for: the feel of his skin beneath my fingers, muscles jumping as I drag my hands down his torso.

"Isla, if I don't get my mouth on you right this second, I may die." He picks me up and throws me onto the bed, crawling up after me, pushing my knees wide. A growl comes from deep in his throat, moisture gushing in response. He pulls my underwear to the side, licking a path up the center of my pussy, swirling his tongue around my clit.

"Fuck, Theo," I gasp, my hips jerking in response. I'm so close I swear I could get there just by him breathing on me.

"So fucking sweet," he groans, dipping a finger into me, massaging my G-spot and chuckling as my back arches.

"Theo, please."

"Tell me what you want, baby girl."

"I need you in me."

"I am in you," he reminds me, crooking his finger. I buck against him, my breath catching in my throat as his touch lights up my nerve endings.

"I need your cock in me. Now." I'm not too proud to beg. "Please, Theo."

"Not yet," he says roughly, adjusting himself in his pants.

"Why not?"

"I don't think you understand that the second my cock slides into that warm cunt, I'm done for. I won't be able to stop until I come. I have to get you there before that."

"I'll get there with you," I promise.

"There's no chance. I have maybe thirty seconds in me. I've been waiting too long for this, Isla."

"And you think I haven't? Just thinking about it has me on the edge. Trust me. We have all night to take it slow. I want the first time to be rough. Wild. I want every single emotion you've been holding back."

"You don't know what you're asking for."

"Yes, I fucking do." I sit up, pushing him back onto his knees. I unbuckle his belt, ripping it out of his belt loops with a satisfying snap before tackling his button.

"Isla-"

"Give me what I want, Theo."

He groans, the sound raising the tiny hairs on my arms. "How can I refuse when it's all I've wanted since I saw you in the bar that night? I think I knew all the way back then."

"Knew what?"

"That you're my endgame, Sunflower. I've been looking for you my entire life, and now that I have you, I'm never letting go."

"I'm going to hold you to that." I pull his cock out, my core clenching as I take hold, squeezing his hard length.

"Fucking hell. Keep doing that, and I'm going to come in your hand." His hips surge, pushing his cock through my fingers. Once. Twice, then he's on top of me, pushing me into the bed, his weight pressing me down.

"I'll regret it for the rest of my life if I rush this, Isla. I'm going to take it slow, treasure your body like you deserve." He positions his cock at my entrance, the crown stretching me, making my body tremble. Every nerve ending in my body goes haywire as he pushes into me, filling me. "Relax, Sunflower."

I take deep breaths, focusing on relaxing my muscles.

"Good girl," he grunts, sliding the rest of the way in. "You're so fucking tight."

I clench around him, my core spasming in response to his praise. One hard thrust and I'll shatter. But he doesn't give in. I wind my legs around him as he withdraws, trying to keep him inside me, but I'm only rewarded with a husky chuckle.

"Not yet, Sunflower." He sits back on his knees, looking down at me, worshipping me with his eyes. A strangled moan twists its way out of my throat as he slides two fingers into me. He watches as he fucks me with them, his teeth buried in his bottom lip. His pinky sliding along my ass crack with his next thrust.

"Theo!" I twist away from him, but he flattens his palm on my lower stomach, holding me still.

"I can tell you like it," he says roughly, circling the pad of his finger, watching me closely.

I cover my face with my hands, my cheeks burning.

"Why are you embarrassed?"

"I–I don't know."

"Has anyone ever done that before?"

"Once."

"Did you like it?"

"Not particularly."

"And now?" he asks, pushing the tip of his finger inside me.

I groan, my hips angling toward him without my consent. "Yes," I whisper, mortified.

"Thank fuck," he breathes, his eyes never leaving my face as he slowly fucks my ass with his finger.

"Why are you relieved?" I ask, my voice trembling.

"Honestly? Because I've been dreaming of the day I get to see you thoroughly fucked by three cocks at once. I want to see your face when we fill you to the point you can't remember your name. We'll fuck you so good you'll never be able to go back."

I whimper as he lies down between my legs, fastens his mouth over my clit and sucks. One more pull and I m breaking apart beneath him, squeezing his head between my thighs as I shatter.

"So fucking beautiful," he breathes, laying his head on my thigh and breathing me in. I don't have time to catch my breath before he's pulling me between his knees at the end of the bed, the full-length mirror directly in front of us. I watch as bends down to lick a line over the globe of my ass cheek, biting hard at the base of my spine.

"Fuck, Theo," I gasp, my entire body spasming. He holds his cock steady with one hand as he guides me down, impaling me as he pulls me onto his lap. He hooks my legs around his knees, spreading my thighs open, both of us getting the perfect view of his cock stretching me wide.

"Oh god," I mumble, trying to rock my hips, but he holds me still, his arm banded across my stomach.

"Don't move," he commands, restraint etched in the lines of his face. His gaze slides down to my pussy, both of us watching as he drags his fingers along my lips, teasing me.

"Show me how you get yourself off."

"What?" I ask, my gaze snapping to his in the mirror.

"You heard me," he says gruffly, taking my hand and moving it between my legs.

"Theo—"

"Show me," he demands, eyes dark, his cock flexing inside me. I squeeze back, moaning at the fullness. I can't imagine three. I'd be so full I wouldn't be able to think, I'd be at their mercy. I clench around him, so fucking turned on I can barely breathe. I slide my hand over my stomach and down between my legs, cradling my clit between my pointer and ring finger, my middle finger riding over my center as I easily slide back and forth, desire coating my fingers, dripping down his balls. The sight is so fucking erotic. Covering my fingers lightly with his own, he memorizes the movement before pulling my hand up to his mouth and licking me off his fingers.

"Look how wet you are for me, baby."

I moan, my breath shuddering out of me as he slides his hand back between my legs. "You take me so good," he groans, tilting his hips, pushing in even deeper. "That's my girl, take every last inch," he says roughly, thrusting hard. I cry out as my muscles tense around him. He jerks me to my feet, both of us breathing hard. "On your stomach, Sunflower. I'm about to blow your fucking mind."

33

Theo's POV*

My entire body is buzzing like a live wire, anticipation coating every inch of my skin, electricity skittering through my body, making it hard to breathe. I tell Isla to turn over on her stomach, and she does, those wide, guileless eyes looking up at me before she lays her cheek on the bed. She's so fucking beautiful. Miles of creamy skin covered in the sexiest smattering of freckles. I want to discover every single one. Connect them with my fingertips. My tongue. My cum. I groan, lifting her by the hips enough to push a pillow under her hips, putting her perfect heart-shaped ass on display for me. I trap her legs between my knees, sitting back, palming the round globes of her ass cheeks and squeezing, spreading her until she pushes back into my hands, her pussy weeping for me.

I've never had a problem with coming too fast, but I know my control will fly out the window the second I'm inside her. That moment I sunk my cock into her pussy the first time is going to be branded into my brain forever. I felt her relax underneath me, her muscles loosening to allow me in before gripping me tight. I nearly embarrassed myself on that very first thrust.

I lick from the top of her crack to the base of her spine. "You've had anal sex before?" I ask, my voice rough, my eyes glued to her ass and the way her muscles ripple under my touch.

She coughs, then clears her throat, making it obvious that the question makes her uncomfortable.

"The truth, Isla."

"I've done some butt stuff," she says, looking back at me, her cheeks scarlet. She's so goddamn pretty when she blushes for me.

"What does that mean?" I ask, sliding my thumbs up her crack, reveling in the way she writhes beneath my hands.

"A finger," she mumbles, burying her face in the bed.

"A finger," I repeat, stunned. Fucking hell. "That's all?"

She nods, gasping as my thumb circles over her puckered skin.

"I wish you had told us that, Isla. It'll take a bit before you're ready for all three of us."

"What do you mean?" She looks over her shoulder at me, green eyes filled with questions.

"I mean that it takes time to be able to fuck someone in the ass and have them like it."

"Oh."

My cock twitches at the thought of claiming her virgin ass. "We'll have to order some things tomorrow."

"Like what?"

I don't answer right away, all of my attention focused on her body. I spit on her, rubbing it in with my thumb before pressing against that tight ring of muscle. Her moan draws a noose around my balls, pulling tight. Fuck.

"We need to order a set of graduated butt plugs so we can stretch you slowly."

"Will three weeks be long enough?"

"As long as we all use them every time, it should be." I crawl backward, lowering myself to the bed and burying my face in her ass.

"Theo!" she shrieks, trying to twist away from me.

"If you don't like it, I'll stop," I pant, breathing in her arousal like it's the elixir of life.

She doesn't say anything.

"Talk to me, Isla."

"I like it," she whispers, her neck flushing.

"There's no reason to be embarrassed. Embrace what feels good. There's no point hiding from it when we only have one life. We need to wring every drop of pleasure from it." I growl as I spread her wide, licking her, fucking her ass with slow, deliberate thrusts of my tongue.

"Fuck, Theo!" she moans, pulling her knees up a little as she pushes her ass back toward me, her body begging for more.

I slide a finger into her pussy, groaning as she clenches around me matching the movement of my finger with my tongue. I add a second finger, turning my hand so my palm is facing down, massaging her inner wall, focusing on the spot that makes her twitch.

"I'm close," she whimpers, her entire body trembling.

I push up to my knees, pulling her hips back. The sound she makes as I slide my thumb down her crack and push inside nearly breaks me. I grip my cock, sliding it up and down her slit, holding the crown on her clit, pulsing there until she's a sobbing, squirming mess. I notch myself at her entrance, giving her a second of warning before I slam into her. I push her chest down into the bed, fucking her ass with my thumb as I rock my hips against her, the ridge of my crown catching on her G-spot with every thrust.

As her body grips my cock, all I can think about is how there's no way I'm going to last as long as she deserves. I had so many plans for tonight, including edging her until the only thing she could remember was my name. But now, with her silky smooth skin beneath me, one hand reaching back to grip my knee, the other fisted in the sheets, and the sounds coming from those perfect lips, fucking hell. I was kidding myself. There's no option but to come and come hard.

"Isla," I rasp, my lips moving against her shoulder.

"I know, me too," she pants, her body moving against mine.

"Will you turn over for me, baby? I need to see your face." I help her turn onto her back, gripping her ankles and wrapping them around my waist.

"Good girl," I murmur, sliding my palms along her calves and up her thighs, need battering me from all sides. "I wanted to last forever for you, Sunflower, but you're too fucking gorgeous. I've been on the edge since your dress dropped to the floor."

"I don't need you to last forever, Theo, I just need you to make me come."

Fuck. I swear my heart nearly bursts from my chest, swelling with love for her. I hold her gaze, drowning in pools of luminous green as I flex my hips, nudging at the entrance to my own personal heaven. I thrust into her, our groans mingling as I press my lips to hers.

"If I die like this—with my cock buried between your legs—I would die a happy man."

"Don't die. Just fuck me. Please."

I can tell she's close by the way she writhes underneath me, her back nearly breaking to get closer to me. I drop my weight, pushing myself forward the slightest amount so my pubic bone rides over her clit as I move over her.

"Look at me, Isla." Her eyes snap open, her gaze spearing me in the chest. Like a knife twisting in my heart, carving her initials into me, branding me as hers. A mark I will wear with pride on my sleeve for the rest of my days.

"Do you feel that?" she whispers, her eyes wide with wonder, her fingers brushing over my jaw.

"Yes," I chuckle, sliding into her, then farther, pressing her into the bed.

"You know what I mean," she gasps, her back arching even as she rolls her eyes at me.

"I do know what you mean," I murmur, tenderly kissing the corner of her mouth. "It's like the stars aligned and our souls locked together." She stares up at me, shocked, not saying anything. I clear my throat. "At least that's what—"

She stops me with a finger on my lips, pushing her hands into my hair and pulling me down. She frames my face with her hands, sucking on my bottom lip before pushing her tongue into my mouth. The tension between us ascending up to dizzying heights as I slowly pull my cock out and then push forward, sliding back in, her clit rolling between us. I swallow her cry, picking up the pace. She rakes her nails down my back, latching on to my ass, pulling me closer until my control breaks.

"Come with me," I say roughly. Our kiss is forgotten, mouths open in desperate ecstasy, breathing each other's air as we reach for the summit. I shorten my strokes, and she rewards me with a moan that has my balls drawing up tight.

"Isla–" I pant.

"Don't fucking stop," she begs, her eyes locking on mine as her face crumples. The first tremor of her pussy around my cock makes me fold. Her eyes close as her orgasm grips her, and I drop my head to her shoulder, slamming into her. I roar my release, burying my cock as deep as it will go, her pussy squeezing out every last drop.

"My ears are ringing," she pants, laughing in the way you do after a mind-blowing orgasm.

"That was incredible, Isla. You're so fucking amazing." I push fiery strands from her forehead, kissing her temple. "Let's get washed up."

"I don't know if I can stand, Theo. My arms and legs are all shaky."

"As they should be. Give me a minute. I'll run a bath." I look down at her, and a peculiar sense of protectiveness washes over me.

"What's that look for?" she asks, pushing to her elbows.

"I know I'm grumpy sometimes–"

"Sometimes?" she asks, interrupting me.

"Fine, most of the time, and I know I'm not the best at communicating, but I hope you know how fucking important you are to me, Isla. I don't know what I would do if I ever lost you."

"You're not going to lose me, Theo. I wouldn't have slept with you if I was planning on leaving."

I sit on the edge of the bed, pulling her into my arms. "Tell me you love me, Isla." My voice is husky, desperation lacing my words.

She places her hands on both of my cheeks, forcing me to meet her eyes. "I love you, Theo. I love you and your brothers more than I ever thought I could love anyone other than family. The three of you have taught me so much. I'll never be able to repay you for what you've given me."

"We'll never be able to pay you back for ripping the pub out from underneath you," I mutter, a bitter edge to my voice.

"You still don't understand, do you?" she asks, shaking her head slowly. "You guys gave me a gift, Theo. I would have been eighty-five and still working in that pub. I would never have had a life. Never taken any chances. Never dated the three of you, that's for sure. Things happen for a reason. Even you snatching the pub out from under me. If you want to pay me back, help me create a successful brewery. Then we can call it even."

"Deal." I can't bear to let her go, so I carry her to the bathroom, sitting on the edge of the tub with her balanced on my thighs as I fill the it with water, dumping in a generous amount of bath salts. I stand, holding her tightly to my body as I climb in, settling her between my legs as steaming rises around us.

"God, that feels good," she sighs, pulling my hands around her stomach and burrowing back into me, resting her head on my shoulder.

"Better than sex?"

"Never." She covers a yawn with her hand, her eyes fluttering closed.

I would do almost anything to stay here like this forever. Just the two of us. But I know from experience that eventually I would want to give her more, and that's where my brothers come into the picture. The three of us are a perfect match for this complicated, feeling, independent woman, and I can't wait to show her what that truly means.

34

I stay snuggled in his arms until the water cools around us, until I can feel him hardening against my back, until need nearly blinds me. I reach behind me, only one thing on my mind. Theo snatches my wrist, pulling it in front of us.

"Not yet, my love."

"Why not?" I ask, not ashamed to beg if that's what it takes.

"Because you need some time to recover."

"Says who?"

"Says me, Isla. I don't want you to be sore."

"Maybe I want to be sore. Maybe I want to be reminded of tonight for the next two days. Did you ever think of that?" He sighs but doesn't say anything, so I turn in his arms, straddling his thighs.

"I poured a bath to soothe your body, Sunflower, not to take advantage of you."

"It's me taking advantage of you, so there's no need to feel guilty." I bite my lip, my gaze glued to the way the crown of his cock is breaking the surface of the water.

"God, Isla," he groans. He squirts some body wash into his hands, spreading it over my chest and breasts, squeezing and kneading, his hands slick against my skin.

"Sit on the edge of the tub," I instruct, scooting back to give him room to move.

"What?" he asks, a wrinkle forming between his brows.

"Please." He raises an eyebrow but obeys, pushing out of the water and perching himself on the side of the tub. I approach him on my knees, pushing his thighs apart with my hands. His breath hitches, and a thrill of power rolls down my spine.

"This is a bad idea," he croaks, even as he flexes his hips toward me.

"I won't get you there. Just having a little fun," I promise, running my nails up his legs, sweeping my thumbs along the soft skin on his inner thighs, chuckling when his cock jumps. I drag my lips from knee to hip on one side, then repeat the motion on the other, running my tongue along the V of his abdomen. I hold his gaze as I push his shaft against his stomach, licking his scrotum and then sucking him into my mouth. I reach out with my tongue, feathering the tip over his taint, his moan quickly followed by a pearl of precum glistening at the tip.

"You like that?" I purr, sliding my tongue along the underside of his shaft and swirling it over the swollen head, focusing my attention on his frenulum.

"Jesus fuck, Isla," he gasps, trying to pull me up. I resist, wetting my hands and rubbing them over my tits, sudsing up the soap Theo coated me with. I lean forward, trapping his cock between my breasts. I don't have a chance to move before he grips the side of the tub and thrusts hard, his pupils blown out with desire.

"Good boy." I bite my lip, watching his face as he struggles for control.

"I'm not a good boy," he growls, pushing me back on my ass. He splashes water over my chest, washing away the soap, and does the same to his cock before lifting me from the tub and carrying me into the bedroom, water streaming down our bodies. I squirm as he carries me out onto the balcony, my head swiveling to make sure nobody can see us. He sets me down on my feet, his gaze dark.

"Don't fucking move." He stalks back into the room, dragging the full-length mirror closer to the sliding doors. Once he has it situated where he wants, he comes back out and pulls me to him, his mouth open as it meets mine, pushing his tongue between my lips, claiming me. He swallows my whimper, pushing my back against the glass door, his cock digging into my stomach. Pulling my knee up to his hip, he adjusts his cock so it settles between my thighs. I rock my hips along his shaft, dragging my clit over him.

"Turn around," he demands, releasing my leg and spinning me around, pressing my tits to the glass. "I want you to watch while I fuck you from behind."

I meet his gaze in the mirror, my breathing ragged as he drags the head of his cock between my ass cheeks. He reaches around me, cupping me, guiding himself to my cunt. He stays poised there, his crown stretching me as he flexes his hips, teasing the sensitive nerve endings before sliding in deep.

"Fuck, Isla," he groans, his breath hot on my ear as he drops his mouth to my shoulder, biting me while he fucks me I whimper as he runs his tongue over the same spot, soothing the sting. "I have to see it," he rasps, desperation in his voice. He tugs me back inside, sitting with his back against the sliding door. He guides my ankles outside his thighs and grasps my hips, keeping me facing away from him as he pulls me down. He wraps one hand around his shaft, keeping himself steady as I sink onto him, impaling myself.

God. He feels so fucking good.

"Look up."

I do as he says, looking up into the mirror, my heart jumping at what I see there. Theo reclines the slightest bit, raising his knees and putting his feet flat on the floor. He spreads his legs, taking mine with them, giving us a perfect view of where I'm impaled on his cock.

"So fucking beautiful," he breathes, the tip of his tongue tracing the shell of my ear. His hand slides between my legs, careful not to block our view, one finger riding back and forth over my clit as he slowly rocks his hips. I watch, enraptured, as his cock disappears, then the way my pussy hugs him as he pulls out, not wanting to let him go. The outer edge of his crown teases at my entrance before he pushes back in, driving me mad.

"Theo," I pant, finding the rhythm and moving my body with his, heightening the friction.

"Look at the way your pretty pink pussy stretches for me, baby." He groans as he pulls almost all the way out, his head dragging over my G-spot, making me tremble. I can't stop watching the way his balls pull up with every thrust, like they're dying for a piece of the action but can't get quite close enough. I slide my hand over my inner thigh, reaching forward until I'm cupping them in my hand. I'm rewarded with a heady moan as I roll them back and forth, massaging, tugging. His fingers speed up, two fingers riding along both sides of my clit while another rides over the top, pushing and pulling with every thrust. I extend my middle finger, pushing up along the back of his scrotum until I reach his taint. I'm not sure what I'm supposed to do, so I experiment with a light touch, light rubbing, and finally massage the spot firmly. His hips spasm in response, and he fucks me hard, an unhuman-like sound ripping from his throat. I don't have any choice but to take what he's giving me, and I fall apart oh his cock, coming harder than I ever have before.

"Jesus," I pant, collapsing against him, trying to catch my breath, my ears ringing.

"Where did you learn that?" he rasps, his hips ghost-spasming.

"From the Internet."

"Is that code for porn?" he asks, chuckling.

"Maaaybe. I know most of it is unrealistic, but I've learned a few things."

"Well, I, for one, am incredibly grateful that you're open to exploring your sexuality."

"Does that mean you'll let me peg you?" I ask, biting my lip to keep in my laugh as I look up at him.

I slide a finger under his chin, pushing it shut, then kiss his neck. "Just kidding."

"Are you, though?"

"That's for me to know and you to find out." I stand up, holding out my hand for him. "Let's get washed up and go look for some snacks."

"Or we can order room service," he says, gesturing to the menu lying on the bed.

"Even better. And then dessert?" I ask, winking at him. "And yes, before you ask, dessert is code for more sex."

"Jesus Christ, Isla. Thank God there are three of us. I don't think I could keep up with you on my own."

"I have years to make up for, Theo. I'd like to make up for them as fast as possible."

"I'll do everything to help you in your quest, princess," he says as he stands, pulling me against his body and capturing my lips with his.

35

I wake up slowly, my senses coming alive one by one. My legs are tangled with Theo's. The contrast of his coarse hair on my freshly shaved legs is absolutely sinful. His chest rises and falls steadily under my cheek, a fluffy comforter cocooning us in downy warmth. I take a deep breath, drowning myself in his scent, wishing we could stay like this forever.

"Morning, Sunflower." His voice is smoke and sandpaper. Goose-bumps race over my body, making me shiver. I crack open my eyes, blinking several times before lifting my chin to look at him.

"Good morning, handsome," I murmur, his sleep-mussed hair and stubble stoking the embers still burning low in my belly from last night. "Did you put me to bed?" I ask, realizing I don't remember falling asleep.

"You passed out ten minutes after we put the movie on."

I wince. "But I promised you dessert."

"Isla, I lost count of how many 'courses' we had last night. We can have dessert another time."

"Another time meaning now?" I ask, biting my lip and looking at him with doe eyes.

He looks at the clock on the nightstand. "We can have dessert now or breakfast. They stop serving in forty-five minutes."

I give him a quick peck on the lips before jumping out of the bed and pulling on clothes. "I love you, but I'm starving."

He chuckles, his gaze worshipping my body. I could get used to this. I toss him a pair of boxers as I head toward the bathroom to brush my hair. Theo wraps his arms around me from behind, kissing my temple before resting his chin on the top of my head. Our eyes lock in the mirror.

"How are you so beautiful when you just woke up?" he asks, tracing my jawline with the back of his fingers.

"Were you expecting a zombie?" I stick out my arms and roll my eyes back. "I want to eat your brainsss," I groan, jerking in his arms.

"Jesus, Isla. Have you been practicing that your entire life?"

"No, but I was a zombie for Halloween when I was fifteen and spent months watching zombie movies to perfect my technique. I guess it stuck with me."

"I see that," he laughs, spinning me around and pulling me to his bare chest. I sigh happily. This is where I belong. I finally release him when I think he maybe won't ever let go and give him a light smack on his ass. "Go get dressed before I get hangry."

"That would be even scarier than the zombie, wouldn't it?" He tips my chin up, kissing me hard before heading back into the bedroom.

My hangry is something nobody should ever have to see. I don't even recognize myself when I get like that. It's like those Snickers commercials. Scary as fuck.

We eat breakfast out on the deck, large umbrellas shading us from the rare summer sun. I could not have asked for a more relaxing couple of days before the stress of Charlie's baby shower. It's like Theo stepped into my head and knew exactly what I needed.

"To our last first dates," Theo says, raising his mimosa, the wind ruffling his hair.

"This really is my last first date with the three of you, isn't it?" I muse.

"This better be your last first date ever, Isla. We're playing for keeps."

I bite my lip to keep in my smile, heat creeping up my cheeks. I love how protective he is. It calls to primitive deep inside me. "To my last first date," I whisper, clinking my glass against his and taking a sip.

"What do you want out of life, Isla?" Theo asks after they lay an incredible number of dishes on our table for a family-style breakfast. I help myself to the fruit salad and French toast, taking time to think about his question before I answer it.

"In the end it all boils down to one thing. I want to feel accomplished in all areas of my life. Love. Family. Business."

"What does accomplishment mean to you?" he presses, taking a bite of scrambled eggs.

"It means I'm happy. That the people I surround myself with are happy. I feel fulfilled, but not at the expense of their wants and needs. And this goes for the three of you as well as Charlie, Jack, Cam, and Lach. And the rest of my family, for that matter." I take another bite, and something suddenly occurs to me. "Have you met Lorna yet?"

"Your sister, right?" he asks. "No, we haven't met."

I cover my face with my hands. I've been so wrapped up in being miserable that I didn't even realize that they haven't met one of the most important people in my life. "She's coming for the baby shower, maybe she'll have time to stop over. Pen will be there, too."

"Who's Pen?"

"Lach's sister."

"We could cook something for dinner over at the Manor House. They could come after the shower," Theo suggests.

"Perfect!" I'm excited to introduce them, but I'm even more excited to catch up with both women. It's been ages since I've had a real face-to-face conversation with them.

"We're not going to get a group date with you this weekend, are we?" Theo asks.

"Probably not, but if you guys want to help me set up, we can still spend time together."

"Of course, we'll help, Sunflower."

I hide my grin by taking a sip of my drink. Just having people in my corner feels so fucking good. It's been lonely since Charlie started dating my brother, Lach, and Cam. Not that I ever told them that. I didn't want their pity, and I sure as hell didn't want to be a fifth wheel on their dates. Ew.

"We should go back to the room and start packing. We only have three hours until we dock," Theo says, setting his napkin on the table.

"I don't think I need three hours to pack my one tiny bag, Theo."

"Maybe not, but I'm going to need three hours to do all of the things I didn't get to do last night."

Fuck. Me.

"Are you two ready for your spa treatment?"

I look up in confusion at the woman standing at the end of our table. "Our what?"

"The person that solves the murder mystery gets exclusive use of the spa utilities on board for two hours," she explains, smiling.

"I completely forgot about that," Theo says, looking over at me apologetically.

"It's not a full-service spa, but we have hydro massage machines, a sauna, and a sensory pool."

"That sounds amazing," I groan, my muscles sore from the workout they got last night.

"If you'll follow me, I'll take you there now." She waits for us to finish our drinks and stand, then leads us inside the ship to the lower level. "I'm the only one with the key, and I promise you I will not barge in unannounced. You have two hours starting now," she says, glancing at her watch.

Theo pulls out his phone and sets a two-hour timer. "Got it."

"Lock the door behind you," she says, grinning over her shoulder at me like she knows exactly what's about to happen.

"What's a sensory pool?" I ask once we're locked inside the spa area. It's a small room with three doors—one at each end and one directly in front of us.

"I have no idea, but we're about to find out." Theo opens the door on the left to reveal two hydromassage machines. The next door we try is the sauna. "Here we go," he says, winking at me as he opens the final door. My first impression is... I'm not impressed. The walls are stark white, the ceiling a deep shadowy black. A small dark pool is sunk into the floor–more like a hot tub. There's room for maybe six people.

"Sensory, how?" I ask, scanning the room for a clue.

"This must be the control panel," Theo murmurs, studying a screen on the wall to our left. He presses a couple of buttons, and sound roars from hidden speakers. I cover my ears, my heart racing. He presses another, and projectors turn on, turning the walls into a jungle. One more button and rain is falling from the ceiling. My hands drop along with my chin as I stand there in awe. It's like we've been transported to a private jungle pool in the middle of a thunderstorm.

"Do you want me to try out the other settings?" Theo asks, scrolling through the control panel's options.

"No, this is amazing," I breathe, shedding my clothes and stepping into the water. The temperature is perfect. I wish I could bring this home with me–I would never leave. I watch Theo undress as raindrops fall around me, water sliding down the planes of his body as he steps into the water.

"I wish I could say I planned this," he chuckles, pushing through the water.

"Maybe the gods planned this." What other explanation is there? It's too goddamned perfect.

Theo pulls me into his arms, and I wrap my legs around his waist, pulling myself up his body so I can press my lips against his. He sits, taking my spot, his pupils blowing wide as I sink onto his lap, my throaty moan drowned out by a clap of thunder.

36

I take Friday completely off. My entire body is still trembling from the incredible dicking down I received yesterday, plus the rest of my escapades during the week. And to be honest, my mind isn't much better. All I can think about is climbing back into bed with all three of them. If I have that much fun with one, I can only imagine what it will be like when we're all together. Fireworks will be flying. Theo serves me breakfast in bed and stays with me while I eat, discussing my plans for the baby shower and getting the details on how much help I'll need. When he leaves to join Henry and Dylan at the castle, I slide back down between my sheets, tug my covers up to my chin, and pull my Kindle from my nightstand, excited to have the entire day to read. Except I can't get my eyes to focus. I keep going back to last night. The way Theo's tongue– Fuck.

After several more attempts at trying to keep myself distracted and realizing nothing is going to work, I run down to Henry's room and snatch my dildo from his nightstand. Maybe once I get myself off, I'll be able to relax a little. I put on some music to set the mood, strip out of my pajamas, and lie down, closing my eyes and thinking about everything that's happened this last week. I slide the silicone up and down between my legs, warming myself up before I turn it on. It doesn't even take thirty seconds before my hips jerk when I drag it over my clit, my body seeking more friction. I turn it on, sliding it down my slit and teasing my entrance.

"Honey, I'm home!"

I freeze at the sound of Henry's voice, my heart racing. This is bad. Very, very bad. His giant strides eat up the stairs two at a time, and then the bulk of his frame is standing in my doorway, two drinks balanced in one hand and a paper bag in the other. To his credit, he doesn't stop and stare. He doesn't even pause to take in what he just walked in on. As heat climbs my cheeks, he sets the food and drinks down, unbuckles his belt, and rips it from his pants, his eyes dark.

"Is somebody being a bad girl?" he asks, his voice husky.

"Is getting myself off bad?" I ask, trying to play it off but failing miserably.

"It is when you have three guys at your beck and call, Freckles." He steps closer, his gaze raking over my body. "Do you know what happens to bad girls?"

"What?" I whisper, trying to control my breathing.

"They get tied up." He puts one knee between my legs on the bed, looping his belt around my wrists before raising my arms above my head and buckling it to the headboard.

Oh God.

"You're so fucking beautiful, Isla. You shouldn't have to lift a finger." I whimper as he drags his lips down my neck, cupping my breasts and lifting them to his mouth, circling my nipples with his tongue. I arch my back, trying to get closer to him, needing more. Just when I think he's going to continue down my body, he gets off the bed. My groan of frustration is cut short when he flips me onto my stomach in one smooth motion and pushes my knees to my chest.

"Henry!" I shriek, struggling against the belt.

"Do you want me to stop?" he asks, his voice low, dangerous.

"No," I pant, hating how exposed I am but loving the thrill. I look over my shoulder at him, watching as his gaze devours my body.

"What else do you keep in your drawer?"

"Don't!" But it's too late.

"What's this?" he asks, turning over a palm-sized vibrator.

"It–" I swallow hard. "I'd show you, but–"

"Tell me, Isla."

"It molds in your hand, so it's easy to hold."

"To hold where?"

"On my clit."

He studies the device, pressing the power button. His grin when it turns on is positively devious. "Oh, this is going to be fun." He drops it onto the bed next to the dildo and climbs up behind me, smoothing his palms over my ass cheeks, squeezing and kneading until I'm pressing back into his hands, whimpering.

"Can I eat you out?" he rasps, desperation dripping from every word. "You're weeping for me, Freckles. I need to taste you."

"Yes," I mewl, burying my face in the bed as he laps up my juices, from clit to ass. The comforter muffles my moan as I draw my knees up farther, pushing my ass up and out to give him better access.

"You're so fucking sweet," he groans, tracing the entrance to my pussy with his tongue before diving inside. My entire body shudders on the brink of ecstasy. He covers me with his body as he reaches forward and releases one of my hands, handing me the vibrator before pulling my knees from under me so I'm flat on my stomach. "You get the front, I'll get the back," he murmurs.

God, this man is going to be the death of me. I lift my hips, sliding my hand under my body and fitting the vibrator at the V of my thighs. I turn it on, waves of pleasure dragging me under in a matter of seconds.

"Ease up a little, hot shot," Henry chuckles, grabbing the other vibrator before straddling my legs. He plays with the buttons for a second before finding the setting he wants, and then he pushes it between my thighs, sliding it along my pussy. I lift my hips, pushing my ass back, my body telling him exactly what to do. He listens so well. He circles my entrance, the pulsing driving me mad. I groan as he pushes it inside me, driving it deep, then pulling out to feather it over my G-spot.

"Henry," I moan, pressing my vibe tightly to my clit, bucking my hips as he fucks me with the dildo.

"Come for me, Isla."

I break apart, my hips jerking as I find release. He follows me as I practically climb up the bed, chasing my orgasm. It's too much and not enough. I cry out as it peaks, riding the dildo until the last aftershocks fade and I sink like a boneless jellyfish into the bed.

"Goddamn, girl." He gently releases my other wrist, setting the toys on the nightstand before lying down next to me, pulling me tight to his chest, and covering us both with the covers.

"We always end up in a bed together, no matter how we start," I murmur, snuggling into him.

"I'd stay in bed with you forever if I could, Freckles."

"You'd get bored with me after a while."

"Bored? With you? How could I ever get bored with you, Isla? You're the only woman that's ever kept all three of us on our toes."

"I'm not sure if that's a compliment," I laugh.

"It's the highest compliment," he says, nuzzling my neck. As I lie there, nestled into his chest, I start to believe him.

37

S aturday arrives way too quickly. I have one full day to set everything up before the baby shower festivities start first thing Sunday morning. I appoint Jack to drive Charlie to the spa appointment I have set up for her. It should take her most of the day, so I won't have to argue with her about helping me. I miss my friend, but I'd rather have her be well-rested and fresh for the baby's arrival than be selfish and have her here so I can talk to her and get filled in on all the gossip I've missed the last few weeks. There will be plenty of time for that once the baby is here.

Since I invited the entire town, I decide to hold the party in the ballroom and the attached terrace. The flurry of activity starts the second I arrive at the castle. The tables, chairs, and linens arrive first, and I just about have those set up with the guys' help by the time the flowers arrive. I give the guys a list of tasks as I start to arrange the flowers into centerpieces, fussing with them until I'm happy.

"Isla?" I glance up to see Penelope's slight frame outline in the doorway, the sun gleaming off her blond hair.

"Pen!" I shriek, running to her and squeezing her tight. "It's been ages! Thank you so much for coming a day early to help me set up."

"Of course! I brought reinforcements," she says, stepping into the room and revealing four gigantic men standing in the hallway behind her.

"Isla, meet my crew."

"*They're* the new crew for the Master Baiter?" I ask, my eyebrows hitting my hairline. I bite my lip to keep from laughing. She's in so much fucking trouble.

"Yeah..." she sighs, her cheeks turning an adorable shade of pink. I turn toward her crew, not bothering to hide the huge-ass grin on my face.

"Thanks for coming to help! If you walk through the ballroom and onto the terrace, you'll see Henry out there, and you can ask him for instructions. He'll be happy to have the help." Truth be told, I'm relieved Pen brought her crew, even if it's a complete surprise. It wasn't until we arrived this morning that I realized just how much work there was to do in the next twelve hours. I wasn't sure how we were going to get it all done, which is exactly what I get for procrastinating yesterday.

"You're an absolute lifesaver!" I squeeze Pen again and then drag her over to the flowers, glad for the help. "How do you feel about helping me make flower arrangements?"

"Sure! I make them for the restaurant every few days. These flowers are a little fancier, but I should be able to manage."

After a few moments of silence, I catch the smirk on her lips, and I know she's waiting for me to ask.

"Spill the beans, Pen."

"There's not anything to spill." She looks at me, a twinkle in her blue eyes.

"Don't lie," I say, elbowing her lightly in the ribs.

"I swear it's not anything yet. Just a lot of flirting. *A lot* of flirting."

"That's all?" I ask, disappointed.

"So far. What about you? Are you going to introduce me to the guys I've heard so much about?"

"Eventually." I smirk, glad to get her back for her lack of information.

"So... how's it going?"

"Really, really fucking well."

Pen sighs a dreamy sigh, looking at me with watery eyes. "I'm so happy for you, Isla. Truly."

"Thank you."

"What's it like?" she asks, picking up several stems.

"What's what like?"

"You know. The romance. Sexy time."

I choke on my spit, coughing until Pen feels the need to pummel me on the back.

"It's a lot. In a good way. More than I ever dreamed of. Better than I could have ever hoped."

"Thank god," she breathes, pressing a hand to her chest.

"Why, thinking about taking on your crew?" I ask, wiggling my eyebrows suggestively.

"I really like all of them, but they're not best friends or brothers. They only met the day they came together to crew the ship."

"But that's been a while now, right?"

"Yeah. A year this month."

"Have you talked with them about it?"

"I haven't even held hands with one of them yet, Isla! I'm not going to ask them all if they want to fuck me together."

"If we want to what?" a deep voice asks, followed a second later by one of the largest men I've ever seen.

Pen squeaks, dropping to the floor and crawling under the table to hide.

"Oh god. I thought there were only four of you," I breathe, worried about how much he may have heard.

He ignores me, bending down to grab Pen by the ankles and dragging her out from under the table. She slaps her hands over her eyes as he lifts her to her feet. When he tries to pry her hands from her face, Pen drops her weight and almost succeeds in sliding back to the floor, except he manhandles her back against the wall, pushing a knee between her thighs to keep her in place.

"What were you just talking about?" he growls, his voice low and raspy. He pulls her hands from her eyes and pinions her wrists to the wall with one hand.

Pen blinks fast, and I decide this is the best entertainment I could have possibly asked for. I switch to the other side of the table, arranging flowers while watching what goes down.

"Isla was talking about her relationship," Pen stammers, licking her lips.

"No, *you* were talking, Penny. Don't lie to me. Was that whole lecture on trusting each other just for show? Or did you actually mean it?"

"Of course I meant it. The job is dangerous. You guys have to trust each other."

"And what about you, Penny? Do you trust us?"

"With what?" she whispers, luminous blue eyes looking up at him like she's either going to run or climb him like a tree. Her gaze locks with mine, silently pleading for help.

"Hey! I'm Isla," I call out, hoping to distract him. "Nice to meet you! Your crewmates are outside helping my– my–"

"Your what, Isla?" Pen says in a sing-song voice, getting me back for watching her drama.

"Guys? Boyfriends? Lovers?" Heat creeps higher on my cheeks with every word. I suppose I'm going to have to figure out what to call them eventually.

"Boyfriends, plural?" he asks, looking over his shoulder at me, one eyebrow cocked.

"Yes, two of Charlie's guys are also here."

"What do you mean 'Charlie's guys'?" he asks, looking between me and Pen.

My mouth drops open as I look back at Pen. "You haven't told them *anything* about us?"

"No," she whispers, covering her face with her hands. "I was scared it would encourage them."

"And that's a bad thing?" I ask, trying to figure out what's going on in her head.

"Not bad. Scary as fuck."

Ah. That I can understand. "Charlie is married to Pen's brother Lach, as well as Lach's best friends, Cam and Jack," I explain, realizing that doesn't even begin to do their relationship justice, so I keep going. "And Jack is married to Lach, and Lach is married to Cam, too," I blurt out.

"And *your* boyfriends?" he asks, surprisingly seeming to understand the relationship dynamics right away.

"They're three brothers."

"Slightly less complicated, then," he says, smiling.

"Yes, thank god."

"Why isn't this freaking you out?" Pen asks him, turning his face toward her, studying him like she's seeing a brand new person.

"Should it?" he asks, smirking.

"I–I don't know," she stammers, stunned.

"Is this the conversation I walked in on?" he asks, holding her gaze. "You were saying you wouldn't ask all of us to fuck you, weren't you?"

"Oh god. I can't do this," she groans, dropping her head back against the wall and closing her eyes.

"We've known each other for a year, Penny."

"I'm your boss," she says, making a last-ditch effort to fend off his questions.

"In name only, and you know it. You've only been on the boat once, and the captain is the one that pays us."

"Are you going to explain away every excuse I have?"

"Yes, so you may as well stop making excuses and tell me what you were talking about before I torture it out of you," he threatens, positioning his fingers against her ribs, ready to tickle her if she doesn't give in.

"You wouldn't dare!" she says indignantly.

"I'll give you to the count of three. One." Pen struggles against him, but he holds her in place, a wicked gleam in his eyes. "Two."

"Fine! Yes, okay? That's exactly what we were talking about."

"And is that what you want, Penny?" he asks, his voice soft, deadly.

Goosebumps race over my arms, and I'm suddenly very aware that I should not be here for this conversation.

"Don't leave," Pen begs when she sees me turning toward the door.

"Answer my question, Penny," he says gruffly, demanding her attention.

"Yes? Maybe? I don't know?" she says, the words rapid-firing from her mouth. "How am I supposed to know what I want when we only ever flirt?"

"I know exactly what I want, and I bet all four of my crewmates do, too."

"Fuck," she whispers, breathing hard. "Let me go, and I promise we'll talk about this later."

"Define later."

"On the drive back home."

"Okay." He bends and pecks her on the cheek before releasing her and going outside to join the guys.

"What in the fuck was that?" I ask her, my eyes wide. I watch as she slides down the wall like a glob of jelly, staring vacantly at the parquet floor. "Pen? Are you okay?" I drop to my knees in front of her.

"Oh god," she groans, hugging her knees. "What did I just do?"

"You just made your life at least five times more interesting," I say, grinning. God, I can't wait to see how this plays out.

38

Sunday morning arrives with the healthy dose of panic that comes with deciding last-minute to make the baby shower co-ed—which means more chairs, more food, more *everything*. The joy in Charlie's eyes when I suggested it more than makes up for the extra work. I would do anything for her. By the time guests start filtering in, I have a gigantic charcuterie table set up, along with tables for drinks and desserts. Pen helped me decorate several round tables for gifts, all of them of different heights, draped in tablecloths and trailing flowers. Peach and green tones are woven throughout the room, giving a unisex vibe, but also one that screams *I Am Woman*. Soft. Elegant. Sexy.

"How did you make this room *feel* like Charlie?" Lach asks, stopping beside me. His chin slowly drops in awe as he takes everything in.

I grin. "It does, doesn't it? That's exactly what I was going for since this is a celebration of her and her body."

"You're amazing, Isla. Thank you so much."

"You don't have to thank me. She deserves it, especially for putting up with the three of you." I grimace, then burst out laughing when he gives me a dirty look.

"Will you be able to relax at all?" he asks, squeezing my shoulder.

"Yes, actually. I wanted to have time to enjoy the party, so I hired some of the local teens and tasked them with refilling the tables with food and drink. It should be pretty laid-back. I really just wanted to create something where she could enjoy herself and her friends and family before the baby is born. Speaking of that, how's the nursery coming? Do you need any help getting things set up?"

"No, but I would like to schedule a dinner with all of us sometime in the next two weeks. Enjoy one last get-together without a little munchkin to worry about."

"My guys were actually considering cooking dinner tonight. Is that too much in one day for Charlie?"

"*Your guys*, hm?" Lach asks, looking over at me, the corner of his mouth ticking up. I can't keep the grin off my face, but I don't say anything, not wanting to encourage him. "As long as Charlie doesn't have to do anything, I'm sure she'd be up for it. Do *your guys* cook?"

"Henry and Theo both do. Dylan doesn't cook much, but God, does he know how to bake."

"I'm proud of you, Isla."

"For what?" I ask, turning to face him.

He shrugs, not sure how to put it into words. "For not being afraid to live outside of the box. You had created such a tidy little life for yourself and then acted like it was nothing when it disintegrated right in front of you."

"Believe me, I didn't act like it was nothing. But in the end, I think it was for the best. I finally feel alive again. I'm excited to wake up every morning. Excited to create something new."

"I can't wait to see what you come up with for the brewery. I'm sure it will be spectacular."

"More like you can't wait to come home and have an unlimited supply of beer at your fingertips."

"That, too," he laughs.

There's a collective intake of breath as Charlie walks into the room, all glowing skin, pink organza, and flowing curls. She looks like a fertility goddess. I glance over at Lach just in time to see his first look, and it makes me all gooey inside. I'm so fucking happy for them.

"You look absolutely beautiful!" I gush, running to Charlie's side and hugging her tightly.

"Look at *you*, Isla!" She turns me around, my moss-colored dress flaring out around my calves. "You're finally getting some, aren't you?" she asks, whispering into my ear.

"Charlie!" I gasp, giggling and looking around to make sure nobody heard her.

"Oh my god! You are!"

"Shhh. We'll talk about it later. Speaking of later, are you up for a family dinner tonight? You, me, Pen, and all the guys?"

"Yes! I wouldn't miss that for the world. I'm dying to get the scoop. I saw them walking in right before I got here, and they were fawning over her like she was in danger of breaking an ankle with every step she took. She was beyond pissed off." Charlie grins with glee, her blue eyes sparkling.

"That's Pen for you," I laugh. " I can't wait to get to know her crew a little better and see how they interact."

"Do you think...?" Charlie asks, not needing to finish the sentence.

"Yes, I *do* think. But five??? Can you imagine?"

"Three is quite enough, thank you," she laughs.

Several hours later, the last of the guests are filtering out, and I'm giving last-minute instructions to the teens on clean-up duty before the guys help me carry the mountain of gifts to the nursery. I catch Henry eyeing the crib, a wistful look on his face.

"What are you thinking about?" I ask, covering his hand with mine on the crib railing.

"How I can't wait to see you pregnant with our child. You're going to be an amazing mother, Isla."

"I think you're jumping the gun a bit," I protest, my heart racing.

"Am I, though?" he asks, tilting his head and looking me in the eye.

"We haven't even talked about whether I want kids or not!"

"Do you?"

"Yes."

"There you go! Now we've talked about it."

"You're infuriating sometimes, you know."

"Pot meet kettle." He smirks, holding out his hand. I go to swat him away, but he wraps me in a bear hug and squashes my complaints with his lips.

"If you guys are cooking tonight, you better get a move on," I say once he releases me, awareness prickling over my body.

"Will you come grocery shopping with us? I've never cooked for this many people before, and I want to make sure we get enough," he asks, lifting my knuckles to his mouth.

"Of course. I'll meet you out front in a second. I need to say goodbye to Charlie first."

With Charlie settled down for a nap, and Pen and her crew helping with the last of the cleanup, I climb into the car with the guys, and we head to the grocery store.

"What are you guys planning on making?" I ask, Theo as he pulls onto the road.

"We couldn't decide if we should go all-American with something like shrimp and grits with strawberry shortcake for dessert or stick to something simple that we know everyone will like."

"I'm sure everyone would appreciate something they haven't had before. I have no idea what shrimp and grits are, but I'm sure whatever you guys make will be amazing."

"You have a lot of faith in us, Sunflower." Theo grimaces, unsure of himself.

"Of course I have faith in you! Have you tasted your food? I don't know that I've ever had food like that before. The flavor!" My mouth is watering just thinking about it.

"Hey, I hope there are some compliments coming for us, too," Henry teases from the backseat, sticking his lip out and pretending to pout.

"All three of you have some serious skill," I amend. "I don't understand why you aren't cooking at the pub. You'd make a fortune."

"Because then we couldn't be with you," Dylan says softly.

"Promise me that once I have the brewery up and running, the three of you will follow your dreams," I say, suddenly worried that they'll be so focused on me that they'll forget what they wanted in the first place.

"We didn't have a dream when we came here, Sunflower. This was a hail Mary. Our last chance at keeping our family together."

"Then promise me you'll put your heads together and create a new dream."

"Pretty sure we've already done that, Freckles," Henry says, chuckling.

"Do you care to inform me?"

"You still don't get it, do you?" Theo asks, shaking his head. "You're our dream, Isla. You're the reason we moved halfway across the world. None of us could stop thinking about you, and it's going to stay that way until the day we die."

"Our dream is for you to be happy," Dylan says, reaching forward and squeezing my shoulder.

I blink quickly, tears threatening to overflow. What did I ever do to deserve them? "Promise me the three of you will come together to discuss a new dream," I push.

"We can promise you that the *four* of us will come together. It's not a dream if it doesn't involve you."

"God, you guys are stubborn," I sigh. "Fine. Just promise me."

"We promise," they say in unison, their voices melding together in perfect harmony. My heart content, I pull my hair into a bun and open the window, taking a deep breath of fresh air. The sun is still high in the sky, warming the air and making the colors on the hills around us pop. I'll never get sick of living here. I don't care that I've hardly been anywhere else. This is home. This is where I belong.

Panic hitches a ride on the coattails of that thought, reminding me that the guys may not get a visa to be able to stay. If that happens, I'll be faced with an impossible decision. I push the thought away, breathing deeply, letting the earthiness of the peat cleanse away the bad thoughts. I'll deal with that when the time comes. No point in worrying about something I can't change.

Grocery shopping with the guys is an experience in and of itself. I can't help falling even deeper in love with them as I watch them bicker over what size shrimp to buy, where the American section of the store is, whether or not they have grits, and how that should have been the first thing we checked.

Dylan and I leave Theo and Henry to duke it out while we gather the ingredients he needs to make the strawberry shortcake. I also grab a bag of marshmallows and some hot cocoa in case everyone hangs around and we decide to have a bonfire later. Eventually, the four of us meet back up at checkout, all three of them refusing to let me lift a finger to put an item on the belt.

Is this what it's going to be like for the rest of my life? Three guys that are absolutely crazy about me? Doting on me? Worshipping me? Not that long ago, I had given up on finding even one.

39

This is hands down one of the most entertaining evenings of my life. It started out awkward since there were so many personalities in one space, but everyone relaxed when we added fantastic food and beer to the mix. Bellies full, we're all sitting around the fire pit, nursing beers—all except Charlie, of course. Jack made her a pitcher of mocktails to enjoy. Her guys weren't going to drink, but she had insisted, saying that this may very well be the last get-together before the baby is born and she wants to see them enjoying themselves and letting loose. I'm sitting across from Pen and her crew–the perfect vantage point to observe them. Over the course of the evening, all five guys introduced themselves to me, and I have to say, I'm more than a little impressed, and I can't fucking wait to watch them figure it all out.

The first to introduce themselves were Spencer and Archer—two best friends who came over together from the US. Benson has a mop of curly brown hair and gray-blue eyes. He's the jokester of the bunch. Archer has a buzz cut, looks like he works out twice a day, and is covered with tattoos, judging by the ink peeking out of his shirt-sleeves. Next up is Sammy, a giant of a man from England. Smooth dark skin wrapped over bulging muscles, complimented by locks to his shoulders, dimples, and an accent to die for. Jamie introduced himself by bringing me a beer when he noticed mine was empty. Bright green eyes seemed to take in every detail as we talked, my eyes constantly drawn to the fullness of his lips, and his cute Irish accent. Liam was the last to introduce himself. He did me the honor of sitting next to me at dinner, regaling me with stories of the ranch he grew up on in Australia, his leather cowboy hat hanging on the back of his chair, ruddy skin blushing every time Pen caught him staring.

NOW THAT WE'RE all sitting around the fire, I finally have a chance to observe the six of them together, and I'm almost positive Pen straight-up lied to me earlier. The way they look at each other and hold back from touching each other. There is something there; she's just not ready to share it with the world. And that's completely fine. Pen has always held things close to her chest, and if this relationship is precious to her, it will be a long while before she's ready to share. Before she's ready for strangers to pick it apart. It makes me feel guilty that I'm surrounded by people that understand *and* support me. I'm so grateful for Charlie paving the path for me, but that means we need to somehow create the same thing for Pen. My guys and I are due for a trip to Pen's pub and an extended stay in town. We'll get people used to poly relationships so she's not the first they've seen. I can handle people judging me, but hell if I let them judge my sweet Penelope. One of the guys gets up, leaving a seat next to Pen, and I jump at the chance to talk with her.

"I've missed you." I grab her hand and squeeze it as I sit in the empty chair beside her.

"I've missed you guys, too. The last year has been an absolute whirlwind."

"Right? We need to make the time to see each other–especially now that there will be a baby in the family again." I take a sip of my beer, eyeing her, trying to decide how much to say. "You guys look pretty cozy," I hedge, trying not to grin but failing miserably.

"I don't want to say something to jinx it, but I really like them, Isla. A lot."

"I can see that."

"I'm insane, aren't I?"

"No more insane than Charlie or I."

"Except I am. How can I give five guys everything they need in a relationship?"

"There isn't a limit to your love, Pen. If they're happy and you're happy, then it's working. Just relax and enjoy it. It's much more fun that way, trust me."

She sighs. "They may not even all be on board with it."

"You haven't had that conversation yet?"

Pen shakes her head. "I'm too scared. Every time one of them tries to bring it up, I do something to distract them, like start a fire or faint."

"Pen!" I can't help but giggle at her panic-stricken features.

"I don't want to lose any of them, Isla. They're my best friends"

"Maybe the guys and I can visit and get the ball rolling. Get them used to the idea and see how a relationship like that would work."

"I think that's an excellent idea." She takes a sip of her beer, the tension leaving her body.

"I think it's time for me to call it a night," Charlie says, stifling a yawn as she tries to stand up. Cam jumps to his feet and grips her forearm, helping her to her feet. I hug her tightly, then watch as she waddles into the house surrounded by her men. I can't believe they're going to have a baby in two weeks. Tears immediately fill my eyes at the thought. I'm so happy for them.

"You okay?" Pen asks softly, swiping a tear from my cheek.

"Yes," I whisper, swallowing hard. "I just can't believe how much things have changed. A year ago, I would have never dreamed any of us would be where we are now."

"It's a fucking miracle, isn't it?" I laugh, grab a paper towel, and wipe my nose, trying to get my emotions back under control. "I hate to leave, but work starts at five in the morning, and I don't want one of the guys to get hurt because they didn't get enough sleep."

"You guys aren't driving back tonight, are you?"

"Yes, but we have to leave now, or we'll miss the ferry," she says, pulling out her phone to check the time.

I wrap her in my arms, burying my face in her shoulder. "I've missed you, Pen. Let me know what day works best for you, and I'll bring the guys out to see your place."

"Deal. Love you, Isla."

"Love you, too," I whisper, releasing her and watching her usher her crew out like a mother hen.

"You're really lucky, you know," Henry murmurs, hugging me from behind, his chin resting on top of my head.

"Why's that?"

"Your family is amazing."

"They are, aren't they? And how lucky is Pen to have found a crew that cares about her so much and gets along so well?"

"It's not hard when they're all united by one thing."

"What do you mean?" I ask, pulling his hand up and kissing each of his knuckles.

"They're all head over heels for her, Isla."

"You think?"

"I know. I was watching them the entire night."

"That makes me happy. She deserves to have people who are willing to move mountains for her."

"I love how you love, baby girl," he says softly, turning me into his chest and hugging me tightly. I breathe him in, relaxing in his embrace. All of the outside noise disappears, and I'm home. I break away from him when I hear the clink of glass bottles as Dylan and Theo start to clean up. Between the four of us, the entire house is sparkling in under twenty minutes.

"Now what?" Dylan asks once we're finished, glancing at his watch. "It's not even nine-thirty yet."

"Well, we all know what the weekends are *supposed* to be for..." Henry says, giving me an exaggerated wink.

"What do you think, Sunflower?" Theo asks, stepping up behind me and sliding his hand inside my pants, palming my ass cheek.

Fuck.

"I think I have a couple more hours in me," I murmur, turning to look up at him. I stretch on my tiptoes to press my lips against his.

"Movie and popcorn?" Dylan asks, threading his fingers through mine, turning my chin to capture my lips with his. I nod, moaning as they sandwich me between them, desire roaring through my blood.

———————

enry heads to the kitchen to make popcorn while Dylan and Theo escort me to the couch, settling my body between them. We bicker back and forth over what movie to watch until a game of rock-paper-scissors decides for us. *The Proposal* it is. Maybe a nice light-hearted comedy will keep the mood light and make it easier to keep to my resolution of waiting to sleep with them until after the masquerade ball. Theo queues the movie, waiting to press play until Henry comes in with two bowls of popcorn, one bigger than the other. He hands me the large bowl, keeping the smaller one for himself, and sits in the chair perpendicular to the couch.

"Henry, we can make room on the couch," I protest.

"We'll take turns, Red. I know exactly where I'm going to end up, and it's not going to be on the couch." The look in his eyes–the way his gaze sweeps over my body, tells me exactly what he's thinking, and I can't fucking wait.

"Where are you going to end up?" I ask, my voice barely a whisper, my stomach clenching.

"You'll see." He grins, reaching over Theo to squeeze my thigh. His wink has me imagining all sorts of naughty things. High on the list is his face between my legs. I clench my thighs together, stifling a groan, shifting my concentration to the movie while I stuff a handful of popcorn into my mouth. Henry's dark chuckle skitters over me, leaving goosebumps in its wake. Theo's eyes stay on the TV screen, but he wraps an arm around me, pulling me into his side, sliding his hand back and forth over my arm to warm me up. Dylan picks up my feet, swinging them into his lap. I groan as he digs his knuckles into the arch of my foot, relieving the incessant ache that comes from being on your feet for the entire day.

By the time Sandra Bullock is dancing around the fire with Betty White, I'm halfway draped over Theo's lap, and Dylan is running his fingertips from the tips of my toes to my ankle. I stretch my legs, the ball of my foot brushing against something hard. Dylan's gaze flies to mine, his hips thrusting slightly, his erection sliding along the bottom of my foot.

Holy mother of god.

Theo feels my body tense and catches on immediately, his hand sliding to my waist, fingertips kneading where the crease of my thigh meets my abdomen. I glance over at Henry and nearly combust. He has a tight grip on his cock through his pants, his hand moving steadily. My moan catches his attention, and he drops to his knees, crawling over to me. Greedy hands pull my feet to the ground; he rips off my clothes as Theo pulls me into his lap, spreading my knees wide.

"Henry!" I gasp, trying to scramble back, but Theo doesn't let me move, reaching over my arms to grab my thighs, spreading them even more, pinioning me in place.

"Fuck." My breath stutters out of me as Henry drags his cheek over the sensitive skin of my inner thigh. Every nerve ending is firing off signals to my brain, making my body feel like it's melting into a puddle of burning-hot magma. The only thought I'm capable of is how I can get Henry's mouth on me faster. I arch my back, trying to move closer, only for Theo to swivel his hips, adjusting himself so his cock rides along my ass crack. I whimper, writhing against them, demanding more.

"Your pussy is so pretty when it weeps for us," Henry rasps, catching a drip with his finger and slowly licking it off, his eyes rolling back as he savors my desire.

"I don't think I can do this," I pant, my chest heaving.

Henry sits back on his heels immediately, giving me space. "What do you mean?"

"It's too much. Not enough."

"What do you mean, Isla?" he asks again, those blue eyes making the butterflies in my stomach riot.

"I mean, I need your mouth on me right this fucking second." I reach forward and grip the back of his head, leaning back as I pull him to the apex of my thighs. The sound that comes out of me when his tongue finally laps at my clit is inhuman, a primal moan that comes from deep in my chest.

"Fucking hell, Isla," Theo groans, his lips grazing my ear.

"Dylan–" I reach for him, and he instinctively knows what I need, climbing off the couch to kneel on my other side, circling my nipple with his tongue before sucking it deep. My body bows under their attention, all vestiges of self-consciousness evaporating as they worship my body.

"You taste so fucking good," Henry growls, the vibrations of his voice doing unmentionable things to my pussy. I jerk against his mouth, my entire body trembling as he fits his mouth against me and sucks.

"Perfect time to give in and fuck me already," I pant, holding Henry's gaze as he does his best to make me fall apart. "No!" I cry out as he pushes two fingers into me, circling them over my G-spot. I come immediately, arousal pouring out of me as he fucks me with his fingers. He waits until the tremors have stopped before breaking contact, a grin pulling at his lips. The way he's looking at me, I swear I could come again. I watch him as he stands, his cock straining against his pants. I need to taste him. I slide from Theo's lap and reach for Henry's waistband, but he grabs my wrists, stopping me.

"Please, Henry."

"Isla, we've already talked about this," he breathes, indecision warring in his eyes.

"Yeah, just like we've already talked about the fact that I'm all in, and that was your only reason for not doing it in the first place."

"I–I can't, Isla."

"What do you mean you can't?" I press.

"I mean, I won't be able to give you the respect you deserve. Maybe after we've been together for a while, but there's this base instinct in me that I just can't get away from."

"Did you stop to think that might be exactly what I'm craving? Maybe I don't want to be respected. Maybe I just want you to let me give you the best blow job of your life."

"Isla–"

"Henry, at least let me decide for myself. If you're going too hard, I'll tap out. No harm, no foul."

He nods tightly, releasing my wrists, his pupils blowing out as he watches me unbuckle his belt. I feel like I've been waiting for this day for ages. I pull him out and immediately take him in my mouth, unable to wait for the silky heaviness of his cock pressing past my lips or the euphoria that comes from making him feel like a god. I slide my tongue over his slit, tasting him, reveling in the way his body trembles under my touch. I press forward until my lips touch his abdomen and then pull back, gripping him with two hands and twisting them over his length.

"Isla," he grinds out, his jaw clenching as he struggles for control.

I suck on his tip like it's my favorite lollipop, hollowing my cheeks, teasing the underside with the tip of my tongue. I move one hand to the back of his thigh, dragging my nails up his hamstring, palming his ass, and squeezing the obscenely tight muscle. I run my finger down his crack, watching his face for a reaction, smiling around his cock as his knees nearly buckle. Who would've guessed my big bad Henry would like a little ass play? Not me, but I can't wait to give him what he wants.

41

Adrenaline races through my system as I lick the crown of Henry's cock, holding his gaze as I lean forward and bury him in my throat.

I've waited so long for this.

The heady muskiness of his scent, the way his fingertips dig into my scalp as his control slips, the sounds he's making. I moan around his shaft, desire pounding through my veins. I sneak a hand between my legs, circling my clit as he fucks my mouth. Theo catches my wrist and brings my fingers to his mouth, his tongue warm and slick as he licks them clean. He kisses my palm before lowering himself to the floor, dragging my body backward until I'm hovering over his face. I grip onto the back of Henry's thighs, pulling him closer. I keep one hand on his leg to steady myself and grip his balls with the other, rolling them in my palm before slipping a finger farther back, massaging his taint.

And then everything happens at once. Theo stops messing around and sucks my clit into his mouth. The pressure has me bucking against his face, screaming around Henry's cock. The vibration makes Henry's back bow, and my finger slips in my saliva, sliding back to nudge against his asshole. His restraint flies out the window. He cups my head with his hands, holding me still while he thrusts into my mouth. Two pumps, and he's pressing deep, finding his release in the back of my throat. I swallow him down, licking the cum from his shaft before pushing him away so Dylan can take his place.

"That's okay–" Dylan protests, looking between me and Henry.

"Dylan. Now," I demand, my body trembling as Theo drags me to the edge again with deft circles of his tongue.

Dylan walks forward slowly, still unsure.

"You're not abusing me. I need your cock in my mouth as badly as I need air to breathe." I mean it. I'm not too proud to beg if he makes me.

"You're sure?"

"Get in my mouth, Dylan." His expression changes as raw desire replaces any lingering doubt. I grab his hand and pull him close, pressing his cock to his stomach and dragging my tongue along the bottom.

"Oh god, just like that," he breathes, his fingers threading through my hair. I flatten my tongue, feathering it over his frenulum, greedy for more praise. "Fuck, Isla," he moans, pulling back. He hooks a finger on my bottom teeth, forcing my mouth open, painting my lips with his precum before pressing between them with a groan. "You look so fucking pretty when your lips wrapped are around my cock," he whispers, his eyes on me as he thrusts.

This is a side of him I haven't seen yet, and I fucking love it. I struggle to take all of him, but he lets me go at my own pace, praising me when my lips hit the taut skin of his abdomen.

"Good girl," he breathes, holding me there as I swallow around him. My core clenches as he gives me all of himself, surrendering to my mouth. To me. I buck against Theo's mouth as Dylan loses his battle for control, pumping into me, losing himself between my lips. Theo jerks my hips away from his mouth before I come, and I groan around Dylan's shaft as his cum hits the back of my throat.

"Please let me fuck you," Theo begs from beneath me, panting against my swollen pussy.

"We have a rule, Theo," I say, pulling away from Dylan and licking him clean.

"Technically, it's just that the three of us can't fuck you at once, right?" Theo asks, his lips brushing my over-sensitized clit.

Fuck. "True. I guess it's between the three of you, then."

"No, that's your decision, Red. I'm going to go shower," Henry says, pulling me in for a kiss, his lips hot and heavy on mine. Dylan is next, his kiss sweet and tender.

"Your choice, Freckles. I'm going to wash up and then put together a little bedtime snack." Dylan gives me one more kiss before walking away.

"Say yes," Theo begs, licking me slowly, teasing me.

"You're sure they won't feel put out by it?" I ask, scared to do anything that will ruin the dynamic.

"They would have told you if that's how they felt, Isla. If they said it's your choice, that's exactly what they mean." He sucks my clit into his mouth as if to make a point.

"Okay," I breathe, riding his face, desperate to come. Theo lifts me from his mouth, scrambling out from underneath me, and then stands, picking me up and throwing me over his shoulder. I squeal, struggling against his tight hold as he walks toward his room. Kicking the door closed, he tosses me onto the bed. Before I can blink, he's hovering over me, one hand pinning my wrists over my head, the other pulling at my nipple as he slams into me. Fuck. Pleasure blinds me, every thrust pushing me higher and higher. I scream as I spasm around his cock, my hips meeting every punishing thrust.

"That's it," he rasps, pressing his lips against mine, deepening the kiss, his hips stuttering as he finds release. I break away from his hold, latching onto his ass, pulling him closer, riding him, wringing every drop of pleasure from both of our bodies.

"Fuck, Isla," he pants, his cock still hard inside me, hips jerking with aftershocks.

I moan as my body goes limp, every muscle trembling, pleasure short-circuiting my nerve endings. "I don't think I can move," I half groan, half laugh, kissing his chin.

"Stay here; I'll be right back." He kisses the tip of my nose and disappears into his bathroom, coming out a minute later with a warm washcloth. He carefully cleans me up, kissing every bit of skin, leaving his mark on me. I love the possessiveness of it—it speaks to something dark and primal inside me. Something that has nothing to do with my independent side and everything to do with the part of me that wants to give up control and be at his mercy.

"Where do you want to sleep tonight?" he murmurs, crawling into the bed with me and pulling me against his chest, his hand splayed over my stomach. I try to answer, but sleep is already claiming me, pulling me down into the darkness.

42

"Morning, sleepyhead." Dylan greets me in the soft light of the kitchen, kissing my temple as he hands me a steaming cup of coffee.

"Morning," I murmur, rubbing the sleep from my eyes. I look at him over the rim of my mug as I blow on the coffee, my gaze drawn to the sweatpants slung low on his hips, the lithe muscles of his abdomen disappearing beneath his waistband. I really, *really* want to find out what's underneath.

"Are you up for a date tonight?" Dylan asks, pulling two bagels from the toaster oven and slathering them with a thick layer of cream cheese. I inhale the yeasty, sweet scent of freshly cooked bagels like a lion scenting its next meal.

"Hungry?" The corner of his mouth lifts, his eyes sparkling as he hands me a plate. I plop down at the table, most definitely looking like Gollum when he finds the ring. I take a gigantic bite, my eyes rolling back as an ungodly moan exits my mouth.

"Please don't ever leave me," I beg around another mouthful. I need his bagels every morning for the rest of my life.

"About that date...I wasn't sure if you'd be too tired after yesterday," Dylan says, reaching over to wipe a glob of cream cheese from my lip.

"What did you have in mind?"

"There's a carnival in Stromness that I thought might be fun. We could go early in the evening so we don't get home too late."

"I'd like that." I lean over and kiss him on the cheek, thankful to have this quiet morning alone with him. "What are your plans for the day?"

"I'm about to head over to the castle with the rest of the bagels. We have a meeting with Charlie in about an hour to review some of the smaller details of the build. What about you?" he asks, sipping his coffee.

"I think I may come over there with you. I need to do some brainstorming and sketch out the interior design of the brewery. I can't really do anything else until I have that figured out. Plus, it'll give my feet some time to recover from the chaos of the last week."

Fifteen minutes later, Dylan and I and a paper grocery bag filled with bagels are walking down the road toward the castle, neither of us wanting to waste a single second of this gorgeous weather. After handing them out and lots of good morning kisses and pats of affection, I scarf down another bagel while watching Charlie and the guys discuss different design elements. I want to listen–should listen–but I can't help but relax into the warmth of the sun streaming through the windows. I balance my sketchbook on my lap and slowly drag my pencil over the paper, sketching out the boundaries of the brewery space. Whenever I imagine it, I think of the brewing area being open to the rest of the building. Shiny copper brewing kettles line the back wall, making it obvious that we craft our own beer and are proud of it. I want the rest of the space to flow seamlessly between the inside seating area and a beer garden. Perhaps most importantly, it has to be family-friendly. Basically the exact opposite of the pub. I'll need to ask the guys how they feel about me offering bar snacks. Obviously, it would have to be different from the food they serve in the pub. And to be honest, I'm not even sure how that would work. I wasn't planning on hiring a chef. Maybe just something simple like charcuterie boards? I jot the word 'food' down at the edge of the paper with a question mark. I'll have to think about it more later.

I'm leaning toward comfortable seating over traditional wooden tables and chairs. Armchairs, sofas, and the like—where people can get cozy and stay a while. Maybe several long tables for bigger groups and shelving for books and board games. What I want most of all is for people to feel at home. I finish sketching my ideas out on paper and end up with a somewhat recognizable bird's-eye view of the brewery and outdoor space.

"What do you think?" I ask Charlie as she pulls up a chair beside me and plops down, wincing slightly. I hand her the sketchbook and drop to the floor, pulling her feet into my lap.

"You're an angel," she groans, leaning back in the chair, balancing the sketch on her stomach as I rub her feet. "This is the back wall?" she asks, making sure she has it turned the right way. I nod, watching her face for clues as she studies it. She takes her time, a grin slowly spreading over her face. "This is going to be amazing, Isla. I'm so fucking proud of you."

"Do you think I should change anything?"

"Not a single thing. What color scheme did you decide to go with?"

"Green and gold."

"It's going to be beautiful. I can't wait to see it finished." She sets the sketch down on my chair and closes her eyes. She looks exhausted.

"How are you feeling? Less than two weeks to go now, right?" I ask, pressing my thumbs into the balls of her feet.

"I'm so ready for this baby to be born. My entire body hurts. I can't sleep. I have to pee every ten minutes."

"Is there anything I can do to help?"

"Absolutely nothing. The men are already waiting on me hand and foot. I'm actually surprised they let me come over here today. They're acting like I'm made of glass and could spontaneously combust any second."

"God. I'd be ready to give birth, too," I say, grimacing.

"I know I act like it's annoying, but they've been amazing. Not that I need to tell you that."

"I'm so happy for the four of you, Charlie. I can't wait to see you start this next chapter of your life."

"So tell me," she whispers, her eyes opening, "how's it going with the four of you?" Charlie glances around to make sure the guys aren't listening.

"Good. Really good. So good, I'm scared I'll jinx it if I talk about it."

"God, I remember those days. I'm here if you ever need to talk. Now go on," she says, shooing me away. "Dylan's waiting to sweep you off your feet." I look up to see Dylan standing off to the side, watching us with a soft smile on his face.

"What?" I ask, laughing as I stand and brush off the back of my jeans.

Dylan smiles, shaking his head slightly. "The bond the two of you have is really special."

"Exactly, so if you hurt her, I'll–" Charlie drags her thumb across her throat, winking at me before standing up and waddling off.

"Wow."

"You heard her." I chuckle as I watch her walk up the terrace steps and disappear inside before I turn back to Dylan. "Ready to go?"

"Yeah, Henry and Theo said they could finish up today's work without me, so if you want to leave now, we can."

"That sounds good to me. I need to grab some things from the house before we go."

"Me, too," he says, his voice dropping an octave, dripping with innuendo. My heart jumps to my throat at the heat in his eyes, and I bolt toward the house, realizing a few steps in that I have no chance against someone who competes in triathlons. He pretends to let me win until I take my first step into the house, and then he's at my back, slamming the door and pushing me against it, his lips roaming over my cheek, my jaw, my neck.

"I could spend forever with my lips on your skin, and it still wouldn't be enough," he murmurs, capturing my mouth with his. I open for him, inviting him in, our tongues tangling, teeth knocking as need drives us closer together. I reach for the front of his pants, closing my hand over the hardness there, my lips curving against his at his swift intake of breath, his pained groan. He kisses his way down my throat to my sternum, pausing to drag his teeth across both of my nipples before dropping to his knees and tugging down my pants. The calluses on his fingertips catch on my panties as he drags his finger along the dampness of my slit. He hums his approval, the sound coming from deep in his chest, making my skin prickle with desire. Hooking his finger in the scrap of lace between my legs, he pulls it aside, tracing me with his tongue, lapping at my clit.

"Let's go to the bedroom," I rasp, my fingers tangling in his dark hair. A slight shake of his head and then two fingers are pushing into me. I roll my hips, pulling him close, grinding on his mouth as my orgasm looms closer. Just as I'm about to come, he pulls back, breathing hard, lips glistening.

"Not yet," he pants, readjusting his cock in his pants, a pained look on his face.

"Why not?" I whimper as he stands and pulls my pants back up.

"Because the longer we wait, the better it will be."

"But it will be good now," I object, my heartbeat pounding between my legs, demanding more.

"Trust me," he growls, pressing me back against the door, his lips covering mine, our tastes mingling on our tongues. I do my best to bring him over to the dark side with my mouth, but his control is infallible. "Grab what you need, and we'll head to the carnival," he says, breaking our kiss.

I take one look at the determination in his eyes and scamper off to my bedroom, grabbing a hair tie, chapstick, and my wallet. As much as I want to sleep with him right this second, I love that he's bossing me around. After being in control for my entire life, it's a relief to give it up in the bedroom sometimes. It allows me to step into my more feminine side and let myself be taken care of. To experience the softer side of life. Nobody has ever given me that option before.

I meet Dylan by the garage door and toss him the keys to the Mustang, ready for the ride of my life.

43

A s much as I adore driving my car, there's something to be said about being a passenger princess for a day. Dylan surprises me by stopping at the café to pick up coffee for the drive–his hot, mine iced. He knows me well. I sneak glances over at him as he pulls back onto the main road, my gaze drawn to how the sunlight gilds the golden hairs on his arms. The way his hand grips the top of the steering wheel, veins riding over the back and up his forearm. And especially the way his hand makes its way to my thigh every time there's a straightaway. I bask in the glow of his love, feeling myself shed layers of my prickly exterior and sinking into the softness of being a well-loved woman. His skin is warm beneath my fingertips as I trace his hand, unable to stand the thought of not touching him. The Isla from a couple of months ago wouldn't recognize this gentle, soft woman content to ride in the passenger seat.

"What are you smiling about?" Dylan asks, noticing the grin pulling at the corners of my lips.

"Myself," I admit, shaking my head. "I'm not sure I recognize who I'm becoming with the three of you."

"How so?"

"I'm losing my edge."

"And that's a bad thing?" he asks, glancing at me.

"I don't know," I tell him honestly.

"Would you like to know what I see?"

I nod. "I'd like that."

"When we met you, you were like a tightly furled rosebud. Ninety percent thorns. Focused on keeping the intimate parts of yourself hidden from the world. Now, you've blossomed into the most beautiful woman I've ever laid my eyes on."

I bring his hand up to my face, pressing my lips to his palm and turning my cheek to rest there for a second, basking in his warmth. God, I don't remember ever feeling like this before. It's thrilling and terrifying at the same time.

THE FIRST THING we do after parking the car is neck like a couple of teenagers. He hooks his fingers around the back of my neck, pulling me closer as he leans to meet me halfway, our lips crashing together like we're starved for each other's touch. His thumb caresses my cheek, and memories from last night come rushing back, blood roaring through my veins, heat pooling between my legs. I gasp, and he takes advantage, deepening the kiss, sucking on my lower lip, exploring my mouth with his tongue.

"Maybe this was a horrible idea," he says, pulling back and pressing his forehead to mine. "We should have stayed home. Made love until we fell asleep in a sweaty, sticky mess."

"We can still do that after the carnival," I remind him, chuckling. I unbuckle, and he springs into action, jumping from the car and racing around to open my door before I can do it myself. I take his hand, allowing him to help me out. He closes the door, and pushes me back against it, his body pressed to mine, his cock hard against my stomach.

"You're right," I pant, running my tongue along the seam of his lips. "We should've stayed home."

A car door slams, and we jerk apart like we've been caught.

"Come on, Freckles, let's go have some fun." His hand dwarfs mine as he pulls me away from the car and toward the entrance. The sounds and lights of the carnival remind me of when I was young and would come with Jack and his school friends. There's nostalgia in every scream of excitement, every whistle, every flashing light. The weight of the world slips off my shoulders as we step foot inside the gates, and I'm back to my younger self with no responsibilities and the rest of my life ahead of me.

"Did you go to carnivals when you were younger?" I ask Dylan as we make a beeline for the cotton candy stand.

"We went to the state fair every year. It was a lot like this. I made a lot of my favorite memories with my parents there."

We trade stories as he feeds me bites of cotton candy, reminiscing about our days of sticky fingers and childhood crushes. I used to think I would give almost anything to be able to go back in time to the days my family was whole, my parents alive. To the days I didn't know the heartache that never quite seems to go away. But as we walk hand in hand, I realize I've grown out of that way of thinking. Like a butterfly emerging from its cocoon, the guys have given me a new appreciation for life. A new purpose.

"Pick out the stuffed animal you want," Dylan says, pulling me out of my thoughts. We're at the beginning of a long thoroughfare lined with booths, all of the workers shouting for people to come to play their games for a chance to win. The second I spot the giant shaggy highland cow, I know I have to have it.

"That one," I say, pointing to it, unable to keep the giant grin off my face.

"You got it." He squeezes my hand before letting go to approach the counter. That's when I realize which booth we're at. It's one of those with the ladder strung up diagonally. To win, you only have to make it to the top. Except I've played this game every year of my childhood, positive I could make it. I never did.

"This is one of those trick ones," I whisper, tugging on Dylan's shirt to get his attention.

"I can do it," he assures me, pressing his lips to my temple.

"I've never seen anybody win, Dylan. It's a waste of money."

"Winning you that cow is not a waste of money." He winks at me before turning back to the attendant, handing him several bills. The attendant gives his spiel and then Dylan is toeing off his shoes and stuffing his socks inside them, approaching the ladder barefoot. He makes it three-quarters of the way up on his first try before falling to the mat, then scrambles back to the start, determined to win. I start chanting his name, and people gather around to watch, joining in. I practically radiate pride as we cheer for him, and just like that, he's at the top, pumping a fist in victory before dropping easily to the ground. When the attendant hands him the oversized stuffed animal, he raises it into the air in celebration, dropping to one knee to present it to me.

"Your cow, milady." His eyes are sparkling, freckles popping in the neon lights, and I'm hit with a blast of love so strong that I don't even take the cow from him before wrapping my arms around his neck and kissing him soundly.

"You made that look easy," I whisper against his lips. He smiles, his mouth curving against mine, but he doesn't release me until I break away to breathe, my cheeks flushed. We barely break eye contact as he pulls back on his socks and ties his shoes, the tension between us thick and heavy.

Dylan carries the cow under one arm, his other wrapped around my waist as we stroll down around the grounds, streaks of pink and orange decorating the sky above us. The Ferris wheel draws us like a magnet, promising relative privacy high above the world. With the cow safely nestled on one side of the car, Dylan and I sit on the other, our sides pressed together, his fingers massaging my thigh as we lift into the air. The moment we're above eye level, Dylan grabs the leg farthest from him and pulls it around his hips so I'm straddling his waist, his lips fitting to mine in a way that tells me that this is all he's been thinking about. He splays his hands over my ass, pulling me closer until the hardness of his cock is nestled in the warmth between my legs. Then he wraps his arms around me, deepening the kiss, groaning into my mouth as I rock my hips against him. We barely notice as the Ferris wheel starts and stops, the outside world disappearing as we hang fifty feet up in the air, lost in each other's arms.

44

I f we had had ten more seconds, I would have come pressed against his leg, thighs squeezing, body trembling. But we didn't. Dylan wraps his arm around my waist as we exit the Ferris wheel, supporting my weight as I flounder on legs made of jelly. Need is racing through my veins, wildfire scorching my insides. I need a cold shower. An ice bath. Anything to cool this lust inferno. I blindly follow Dylan as he walks away from the bright lights of the carnival, sticking to the paved path at first and then veering off to follow the edge of a pond until we come to a thick copse of trees. A quick look around to make sure we're well and truly alone, and then he has me pressed against a tree, his knee between my legs, pinning me there while he licks a path up the column of my throat, murmuring my name like a prayer.

Any last illusion of control shatters. I push my hands beneath his shirt as he captures my mouth with his, every move wild and untamed. His teeth sink into my bottom lip as I yank his shirt up, only letting go long enough for me to pull it all the way off and drop it to the ground. His skin is so warm–like there's a furnace heating him from the inside.

"Will you run for me, Freckles?" he rasps, his breath hot on my ear, his stubble scraping the tender skin of my jaw.

"Run?"

"I want to chase you. Catch you. Fuck you in the forest like a wild animal." His eyes glint in the moonlight, dark and dangerous. My adrenaline spikes.

"Yes," I breathe, my muscles tensing, getting ready to put up a fight. This feeling–blood rushing, heart pounding–is what I live for.

"Then run," he growls, backing up a step and setting the stuffed cow safely against a tree.

I take off as fast as I can into the gloom of the forest, keeping the pond in sight so I don't get lost. The first time I trip, I scramble back to my feet and keep going. The second time, my toe catches on a root and sends me careening into the dirt. I desperately try to suck air into my lungs, gasping and choking as I stand up and brush myself off. Something crashes through the trees behind me, and my heart jumps to my throat, fear and excitement mixing into an addictive cocktail. I see his arm a second too late as he pops out from behind a tree and hooks me around the waist, my momentum bringing us both to the ground. We tear at each other's clothes, our breathing ragged. Pants tugged down our thighs, he flips me over, capturing my wrists in one hand, notching his cock at my entrance with the other, and slamming into me. I arch against him, crying out as his cock fills me, stretching me, completing me. Euphoria floods my bloodstream as I arch my back and meet him thrust for thrust.

"You're mine," he growls into my ear, pulling me to his chest as he sits back on his knees and impales me. "Arms around my neck," he commands, reaching between my legs to circle my clit with his fingers. I melt back against his chest, finding the rhythm, and then he slips his fingers farther back, anchoring the heel of his palm on my clit as he stretches me even more with two of his fingers, rubbing my G-spot as he thrusts into me with his cock. His other hand skates up my stomach, cupping my breast before tweaking my nipple, sending a lightning bolt of desire shooting straight to my core, igniting my orgasm. I cry out as we fall to the dirt, my muscles squeezing around him, his hips stuttering against mine, ramming me into the earth as he falls apart. He drops his forehead to my back, hard breaths fanning over my shoulder blades as the last of the tremors rock our bodies.

"Dylan–"

"I'm sorry," he rasps, raining kisses over my bare skin.

"Sorry for what?" I ask, squirming out from under him to see his face.

"For that. You deserve better."

"Better? The only thing better would be if all three of you were chasing me."

"You mean that?"

"I wouldn't lie to you. I thrive on adrenaline, Dylan. I need it. That was fucking amazing."

Dylan straightens himself up and then bends down to tug my pants back up, sliding his arms underneath me and lifting me so I'm nestled against his chest.

"Where are we going?"

"To find a bathroom." After circling back to grab the cow, we come across a community pool at the edge of the fairgrounds, and he slips into the locker room, sliding the bolt behind us. "Sit," he commands, pointing to the bench just outside a shower stall. I do as he says, staring up at him as he closes the distance between us, squatting down to take off my pants, folding them neatly before doing the same with my shirt and then my undergarments. He sheds his clothes quickly, setting his glasses carefully on top of them, and turns on the shower. Once the steam is billowing around us, he takes my hand and tugs me underneath the stream of water, wiping at the streaks of dirt. He moves down to my legs, gently splashing water between them, washing away the evidence of our tryst with gentle hands. I turn in his arms and do the same for him. I rub my thumb over his cheekbone, dislodging a smudge of dirt, and then I run my hands over his forearms and knees. Lastly, I cup my hands, making a waterfall that runs down his happy trail and over his cock.

"I think he needs a more thorough cleaning," I rasp, watching as his shaft slowly thickens, the tension ratcheting up by the second.

"Again?" he asks, his eyebrows climbing up his forehead. "I think I know exactly what you need." He turns off the water and throws me over his shoulder, his arm tight against the back of my thighs. I start squirming in his arms when he heads toward a different door than the one we entered through.

"Dylan! Somebody will see us!"

"It's closed. Nobody is going to see us, Freckles." He pushes through the door and out into the night air, chuckling as I shiver against him. Before I realize what's happening, I'm soaring through the air and splashing into the pool, the water closing over my head. Dylan splashes in next to me, pushing hard off the bottom and pulling me to the surface with him. I don't even take a second to catch my breath before I'm climbing him like a tree. Instead of kissing me, he grips my waist and lifts me onto the edge of the pool.

"Lean back on your elbows, Isla. I need to taste you."

My nipples harden in the cool air as I lean back. He pushes my knees open wide, his dark gaze meeting mine for a second before his face is between my legs, devouring me. His hair is slick beneath my fingers as I try to maneuver his head exactly where I want it, but he refuses, instead insisting on taking his time, moving his tongue in lazy strokes along the crease of my thigh, then my outer lips, the light scrape of his teeth on my clit. A low moan rips from my throat as he pushes a finger into me and finally, *finally*, circles my clit with his tongue. He fits his lips around me and sucks hard. I buck against his face, digging my fingers into his scalp to keep him where I want him.

"Whyyy," I groan when he stops, my fingers slipping over his skin as I try to draw him back to finish what he started.

He looks at me, his dark gaze caressing my body. "Because I want to see you beg."

45

"I'll gladly beg for you now."

"That won't work, Freckles." He lifts me by the waist, sliding my body over his as he lowers me into the water, every ridge, every bulge sending zings of desire racing through my bloodstream. He stops me high on his waist, chuckling when I try to drop down farther, needing to feel him fill me, stretch me. He captures my groan of frustration with his lips, the kiss wild and frantic.

"Is this what you want?" he murmurs, pressing me back against the side of the pool, holding me still while he notches the head of his cock at my entrance.

"Yes," I hiss, struggling against his grip.

"Stop," he demands, his eyes dark.

I don't have any other option but to obey, stilling beneath him.

"Good girl," he breathes, pressing into me, steady and slow. I can feel every inch, relishing the burning stretch as he bottoms out, filling me completely. I would stay like this with him forever. His forehead presses to mine, our pants mingling, ecstasy sparking in the air, coating our skin. He slips a hand between us, putting pressure against my clit with a fingertip, rolling it as he slowly pumps back and forth. Almost too much but never quite enough. He doesn't stop until I'm writhing beneath him, desperate to break from his grip, to take, take, take. His muscles tense beneath my hands, and then he's ripping away from me, and I'm empty, and he's standing three feet away, chest heaving.

"That was too close."

"Not fucking close enough," I pout, my cunt squeezing around a phantom cock, desperate to come.

"If you're patient, I'll give you the best orgasm of your life, Freckles."

"That better be a promise." I fold my arms over my chest, staring daggers at him.

"It's more than a promise." He sees my teeth chatter before I can clench my jaw and shakes his head slightly like he's disappointed in himself for not catching on sooner. He twines his fingers with mine, pulling me to the stairs, and then we're running into the locker room, back to the steaming hot shower. It's impossibly romantic being here with him like this. Desire thick between us despite our earlier romp in the woods, despite his cum still dripping from between my thighs. I back him against the tile wall, pressing up on my toes to fit my mouth against his, our goosebumps slowly melting away. He kisses the top of my head and walks me into the shower spray, pumping body wash into his hands, lathering it between his palms before scrubbing the chlorine from my skin.

"What would you like to do?" he asks, squatting down to run his hands over my legs. "Go back to the carnival? Go out to dinner?"

"Go home?" I ask hopefully.

"Or go home," he concedes, chuckling.

"We can stop by the pub for dinner if you're hungry," I say, hoping to God it will be takeout—whatever will get us home the quickest.

"Sounds perfect." We switch places, and I soap him up, making sure to get every nook and cranny so I don't taste chlorine when I'm licking him from head to toe later. I have so many plans for him. There are so many things I need to know if he likes. Heat pools between my legs just thinking about it.

"Before we go home, we have to make a quick stop," Dylan says, his breath hitching as I run a soapy hand back and forth over his cock.

"A quick stop where?" I ask, reveling in the way his throat bobs, the way he licks his lips and the way his eyes roll back as he closes them.

"Fuck, Freckles," he groans, thrusting into my grip before pulling out of my reach.

"Theo told me we need to find a sex shop and buy you a butt plug."

Fuck.

WE'RE soggy and damp from pulling on our clothes without drying ourselves off, forcing us to keep the windows down as Dylan helps me navigate to a cute gingerbread-looking house on the edge of town. I've never been anywhere like this before. I've ordered things online, of course, but to see walls and racks and displays of all manner of sex toys? It's a little intimidating.

"Never been to one before, have you?" Dylan asks, reading my face like an open book.

I can only shake my head as I take everything in.

"It's overwhelming the first time. Well, the first few times. But eventually, it won't be a big deal."

"How many times have you been in a sex shop?" I ask, wondering exactly how much I don't know about him.

"I used to work at one."

"You what? I thought you were a baker."

"I was. But I also needed a part-time job, and they were the only place hiring. It was only for one summer. An incredibly informative summer."

"I'm sure it was," I say, sarcasm dripping from my words. What is this feeling? Jealousy? Am I jealous that Dylan had a life before me–that he learned how to use toys with someone before me?

Yes. Yes, I am.

I tuck that little fact away to think about later. I don't remember a time I've ever been jealous of past sexual partners before. I don't know if I ever cared enough to be jealous, if I'm being perfectly honest.

"Okay, Mr. Expert, lead the way." I follow him into the store, the intimidation slowly turning into something that heats my blood and sets my heart pounding. We stop along the back wall, which is entirely filled with anything you could possibly want for butt stuff. "What's the best thing to start with?" I ask, wondering how some of these things can even fit in a human body.

"Something like this," Dylan says, pointing to a set of three magenta butt plugs, the first one barely wider than my thumb, the biggest one about three times bigger, both with a flared base.

"But that's not even as big as you."

"And that's why we would get something like this for after we make our way through those." He picks up a string of anal beads, starting small at the tip and moving up in size until the last one, which is about the size of a golf ball.

"I know it looks weird, but it will feel so good coming out, Isla."

"I'll have to trust you on that one."

"We can also get a dildo that's about the same size as us to help get you used to the feeling before we try for the first time."

"Okay," I whisper, the heat pooling in my core almost unbearable.

"Hey." He slides a finger under my chin, tilting my face up to his. "Are you okay? We don't have to get any of this if you don't want to."

He's misreading me. I feel like my body is on fire, my heartbeat pounding between my legs. "I'm fine. Just grab what you want. We need to go."

Understanding flares in his eyes, and his cheeks flush, pupils blown wide. "Go wait in the car," he says, handing me the keys. "I'll be fast."

I track him as he comes out of the store, the surprise in his eyes when he sees me in the driver's seat, the grin of understanding. I'm pulling out of the parking space before his seatbelt is buckled.

"In a hurry for something?" he asks innocently, blinking those big brown eyes at me.

"I'm in such a hurry that I booked us a hotel."

Dylan's smile is blinding.

46

When I booked the hotel, I didn't stop to research; I just picked the closest one and paid, knowing I would have spent an exorbitant amount just to have him inside me five minutes faster.

"You weren't kidding about being in a hurry, were you?" Dylan asks, laughing as I put the car into park thirty seconds after pulling out of the parking lot.

"You have no idea." Three minutes later, he's pressing me against the side of the elevator, and we're making out, our heartbeats in sync, lust a heady drug pounding through our systems. We collide with every wall on the way to our room, my knee hooked around his waist here, his hand up my shirt there. By the time we're crashing through our door, my top is lying forgotten in the hallway, and his pants are riding low on his hips. I'm pulling his shirt over his head before the door closes, pressing my palms to the hard planes of his chest, smooth skin jumping beneath my touch, his breath trembling against my temple. I take a deep breath, trying to get a hold of myself and reel it back.

"Don't," he rasps, cupping my face between his hands, his thumbs caressing my cheeks. "Don't hold back. I want all of you, Freckles."

God. How does he already know exactly what I need to hear? "It doesn't scare you?" I whisper, dropping my gaze.

"Does what scare me?"

"This–this desperation. This ache." I press my hand to my chest, words escaping me.

"How can it scare me when I feel the same way?"

Words disappear as we stare into each other's eyes, desperate need flowing between us like electricity. He holds my gaze as he dips his head, brushing his lips over mine in the most tender of caresses. I curl my fingers into his hair, sinking into him as we deepen the kiss. He hoists me into his arms, fingertips digging into my ass, holding me close. He presses me into the wall, freeing his hands, and kisses me like I'm the most important thing in his life. A treasure he's spent a lifetime looking for, and now that he's found it, he's never letting go. I lose myself in his sighs, the whispers of his touch, the soft insistence of his lips, the scrape of his teeth.

"I don't think I'll ever get enough," he says, his breath trembling against my ear. He presses kisses to my jaw, my neck, and the hollow of my throat. I squirm against him, trying to get impossibly closer.

"I need you in me," I groan, not recognizing the throatiness of my voice.

"I know, love. Soon." He carries me to the bed and gently lays me down, slowly removing the rest of my clothing. His touch is soft. Reverent.

"You are the most beautiful woman I've ever seen, Isla," he breathes, wrapping a strand of red hair around his finger, marveling at the color.

"Dylan–"

"Let me worship you, Isla." He pulls away from my greedy fingers, holding me down as he kisses his way from freckle to freckle, creating constellations on my skin. Shooting stars cloud my vision with every brush of his lips, every touch of his tongue. My thighs open for him as he lowers his knees to the floor, squeezing and massaging my flesh as he works his way to the very heart of me.

"I could spend a lifetime between your legs, Isla. Those little sounds you make. The way you move beneath my hands. Beneath my tongue." He licks a path up my slit, flattening his tongue when he gets to my clit and sliding it back and forth over me, chuckling as I squirm beneath him.

"How do you feel about breaking out some of the things I bought today?" he asks, his lips moving against me.

"As long as you get me there, I don't care," I pant. He keeps me right on the edge, so close to tumbling over that I can't catch my breath.

"Don't move." He presses a kiss between my legs before standing. I throw my arm over my eyes, breathing deeply as I listen to him open boxes; then the water is running, the whisper of his pants falling on the floor, the bed dipping beneath his weight.

"Let me see," I say, peeking at him.

He holds up the smaller of the butt plugs and a vibrating wand. "You can still say no."

"I don't think that word is in my vocabulary when it comes to the three of you."

"Turn over for me, beautiful." I flip over onto my stomach, goose-bumps racing over my body as the low sound of his desire surrounds me. He grips my waist and pulls me back so my ass is in the air, and then his mouth is on me, stealing my soul.

"Fuck, Dylan," I moan, pressing back against his face, my entire body shuddering. He stands, my protest dying on my lips as he pulls me to the edge of the bed, notching his cock at my entrance and slamming into me with a choked sound. He stretches me like nobody has before, filling parts of me I didn't realize were empty.

"I swear you were fucking made for me," he says, rolling his hips.

"Dylan," I beg, so close.

"Not yet. I need you close so I don't hurt you, but you're not allowed to come yet. Do you understand?"

"Yes," I groan, pressing back against him. "Just hurry." His low chuckle skates up my spine, my back arching as if he commanded it, giving him easy access.

"Relax and breathe deep," he instructs, his palm warm on my ass cheek.

I clench all my muscles, loosening them one by one until I'm sure everything is as relaxed as possible, then nod my head as I take a deep breath. I tremble as he squirts lube onto me, my body jerking as he circles my ass with the plug, then slowly puts pressure on it, easing it in slowly.

"You're doing so well, Isla. Breathe."

I focus on taking long, slow breaths as he slides the plug in, the feeling of fullness like nothing I've ever experienced. I clench the comforter in my fists, pushing back, my body strung tight as a bow.

"Fuck," I groan into the mattress, my limbs trembling as my body strains against him.

"Good girl, Isla. God, I wish you could see the way you move. You're so fucking sexy."

The reward centers in my brain go off like I just won the billion-dollar jackpot. I rock forward and then slam back onto him, my reality slowly narrowing until the only thing that exists is the way he stokes the flames of my orgasm with his perfect cock. He anchors himself with one hand on my hip and reaches around with the other, circling the pads of his fingers over my clit. I take him all the way in and then rock forward, dragging my clit over his fingers, then back again. I squeeze tight around his cock, his answering groan sending tremors through me, sky-high flames of a wildfire burning me alive.

"There she is, my very own Aphrodite," Dylan whispers, his voice deep and raspy with desire. "Yes," he groans as he thrusts hard, his fingertips digging into my hip. He pulls out so suddenly I don't have time to protest, flipping me onto my back and tossing me higher on the bed. He shoves a pillow beneath my hips, and then he's on top of me. In me. His eyes lock on mine as he catalogs every expression I make, every bite of my lip, every roll of my eyes, stoking the flames higher and higher. We combust, rutting against each other, wringing out every drop of pleasure until he collapses on top of me, our skin slick, lungs battling for air.

"Fucking hell, Freckles," he pants, his breath puffing against my neck. "I've never had sex like that before."

"Like what?"

"All consuming. So fucking perfect I could cry."

I cup his face, staring into those big brown eyes, letting myself get lost in the joy and happiness radiating between us. "I love you, Dylan," I whisper, kissing him as I blink away the tears welling in my eyes.

47

I'm dragging as I make my way over to the brewery space Friday morning. With all the decisions to make, I've been finding it hard to sleep on the nights I'm not with one of the guys. And if I'm being honest, it has nothing to do with the decisions and more to do with the fact that I *want* to be with the guys. I want to cuddle with them in bed, wake up to the brush of their lips over mine, to the smell of warm skin. If there's one thing I'm looking forward to after the masquerade party, it's that I won't have to divide my nights between them.

"Morning, Sunflower." Theo looks up at me as I walk through the door. He's sitting cross-legged on the floor, a shaft of sunlight turning his eyes to melted caramel. Pieces of paper, sketches, and magazines litter the scarred wooden planks around him.

"What are you doing?" I ask, surprised.

"I saw how stressed you were at dinner last night, so I thought we could make a list of what needs to be done and work through it today."

"You don't have anything else you need to be doing?"

"Nothing more important" He pushes to his feet and envelops me in his arms, kissing the crown of my head.

"What's that?" I ask, spying two cups and a box sitting on a table tucked into the corner of the room.

"Just a little something for my best girl." He links his fingers in mine and pulls me to the table, handing me one cup and opening the box. "Vanilla lattes and strawberry rhubarb hand pies."

I groan, my mouth already watering. "These are my favorite." I carefully pick up one of the tarts and take a gigantic bite, moaning as the taste explodes over my tongue.

"I don't think I'll ever get over the way you appreciate food," Theo murmurs, his gaze glued to my mouth as I lick a crumb from my lips.

"What does that mean?" I ask, taking another bite.

"It means that every time you take a bite and moan in appreciation, all I can think of is you making that noise with my cock in your mouth."

Heat rushes to my cheeks. "Oh." I can't stop my eyes from sliding down his chest, latching on to the bulge in his pants. I take a deep breath, trying to decide if I want to eat the rest of my pie or drop to my knees and suck him off.

His finger nudges at my chin, raising my gaze to his. "We can do that later, Sunflower. Right now, we're working through your to-do list. I won't be happy until I know some of that stress is off your shoulders."

"Thank you, Theo." I push up on my tiptoes and wrap my arms around his neck, squeezing tightly. The position of my hands means the pie is about an inch from my mouth, so I lean forward and take a bite without letting him go, my mouth right next to his ear when I moan.

"Careful, Isla. You're treading a dangerous line."

"I like danger, Theo. You should know that by now."

He bites his lip, indecision warring on his face. My shoulders drop in disappointment when he only guides me back to the magazines, motioning for me to sit on the floor.

"Okay, what's the number one thing you're worried about right now?" he asks, picking up a pen and a pad of paper.

"The kettles," I say without hesitation. I've done so much research—too much research, really, and I'm more confused than ever.

He draws three columns, labeling the last two PROS and CONS. "Which ones are you considering?" He writes the brand names in the first column as I spout them off. After about 20 minutes, there's a clear winner. I roll my shoulders, feeling some of the weight slide off. Theo moves to sit behind me, digging his fingers into the top of my shoulders, releasing the bulk of the tension. I hear him take a breath as if he's going to say something, but he only breathes out, his breath ruffling the tiny hairs on my neck.

"What?" I ask, twisting to look back at him.

"It's just–"

"Just what?"

"This will sound stupid, but your brain is the sexiest part of you."

I snort.

"I'm serious, Isla. Watching you work through that list, neatly categorizing all of the small important details, and then breaking it down even further to come to the perfect conclusion."

"You're the one that suggested the pros and cons list," I protest, turning in his arms.

"Yeah, but I've never seen anybody approach it like that. I wish I could get inside your head and see how it works. What you're thinking. How you're feeling."

"You could ask."

"See, there you go again. So smart." His gaze dips to my lips, and I know without a shadow of a doubt that he's thinking about every part of my body *except* my brain. "Well, go on, tell me," he rasps, his hands sliding down my arm, thumbing my hipbones before palming my ass cheeks and pulling my legs around his hips. Before I can answer him, he drags his hands up my back, cups my face and draws me into a passionate kiss.

"We'll try again later. In bed. When my face is between your thighs."

Oh God.

"What's next, boss?" he asks, tucking a strand of hair behind my ear.

"Furnishings."

"Perfect. Sit."

I plop onto the floor, holding out my arms as he stacks magazines in my arms. "These are all industry magazines. There are tons of pictures that will help with inspiration. I was thinking we could tear out the ones we like, narrow them down, and then find something similar from one of these." He plunks down a stack of restaurant supply catalogs.

"You're a lifesaver," I choke out, blinking back tears at the fact that he took the time to scrounge up all of these just to relieve the pressure I'm feeling. We spend the next couple of hours poring over the magazines, bouncing ideas off each other, deciding on a color scheme, and then finally finding the items that match my desired aesthetic.

"We can go antique shopping in Glasgow to look for some of these older-looking pieces," Theo says, pointing out the vintage lamps and glasses I ripped out of a magazine.

"That sounds fun!"

"When do you want to go?"

"All of us could go this weekend if you don't have plans," I suggest, biting my lip as dirty thoughts flood my mind.

"You sure that's a good idea?"

"What do you mean?" I ask innocently.

"You said you wanted to wait for all of us to be together until after that party. Has that changed?"

"I mean, I haven't really thought about it." That's a lie. I have. A lot.

"I'm worried we'll get carried away, Isla. There's something about seeing you ravished that flips a switch inside us. I don't know how much closer we can get without going all the way."

I pull in a shaky breath, heat crawling up my body as my mind takes over, imagining the four of us in every position possible. "That's probably a good point."

"If you want to go to Glasgow, then that's what we'll do. We just need to be careful. And because we obviously need a reminder, you chose that day because you want it to be magical, and I can't think of anything more magical than our first time being after a masquerade party, if I'm being truthful."

"Out of the three of you, I never thought it would be you reeling me back in," I say, laughing shakily.

"I'll always have your best interests at heart, Isla."

"Hold that thought." I pull out my phone and hold up a finger when I see Charlie's name on the screen. "Charlie?"

"Isla. It's time."

48

I hear the panic in Charlie's voice as she says those two little words, and my phone slips out of my hand, crashing to the floor. I pick it up, slicing open my trembling finger on the glass as I hold it back up to my ear. Nothing. "No. No, no, no, no!"

"Isla! What's wrong?" Theo yells after me as I take off, running toward the castle.

"No time!" I pound up the steps and tear inside, running from room to room, looking for them. I finally give up and scream Charlie's name, hoping she'll hear me.

"Jesus Christ, Isla," Theo pants, catching up with me. "Jack texted me. They're at the hospital already."

"What! This wasn't the plan! I was supposed to go with them. I was supposed to be there for her."

"He said they were out on errands when her water broke, and they went straight there. He said it's progressing fast. They're getting ready to have her start pushing."

"They what?!??" I run back to the foyer to grab the keys to the farm truck off the table. "Fuck. Fuck!"

"Give me those," Theo says, snatching the keys from my hand.

"What about Dylan and Henry?" I ask as he buckles me into the truck.

"Let me worry about them. For right now, let's focus on getting you to the hospital before she has that baby."

"Right. God. I didn't realize my brain would shut down like this. What will I do when it's *me* having a baby? I'll be a total mess!" I look over at him just in time to see his eyes soften, the corner of his mouth pulling up. "What?"

"A baby? With us?" he asks, hope sparkling in his eyes.

Alarm bells go off in my head. Did I just say that out loud? Did I really imply I'm going to have kids with them when we haven't even had that talk yet?

"Yes?" I drop my head into my hands, peeking up at him through my fingers.

His grin sets my heart racing, a curious fluttering starting in my stomach—like butterflies, but deeper, more profound.

"I love you, Isla MacLeod," he whispers, emotion thick in his voice as he gently closes the door and rounds the truck to the driver's side. The tires squeal as we pull out of the driveway, his foot heavy on the accelerator. "Hang on, baby."

I shriek as he drifts around corners, my heart in my throat. Ten exhilarating minutes later, we pull into the small community hospital. Theo drives right up to the emergency entrance, ignoring the no-parking signs. "Go!"

"Thank you, Theo." I give him a quick kiss, but he captures the back of my head with his palm, deepening it for just a few moments, like he can't bear to let me go.

"I'm going to go get Dylan and Henry," he says roughly. "We'll be in the waiting room when you need us."

I nod, giving him one last kiss before jumping out of the car and racing inside. The woman at the counter recognizes me from the gym, slaps a visitor sticker on my shirt, and points me toward the correct room. I push open the thick wooden door, poking my head inside the room. Charlie sees me before I see her.

"Isla, you better get your ass in here right now. I need you." Her auburn hair is plastered to her face, her cheeks rosy, blue eyes sparkling with excitement and fear. I rush to her side, ignoring everyone else as I squeeze her hand.

"The guys are useless," she says, wincing as a contraction starts.

"Good, Charlotte. Breathe through it. The doctor is almost here, and then you can push."

I glance over, noticing the nurse standing between her legs for the first time.

"Push?" I feel the blood rush out of my head, and I sit heavily on the edge of the bed. "How long did you wait to call me?"

"We only got here thirty minutes ago," Lach says from where he's standing by the window. "*Somebody* thought it was Braxton Hicks contractions when she was actually in active labor."

"Jesus Christ, Charlie. What do you need me to do?"

"Just stay by my side and don't faint."

I look up at the guys then, taking in their pale faces, absolute terror mirrored in their eyes. "You three better get it together," I say, giving them hard looks.

"Fuck!" Charlie gasps, her chest curling forward as a contraction grips her in its clutches. I push her hair away from her face, keeping my eyes locked on hers as I guide her through her breathing. Once it passes, I pull her hair to the top of her head, tie it into a messy bun, and then hand her the cup of ice sitting on the table by the bed.

"What else do you need?" I ask her, wanting to do anything possible to ease her discomfort, trying not to think about everything that could go wrong.

"All I want are the four of you by my side when this baby takes its first breath."

We all turn toward the door as it opens, staring down the older woman wearing a white coat who hurries in.

"Hello, everyone! Hello, Charlie! Today is a great day to have a baby!" the doctor sings, a wide smile on her face. The snap of her gloves echoes in the room, and I let out a startled giggle, which promptly results in all of us laughing until the doctor sobers us up by sitting between Charlie's legs and telling her she can push with the next contraction.

Charlie nods, squeezing my hand in a hulk grip.

"You have this, beautiful," Jack murmurs, taking her other hand. Lach approaches my side of the bed as Cam stands next to Jack. We all stare at the monitor in complete silence. It feels like the whole world is waiting for this baby with bated breath. As that little black line starts to climb, we all turn back to Charlie, watching as she takes a deep breath and pushes with everything she has.

"Good," the doctor says. "Again." Charlie takes another breath, holding it as she bears down. "Perfect. Now rest until the next one. You're so close, Charlie."

I swear my heart grows tenfold as I watch Charlie trade loving glances with all three of her men. This baby is going is going to be the luckiest kid alive.

"You're fucking amazing," Lach says, dropping to his knees by her head and tracing the sweep of her jaw with one finger. The next contraction starts, and we all tense as she pushes, like we can somehow lend her some of our strength.

"Perfect, Charlie," the doctor beams. "You'll meet your baby with the next push."

Tears start running down Charlie's cheeks, and then I'm sniffling, blinking quickly, trying to hold myself together.

"Who wants to put the baby on Charlie's chest once he or she is born?" the doctor asks, looking between us.

"Isla, will you do that, please?" Charlie asks, giving my hand a tight squeeze.

"Yes, of course."

"Go with the nurse; she'll get you ready," the doctor instructs, turning back to Charlie as I follow the nurse into the hallway. She rushes me to a room with a huge washtub, instructs me on how to wash up, and then helps me into a gown and gloves.

"All you're going to do is take the baby from the doctor and gently lay him or her on the mother's chest. Then you can take the gloves and gown off and put them in the red wastebasket." The nurse leads me back to the room, motioning for me to stand on the left side of the doctor while she takes the right.

"This is it, Charlie. Take a deep breath and push."

The guys bend toward her like the petals of a flower, words of encouragement flowing from their lips. Charlie takes a deep breath and closes her eyes as she makes that last final push.

"Good, Charlie! Harder!" the doctor encourages, her voice echoing in the room.

A cry erupts, and my gaze flies to the doctor's hands and the wee little creature cradled between them.

"This is your big moment," the doctor says, standing and handing me the most precious baby girl I've ever seen, eyes already open, face scrunched up, mad as hell. The nurse tugs down Charlie's gown, and I step forward, gently laying their baby girl on her bare skin.

"What's her name?" I ask, looking between the four of them, gently tracing the slope of the cutest nose I've ever seen with the tip of my finger.

"Summer," Charlie says softly, looking down at their baby with wonder. The guys cover Summer's back with their hands, giving her skin-on-skin contact with all four of them.

"I'm so fucking proud of you, Charlie," Cam says, breaking out of the stupor first.

"I can't believe you made her inside your body," Lach says, stunned.

Jack struggles to hold back tears, his chin wobbling, his eyes bright. He presses a kiss to Charlie's temple, then tilts her lips up to his. "Incredible," he whispers, catching one of her tears with his thumb.

There's too much emotion for me to keep it together, so I murmur something about taking off the gown and step out of the room. I break down the second I close the door behind me, uncontrollable sobs wracking my body.

"Isla, what's wrong?" Henry jumps up from a chair in the hallway and wraps me in those strong arms I've come to rely on.

"Nothing's wrong, Henry. She's perfect."

As soon as I get the text from Jack confirming that Charlie is home and settled, I feel some of the stress slide from my shoulders. Now that I'm not waiting by my phone, I take a shower, the scalding water washing away any remnants of worry. I know they'll take excellent care of Charlie and sweet little Summer. I have no doubt Charlie will call me if she needs a break from their fussing. I step out of the shower feeling like a new woman.

I wander down to the kitchen, rummaging through the fridge and then the cabinets, looking for something good to snack on. The house is dead silent, which means the guys must be working at Jack's. I could go over there and bug them, but I don't want to be a distraction when they're so close to finishing up. I plop down at the table, feeling oddly dejected. There was such a huge swell of emotion early in the day that it's making the afternoon seem dark and dreary in comparison. What I need is to get outside and get some exercise. I grab an apple from the bowl in the middle of the table and jog upstairs to grab a sweatshirt. Tying it around my waist, I head outside and down the path to the beach, mentally ticking off the things I need to check on before the ball next weekend. Now that I've been putting on these events for so many years, everything runs like a well-oiled machine. The only decision I had to make this year was the theme; this year, it was easy because I knew exactly who I wanted to dress up as.

I stop dead in my tracks as the cottage comes into view. The most delicious smell is wafting through the open windows, along with Post Malone's crooning voice. "Hello?" I call, poking my head through the door.

"There you are." Theo practically bounds out of the kitchen, enveloping me in a giant bear hug.

"What are you doing?" I ask, looking up at him. His hair is curling over his forehead from the humidity of the kitchen, making him look soft and boyish.

"I figured you wouldn't be in the mood to go out, so I'm making our dinner and then bending you over the back of that couch later."

Desire immediately tightens my stomach, warmth sliding through me like honey.

"Were you headed for a walk on the beach? I'll join you unless you'd like to be alone." He tucks a lock of hair behind my ear, tracing my jaw with the tip of his finger.

"I'll never choose to be alone over having your company, Theo."

"Good. Because I just put the roast in the oven, so I have a couple of hours before I need to do anything else."

"I'm sorry for the way I acted before," I blurt, needing to apologize and get some of this guilt off my chest. It's been weighing on me more every day. Especially now that I really know him. Yes, he's grumpy, but he's also the most loyal person I've ever met.

"Before? What do you mean?"

"When you guys first came to the house. And the weeks after that."

"Oh, you mean when Feisty Isla came out to play?" he asks, grinning.

I raise an eyebrow. "If that's what you want to call it."

"What would *you* call it?"

"Being a total bitch," I say honestly.

"You could never be a total bitch, Isla. You care too much about people."

"But I was, Theo. I was awful to you."

"Only because we ripped your life apart. Plus, I like that side of you," he admits, closing the door behind us. "You can knock a croissant out of my mouth anytime."

I do a horrible job of hiding my smile as we scramble down the path to the beach.

"There's no way you liked me back then."

"I assure you that I did. I had to rub one out in the shower that night just to get you off my mind for two seconds."

"You did not!"

"Did, too. Just talking about it is making me hot." He flattens my hand over the bulge in his pants, proving his point. "You're blushing," he says softly, pressing me against a rock and wedging his knee between my thighs. He nudges my chin up with his knuckle, holding my gaze. "I like every mood because it means I'm still by your side. And that's the only place I want to be."

"Theo–"

"No. I mean it, Isla. You're it for me. There is no other woman on the face of this earth that could ever mean as much to me as you do. You give me purpose." He wipes a tear from my cheek, licking it off his thumb before capturing my lips with his. When we finally break away from each other, he presses his forehead to mine. "Marry me, Isla."

Shock rushes through my system, the world spinning around me as I struggle to remember to breathe. "We barely know each other," I protest, my voice raspy.

"That's a lie."

"It hasn't been long enough–"

"Says who?"

I stamp my foot, beyond frustrated. "This isn't the way I imagined my proposal, Theo."

"You wanted a ring?" he asks, dropping to one knee and pulling a tiny box from his pocket.

Fuck. Suddenly, this is exactly how I wanted my proposal to be, with the ocean waves providing a soundtrack to one of the most important moments of my life.

"Isla MacLeod, you're everything I never knew I needed. My best friend. My hope. My light. Please say you'll marry me so we can spend the rest of our lives annoying the shit out of each other."

"Yes, Theo." The words slip from my lips before I can even think about them because if there's one thing know, I know I don't want a life without him in it. "A thousand times, yes." He opens the box and pushes the ring on so fast I don't get to look at it before he sweeps me into his arms, spinning me around and around.

"What do you think?" he asks the second my feet touch the sand.

"I haven't even seen it yet!" I laugh, holding my hand out and taking my first glimpse. It's the most beautiful ring I've ever seen. A large starburst cut green pear-shaped sapphire is set in the middle, flanked by diamonds on a simple gold band.

"I knew the second I saw it that it was the one. I've never seen a stone the exact color of your eyes. It's made for you."

"It's beautiful, Theo." I want to say more, but I'm at a complete loss for words. It's perfect.

"I've been carrying that with me just in case the right moment presented itself."

"And this was the right moment?" I tease, pushing up on my tiptoes to press my lips to his.

"Every moment was the right one, Isla. I couldn't wait any longer. I needed to know we were forever. Come on." He tugs on my hand, pulling me toward the water.

'Where are we going?"

"We came down here for a walk."

"Walking is the last thing on my mind right now."

"Thank fuck," he groans, his shoulders sagging in relief. "Do you want to go back up to the cottage?"

I shake my head. "There's nobody down here, and there's a nice flat rock over there. But first, I want to skinny dip to commemorate the occasion." I drop my sweatshirt to the ground and pull my shirt over my head, the ring glinting in the sun, reminding me of the green flash at sunset. "Last one there has to do the dishes!" I yell, running backward toward the water as I unhook my bra, tossing it to the side. He's too busy watching my tits bounce to even try to catch up.

50

I feel like I'm in the cast of Baywatch as I run along the beach, my clothes scattered across the sand, one of the hottest men I've ever seen watching me like I'll disappear if he dares to blink.

"What are you waiting for?" I call out, looking over my shoulder at Theo, grinning at the way his mouth is hanging wide open. "Theo!" I laugh. Come on!" His only response is his throat bobbing and several slow blinks. I jog back toward him, completely failing to keep the dopey smile off my face.

"Need some help, big guy?" I push the hem of his shirt up his torso, tugging it over his head and discarding it on the sand. I shriek as he suddenly comes alive, muscled arms shooting out and pulling me close, his hands sliding down my back, cupping and kneading my ass.

"God," he groans, his voice muffled against my neck. "I don't think I'll ever get enough of how you feel in my hands. Your skin is so fucking soft." He grips the back of my thighs and pulls my legs around his waist, banding one arm around my back to hold me in place while he cups my face with his other hand, those caramel eyes staring into my soul. "Do you have any idea how gorgeous you are?"

he rasps. "Your freckles. Your eyes. And, god, your hair. Holy fuck. I could spend forever exploring you, and it would never be enough." He savors my lips like he would vintage wine, his tongue sweeping softly and slowly over my bottom lip. I take the reins, pushing my tongue into his mouth, deepening the kiss. He walks us toward the rock I pointed out earlier, his fingers brushing between my legs, igniting my body with the heat of a thousand suns. I squirm against him, frustrated that he still has his pants on. He hikes me up onto the rock, his muscles bulging. I trace the vein that rides over his right bicep with my fingertip, then with my tongue. He growls, pushing my body down flat and my knees wide.

"Are you wet for me, Sunflower?" he asks, running his nose along the soft skin of my inner thigh.

"Why don't you find out?" I breathe, straining toward him. He doesn't tease, just pushes his middle finger straight into my drenched pussy, dragging his fingertip over the spot I love before pulling it out and leaning over me. "Suck."

I open wide, closing my lips over his finger and sucking him clean, then grip the back of his neck and pull him down, sliding my tongue over his.

"Fuck, Isla. You taste so goddamn sweet. I'd live with my head between your thighs if you'd let me."

"I'm not saying no." My laugh turns into a moan as he buries his face in my pussy, flicking his tongue over my clit. I thread my fingers through his hair, pulling him closer, grinding against his mouth as he flattens his tongue and gives me what I want. I throw my arm over my face, the flashing green of the rock on my finger giving me that extra burst of emotion that sends me over the edge into oblivion. I clamp my thighs around his head, riding him hard. Instead of coming up for air when I release my hold on him, Theo licks me gently as I come down.

"I swear all I'll be able to think about is when I can make your body move like that again," he says, his voice husky with desire.

"My turn." I sit up, locking my heels around his ass, sliding my palm over the bulge of his cock.

"I don't think so." He bends down, pressing his shoulder against my stomach and standing, lifting me effortlessly. He ignores my shrieking curses, slapping me hard on the ass before jogging toward the water. I stop struggling when I realize the spectacular view I have of his ass. The only thing that could have made it better is if he was naked. I scream in earnest as he kicks off his shoes and splashes into the freezing cold water.

"Your pants!" He's going to regret that later when we have to walk back up to the cottage.

"It's worth it." After a couple more steps, he's up to his ribs. He sinks down fast, submerging both of us. I burst back up to the surface, spluttering, hair and water streaming over my face. I duck down once more, sweeping my hair back before I come up. I wipe the water from my eyes, opening them to find Theo's gaze glued to my nipples as the water laps at them.

"Come here," he rasps, grabbing my hand and pulling me close, ducking down and closing his mouth around the sensitive peak. I cry out, my back bowing. After he pays equal attention to the other nipple, he straightens, his eyelids heavy with desire. Wonder flashing across his face before he presses his lips to mine, drinking me in like I'm the elixir of life.

"I don't think I've needed anything as much as I need you right now," he pants, breaking the kiss.

"Then have me." I unfasten his pants and pull out his cock, wrapping my hand around his shaft and squeezing hard. In one swift movement, he lifts me, impaling me in one hard, deep stroke. My groan is muffled by his shoulder, my body adjusting to his size, pulsing around him. He pushes my hips down, sliding me along his shaft until the head of his cock is at my entrance, rocking back and forth, driving me crazy.

I whimper, sinking my teeth into his flesh as he slides his hand down my crack, his finger grazing over my asshole, teasing me.

"I have the butt plugs in the cottage," he murmurs, sliding his tongue over the shell of my ear. "I can't wait to bend you over the couch, slide it in, and fuck you hard." He punctuates his sentence by pushing his finger past that ring of muscle, keeping still while I buck against him.

"Too much, Theo. I need to come," I pant, contorting my body in every possible way to try to get him deeper.

"If you think this is too much, just wait until later." He slams into me, once, twice, then pulls out, breathing hard. He hikes me far up on his torso and carries me out of the water, not putting me down until we're back at the rock. He climbs up and lays me down gently, spreading my hair around my head before shucking off his pants and lying down next to me. The warmth of the rock seeps into my bones, lulling me into a deep state of relaxation. Theo grabs my hand and holds it above him, looking at the ring.

"It looks good on you."

"It's perfect, Theo."

He pushes up onto his elbow, his gaze lazily sweeping down my body and then back up. He readjusts my hair and then bends down, lightly brushing his lips over mine. I cup his face, stubble rough against my palms, and keep him there, deepening the kiss. I use the element of surprise to push his shoulder until he's lying flat on the rock, and then climb on top of him, sliding my pussy along his shaft until he's notched at my entrance. I watch the ecstasy flood his eyes as I lower my weight, groaning as he stretches me, touching every part of me.

"I swear we were made to fit together," I pant, rolling my hips. He groans in agreement, fingers digging into my hips as he tries to keep control. I pick up my pace, dragging my clit over his public bone, climbing for the peak strong and fast.

"Jesus Christ, Isla!" His hands clamp down, freezing me in place. With a growl, he lifts me off his body, setting me down on all fours beside me. Before I can protest, he's behind me, spreading my cheeks and licking me from pussy to ass. I can't even pretend to be embarrassed when it feels so fucking good.

"You like that, Sunflower?" he murmurs, running his tongue along that tight muscle.

I drop to my elbows, pushing my ass out to give him better access, muffling my moans against my arm.

"Don't be shy. I want to hear you, baby."

He pushes two fingers into my cunt, then presses his tongue against my ass, breaching the muscle, and I swear I see God. My moan echoes off the surrounding rocks, and I feel him smile against me. "Good girl. I think it's time to go back to the cottage so I can fuck you properly."

51

"What do you have going on for the next week?" Henry asks me as I take my place at the dinner table. I ease myself down, mindful of the slight soreness from the thorough workover Theo gave me last night. I snatch a piece of fresh-baked bread out of the basket Dylan sets on the table, my ring catching my eye. Theo thought we should wait to mention it so it didn't pressure his brothers, but I refused to take the ring off. I told them over breakfast this morning, and they answered with whoops, hollers, and long, drawn-out kisses. It was the best response I could have possibly asked for. I blink back tears as I chew my bite of bread, stalling so they won't hear the emotion in my voice.

"It will mostly be getting ready for the party. I have people to do the set-up and tear-down, but I still need to be there to make sure it's done right. Plus, I always make the flower arrangements myself."

"Why's that?" Dylan asks, sitting beside me as Theo brings a heavenly-smelling dish to the table.

"Because I've never felt like I got my money's worth when other people do it. It's not like they did a bad job, it's just never what I envisioned."

"In other words, you weren't in control," Henry says, his voice low and raspy. "Do you like being in control, Isla?"

I lick my lips, and his pupils blow wide. "It depends on the situation." I wink, smiling as an adorable blush creeps up his cheeks.

"So what does that mean for our date schedule?" Theo asks, plunking a glass of water in front of me and ordering me to drink as he sits down.

I obey, taking several gulps before I answer. "It means it's going to be completely screwed up. I don't know why I didn't think about that when I originally suggested it."

"We'll survive. Henry needs the time with you. Why don't the two of you take the weekend? Then we can focus on helping you get everything ready next week."

"Really?" I ask, looking between him and Dylan. They both nod.

"It's important you're with Henry before next weekend, Isla. If this weekend is the only time you have open, then that needs to be a priority."

I look over at Henry, and I'm not going to lie—it looks like he's going to have a heart attack. "Are you okay?" I laugh, reaching over to pat his hand.

He swallows hard. "I knew it was coming, but I wasn't expecting the day after tomorrow. I have some planning to do."

"We can just stay here," I suggest, wanting to take the stress out of the situation for him.

"Absolutely not. This needs to be one of the best nights of your life. I want you to remember it forever."

"I'm sure I'll remember it forever, no matter where we are."

He lifts my hand to his lips, kissing the base of my thumb. "Only the best for my girl," he whispers, his lips moving against my skin.

"When you have time, why don't you write to-do list for next week so we can stay organized?" Theo suggests, motioning for me to take a bite of food.

"Will do. How are the guest suites coming?" I ask, taking a giant bite, chewing and then opening my mouth like a sassy brat to show him I swallowed it. I roll my eyes at his scowl.

"We only have trim left unless Jack comes up with a new project for us," Henry says, relief in his voice.

"Have you heard anything on the visa yet?" I ask, looking between them.

"We have an appointment in Glasgow in two weeks. They refused to give us a visa just for the pub. If we open a construction business, they'll allow residency. It has something to do with the skills needed in the community," Dylan explains.

"Seriously?" I squeak, bouncing up and down in my chair. "So I can stop worrying?"

"Were you worrying?" Theo asks, his brow creasing.

"Of course I was worrying!"

"I'm sorry we didn't tell you the second we found out. You seemed so confident that we wouldn't have an issue, I didn't think it was keeping you up at night," Theo says, reaching over and squeezing my thigh.

"Being confident and being sure are two different things," I protest.

"True."

"Does anyone want some brownies?" Dylan asks, stacking our dishes and carrying them to the sink.

"What kind of question is that?" I laugh. "Not sure I've ever said no to a brownie in my entire life."

Dylan grins. "Fair enough. Give me about an hour."

"Come with me," Henry says, grabbing my hand and dragging me out the front door.

"Where are we going?"

"You'll see." He brings me into the garage and hands me the helmet from the back of the motorcycle before swinging his leg over, his jeans stretching tight over his ass.

"Get on."

Yes. Please, sir. Instead of climbing on the back, I set the helmet down and climb onto his lap, straddling him.

"Isla–"

"Henry–" I breathe, framing his face with my hands, staring at him, drinking in his dark blue eyes, the angular planes of his face, the dimple in his chin. I'll never have any idea how I managed to make this man mine.

"Kiss me," I demand. And god, he does. There's no hesitation, only unbridled passion. He moans into my mouth, catching my bottom lip with his teeth, his hands tangling in my hair, tugging my head back to expose my throat. The softness of his lips, coupled with the roughness of his stubble, has my nerves misfiring. My breath hitches, and I go limp in his arms, sinking into him. He chuckles against my throat, raising goosebumps all over my body.

I want him.

Now.

"Patience, Isla." He reaches back for the helmet and slides it down over my head, starting the motorcycle while I hang onto him like a koala. I squeal as he pulls out of the garage and onto the road.

"We're only going to the castle. Hang on tight."

I cling to him, pressing my chin to the outer edge of his shoulder, our bodies plastered together, making it hard to think. Hard to breathe. Once we're parked in the castle drive, he plucks off the helmet and smooths back my hair. He wraps his arms around me and stands, his height making it easy for him to throw his leg over the motorcycle and step away. He releases me slowly, groaning as I slide down his body. I try to cling to him when I feel the bulge in his pants press between my legs, but gravity insists on pulling me down. I mewl in protest, and his answering chuckle is the sexiest thing I've ever heard.

"You'll get all you want in a couple of days, baby. We need to hurry before it gets too dark."

For the first time, I notice that the sun is close to setting. I swear everything else disappears when I'm with him. All I can think about is rubbing on him like a goddamned cat. He links his fingers with mine and pulls me toward the side yard, the pink and purples of the sky reflecting on the loch. I hate to admit it, but I miss living in the castle. I don't miss the lack of privacy, but the beauty is unmatched.

"Where are we going?" I ask as he tugs me through the orchard and toward the woods. "You're not dragging me out here to murder me, are you?" I tease.

"Not when we haven't even had sex yet," he says, winking.

God, he's so fucking sexy. All I want to do is push him down on the forest floor and ride him until we both sink into oblivion. I don't care about whether it's special or romantic. I want him. All of him. Now.

Henry stops suddenly, turning toward me. "Close your eyes."

52

Henry covers my eyes with his hands, shuffling me forward several yards before removing them. "You can look," he whispers, a catch in his voice like he's nervous.

I open my eyes, blinking several times until they adjust to the light streaming through the leaves. And then I see it. Something that looks like a moon gate sits to the side of Charlie's studio, copper and gold burnished metallic sunflowers twining in a gigantic circle, a gorgeous macrame and wood swing set in the center.

"You made me a swing?" Memories of my mom immediately come flooding back, forcing me to blink away tears.

"Let me show you how it works."

"It's a swing, Henry."

"No, look." He fiddles with a locking mechanism on both sides of the swing, which allows the seat to move up and down. "That way, Summer can use it, too."

I really do start crying then. I try to stifle the first sob with the base of my palm but fail miserably.

"Please say your crying doesn't mean you hate it." Henry chuckles into my hair, scoops me into his arms, and holds me tight.

"It's perfect, Henry. And for you to think of little Summer. And the sunflowers. God, the sunflowers." I sniffle, wiping my eyes.

"I know how much they mean to you. I thought it would be a little piece of your mother here in the forest while you're playing with her grandbaby."

"Oh, Henry." I press my salty lips to his cheek, breaking away as the sobs come harder. What did I ever do to deserve him?

"I worked on it every night we weren't together," he admits.

"Wait. You made this? By hand?" I ask, ducking out of his arms and walking closer. The petals look like they're made of spun gold, the middle of the flower is copper, and the leaves and stems are a beautiful shade of burnished green. "How?"

"I'll show you sometime."

"Can *I* show you something sometime?" I ask, biting my lip, trying to look sexy despite the tears dripping from my chin.

"You can show *something* tomorrow night," he replies, his voice deep and raspy. He lifts me so my feet are on top of his and walks me back into the forest, pressing my body against a tree.

"Not tonight?" I ask, giving him my best puppy dog eyes and a quivering lower lip.

He growls deep in his throat, and my knees would have buckled if he wasn't anchoring me against the trunk with his hips, something long and hard pressing into my stomach. I start to reach between us, but he's faster than me, capturing my wrists and pinning them over my head. He dips down, grazing my jaw with his nose, then dragging his lips down my throat.

"My naughty girl," he rasps against my skin, nipping at my neck. He captures my groan with his mouth, cupping the side of my head with his free hand, my head and deepening the kiss.

I break away, chest heaving, needing to put some space between us before I combust. I walk to the swing, testing it with only some of my weight before sitting down fully.

"Did you really just do that?" Henry asks, eyes dark. I don't have time to react before he tackles me out of the swing and onto the ground, taking the brunt of the fall. "You don't trust me? Is this how it's going to be?" he asks, digging his fingers into my ribs and tickling me until my eyes are streaming. "Are you going to test out the guest suites to make sure they don't fall down before the first guest stays in them?"

I slither out of his grip, scrambling to my feet, and make a break for it My feet are nearly silent on the bed of pine needles, but I have no idea if I'm making any headway because I'm scared that if I look back, I'll crash headlong into a tree, which is not on my bingo card for today. I break out into the openness of the orchard and stop running, listening for any signs of him behind me. Nothing. I turn back toward the woods, scanning the trees. He slams into me from the side, cradling me against the mass of his body as we fall.

"No more tickling!" I shriek, trying to wiggle out of his grip.

"I won't," he laughs, holding onto me tight. "But now I know what punishment to use when you're a bad girl."

"I'd prefer a slap on the ass, thank you very much."

His hand makes contact with my butt, his palm flat, the loud clap echoing off the trees.

"Like that?" he growls, squeezing and kneading my ass cheek.

"Just like that," I breathe, pressing up into his hand, burning for him. He hums deep in his throat, like he's cataloging that information for later, then moves his hand up to my lower back, moving it in slow circles. We gaze at the sky together, watching as the sunset slowly seeps into twilight. I'll miss these long summer days with my guys when winter steals the light.

"What do you have planned for us this weekend?" I ask, tipping my head back to look at him.

"That's for me to know and you to find out," he says, his eyes sparkling.

"You don't even have anything planned, do you?" I tease, stroking my fingertip over the dimple on his chin.

"I've had this planned since the moment I met you, Isla."

Something in his face stops me from blowing him off. "What do you mean? You planned how you were going to have sex with me the first second you saw me behind the bar last year?"

"I planned exactly how I was going to do a lot of things with you, Isla. To you. For you."

"That's ridiculous, Henry."

"I didn't believe in love at first sight until that night," he says, the admission tumbling from his lips.

My heart thumps, and I bury my head in his chest, my cheeks on fire. What do I say to the man who just said the words I've dreamed of hearing since I was a little girl?

"Thank you, Henry. Thank you for not playing it cool, for not pretending to be someone you aren't. You have no idea how much those words mean to me. And for what it's worth, I think I fell in love with you a little that day, too." I push myself up on my elbow, stretching to kiss him. The warmth of his hand cupping my neck makes me shiver.

"Time to go home, baby. You're cold." He helps me up, then lifts me into his arms like I barely weigh anything.

"Sleep with me tonight?" I ask, pressing my cheeks to his chest.

"Isla–"

"Just sleep, Henry. Nothing else."

"How can I refuse when you look at me like that?"

"The same way you can refuse to have sex with me for what seems like an eternity."

"Just wait, Isla. In twenty-four hours, I'll be blowing your mind." He looks down at me, a dark gleam in his eyes.

"Is that a promise?"

"It's an oath."

53

*H*enry's POV*
     I wake up with a web of scarlet hair tangled over my face, shining like fire in the morning sun. I'm on my side with Isla tucked into my shoulder, her forehead pressed to my chest. She's such a tiny thing. It makes me worry about tonight. I'm wavering between fear that I'll hurt her and the absolute burning need that's been scorching my insides since the moment I met her. I lightly trace the freckles on her cheek with my thumb, rocked by the realization that I would do anything for this tiny, prickly, snoring creature. And I do mean anything. I push myself up on my elbow, trying not to disturb her. Swinging my legs over, I straddle her calves with my knees as I slowly slide my arm from beneath her. I freeze as she shifts in her sleep, mumbling something, then sighing. She's so fucking beautiful that it makes my heart hurt. I replace my body with a pillow and tuck the covers around her before tiptoeing out of the room.

Today has to be perfect, and every perfect day begins with a good breakfast. At least that's what I'm telling myself right now. I start the coffee first, then rummage around the kitchen, filling my backpack with everything I need before scrawling a quick note for Isla, filling the thermos with coffee, and heading down to the beach.

Forty minutes later, I have a fire going on the sand, and everything is laid out and ready to go. The second I see her silhouette high on the cliff, I put the griddle over the fire, heating it until it's smoking before laying out six strips of bacon. Next, I dip the bread Dylan made the other night into an egg mixture, coating it well before tossing it on the griddle. I don't add the eggs until I flip the bacon and French toast, careful not to overcook them. I'm plating the food just as Isla steps onto the beach.

"Perfect timing," I murmur, grinning up at her as I slide her eggs onto the plate and hand it to her.

"Good morning to you, too." She takes her plate and, not waiting for me to stand, wraps her arms around my neck, burying my face in her breasts. I breathe her in like an absolute maniac, my mouth watering at the thought of pulling one of those perfect nipples into my mouth. She pulls away, takes the fork I hand her, and plops down on the sand, moaning as she takes her first bite.

"You didn't need to do this, but I'm not complaining. You cook a damn good breakfast, Henry."

"I'm glad you think so since I'm going to cook breakfasts for you for the rest of your life." I chuckle as she raises an eyebrow as if she's expecting a proposal right here and now. And hell, maybe I should. It's not like I haven't been thinking about it since I saw her behind the bar last year. No other woman has even crossed my mind since then.

I take her left hand and hold it up to the morning light, admiring the ring that somehow mirrors her personality. "He did good, didn't he?"

"Did you notice the prongs that look like thorns?" she asks, eyes sparkling. I take a closer look, and sure enough, the prongs are sharp little claws clasping a stone the same color as her eyes.

"It couldn't be more perfect, could it?" I pull her hand to my mouth, kissing her ring finger. "Finish up before it gets cold," I say, picking up my plate and taking a gigantic bite. I pour a mug of coffee from the travel thermos, and we share it as we stare out at the waves, the tranquility of the morning muffling everything but right this moment.

"Thank you, Henry," she whispers, the softness of her voice barely breaking the silence. "This is incredibly romantic."

"What's romantic is you and me rolling around on this beach," I mutter under my breath. I grunt as her body slams into me, taking me by surprise. She tries to push me down, but I hold her beneath me, pinning her down with my hips, her wrists locked over her head.

"You're fast," she laughs, chest heaving. I watch the way her shirt stretches across her breasts with every breath, those perky nipples begging for attention.

Her soft 'please' is all the permission I need. I wrench her shirt up to her neck, growling deep in my throat when I realize she doesn't have a bra on.

"God damn it, Isla. You're absolute perfection." The last word is muffled as I close my mouth over the tip of one breast, circling her nipple with my tongue before drawing it in deep. She moans, her body arching, reaching for me, demanding more I move my way up to her mouth, unable to resist drinking in the sweet moans flowing from her soft lips. She tastes like sunshine and maple syrup, with the slight bitterness of coffee, and I'm obsessed. I grab her chin, coaxing her mouth wider, delving into her heat with rough strokes of my tongue. The second I release her wrists, she wraps her arms around my neck, drawing me closer until I'm sure we'll sink through the sand to the other side of the earth. I groan into her mouth when she starts rocking her hips against mine, the heat between her legs like the Bermuda triangle. I know once I go there, there's no going back.

I can't fucking wait.

"I need to cool down before I combust," I pant, climbing off her, holding my hands out to help her up. She rolls her eyes and pouts, but I'm used to it by now. Staying in control for both of us hasn't been easy. There have been so many times where I've wanted to say fuck it and bury myself nine inches deep. I take a deep breath, willing my cock to settle down.

"Are you okay?" she asks, looking up at me with bright eyes, her cheeks pink, lips swollen from kissing.

"No."

"We could–"

"No, Isla."

She lifts her shirt, flashing her tits, before flipping me the bird and running like her life depends on it. I chase her up a dune and into the grass, tackling her to the ground, and rip off her shorts and panties. My head is buried between her legs before she has time to process what's happening. I groan against her pussy lips. She's already wet and so fucking sweet. The sound of the waves swallow up her cries as I devour her, licking, nipping, and biting until she's a squirming mess. Until her body is straining toward my mouth, every cell yearning for what only I can give her. I push up her shirt, palming her breast, worshipping the only woman I'll ever want for the rest of my life.

"Come for me, baby," I murmur, lapping up her juices before sealing my mouth to her clit and sucking. She scrapes her nails over my scalp, clenching her fingers in my hair, pulling me closer. I slide two fingers deep inside, and she explodes, soft skin and lithe muscle spasming beneath me, around me. I keep up the rhythm and then slowly ease her down, resting my cheek against the soft skin of her inner thigh, breathing hard.

"I could do that forever. I swear to god," I pant, my pulse pounding, demanding more.

"You have me forever if forever is what you want, Henry," she says, licking her lips, her color high in her cheeks.

"If?" I throw my head back and laugh, standing and lifting her into my arms. "*If* was never part of the equation, baby girl. Do you know how long I've been waiting to hear you say that?" She shrieks as I carry her across the beach and wade into the water, trying to climb my body to escape the waves. Neither of us is ready for the shock of cold water, but I know we both need to cool the fuck off. If I'm not careful today, all of my plans will go to crap, and I'll be buried deep inside her in a gas station bathroom. I only have to stay in control for 12 more hours. I can do this.

I think.

54

I throw my arm over my face, blocking the morning sun from searing my eyelids. I sneak a look at Henry, and I'm pretty sure I ovulate right then and there. He looks like a statue carved from marble–all supple skin and mouth-watering muscle. His arms are stretched over his head, drawing my attention to his perfectly formed abs. I've never wanted to lick someone as much as I want to lick him. All the way from the hollow of his neck down to that magnificent cock.

"Can I help you?" he rasps, opening one eye and squinting at me like he knows exactly what I'm thinking.

"You can help me by fucking me," I say, not mincing my words.

"I'll *make love* to you tonight, Isla."

Hmph.

"*Then* I'll fuck this goddamned frustration out of both of us." My breath catches in my throat, and I choke, nearly coughing up a lung. "Is that what you want, Isla?" he asks, looking at me.

"I want everything you're willing to give me, Henry, and I want it hard." He bites his lip, his gaze slowly sliding down my body. My insides clench like I'm on the verge of a full-body orgasm. "You can't look at me like that."

"Like what?" He pushes up on his elbow, the tip of his tongue poking out to moisten his lips. His eyes are glued to my tits, trying to coax my nipples to attention. And it fucking works. I close my eyes, breathing deeply, desperately trying to wrangle the need before it shreds my control. When I open my eyes, the first thing I see is Henry's cock nearly touching his stomach, and restraint flies out the window. Before he can protest, I'm straddling his torso, his cock snug against my ass crack.

"Don't you dare," he breathes, swallowing hard, his hands convulsing on my hips.

"I won't." I lie down on top of him, cradling his head between my arms, tucking my face into the crook of his neck. He wraps his arms around my waist, his breath ruffling my hair. And we just lie there with the salty breeze kissing our bare bodies. In all my years, this may be the most intimate thing I've done with a man I haven't slept with.

"Can we just lie here forever?" He presses his lips to my hair, his voice rough. "We can hide away from the world, just you and I."

"What about your brothers?"

"They don't have to know."

"Would you rather not share?" I ask, terrified to ask the question that's been in the back of my mind for a while now.

"That was never in the cards for us, Isla. I always knew this was going to happen."

"That wasn't my question," I whisper, my lips moving against the saltiness of his neck.

"The simple answer is yes."

"And the not simple answer?" I ask, holding my breath.

"I have certain appetites that involve watching you get absolutely ravished in the bedroom. And I'm not willing to do that outside of a committed relationship."

That's the only explanation I need to make that niggling sense of worry in the back of my head completely disappear. I push to my elbows, drowning in his baby blues, seeing the truth written there plain as day.

"Thank you for being honest with me."

"While I'm being honest, I'm just a man, Isla, and your ass pressed against my cock is making me feral." He lifts me off his body, depositing me on my knees beside him, and pushes to his feet.

"What are your plans today?" he asks, helping me up and handing me my clothes.

"My sister Lorna wanted me to stop by today for lunch and a chat. Do you want to come with me?"

"Yes."

The lack of hesitation in his voice gives me the warm fuzzies, and I grin up at him, not even trying to hide how fucking happy I am. "You may regret that decision when you meet Daniel and Lorelei. They're absolute hellions."

"Try me. I've never met a kid I didn't like."

Fuck. This man. My insides are in a constant state of bonelessness with the way he talks.

"Tell me about Lorna."

Memories of my childhood flash through my head as I try to think about what to say. "She's kind. Brilliant. The most loyal person you'll ever meet. She loves with her entire heart."

"Is she married?"

"Her jackass of a husband left her when she was still pregnant with the twins."

"Jesus," Henry mutters, his jaw clenching. "What does she do? Hobbies? Work?"

"I actually think that's what she wants to talk to me about. She finally got her doctorate about six months ago and then took a bit of a break. She's been dabbling in gardening the last few years, and I have a feeling she's thinking about taking it full-time."

"Is that what her doctorate was in?"

I cough, my cheeks flushing. "I'll let you ask her about that." There's no way I'm having a conversation with Henry about how my sister is a literal doctor of orgasms.

Henry raises an eyebrow but doesn't press further. "I will. Should we go up and change and head that way?"

I nod, turning to head back up the path, but he grabs my hand and jerks me toward him, enveloping me in a gigantic bear hug.

"Thank you for coming down and eating breakfast with me," he murmurs into my hair.

"Thank you for cooking breakfast for me and for making this morning so romantic."

"This is only the beginning. Just wait till tonight."

My heart jumps. I'm sure I'm going to love every single thing about tonight, but most of all, it will be the moment he slides inside me, and we make that connection I've been yearning for. I help Henry pack up the breakfast things and then watch as he slings the huge pack over his shoulders like it weighs nothing. I wish I could say I'm being discreet as I flatten my palm to his shoulder and drag my hand over his ridiculously large bicep, tracing the veins riding down his lower arm before I lace my fingers with his. He's so goddamn sexy it hurts.

"You okay?" he asks, chuckling.

"Not at all," I whisper, practically salivating.

We take the motorcycle to Lorna's, and I'm not going to lie, wrapping my arms around his torso and feeling him between my thighs does things to me that I'm not proud of. Lorna lives on a beautiful farm at the very far end of the Isle of Lewis, right on the water. Jack and I have both begged her to move back to the castle, but I can't blame her for not wanting to leave her little slice of heaven. Plus, the kids love their school and their friends. But I miss my sister.

I can't help but laugh as we turn into her driveaway. There are flowers and animals *everywhere*. To our left, a family of short, hairy pigs tries to keep up with us, lumbering through the tall grass, their babies squealing. Lorelei pops out of the woods on the right, holding a duck under one arm, waving so hard I'm scared she may dislocate her shoulder. She sets the duck down as we pass and runs behind us, the duck taking flight and beating us all to the house.

Lorna is waiting for us just outside the front door, Daniel on her hip, both framed by thick, glossy jasmine that has taken it upon itself to absolutely cover the front of the house. A thick brunette braid hangs over one of Lorna's shoulders, loose pieces of hair framing high cheekbones. Her peaches and cream complexion sets off navy blue eyes and rosebud lips. I may be biased, but she is truly the most beautiful woman in the world. I nearly trip as I'm getting off the motorcycle, tossing Henry my helmet as I run to her. She sets Daniel down just in time for me to barrel into her, and I squeeze her as tightly as I can.

"God, I missed you," I whisper, breathing her in. She's been using the same perfume since I can remember, and I inhale the peppery, salty scent and feel like I'm home.

"First, let me see that ring," she says, kissing me on the cheek before pulling back to grab my hand. "Oh, Isla. It's perfect!" She admires it, turning my hand side to side to see all the colors in the stone.

"And you must be Henry," she says, putting her hands on her hips as she cranes her neck to look up at him. "What are your intentions with my sister?"

"To marry her and knock her up," Henry says without preamble.

Lorna snorts. "I was joking, but damn. Good for you." She grins up at him, studying his face before giving him a quick hug. "If you're a friend–or more–of my sister's, you're a friend of mine. Just don't hurt her, or I'll have to kill you." She drags her thumb across her throat, winks at him, then turns away from us both, extending her arm toward the beauty she's created. "Welcome to Misty Meadows Farm."

"It was quite the welcome," Henry chuckles. "I would love a tour if you have the time. Growing up, I was one of those kids who always wanted animals but never had any. This seems like heaven to me."

Daniel tugs at the hem of my shirt, and I haul him into my arms, kissing his chubby cheeks. He immediately tries to push a sticky finger into my mouth.

"Of course! I made a light lunch. I can give you a tour after we eat," she says, ushering all of us inside the house.

She leads us into the dining room, where she has a table set with beautiful china and a huge bouquet of gorgeous flowers in the center. "It's nothing fancy, just some sandwiches and a fruit salad. There's ham salad, egg salad, and tuna salad. White and whole wheat bread."

"You didn't need to do this, Lorna," I protest, my mouth watering at the spread.

"You know I like to spoil you," she says, winking, motioning for us to sit.

"Isla says I should ask you about your doctorate," Henry says, eating his sandwich in two bites.

"She did, did she?" Lorna asks, giving me a look I know well—one that means she'll get me back later. I can't help the grin that pulls at my lips, and I try to hide it with a huge bite of ham salad sandwich. This is going to be fun to watch.

55

I feel the same pang I always do as Henry and I leave Lorna's to head home. We only live thirty minutes apart, but with each of us having our own lives, we don't get to see each other as often as I would like. After practically begging, I finally convinced her to get a babysitter and come to the masquerade party next weekend. I'm excited to watch her let loose and relax for a change.

I can't help but be in awe of what she showed us on the farm. In addition to all of the animals, she's been hybridizing dahlias. She had fields and fields of new colors and types in development, the buds just starting to bloom in a gorgeous display. Her dream has always been to be able to make a living off the farm, and this year, she'll finally be able to do that. Instead of selling the flowers like most people would, she's focusing on selling the tubers, which she said provide an exact clone of the plant, so the customer will know exactly what type of flower they're buying. It's also much less labor-intensive since she doesn't have to worry about cross-pollinating. I'm incredibly proud of her, but I worry that so much time spent on the farm means she won't be putting herself out there to meet someone. She deserves a guy that who will take care of her and appreciate what an amazing woman she is.

· · ·

IT's late afternoon by the time Henry and I get home, and I can sense the nervous energy flowing through him. He's jumpy, his muscles rippling every time I touch him, his cock permanently tenting the front of his pants. It's not just him, either. My body feels like a live wire, electricity crackling through me every time I think about what's happening tonight. My heartbeat has taken residence between my legs, creating an ache that only one thing will fix.

"What are the plans for tonight?" I ask, sliding off the motorcycle and setting the helmet on the seat. "Because I'd be more than happy if you throw me over your shoulder, take me to the cottage, and have your way with me right this very second."

"Do you really think I waited all this time not to have this planned out down to the tiniest detail?" he asks, holding the door for me.

"No." I pout, sticking out my lip.

"Pack for two nights while I go and run an errand. We'll be alone, so bring whatever you'll be comfortable wearing. And a swimsuit unless you want to swim naked."

"Can you give me a little clue?" I beg. I need some idea so I know what to pack.

"We'll be on a sailboat."

"You know how to sail?" I ask, surprised.

"Not exactly." He winks, then leaves me wondering what the heck he means by that. Eventually, I give up trying to puzzle through it and pack some comfy clothes and a swimsuit. I take a quick body-only shower, throw on a sundress, and grab a sweater to ward off the chill. Glancing in the mirror, I fuss with my hair for a couple of seconds before giving up and clipping it back in a messy bun. By the time I'm heading back downstairs, my overnight bag in hand, Henry is just coming back, entering through the front door looking windswept. All rosy cheeks and sparkling eyes.

"Ready?" he asks, giving me an appreciative look from head to toe.

"I don't think I've ever been more ready for anything in my life," I confess, stretching on my tiptoes to give him a kiss before walking out the door. He stows our bags in the trunk and jogs around the car to the passenger side just as I'm reaching to open it. He swats my hand away and cages me against the car, the little growl in his throat setting me on fire.

"If you do that again, I'll have to punish you. I want to take care of you, Isla. Let me."

"Yes, sir," I say, covering my mouth to hide my smile. I melt as his fingers circle my wrist, tugging my hand down.

"Say it again," he commands.

"Yes, sir." My breath catches in my lungs as heat pools low in my belly. He rolls his hips against mine, groaning as I reach up to rake my nails through his hair.

"Get the fuck in," he rasps, wrenching open the door. My pussy quivers at the command in his voice, and I plop into my seat, anxious to get wherever we're going so I can impale myself on his cock and ride him until I forget my name.

We haven't even been on the road for ten minutes before Henry turns down a gravel road. Fields of heather spread out on either side of us, painting everything with a romantic lavender haze. The lane ends abruptly, butting right into the water, a narrow wooden dock and a gorgeous sailboat the only things in sight.

"Whose boat is it?" I ask, taking in the sleek lines.

"Someone owed Lach a favor."

"So now *you* owe Lach a favor?" I ask, laughing.

"Pretty much." He takes our bags from the back, grabs my hand, and leads me onto the dock. I gasp as we turn toward the boat, and the part of the dock hidden by the boat comes into view. Rose petals are scattered across the weathered boards, leading to a small round table covered in a white tablecloth and glowing candles. A few pizza boxes sit on the edge of the table, along with two cans of Irn-Bru and a bottle of champagne.

"I was planning on cooking a fancy dinner, but meeting your sister was more important than me looking like an absolute stud tonight, so I hope pizza is okay," he says, nervously raking his hand through his dark hair.

"The fact that you changed your plans and went with me means more to me than you'll ever know, Henry. Much better than a fancy meal." I turn to face him, standing toe to toe, and slide my fingers over his five-o'clock shadow, cupping his face. And then I look at him, taking in his sun-kissed skin, the brilliant blue of his eyes, the dark curl of hair falling over his forehead. Taking in this moment. This incredible life. I don't blink fast enough, and a tear drops from my eye, sliding down my cheek. He catches it with his thumb, licking it from his fingertip before pressing his lips to mine.

"Your eyes are the most stunning shade of green when you cry," he murmurs, lifting my hand to his lips before drawing me toward the boat. "Would you like a tour of our home for the next two nights?"

"Yes, please."

"Like I told you before, I don't know how to sail, so we're going to stay tied to the dock the whole time."

"May I ask why you chose a sailboat?" I ask, laughing.

"Because there's nobody around to hear you screaming my name."

Fuuuuck. My legs immediately turn to Jell-O, and I swear to everything holy that I would push him down right here on the dock and have my way with him if he'd let me. He's so goddamned thoughtful.

"Watch your step." I take his hand, willing my legs to work as I step on board. I wasn't sure what to expect before we arrived, but this wasn't even on my radar. Sleek, gleaming wood nearly blinds me as he shows me around the deck. The mast is so tall that I get dizzy when I look up at it. I follow him inside and down a short flight of stairs to find what may as well be a house. It has a large open living area, a galley kitchen, a bathroom, and sleeping quarters big enough for a king-sized bed. Rose petals are scattered across the bed, electric candles covering every flat surface, lending soft, romantic glow to the space.

"You've thought of everything, haven't you?" I squeeze his hand, blinking back more tears.

"Do you like it?"

"Like it? It's perfect."

"Should we take advantage of the rest of the daylight? Swim, eat dinner, make some dessert?" He presses a finger over my lips when I start to protest. "I know you would rather go straight to the bedroom, Isla, but this day is so important to me. I want to draw it out as long as possible. I want to have fun with you. Make memories." He squats down and rummages through his bag. "Speaking of memories–" He holds up a Polaroid camera. "Smile!"

I grin at him and flash my tits just as the shutter clicks. This is going to be one hell of a night.

56

I hear the shutter of the camera click as I strip and jump off the dock, naked as the day I was born. The cold water relieves the scorching need pumping through my veins. I plant my feet on the bottom and stand, slicking my hair back and looking up at Henry. I've never been with someone who is so careful with me—with our relationship. I must admit it annoyed me initially, but I know I'll treasure our first time for the rest of my life.

Before the guys showed up, it was mostly one-night stands, maybe a second date here and there. And now? I could have never dreamed I would be in a stable relationship with one guy, let alone three. I even told Charlie at one point that I would never be in a relationship like hers, and to her credit, she's never said 'I told you so.' I didn't understand till the guys showed up and gave me a reason to care about how relationships like this work. How each guy fulfills a different part of me, how we work together like a well-oiled machine.

I SHRIEK as Henry plunges into the water next to me, his knees pulled to his chest, a gigantic wave of water hitting me square in the face. He bursts through the surface and flings his head to the side to get his hair out of his eyes. Dark eyelashes stick together as he blinks the water away, framing eyes the color of the sky.

"You look like you're straight out of a Disney movie," he says, sinking into the water until it's lapping at his chin. "My favorite movie used to be *The Little Mermaid*. I was obsessed with Ariel. Maybe I manifested you."

"If that's the case, then I manifested you, too. I was enamored with Prince Eric, and you could be the live-action version of him."

"Well, fuck. Maybe we were always meant to be then, Red. Does that mean Dylan and Theo are Sebastian and Flounder?" he asks, a smile tugging at the corners of his mouth.

"I'll let you tell them that and see how they take it."

"No, thanks," he chuckles, reaching out and pulling me closer.

"Just promise me you'll never lose your voice. It would be a sad day not to hear that sassy mouth running off about something." He slides his thumb over my bottom lip, tugging lightly.

"That wasn't very complimentary," I pout, crossing my arms over my chest.

"Your feistiness is what drew me to you in the first place, Isla. Trust me, it's a compliment." His arm shoots out, his fingers wrapping around the back of my neck, and he pulls me to him, covering his mouth with mine in a sizzling, possessive kiss. The prickliness melts away as my body molds to his. I wrap my arms around his neck, tilting my head and deepening the kiss. He strokes his tongue over mine, his groan of need settling low in my stomach, stoking the fire. He walks us backward, pressing me against one of the dock piers. I whimper as he wraps my legs around his waist, sliding his cock up and down my slit, crushing his body to mine, grinding on my clit.

"Fuck, you feel good," he groans, peppering kisses over my jaw and down my neck. I squirm against him, dragging my clit up and down his shaft. Just as I tense, right on the edge of orgasm, Henry drops his weight, dragging us both under the water. I hit his shoulders with my fists, pushing away from him, taking a deep breath as I break through the surface.

"Asshole!" I use my arm to send a wave of water directly into his face.

"Do you know how close I was to saying screw it and ramming inside you, rutting until we lost ourselves?"

"That was the goal, Henry." I wipe under my eyes, hoping I don't look like a raccoon.

"No, it wasn't. The first time I come inside you, I want you screaming my name, Isla. I want to feel the walls of your pussy spasming around my cock, both of us wringing every single drop of pleasure from our bodies. Understand?"

I roll my eyes, trying to ignore the throbbing between my legs.

"Did you really just roll your eyes at me?" he growls, reaching me before I can react, pinning the front of my body against the pier, his cock nestled against my ass. "Just for that, I'm going to tease you until you're on your knees begging," he rasps, his voice taking on a dangerous edge. I moan as he cups my tits, rolling my nipples between his fingers, squeezing and pulling until I'm rocking against him, desperate for him. Just as I'm about to beg, he slides his hands down, squeezing my ass, spreading me as he pulls his hips back, giving his cock room to slide down my crack and notch itself at my asshole. I whimper as a shiver of need wracks my body. Henry sinks his teeth into the space between my neck and shoulder in response, careful not to break my skin.

"Has anyone fucked your ass yet?" he asks, pressing his lips to my ear before sucking and biting my earlobe.

"No," I moan, sneaking my hand between my legs. He notices immediately and pins my wrists above my head with one hand, the other steadying his cock. He growls as he pushes forward slightly, the head of his cock spreading but never breaching my tight ring of muscle. I take a deep breath, forcing my body to relax, and I'm rewarded with the head of his cock slipping inside me the next time he pushes forward.

"Holy fuck, Isla," he breathes, his body going rigid against mine as he fights for control. His moan turns into something deep and guttural as I squeeze as tight as I can, pushing my ass back to take more of him. He jerks his hips back, sliding out of me. I turn to face him, smirking.

"Nothing has ever felt that good." The admission slips from his lips, his eyebrows popping up like he's surprised the words came out of his mouth.

"Not even when you're strangling your cock with your hand?" I ask, biting my lip to keep in my laugh.

"Not even then. You just gave me enough spank bank material for years, Isla. Fuck." I make my way over to the ladder, looking over my shoulder at him as I climb it, wondering just how much restraint he has left. I only make it to the second rung before he circles my ankle with one hand, bringing it down so both feet are on the same rung.

"Hold on with your hands and sit back," he commands, guiding my hips back. My body quivers with anticipation as he kneads and spreads my ass cheeks. The first touch of his tongue at the base of my spine has my body shuddering. He drops into the water and buries his face between my cheeks, eating me like his last meal. I push against him, greedy for more. He chuckles and sinks three fingers inside my pussy, his pinky sliding over my clit as he pumps. My body seizes as I teeter on the edge of orgasm, nearly losing my grip. He climbs up behind me, looping his arm around my middle, and lifts me onto the dock. He's on top of me before I can move, my chest pressed to the dock, his hand snaking around my hip and diving between my legs, anchoring on my clit and pressing me into the dock. His cock nudges at my entrance, pulsing with need.

"I wanted our first time to be in a bed, but this feels so fucking right," he groans, his lips brushing my ear. "Are you okay with this?"

"Yes, Henry. Please. I need you inside me." I whimper as he increases the pressure on my clit, bucking against his fingers. He pulls his hips back and slams into me, his cock filling, stretching me, completing me. I call out his name, straining against him, meeting him thrust for thrust.

"You're so fucking perfect, Isla," he groans. "The way your pussy hugs my cock, god. I'm close already, and I've only been in you for ten seconds."

I groan in frustration as he pulls out, but it quickly turns into a moan as he slides his shaft along my slit. I lift my hips and he holds the head of his cock against my clit, rocking back and forth.

"That's it. Good girl," he whispers, his lips moving against my neck as I rock my hips against him. I cry out as he thrusts back in, my pussy clenching around the wide girth of his shaft, milking him. He keeps his fingers pressed to my clit as he thrusts, bringing me higher than I've ever been before.

"Yes, baby. Just like that." He pounds into me over and over, biting my neck with a growl as his hips stutter, my pussy spasming around his cock as we find heaven together.

"Jesus Christ, Isla," he pants, licking my skin to soothe the pain. "That was not how this was supposed to happen."

"It was fucking perfect," I pant, turning on my side and snuggling into his body as he settles on the dock beside me.

"We'll be picking splinters out of each other for weeks." He grips my chin, turning my face up to his, and kisses me deeply, his tongue sweeping over mine in a rhythm that sets my body trembling, making me wonder if I'll ever get enough.

57

We lie on the dock in a post-coitus daze until the sun sinks low enough that we're shivering in each other's arms.

"Come on, baby. Let's go warm up." Picking me up, he cradles me against his chest as he carefully steps onto the boat, ducking as he goes down the stairs. He makes a beeline to the bathroom, depositing me on the toilet and instructing me to pee as he turns on the tub and heads back upstairs. I'm flushing the toilet as he reappears holding the bottle of champagne. My gaze slowly slides down his body, taking in his still erect cock, the rippling muscles, the god-like physique. I drop to my knees with a sudden, desperate need to have him in my mouth, his cum sliding down the back of my throat.

"Isla–"

"Please, Henry," I beg, wrapping my hand around his shaft, my fingertips not quite touching. He must see the absolute desperation on my face because he gives in, nodding slightly before leaning back against the counter as he unwraps the foil from the top of the champagne bottle. My tongue passes over his slit as he pops the cork off the bottle, and I taste him for the first time. He cups the back of my head with one hand, nudging past my lips as he takes a deep swig from the champagne bottle. Tugging my head back, he forces me to look up at him, slowly dribbling the champagne from his mouth to mine. He pushes the head of his cock back into my mouth.

"Swallow." The combination of his taste, the bubbles of the champagne, and how fucking erotic this is makes me absolutely feral. I grab the backs of his thighs, holding myself steady as he guides my head back and forth, his gaze never leaving mine, dark desire practically dripping from him.

"Be a good girl and take me all the way," he says, his voice hoarse. "Please, Isla."

I take a deep breath through my nose, flatten my tongue, and slide my lips down his shaft. He flexes his hips, plunging into my throat, his hands cradling my head.

"Fuck," he rasps, the head of his cock pulsing at the back of my throat. Eyes watering, I swallow, squeezing him with my throat. He thrusts one twice, then pulls out, replacing his cock with his thumb.

"You're so pretty," he whispers, tracing my lips and coating them in my saliva.

"Use me, Henry," I practically beg, feathering the tip of my tongue over his frenulum. He growls deep in his throat, his hands spasming in my hair. Picking me up, he turns the water off, carries me to the bedroom, and tosses me on the bed.

"Don't move." I shiver at the command, not moving a single muscle as I lie there wondering where he went. When he comes back into the room, he's holding a vibrator in one hand. He tugs me to the edge of the bed, positioning me so my head hangs off. "Pinch the back of my leg if you want to stop," he says, his cock bobbing as he takes a step toward me. "I need to hear that you understand, Isla."

"I understand," I whisper, my mouth watering as the head of his cock presses against my lips. He turns the vibrator on, sliding it over my clit before slowly sinking his cock into my mouth. This position makes it seem like he's twice as long, and I silently thank the gods for a practically nonexistent gag reflex as he bottoms out. I moan around him as he drags the vibe back and forth between my legs, taking turns between concentrating on my clit and dipping it inside, teasing my G-spot. I take a deep breath as he pulls back and then promptly gag as he shoves back in with a grunt, his control cracking. I keep a grip on his thigh with one hand, steadying myself as I wrap my other hand around his balls, massaging and tugging, discovering what he likes. My thumb slips up the back, barely brushing his perineum, and his entire body tenses, a guttural sound slipping from his mouth. I wait for him to tell me to stop, but the request never comes.

Gaining courage, I slide my thumb over his taint in slow circles. He shudders against me like he's shaking off the restraint that's held him back for as long as I've known him. Pulling my legs toward him, he practically folds my body in half, pressing my head against the side of the bed with his hips and fastening his lips over my pussy, sucking on my clit like it's a goddamned Jolly Rancher. I increase the pressure on his taint as he thrusts, doing my best to keep up with him as he uses my mouth to find relief. I hear the vibrator start up again, and I'm a goner the second he slides it inside me and flattens his tongue against my clit. My cry is muffled by his cock as he pushes deep. One more pump, and he's pulsing inside me, hot cum pooling in the back of my throat as he comes. He pulls out the second he's finished, lifting and tossing me higher onto the bed and crawling up after me, looks of concern and wonder battling for dominance.

"You're fucking amazing, Isla." He swipes his thumbs under my eyes, wiping away the tears and the rest of my mascara, then cradles my head between his hands and kisses me dizzy. I reach between my legs, trying to take out the vibrator, but he wraps his fingers around my wrist, stopping me. His mouth is hot as he makes his way down to my breasts, sucking my nipples into his mouth before kissing his way down my stomach.

"Henry! I just got there!" I protest, trying to squirm out of his grip.

"Let me make you feel good, Isla," he murmurs, his lips brushing against my clit. I relax into the bed with the first touch of his tongue, my legs falling wide open. "Your pussy is so pretty," he whispers, running his nose along my slit before sucking my clit into his mouth.

"Henry!" I don't like him looking. I'm not dumb. I know it's not pretty down there.

"Have you thought about how it will feel to have two cocks stretching you?" he asks softly, sliding two fingers inside me, joining the vibrator. He spreads them out, a delicious stretch making me forget everything I was about to say. He shifts, and then I feel the thumb of his other hand sliding up my crack and pushing gently against my asshole.

Fuck. My breath hitches as he works me over, playing my body like a violin, making me feel good in so many ways that I can't do anything but go along for the ride.

"Oh, god," I whimper as he forces me higher, his lips curling against me just before he tears my world wide open. I buck against his hands and his mouth, my body not knowing what to do, where to press, where to pull, to get the most pleasure. I suck in a ragged breath, tears streaming down my face as he brings me back down gently, slowly removing his fingers, then the vibe, kissing just below my belly button before crawling up next to me and gathering me into his arms.

"Where the hell did you learn that?" I ask, breathing hard. "Wait, don't answer that. I don't want to know."

Henry chuckles, pressing his lips to my hair. "I can tell you with absolute certainty that I've never done that with anyone before, Isla."

God, I hope he's telling me the truth. I've never been a jealous person, but thinking of him doing that to someone else practically crushes my soul.

"Good, because you're mine," I whisper, pressing my lips to his.

58

My stomach rudely interrupts our kiss, and Henry's lips curl against mine as he pulls away.

"Does somebody have a little rumbly in their tumbly?" He grins, tickling my belly. I clench my jaw, refusing to give in to laughter. I finally break when he moves to my sides, digging his fingers into my ribs, demanding surrender. I shriek, twisting away from him, nearly falling off the bed. "We better get washed up and eat. You need keep your energy up for later," he says, grabbing my ankle just in time.

Later?

LATER?

How many times can this man get it on before he needs a break? I take his hand and let him help me out of bed, trailing him to the bathroom. I follow him into the bathtub, and he turns me away from him, pulling me down between his legs. His hand flattens over my stomach as I lean back against his chest, my body pleasantly humming. He lathers body wash in his hands and runs them over my limbs and torso as the tub fills, rinsing the soap away before using just water to clean between my legs.

"Tilt your head back, love." His fingers press against my chin, guiding my head back until it's resting against his chest. He takes a cup from the side of the tub and carefully pours water over my hair, then he squirts shampoo into his palm and works it into my scalp.

"Thank you, Isla," he murmurs, the moment somehow turning even more intimate as he rinses the soap from my hair.

"For what?" I ask, opening my eyes, tilting my head back, and looking up at him. The only thing I can see is the underside of his chin and the way his throat bobs as he swallows.

"For being you. For letting me fuck your face like a lunatic." A hint of remorse in his voice puts me on my guard.

"No, we're not doing this," I say, turning to face him. "I liked it. I liked it a whole fucking lot. You don't need to say thank you. You don't need to feel bad. If you ever ask me to do something that I don't like, I'll tell you, Henry. Scout's honor."

He breaks out into a smile so big it takes my breath away. "Honest?"

"Honest. I mean it when I tell you I want everything you have to give me." I stand, holding my hands out to him to help him up. "Let's eat before my stomach decides to revolt and consume itself."

THE PIZZA IS COLD, but it's fucking delicious. I don't think I've ever been this hungry in my entire life. Three-day-old bread would taste like a gourmet meal at this point.

"What did you have in mind for dessert?" I ask, swallowing the last bite of my fourth piece of pizza.

"We used to do something called campfire cones when I was younger. I brought a portable grill we can set up on the shore. They'll only take about ten minutes once the charcoal has burned down a little." He pops the top off another bottle of champagne and fills my empty glass before trekking back to the car to grab the grill and charcoal. I join him with the intention to help but quickly realize I'll only be in the way. Instead, I sit on the dock with my feet hanging over, nursing my glass of bubbly and getting shivers every time I think about what we just did.

"Are you cold?" Henry asks, coming up behind me and rubbing my shoulders.

"No, I just keep getting flashbacks."

"Of what?"

"Your cock down my throat."

He coughs, then clears his throat, blushing. "Oh."

The sun is just starting to dip below the horizon when he pops two foil-wrapped packages on the grill, sets a timer on his phone, and sits beside me, the champagne bottle in hand.

"I really enjoy spending time with you, Isla. I know that seems stupid to say at this point, but I mean it. There's always been a level of anxiety in other relationships. I'm scared I'll do something wrong or won't be enough somehow. Not with you."

He keeps talking, but all I can concentrate on is how his hand squeezes around the neck of the bottle, making his veins pop. I look over at him from beneath my lashes, biting my lip. "You need to be careful saying things like that."

"Why?" he asks, his eyes darkening.

"Because it makes me want to do dirty things to that magnificent body of yours."

"Nobody is stopping you, Isla."

Fuckkk.

"Is that so?" I ask, swinging my leg over his hips and straddling him. He lies down, hands behind his head, staring up at me like I'm the most beautiful thing he's ever seen.

"Never stop looking at me like that," I whisper.

"I couldn't even if I tried."

"Even when I'm old and gray, and my boobs are hanging down past my belly button?"

"Especially then." He smiles up at me, his eyes crinkling. "I love you, Isla MacLeod."

"I love you, too." I melt into his body, snuggling against his chest, breathing him in. Just as the scent of charred sugar starts drifting over to us, Henry's alarm goes off. We hop up, and he flings the little packets from the grill onto the rocks, instructing me to let them cool down before I try to open them. God, he knows me well. The smell is almost impossible to resist. When they're finally cool enough to pick up, I shake the debris from the outer layer of tinfoil and unwrap the first layer, discarding it before I start on the second layer. Inside is a waffle cone coated in melty peanut butter, stuffed with bananas and chocolate chips. It's the most delicious-looking creation I've ever seen.

"Whoever invented this is a goddamn genius," I mumble around a giant bite, scalding my tongue and not even caring.

"It's good, isn't it?" Henry asks, blowing on his before taking a bite.

"It's freaking amazing."

"Someday, we'll be making these with our kids," he says, looking up at me, eyes sparkling.

"Someday." I smile, loving the thought of a little Henry running around. "But for now, I want to enjoy the four of us before we bring a baby into the world."

"Totally agree. I'm going to be selfish with your time for a long while. I already feel like I don't see you enough."

"After this weekend, we'll all be sleeping in the same bed, right?" I ask, licking chocolate from my finger.

"If that's what you want, yes."

"Is that what you guys want?"

"I'm not going to speak for Dylan and Theo, but that's what I'd prefer, yes," Henry says, raking his hair out of his face.

"So, how is that going to work? With Charlie, it's easy because the guys are in relationships too, so everyone is cuddling."

"We'll just have to rotate," he says, shrugging. "We could keep a schedule if it's easier, or we just fall asleep how we fall asleep, and that's that."

"We'll all have to sit down and hammer out the details."

"Speaking of that, are we going to push two beds into one room? I don't think four of us would fit on any of the beds you have in the house right now."

I take another bite, giving myself time to think. "I thought maybe we could move back to my old bedroom at the castle if the three of you are willing to try that. It's in a different wing from Charlie's room, so we'd be pretty much on our own, and it's plenty big enough for the size bed we need. Plus, I'll be there to help Charlie when she needs it. And then with the brewery–"

"You can stop there," he says, chuckling. "You don't need to convince me. Who would say no to living in a castle? We can ask Theo and Dylan what they think when we get back." He takes my hand, threading his fingers through mine. "What will you do with the Manor House and the cottage?"

"If I can't convince Lorna to move, then probably just rent them out."

"Do you think she would?" he asks, bringing my hand to his mouth and pressing his lips to my fingers.

"If we make it easy for her, maybe."

"What does that mean, exactly?"

"Setting up a part of the farm for her. Making her flowerbeds, putting in irrigation, figuring out what else she needs without her knowing what we're doing."

"You want to surprise her?" he asks, eyebrows jumping up his forehead.

I shiver as he drags his lips over the back of his hand, struggling to keep my thoughts on topic. "I think that's the only way I'll get her to say yes. If she has too long to think about it, anxiety will get in the way. If we can make it as seamless as possible, there won't be a reason for her to say no."

"All the kids will be able to grow up together, too," Henry adds, his face softening.

"True. That may be the best selling point when it comes down to it."

"We'll start planning when we get back. I'm sure between the eight of us, we can come up with something."

"You'd really help me with that?" I ask, blinking back a sudden onslaught of tears.

"If you asked me to get you the moon, I would figure out a way." His blue gaze collides with mine as he sweeps a strand of hair behind my ear, his thumb gently sweeping over my cheek. "You're my entire world, Isla." Overwhelmed by emotion, I flop on my back, staring up at the darkening sky, not quite able to believe this is my life. He kisses my forehead before lying next to me, interlocking our fingers as we watch the stars slowly appear.

"I have something for you," he says suddenly, sitting up and reaching into his pocket. "Hold up your hair." I lift my hair from my neck, unable to see what he has in his hands. "There." I feel around on my chest, lifting the necklace toward my face. I nearly drop it when I see the brilliant diamond shining back at me.

He pulls me to my feet and then takes my hand, getting down on one knee. "Marry me, Isla. Be my wife. My best friend. My forever."

I sniffle, hastily wiping at the tears streaming down my cheeks. "Yes, Henry. I'll marry you." I would marry this man over and over again if I could. I've never felt so treasured in my life.

"Thank fuck," he breathes, pressing his hand to his chest. "I chose a necklace because it's closest to your heart, but if you'd like it made into a ring, we can do that, too."

"No!" I say, holding tight to the pendant. "It's beyond perfect."

Getting back to his feet, he looks down at me, eyes shining. "I was hoping you would say that." He cups my chin and lowers his lips to mine, leaving me breathless. "Do you know what I haven't been able to stop thinking about?"

"What?" I breathe, toying with the hair at the base of his neck.

"How that diamond will glitter against your skin while I'm eating you out."

59

When we return home Sunday afternoon, Dylan and Theo are standing in the driveway waiting for us. They look so much like two little lost puppy dogs that I can't help but laugh as I leap from the car and throw my arms around them, peppering their faces with kisses.

"Better?" I ask, looking between them.

"It will only be better when we stop splitting up for dates," Theo grumbles.

"Well, I have good news for you then, grumpy, because that was my last single date, remember?" I can see the relief spreading over his face, and it tugs at something in my heart.

"Thank fuck. You have no idea how much I hate being separated from you."

"Pretty sure that's how we all feel, dumbass," Dylan says, elbowing Theo out of the way, practically bending me backward as he crushes his lips to mine.

"What do you guys think of living in the castle?" I ask, springing the question on them without warning as I straighten my skirt and top.

"Her old room is in a separate wing of the castle from Charlie and the guys. We'd have all the privacy we want," Henry adds, grabbing our bags from the car.

"Can we see it before we give a final answer?" Dylan asks, his big brown eyes luminous in the afternoon light.

"Of course. I was planning on going over today so I could make a to-do list for the party. Do you guys want to come with me?"

"Speaking of the party, is it adults only?" Theo asks, holding the door as I walk inside.

"Yes, it's adults only. Your costumes can be as raunchy as you want," I answer, hoping they'll take that as a suggestion. I'd love to see them dressed like absolute sex gods.

"Will we get dressed together, or do you have other plans?" Henry asks, winding a strand of my hair around his finger.

I shake my head. "I'll be getting dressed with Lorna at the castle. It'll be a great way for me to remind her of the good old days, plus I want my outfit to be a surprise."

"Intriguing." Dylan's gaze rakes over my body like he's imagining all the possibilities of undress I could show up in.

"Do you guys want to head over there now?" I ask, antsy to get organized before the week officially starts.

"We may as well. Dylan and I bought stuff to make dinner, so we can work on that when we get back."

"Thank you both." They're truly lifesavers. I hadn't even thought about dinner. I probably would have nibbled on cheese, crackers, or something else equally unsatisfying.

MY HEAD IS SPINNING by the time we make it over to the castle. I can't stop thinking about everything I need to do, whether I ordered enough linens or planned for enough food. I'm so preoccupied that I don't notice Theo holding me back as Dylan and Henry go inside.

"You okay?" he asks, backing me into the corner of the entrance, tipping my chin up, and studying my face.

"Yeah. There's just a lot to juggle right now."

"We can sit down and make a list when we get home. Maybe it'll help make you feel a little more organized."

"I'd like that," I breathe, already feeling a little less weight on my shoulders.

"I miss you, Sunflower." His caramel eyes are deep brown in the low light, his fingertips rough on my cheek as he sweeps a strand of hair off my face.

"I'm right here." I stretch up on my tiptoes, wrapping my arms around his neck and hanging on tightly. I practically purr when he buries his face in my neck, and breathes me in. He fiddles with the chain around my neck, eventually leaning back so he can look at the pendant.

"He did good, didn't he?" I ask softly.

"It looks stunning on you, Sunflower."

Dylan pokes his head out of the door, giving us a dirty look. "You do know you're running the show here, Freckles?"

"Sorry!" I squeak, ducking out of Theo's arms and rushing inside. "Room tour first?" I ask, wigging my eyebrows suggestively.

"Yes, please," Henry growls, coming up behind me and pulling me against the hard planes of his body. I practically melt in his arms, my muscle memory convinced I'm about to have a *really* good time.

"If the three of you keep touching me, we're not going to get anything done today," I say sternly, disentangling myself from Henry and skipping ahead several paces to distance myself from them.

"Oh no, you don't." Dylan watches me with eagle eyes as he takes a predatory step my way. I mirror him, taking a step back, keeping us far enough apart so I'll have a chance to run if he pounces. And boy, do I want to run, because I know exactly what he'll do. Dylan takes another step toward me, and I explode into action, turning and bolting down the hall. My only advantage over them is knowing where I'm going, but it ends there. I take the stairs two at a time, swinging around the banister and propelling myself down another hallway to the right. I duck into a room on my left, closing the door after me and running through to the next room. I duck through the servants' entrance and follow the tiny hallway until I get to my room and crack the door, ready for the mustiness of an old, unused room to hit me in the face. That's not what happens at all. My old, outdated furnishings from my childhood are gone. They've been replaced by beautiful, earthy furniture. A brand new gigantic bed sits where my queen bed used to be. My mouth falls open as I take everything in, spinning in a slow circle. I spy a tiny cream envelope nestled in the bedspread and pick it up, running my fingernail under the flap.

Isla, I don't know if or when you'll come back to this room, but I couldn't pass up the chance that you would come home someday. Charlie helped me pick everything out. I hope you love it.
   Love always,
   Jack

I'M WIPING the tears away from my eyes as the guys burst through the door, all three stopping dead in their tracks.

"What's wrong?" Dylan asks, the first to spring into motion.

I sniffle, waving the card in the air. "Jack redecorated the room for me. For us. Just on the off chance I decided to come back." I turn toward the bed, taking in how big it is and how perfect it will be for all four of us. "He even had a bed made that we'll all fit in."

"Maybe we should make sure we all fit," Henry says, his voice rough. He grips my wrist and tugs me toward the bed, his eyes dark with desire.

"It's–It's not the masquerade party yet," I stammer, looking between the guys, my heartbeat ratcheting up when I see the need radiating from them.

"We can help take the edge off, baby," Henry whispers, his teeth sinking into his lower lip as he pushes me down onto the bed. Cotton candy clouds envelop my body. I moan indulgently as I sink into the mattress. I don't know what this bed cost, but whatever it was, it was worth it.

The guys must have some unspoken code because they don't say a word as they take position–Dylan and Henry sitting on each side of my head while Theo kneels at the end of the bed, kneading my thighs.

"I know we're waiting to have sex together until after the party, but what if we have sex with you one at a time?" Theo rasps, skating his lips up the inside of my thigh, his tongue sneaking out and delving inside the crease at the back of my knee.

One at a time? I can barely think with his hands on me like this. With Dylan and Henry's cocks only inches from my face, already tenting their pants and ready to go. I whimper as Theo pushes up the fabric of my skirt, pressing his thumb against my clit and moving in slow circles.

"It'd be a perfect time to test your ass," Theo murmurs, his tongue licking a long line up my inner thigh.

"Test my–?" I stop trying to talk when his mouth reaches my pussy.

He pushes my legs to my chest, Dylan and Henry holding them there, then pulls my underwear to the side, licking a long, slow line from my ass to my clit.

"To see if you're ready for us to ass-fuck you, Sunflower." The dirty words with my sweet nickname in one sentence do indescribable things to my insides. Fuck.

"Okay," I rasp, not even caring what they do as long as we all get there.

Theo holds his hand out to Henry, and Henry plops a vibrator and a tiny bottle of lube into his palm. He must have had it in his pocket this whole time. I love a prepared man.

"Dildo first," Theo says as he stands, shucking off his clothes before pulling my underwear off as well. The guys drag me higher on the bed, pushing my thighs to my chest. Theo kneels between my legs, squirting lube first on my ass and then on the dildo. Just as Theo slides the dildo back and forth over my asshole, Dylan bends over my torso and slides his tongue down my slit. I arch toward his mouth, desire pounding in my veins.

"Deep breath," Theo says, gripping the back of my thigh with one hand, the dildo ready to go in the other. I take a deep breath, squeezing my eyes closed and focusing on relaxing my muscles. Theo puts pressure on the dildo, and I can feel it slide in little by little. Dylan seals his lips over my clit and sucks hard. My body convulses, opening up and allowing Theo to push the dildo all the way in.

"Look how good you're doing," Theo breathes, looking down at my ass, nostrils flared, color high on his cheeks. "You're dripping for us, Sunflower." He dips a finger inside my pussy, sliding it along the stretched skin of my asshole, massaging me.

Fuck me. I'm never going to survive them.

60

I reach between my legs, threading my fingers through Dylan's hair, my body undulating with the push and pull of the dildo as Theo works it inside my ass. My pussy squeezes around nothing, desperately needing to be filled. Only one more week and I'll know what it'll feel like to have all of my holes filled at once, and god, it will be transcendent. I gasp as Theo seats the dildo to its hilt, dropping to his knees and slowly running his tongue over my stretched skin as I spasm around the silicone, lightning bolts of pleasure making me breathless. I whimper as he pulls the dildo out, plunging his tongue in its place, teasing me until I'm incapable of using words to tell him what I need.

The sound of Theo's zipper sends a thrill of anticipation down my spine. Yes. This is what I want. My guys surrounding me. Taking care of me. Loving me. Henry squirts lube into Theo's palm. I watch as he coats his cock and then spreads the rest over me, working it inside with his thumb. Dylan moves out of the way as Theo drags me to the edge of the bed, trapping my legs to my chest with his torso, his cock nudging at my asshole.

"You're sure?" he asks, his voice like smoke and whiskey.

"Yes, Theo. Please."

Using gravity as his guide, the weight of his body has his cock pushing slow and steady against that tight ring of muscle. "Fuck," he grunts, his eyes locking with mine, ecstasy swirling in their depths. "The head of my cock isn't even in. You're so fucking tight, baby."

I blow out a slow breath, gaining control of my body and relaxing my muscles one by one. He presses with his hips, and the head of his cock pops inside me, filling me in ways I've never been filled before. I whimper, squeezing around him.

"Don't move," he rasps, pinning me to the bed with his hips, doing everything he can to gain some semblance of control. He drops his forehead against mine, breathing hard. "You feel so goddamned good, Sunflower."

I sneak a hand between our bodies, rubbing my clit before impaling myself on my fingers. I anchor the heel of my palm and rock my hips, moaning as my muscles clench, bucking against Theo faster and faster until he finally surrenders. I scream his name as he bottoms out, riding my hand and his cock until the dam breaks, a tsunami of pleasure washing over us.

"Fucking hell, Isla!" Theo grunts as I come, my ass squeezing around him like a vise. One pump, and his hips spasm as he fills me. We lie there, breathing hard, aftershocks rocking our bodies. No sooner does Theo climb off me than Dylan shucks his clothes and tells Henry to help me up higher on the bed. Dylan takes his time, kissing the arches of my feet before making his way to my ankles, the backs of my knees, and the insides of my thighs. My back arches, my center yearning for his touch by the time he makes it to my pussy, the softness of his tongue making me gasp. He flattens it against me, licking lightly, giving me time to recover from my last orgasm. I move against his mouth, greedy for more.

"Already?" he breathes, the corners of his lips pulling up in a satisfied smile as he crawls up my body. My eyes roll back in my head as he slams inside me, giving the greedy nerve endings in my slick channel what they want. I squeeze around him milking him, taking all the pleasure I can as he pumps his hips. When I'm whimpering beneath him, he shifts forward slightly, dropping his weight so his pelvic bone is pressing against my clit. Every thrust has the head of his cock sliding over my G-spot, my clit rolling between our bodies.

"Isla, come for m–"

I explode before he can finish his sentence, locking my heels around his ass, holding his body to mine. He captures my mouth with his lips, our kiss sloppy as we wring pleasure from each other's bodies. I swallow his groan as he gives in, rutting hard as he falls apart, filling me with his cum.

I try to catch my breath, my body humming. There's no way Henry will be able to get me there after this.

"Yes, I fucking will," Henry growls.

Fuck. I didn't mean to say that out loud. He's still fully clothed as he takes his place at my feet, gripping my ankles and flipping me onto my stomach in one smooth movement. He doesn't give me time to protest as he grabs my waist, pulling my hips in the air. I struggle in his grip, but he holds me still. "I want to see, Isla."

"See what?" I pant, breathless.

He practically purrs with satisfaction as he spreads my ass cheeks, pushing his thumbs down to slide along my pussy lips. "So fucking pretty," he murmurs, squeezing and kneading, watching the cum drip from me, then gathering it with his fingers and pushing it back in. Oh god. My core clenches hard. I'm more turned on than I've been in my entire life. The long swipe of his tongue from my clit to my ass leaves me trembling. He hears my gasp and chuckles against me, the vibrations ratcheting the tension even higher.

"A little cum isn't going to stop me from putting my mouth on you, baby girl." He proves his point by delving his tongue inside me before fastening his mouth over my clit and sucking hard. "Such a pretty dripping pussy," he rumbles, spreading my cheeks even wider and burying his face in my ass. He finally stands, undoing his pants and letting them fall to his ankles. "Legs together, pet." I obey, whimpering into the mattress as I wait for him to ravage me. He wraps his hand in my hair, tugging my head back as he slides his cock into the triangle below my pussy, fucking my thighs with hard thrusts. My breath stutters as the head of his cock pushes against my clit, my entire body trembling as he starts dragging me to the summit. My core clenches, Dylan and Theo's cum leaking out of me, making my thighs even slicker. Henry's groan is primal as he lifts my back to his chest, holding me there as he pushes into my pussy inch by incredible inch.

"Fuck. Me," he groans, his hips stuttering for a second before he gains control. Reaching between my breasts, he grips my neck, the fingers of his other hand pushing between my legs, massaging my clit, working me hard.

"Too much," I pant, my body throbbing in time to the frantic beating of my heart.

"No. It's not," Henry growls, slamming into me over and over. "Be a good girl and come for me."

My body overrides my brain, an insatiable black hole opening inside me, greedy for every drop of pleasure. We topple onto the bed, the crush of his body heightening my orgasm as he ruts into me, finding release.

"Fuck," I gasp, sucking in huge lungfuls of air, trying to catch my breath. Henry kisses my temple and slowly peels his body off mine. He sits back on his heels, grasps my ass cheeks, and spreads me, watching his cum leak from my pussy.

"So pretty," he practically purrs, kneading my flesh. I bear down, giving him what he wants, and I'm rewarded with a moan that sends goosebumps skittering over my body. He's quick to slide his thumb up my slit, coaxing the cum back inside. "Again," he rasps.

I obey, and this time he slides his thumb inside me, teasing my G-spot. My body clenches around him.

"Give me one more orgasm, Isla," he rasps, pushing his thumb in farther, sliding his fingers beneath me to cradle my clit.

"Henry–"

"Please, Isla. I want my cum deep inside you, and I want to know it's going to stay there."

He lowers his weight onto my hips, pushing his hand with his pelvis in a punishing rhythm. He sinks his teeth into the space between my neck and shoulder, riding me hard. His growl unlocks something in me, and I let go of everything except the feeling building deep inside. He crooks his thumb, putting pressure on my G-spot, and I crumble. I sob out his name as my orgasm rips through me, tears streaming down my face, my throat raw.

Holy fucking god.

My world spins as he gathers me into his arms, cradling me against his chest. "That's my girl," he murmurs, his lips moving against my hair. "I'm so goddamned proud of you."

If this is what it's like fucking them separately, I don't know how I'll ever manage all of them together.

61

By the time Thursday rolls around, I'm going through cycles of feeling like the party preparation is on track to absolute panic over being behind. Henry and Theo run into town to grab some last-minute supplies, which means Dylan is the only one here to deal with my crazy moods.

"Why don't we take a drive and then go to the pub for dinner?" Dylan asks after I sign one too many times, taking my hand and tugging me into his arms. "It'll be like old times. Plus, I think a few beers may help take the edge off."

I laugh at his understatement. There's no *thinking* about needing a beer right now. I definitely need one. Or five. "That's a great idea. It feels like it's been forever since I've been to the pub. It'll be nice to see everyone."

I toss him the keys as we head out the door, my nerves so shot I don't think I should even be driving. I know part of the way I'm feeling is what's happening the night of the party. The pressure and anticipation are going to kill me.

"Isla?"

I look up, realizing we're parked in a small gravel parking area, a sign for Luskentyre Beach directly in front of us. "Sorry," I mumble, but Dylan is already outside the car, scrambling to open my door before I do. I take a deep breath as he pulls me out of the car and wraps a protective arm around my waist, willing my brain to chill out. When I toe off my shoes and dig my toes into the sand, the cobwebs finally start to clear from my mind, and I feel like myself again. We walk the half mile to the water and chase each other in and out of the waves, trying not to get wet. Dylan stops to pick up something, running to me with his find.

"What is this?" he asks, poking at the round ball in his palm. "Some sort of seed?"

"Sheep shit, Dylan. That's sheep shit."

He drops it like it burned him, glaring at me when I start laughing. "Why is there sheep shit in the ocean?"

"Have you seen any fences on the entire island? The sheep go where they want, including the beach. It's just the way it is."

"Gross. Maybe I don't want to live here after all."

I spin on my heel. "I can't believe you'd say–!" My heart nearly stops when I see him on his knee.

Tying his shoe.

Fuck. I slap my hand over my heart, bending at the waist, sucking in air. "Don't do that to me," I say raggedly.

"Do what?" he asks innocently, standing back up and having the audacity to look completely confused. I shake my head, too embarrassed to explain what just happened. I'm an idiot.

"Let's go get that beer you promised me," I say instead, grabbing his hand and tugging him back toward the car.

We get to the pub early enough in the evening that it's still fairly quiet. Dylan follows me to a booth in the corner, and once I'm seated, he heads to the bar to grab our drinks.

"This was a good call," I admit, taking the glass from him.

"Yeah?" he studies my face to make sure I'm telling him the truth.

"The second I stepped in here, it was like all the worry about the party disappeared. I don't feel guilty for sitting and relaxing like I did at home."

He takes a huge gulp of his beer. "Good." He gives me a goofy smile, foam covering his upper lip, before licking it off. My gaze follows the path of his tongue, remembering with vivid detail what that tongue can do between my thighs. I bury my face in my hands, attempting to cover the blush crawling up my cheeks.

"What's wrong?" he asks, reaching across the table to pry a finger from my eyes.

"What's wrong is that the three of you decided—wrongly, might I add—that my body needs a break until after the party."

"Isla, you were sore after the last time. Heck, you barely got off the couch the day after. The last thing we want is for you to be sore on the night we've been planning for so long. We want it to be perfect for you."

"I know," I sigh, taking a long drag of my beer. I realize they'll only ever do what's best for me, but right now, riding a hard cock seems like a great way to unwind.

Dylan expertly steers our conversation away from sex for the next couple of hours. I'm pleasantly buzzed by the time the pub regulars arrive, thoroughly enjoying the constant stream of visitors at our table for the next hour. When the band winds up, I pull Dylan to his feet, and we join everyone in the middle of the floor. Every single person is stomping and clapping, waiting for the next brave soul to jump into the circle and dance to the fiddle. After about ten minutes, Dylan tugs on my hand, drawing me into the center of the circle, twirling me around and around. After several minutes, he pulls me to a stop and claps loudly, getting everyone's attention.

"I want to thank everyone for the welcome you gave my brothers and me, even after the fiasco with our precious Isla here. I'm making a promise to all of you tonight that we will do right by her and keep running the pub the way she envisioned." He stops when a cheer goes up, smiling down at me. I swallow hard, my heart beating loudly in my ears. "I also want to let you know that Isla isn't going anywhere. She's opening a brewery at the castle later this year, and her offerings will be on tap here at the pub." Another cheer goes up, the fiddler playing a little ditty to show his excitement. "Lastly–" He turns to me, taking my hands and lowering his voice. "I had planned to do this privately, but it feels right to do it in front of all these people who love you." He clears his throat, those big brown eyes locking with mine. "Isla MacLeod, will you do me the honor of being my wife?"

I cover my mouth as he drops to one knee, fishing a box from his pocket. He flips the top open to reveal a band of alternating baguette diamonds and pieces of polished wood. It's gorgeous and earthy and will look absolutely amazing nestled against the ring Theo gave me.

Before I can say anything, he raises a finger, making me pause. "The diamonds are from a necklace that belonged to your mother. I took the wood from the bar behind you. I wanted to give you a ring that would have sentimental value."

My legs shake, and I drop to my knees in front of him, tears streaming down my face. "Goddammit, Dylan." I sniff, wiping my cheeks with the back of my hand.

"I would have proposed earlier, but it took a while for the jeweler to make it," he says softly, cupping my face and wiping my tears away with his thumbs.

"Answer him!" someone calls out, his voice echoing around the room, others joining in until they're chanting it.

I hold my hand up, waiting until everyone quiets down. "Yes, Dylan. It will be the honor of my lifetime to be your wife." He takes my hand and slips the band on my finger before drawing me into his arms. Cheers and stomping feet shake the floor, and we break away from each other, laughing. Dylan stands, drawing me to my feet. The band starts up again—a slow song this time—and Dylan cradles me in his arms, swaying to the beat.

"I love you more than you'll ever know, Freckles." He presses his lips to mine, kissing me gently. "Thank you for saying yes."

"Thank you for asking," I whisper, grinning up at him.

"Like I ever had a choice," he scoffs, eyes sparkling. "I was a goner the second I laid eyes on you."

62

I bounce on my toes in anticipation as Lorna pulls into the castle
drive. I wrench her car door open before she stops completely,
tackling her in a crushing hug.

"God, it's good to have you back here."

"We just saw each other, Isla," she admonishes, squeezing me
tightly anyway.

"I know, but it's not enough. I miss my big sister."

Lorna rolls her eyes but can't quite hide her smile. "I miss you,
too, wee shrimp."

I groan. "That nickname is one thing I haven't missed."

She laughs, perfectly aware of how much I dislike it. "You *are* the
shortest one in the family, Isla."

"And how is that my fault?" I ask, helping her grab her bags from
the car and following her inside.

"It's not, but it's still fun to tease you about it."

"Who's watching the kids?" I ask as we make our way to the guest
room with the biggest bathroom. It's the same one we've been using
to get ready in since we were kids.

"The neighbors."

My brows pull together in confusion. "Neighbors? Since when do you have neighbors?" The last I knew, Lorna didn't have any neighbors. The only farm close to hers has been abandoned for years.

"They bought the farm next to mine at the start of winter."

"And you know them well enough to leave your kids with them?" I realize my mistake the second the words leave my mouth. She's a fantastic mother, and I have no reason to question her decision. "Don't answer that. Obviously, the answer is yes. Why haven't you mentioned them before?"

Lorna scowls but ignores the foot I just put in my mouth. "I haven't?" she asks, her eyes wide, trying to look innocent.

"You know you haven't," I say, narrowing my eyes.

"You're sure? I could have sworn I did." She drops her gaze, unzipping her garment bag.

"You're such a bad liar. What are you hiding? Tell me about them."

She throws up her hands. "God, you can be so stubborn sometimes! There's nothing to tell. It's a single dad and his two stepsons. Well, kind of his stepsons—they're really close in age, so it's kind of complicated. Their house burned down in a fire in Australia two years ago, killing his wife and their mother. They decided to move somewhere that didn't have wildfires and ended up here."

"Three *guys* are taking care of my niece and nephew right now?" I ask, my eyes nearly bulging out of my head.

"The kids love them, Isla. And I swear they're more careful than I am. I've had to tell them to ease up a bit, or I swear they wouldn't even let them run."

My brain is racing, trying to put all of the pieces together. "Let me get this right. You left your kids with your three guy neighbors who you seem to know very well, yet you've never mentioned them a single time," I say, ticking the facts off on my fingers.

"Whatever you're thinking, you're wrong," Lorna huffs, getting irritated.

"Okay, okay. I'll drop it. But next time I'm out there, I want to meet them."

"Fine."

"Fine."

Lorna's gaze finally lifts enough to notice my necklace, and she comes closer, lifting it gently. "Did Henry give you this?" I nod. "It's beautiful. What about Dylan? Has he proposed yet?"

I hold up my left hand, showing her the band. "He asked Jack for something that was Mother's. The diamonds are hers, and the wood is from the bar at the pub."

"Oh, Isla!" Tears are already running down her face as she throws her arms around me. "I'm so glad they found you and that you didn't give up on each other."

"Me, too," I sigh, squeezing her tightly. My alarm goes off in my pocket, startling both of us. "Two hours until show time. Are you ready for this?" I ask, nerves bubbling in my stomach.

"You have no idea. I haven't let loose in way too long."

An hour and a half later, Lorna and I are staring into the mirror, transfixed. "Damn, you look fucking hot. Too bad your neighbor-dad isn't here to see you."

"It's not–" she snaps her mouth closed, refusing to finish the sentence.

"One of the stepsons then," I amend, watching her closely. Her cheeks flame, but she doesn't say anything. "Both of the stepsons?" I can read her like a book and know I haven't quite hit the nail on the head. "All three?" I whisper. Her head snaps up, her eyebrows forming points over her deep blue eyes.

"Enough, Isla."

Oh shit. "Do they know you have a crush on them?"

"Isla!"

"You need to tell them, Lorna. Life is too short not to embrace a chance like this. And Lord knows, most of us don't get an opportunity to live next to a hot dad and his two hottie stepsons"

"God, you're never going to stop, are you?" she groans, covering her face with her hands.

"Do they know what you went to school for?"

"I swear to god, if you breathe a word when you meet them, I'll cut out your tongue," she threatens, her eyes flashing.

"Jesus Christ!" I take a step back, holding up my hands. She must really like them. Interesting. I bite my lip to hide my grin and turn back to the mirror, inspecting my reflection. My costume is barely more than a scrap of diaphanous fabric. The neckline of the dress attaches to a gold ring around my neck, the fabric draping over my breasts, falling in soft folds to the floor. It covers all the critical parts but leaves an incredible amount of skin bare. My skin has a soft golden sheen thanks to gold-flecked body oil. I meticulously painted over my freckles with gold paint, leaving my hair down, allowing the copper ringlets to fall down my bare back. A large gold headpiece keeps my hair off my face, golden spikes radiating from my head like rays of the sun.

"Do you think I'm missing anything?" I ask, turning to Lorna.

"Not a thing. You look magnificent. What about me?"

Lorna is dressed as Diana, the goddess of the hunt. She looks like a wood nymph with a lust for revenge. Her gown is less revealing, layers of breezy, cool-toned fabrics flowing over her curves like water over rocks. A silver chain is fastened around her waist, revealing the swell of her hips. She has a huge bow slung over her back, fastened by a thin strap across her chest that blends in with the dress. Her hair is piled on top of her head, curls falling down in a way that makes it look like she just ran through a forest. I lined her eyes with a reddish-orange, making the blue of her irises pop, finishing her look with a swipe of brown mascara and lip gloss. She is absolute perfection.

"You look beautiful, Lorna. Now, tell me about your neighbors before we have to go downstairs."

"Isla-"

"Please? At least show me some pictures!"

She rolls her eyes at me, turning back to inspect her reflection.

"Don't even tell me you don't have pictures of them. I know you better than that. Don't make me steal your phone."

She sighs, snatching the phone away from my outstretched hand. She opens her camera roll, scrolling back a couple of pictures. "This is the dad."

I look down at a picture of a man about the same age as Lorna.

He's ruggedly handsome, gray hair just starting to show at his temples. "How old is he?"

"Thirty-five," she says softly, staring at the picture.

"How old are his sons?"

"Stepsons," she corrects. "His wife was older than him. They're twenty-eight."

"They're twins?" I ask when she doesn't give another age.

She nods, holding out the phone to show me a picture of two guys who look like runway models.

"Ohhh, this is trouble," I breathe, my eyes widening more with each picture she scrolls through.

"So much trouble," Lorna whispers, her gaze lingering on a picture of all three of them.

"Good luck with that." I grin at her, excited for this new side quest in her chaotic life. "Are you ready to dance your ass off?" I ask, excitement swooping in.

"I've never been more ready for anything in my life."

"Wait." She looks so beautiful that I can't help myself. I grab the phone from her hand, open the group chat that shows three tiny little guys at the top, snap a picture of her, and send it to them before she can protest. I throw both of our phones on the bed and drag her out the door, heading down to where I can already hear the music thumping away.

63

People have been arriving for about twenty minutes, and the guys should be just pulling in. Charlie and her men decided to forgo the party this year–Charlie wasn't willing to leave the baby with a sitter yet, and the guys weren't willing to leave her. Jack is taking his host duties seriously, though–I can hear him greeting every single guest as they come through the door.

"Let's go!" Lorna begs, dragging me down the hallway. I get more nervous with every step, butterflies going wild in my stomach. Pausing in front of a mirror, I take one last look, breathing deeply through my nose, the diamond around my neck glittering as my lungs expand. I look down at my rings, twisting them around my finger with my thumb, remembering the moments they proposed.

"I can hear them calling for you, Isla." Lorna pushes me ahead of her, prodding me down the hallway, not stopping until we're at the top of the stairs. And there they are. My men. They look up at the same time, and it feels like all the air is sucked out of the room.

Dylan is standing on the left, torso bare except for a gold strap holding a bow to his back. Small wings poke past his shoulders, the feathers matching the white fabric draped around his waist. It stops mid-thigh, leaving a tantalizing amount of skin bare. My gaze slides to Henry, my mouth dropping open even more as I take in his burnished gold body, the gold circlet of leaves around his head, and the large wings protruding from his back. And then there's Theo. His whole body is highlighted in a deep reddish gold, the metallic paint catching the light, making me want to drag my fingers over him so I can see every place I've touched. The fabric draped over one shoulder and around his waist is a deep dove gray, matching the wings peeking from behind him. The feathers are edged in the metallic paint, making them look like they're on fire. I snap my mouth closed as I walk down the stairs, my heart in my throat. Henry is the first to step forward. He takes my hand and spins me in a circle, admiring my costume.

"Ravishing," he whispers, his voice deep and so fucking sexy it has me clamping my thighs together.

"What do you think of our costumes?" Dylan asks, turning my head and kissing me soundly. "We're the three different parts of Eros. I'm love, Henry is longing, and Theo is desire." I swallow hard, my mouth like the desert as I look them up and down, studying their costumes for far too long, wanting nothing more than to undress them right this very second.

I clear my throat. "You all look fucking amazing."

Theo closes in, drawing me into a passionate kiss. "I don't think I could have waited one more day, Isla." He cups my jaw, his fingers gripping me in a desperate hold. "I can't fucking wait until we're married, and I can stop worrying about you realizing what you're getting yourself into."

I pull back, meeting those honey-colored eyes. "I know *exactly* what I'm getting myself into, Theo. I'm not going anywhere. Even when you're an asshole." The corner of his mouth twitches, and he kisses me again, softer this time.

"You're Aphrodite?" Henry asks, more of a statement than a question. I nod, spinning in a circle so they can see the entire costume as well as my ample side-boob. As I turn, I realize Lorna is still behind me, and my cheeks flame.

"Dylan and Theo, this is my sister Lorna," I say, quickly stepping to the side so she can come forward.

She gives them a wide smile. "It's so nice to meet the other half of the relationship." After giving them hugs, she turns to Henry and slaps him on the shoulder like an old friend. "Are you ready to have the night of your life? I know I am." She grabs a flute of champagne from a passing server and downs it, wiggling her fingers at us before disappearing into the crowd.

"You look fucking amazing," Henry breathes, his hand sweeping over my bare back as we head in the same direction as Lorna. "You're sure we can't have sex now?"

I glare at him. "I did *not* spend as much time as I did planning this party only to miss it."

He gives me a guilty grin. "I knew that's what you'd say, but you can't blame me for trying. Especially when you look like *that*."

We're swept into the fray of dancing couples as we enter the ballroom, but we quickly realize there is no way for us to dance without it feeling awkward. We're either bumping into people or getting separated. I give up and guide them out onto the terrace, where we tuck ourselves into a dark corner, the guys crowding around me as we sway to the music. The more glasses of champagne that slide down my throat, the less I'm able to tear my gaze from their incredible bodies. Just when I'm about to screw it all and drag them up to the bedroom, the dinner bell sounds.

I'M PUSHING my food around my plate, my stomach a ball of nerves, when Lorna shows up.

"You guys certainly look like you're having fun," she says, rolling her eyes as she steps up behind me, resting her hands on my shoulders.

"I think it was a bad idea to save what's happening tonight for the party," I whisper.

"Maybe, but it's certainly fun to watch. You could cut the tension with a knife from across the room."

I lick my lips, noticing how all three sets of eyes follow the motion of my tongue.

"Why don't the four of you go take a walk in the garden? Cool off a little. Relax. I'm more than capable of taking care of the host duties. Or if it's something I can't handle, Jack's waiting in the wings to help if needed." She squeezes my shoulders playfully. "Have fun, Isla. *Enjoy yourself.* Tonight is special, make the most of it." She gives my shoulders one last squeeze and then walks over to the next table, greeting family friends she hasn't seen in years.

I take a deep breath, trying to steady my nerves. "Garden walk, anyone?" They jump up as one, Dylan's chair tipping backward and cracking loudly on the hardwood.

"Fuck," he mutters, raking his hand through his hair nervously, looking down at the chair like it appeared out of thin air. Theo picks it up for him, slapping Dylan on the back. "You okay, bro?"

"Not even a little bit."

I giggle and grab Dylan's hand, tugging him toward the bar. We each grab a bottle of wine and then head out toward the garden.

"We're embarking on operation 'Get Buzzed'," I announce, popping the cork off a bottle of prosecco and taking a long swallow before handing it to Dylan. I laugh as he downs nearly half of it, his hands shaking from nerves. Henry opens another bottle and shares it with Theo. I can feel my nerves settling down as we walk, the night air a balm to my soul.

"You guys should have seen the gardens when I was little." I look around wistfully, remembering when I would come out here and get lost among the flowers.

"Who takes care of it now?" Henry asks, picking a spent rose off a bush.

"Jack mostly. But I'm sure he hasn't had as much time since Summer was born."

"What about Lorna? Could she use this space for her flower farm?"

I turn in a circle, looking at the beds through a completely different lens. "I think that could work. I'd have to do some research, but I don't see why not."

"Good," Henry murmurs, studying the garden like he's memorizing it so he can brainstorm ideas later. We wander down another pathway, the silence only broken by the soft music floating through the air.

"Should we try dancing again?" Theo asks, setting down his bottle and holding his hand out to me. I look up at him as I take it, my heart flip-flopping. He pulls me close, cradling me in his arms. Dylan and Henry angle themselves at both of my shoulders, their hands roaming over my stomach and back.

So many hands.

I take a shaky breath as goosebumps race over my skin, close my eyes, and lose myself to them. Theo presses his lips against mine, his tongue delving into my mouth, teasing out a moan. Dylan nibbles at my ear, tugging lightly. Henry drags his lips down my throat and over my collarbone, one hand sliding up my stomach to cup my breast. The four of us freeze when we hear someone call out, a man's faint response, then a woman giggling softly. We jump away from each other as their footsteps come closer.

I press my hand over my heart, breathing raggedly. "I know somewhere we can go. Follow me."

64

I lose my hairpiece as we run through the grass to the standing stones, but I don't stop to retrieve it. Henry presses me against one of the monoliths, pinning me with his hips, his cock hard and ready, digging into my stomach.

"The way your tits look in this dress, Isla...holy fuck." He covers my breasts with his hand, kneading and pinching, my back bending until I feel like I'm going to break in half.

"You need to share," Dylan says roughly as he and Theo approach from both sides.

Henry picks me up and turns us around, putting his back against the rock, never letting up on his exploration of my body. Dylan presses his lips beneath my ear, murmuring something I can't understand before kissing his way to my throat and using his teeth to unhook the clasp at my neck. The fabric catches at my waist, my nipples perking up in the cool air. I whimper as his calloused hands scrape over the tender skin of my breast. He ducks to the side, his breath warm against my skin as he closes his mouth over my nipple. Henry catches me when my knees buckle, pressing his thigh between my legs to help hold me up.

"Should we go back to the bedroom?" Theo asks, taking my hand

and kissing my palm before pressing it over the front of his pants, groaning as I trace the outline of his cock.

I shake my head as I lean over and press my lips to his, rubbing my palm up and down his length. He growls deep in his throat, his hand clenching on my hip, tugging at my dress.

"This needs to come off."

I shimmy a little, and the fabric slips over my hips, leaving me completely naked.

"Fuck," Dylan whispers, swallowing hard, his gaze roving over my body, then rising up to meet mine. "Turn around."

I turn, pressing my back against Henry's chest, and Dylan drops to his knees, shuffling closer until his mouth is in line with my pussy. He peppers kisses over my lower stomach, his hand sliding up my thigh so slowly it makes me want to scream. It seems like ages before his hand brushes between my thighs, his middle finger sliding in the moisture along my slit before slipping inside.

Fuck. I moan, my back arching, need roaring through my veins.

"Henry, hold her leg." Dylan pushes my knee up, and Henry grips the back of my left leg, pulling my thigh to my chest and opening me wide.

Oh god. I drop my head against Henry's shoulder, trying to remember to breathe as Dylan slowly fucks me with his finger, his mouth hovering over my clit.

"Dylan!" I half cry, half beg, delirious with need. He slides his tongue between my lips, teasing my clit. I palm his head and pull him closer, riding his face, taking what I want.

"My dirty girl," Henry murmurs, his lips grazing the top of my ear. "I bet you wish you had a cock inside you right now, don't you?"

I feel him reach between our bodies, stroking his cock before he brings his fingers to my lips. I open for him, licking the precum from his fingers, my eyes rolling back as his taste explodes over my tongue.

His breathing grows ragged as I keep sucking on his fingers like they're his cock. "Fuck, Isla." He fumbles between our bodies, his pants falling at our feet. "Dylan, hold her steady," he says roughly.

Dylan grabs my hands and brings them to his shoulders, holding my gaze as Henry drags his cock down my crack and notches himself at the entrance to my pussy. One hard thrust and I'm seeing stars. My arms tremble as my body tries to keep up. Theo steps in, taking my hands and supporting me as Dylan moves out of his way. Theo pulls one of my legs around his waist, making sure Henry is holding onto me before doing the same with the other leg, his cock pressing into my stomach.

"Better?" he asks, his gaze roaming over my body as I lean back against Henry, his long, slow thrusts burning me alive. Theo reaches between our bodies, pressing the pad of his thumb to my clit. He leans back, hooded eyes watching as Henry fucks me.

"Fuck, Isla," he groans, dragging his thumb down my slit and pressing inside along Henry's shaft. Henry sucks in a sharp breath, his hips hitching. Dylan makes a noise, and I look up to see him slowly jerking the length of his cock, eyes dark with desire.

"Come here." I motion for him to come closer.

"We have all night for that, Isla. Right now, Theo really wants to fuck you. Are you going to let him?"

I look down just as Theo slides the head of his cock over my clit. I buck against him, so fucking close I could cry. He presses his cock down my slit until he's nestled against Henry's shaft. He doesn't move a muscle while he waits for my answer.

"Yes," I sob, arching my back, trying to help him. He holds his cock steady and presses forward, stretching me around his swollen head. "Fuck," I whimper, my entire body trembling as he pushes deeper. The burning fades as I squeeze around them, a fresh flood of desire allowing him to slide the rest of the way in, anchoring me against Henry.

"You're so fucking tight," Henry pants, gripping my hips as he wrestles for control.

"Ready, baby?" Theo asks.

I nod, losing myself as ecstasy drowns my senses. My body travels to another plane as they make love to me, stars sparking behind my eyelids.

"You're doing so good," Dylan says roughly, rolling my nipple between his fingers before sliding his hand between my legs, moving his fingers in a circle over my clit. I swat his other hand away from his cock, taking hold, and then I grab the back of his neck, pulling his mouth to mine.

"You feel so fucking good," Theo groans, punctuating each word with a thrust. I keep my hand pumping on Dylan's cock, my eyes rolling to the back of my head as pleasure swallows me whole. I can feel their cocks sawing back and forth, breaking me apart and rebuilding me again.

"Come for us," Henry whispers in my ear before biting my shoulder and increasing his rhythm. We all start climbing together, our breathing stilted, bodies slick with sweat, limbs shaking as we push each other to the limit. Dylan folds first, hot ropes of cum painting our sides as his hips jerk against my hand. His moan sends the rest of us over the edge. Theo thrusts hard, staying deep inside as Henry fucks me.

"Don't move," Theo murmurs to Henry as he slowly pulls all the way out.

I whimper, squeezing around Henry's shaft. Theo pushes the thick head of his cock against my entrance, pulsing against my G-spot, shoving himself in little by little until Henry and I both give up on not moving. Henry pulls back and slams into me at the same time as Theo bottoms out.

"Yes, Isla." Theo grabs my chin and shoves his tongue into my mouth, possessing me. I bite his lip as I explode around their cocks, coming hard.

"Fuck," Henry mutters, slamming into me once, twice, before his hips stutter against my ass and he empties himself inside of me. Theo growls my name as he comes, gripping my neck and kissing me roughly as he grinds his hips against me, giving me every last drop.

65

Everything is dark by the time we make our way back to the castle. The four of us creep back in, wrapped in our costumes, trying to make the least amount of noise possible.

"Look what the cat dragged in."

Charlie's voice stops us dead in our tracks. She's sitting on one of the couches pushed against the wall, Summer snuggled at her breast.

"Hello," I whisper, waving at her awkwardly, completely failing to keep the grin off my face. Hell, I'll probably be grinning for years after what just happened.

"Did the four of you have fun?" she asks, raising an eyebrow, eyes sparkling.

"Yes, but the real question is, did Lorna have fun? I feel bad for abandoning her," I say, changing the subject.

"Jack told me some she was whisked off her feet by a man dressed in all black." She holds up her hand before I can start worrying. "She shared her location with Jack before she left and said she'd call you first thing in the morning."

My heart rate settles a bit, and I let out a relieved sigh. "Good. I hope she has the time of her life."

"Speaking of the time of her life, shouldn't that be what the three of you are doing?" Charlie asks, looking pointedly at the guys.

"Message received," Henry says, picking me up and throwing me over his shoulder before jogging from the room.

"Put me down!" I shriek, banging my hand against his back. The pounding quickly turns into me marveling at this man's ungodly amounts of muscle.

"If you keep stroking me like that, I'm going to fuck you right here in the hallway," he growls, slapping my ass.

"Again, Daddy," I tease. He stops dead in his tracks, his body practically vibrating.

"We'll just go ahead and start the bath," Theo says, dragging Dylan away, looking back at me with a smirk.

"When you say things like that–" Henry says roughly, the muscle in his jaw jumping as he struggles for control.

"What, Henry?" I ask, trying to get out of his grip, but he only tightens his hold on me.

"You don't understand," he growls, reaching up to massage my ass cheek, then spanking me again before lowering my feet to the floor, the remnants of my costume falling to the hardwood. He turns me around, his hand circling the base of my neck. I look up, meeting his gaze in the window reflection, my heart racing.

"I will never get enough," he says roughly, leaning over me, and placing my hands on the window ledge. "Cross your legs," he demands, tapping my heel with his foot. He fumbles with his costume, then wraps his hand around his cock, sliding it through the mixture of desire and cum between my legs, fucking my thighs. "My appetite for you is insatiable, Isla MacLeod. Every time you touch me, it makes my cock hard. So, when you say things like that, you better fucking mean it." He pulls back and plows into my cunt, making my pussy spasm. "Are two cocks not enough, my dirty little red-haired devil? Do you need two in your pussy and one in your ass?"

"Fuck, Henry," I moan. His words. His cock. God. I'm trying to hold it together, but he's making it nearly impossible.

"Answer me," he growls, wrapping his hand in my hair and

pulling me up, his hand going back to my throat as he punishes me with his thrusts.

"Yes," I cry.

"Good, let's find the others and tell them what you want."

He pulls out, leaving me empty and needy. My legs nearly give out as he releases me, but he scoops me into his arms before I can stumble. He doesn't put me down until we reach the bathroom, carefully testing the bathwater before sliding me in. He kisses my forehead and tells me to relax before leaving the room. Dylan appears soon after, skin glowing, brown eyes luminous.

"Can I join you?" he asks softly, crouching next to the tub and sweeping my hair behind my ear.

"Of course," I murmur, kissing him softly before scooting forward to make room for him. Once he's settled behind me, I lean back, snuggling into his chest.

"You were amazing," he whispers, strong fingers digging into my shoulders.

"I didn't know it would be like that," I confess.

"Like what?"

"It was like an out-of-body experience. So many hands, so many feelings, with no beginning and no end. It was incredible."

"It'll get even better the longer we're together, Freckles. Just wait."

I drop my head onto his shoulder, close my eyes, and try to wrap my head around how the sex could possibly get better.

"Let's get you washed up so we can go cuddle in bed," he murmurs against my ear, squirting some body wash into his hands. He washes my limbs one at a time, then my stomach, saving my breasts for last. I try to play it cool, but my body betrays me, my back arching as he slides his palms over me, just shy of my nipples. His raspy chuckle has goosebumps streaking over my skin as the embers of need low in my belly roar back to life.

"I wish you could have seen the moment you came, Freckles. The sounds you made. Fuck. I'm going to remember it forever."

His words stoke the flames of my desire even higher. I lift my hips as he slides his hand down my stomach, eager for his touch. He stops just shy of the apex of my thighs, my groan of frustration doing nothing but making him laugh.

"Please, Dylan," I beg.

"Such a needy girl," he purrs, teasing me with the lightest of touches, his fingertip sliding along my slit.

"Time to eat," Theo says, poking his head in the bathroom, his eyes darkening when he sees Dylan's hand between my legs. He smirks as he helps me from the tub, wrapping me in a fluffy towel before carrying me to the bedroom. They must have raided the leftovers from the party, judging by the huge charcuterie board sitting at the foot of the bed. Henry is picking through it, putting choice pieces on a plate.

"How are you feeling, Red?" Henry asks, his gaze sliding over my body as Theo sets me on the bed.

"I feel good. Really good."

"Here." He shoves the plate into my hands. "I picked out all the best bits. You need to eat."

"Thank you," I whisper. Normally I would have told him he didn't need to do that, but I'm starving. I eat one of the bites he assembled– a tiny cracker with cheese and some sort of jam. I moan as the flavors explode in my mouth.

"Didn't realize how hungry a good fucking could make you, huh?" Henry asks, a smile pulling at the corners of his mouth. I make a face at him and then proceed to devour the entire plate of food.

"A little something to wash it down?" Theo hands me a bottle of water, watching to make sure I take several large swallows while Henry clears the food from the end of the bed.

"Good girl," Dylan murmurs, climbing onto the bed next to me, taking the water bottle from my hand and giving it to Theo. Before I can blink, his hands are cupping my face, pulling me roughly to him, his mouth crashing against mine. He tastes like champagne and sex, my new favorite combination. I tremble as his fingertips trace a line over my ribs, skimming over the dip of my waist, coming to rest low on my hip. He sinks onto the mattress, and I follow him down, both of us lying on our sides facing each other. Our legs tangle as we kiss, the position allowing his cock to align perfectly between my legs. I roll my hips, gasping as the head of his cock brushes my swollen clit.

"Will you make that noise for me, too, Sunflower?" Theo asks, lying down behind me, propping himself up so he can lean over me. He turns my chin toward him and captures my lips in a searing kiss.

66

I feel like I can't breathe with Theo plastered to my back and Dylan to my front. Frissons of pleasure sizzle over my skin, colliding and exploding as they run their hands over my body, squeezing, kneading, pulling, caressing.

Theo grips my hip, pulling me flush with his body, his cock digging into my ass. I arch against him, extending my head back as a silent invitation to kiss my neck. The warmth of his tongue flicks over my pulse before dragging down to my collarbone, slowly stoking the flames beneath my skin. Dylan captures my face between his hands, his fingers strong and firm. The heat in his gaze makes my heart flip-flop, a fresh wave of desire gushing from between my legs. He groans as he captures my lower lip between his teeth, sucking and biting before pushing his tongue into my mouth. I cling to him, angling my head to deepen the kiss. He slides his hand between our bodies, positioning his cock between my legs, holding it in place as he drags the head of his cock back and forth over my clit.

"Please, Dylan," I beg, hitching my leg over his hip, and opening myself up to him. He groans, pushing his hips forward until he's nudging at my entrance, and then with one smooth motion, he buries himself deep. The walls of my pussy convulse around him as I adjust to his size, pleasure smothering my senses. I vaguely register hearing the pump of the lube bottle, and then Theo is sliding his cock along my crack, coating me with lube before pressing himself against my ass. I can feel his body tense behind me, a live wire vibrating with sexual energy.

"Deep breath," he murmurs, nibbling at my ear. I breathe in deep, focusing on how good Dylan's cock feels as he slowly slides in and out of me.

"Good girl. Now relax."

I release the hold on my muscles one by one until I'm loose and pliant in their arms. His growl sends a thrill down my spine as I push my ass back, the head of his cock slowly pinning me in place.

"Fuck, Isla," he breathes, going still. "You feel so fucking good."

I push back more until my ass swallows the head of his cock, then surge forward, sawing my hips back and forth on their cocks. The end of the bed dips, and I look up into Henry's face, his eyes dark with need. He straddles mine and Dylan's legs, pushing my left leg to my chest, making room for his hips.

"You ready to come so hard you forget your name, Red?" he growls, coating his cock in the moisture between my thighs. I whimper as he notches himself along Dylan's shaft. He presses his hips forward, slowly working his way in.

I forget how to exist as my world contracts to one tiny pinprick where there's only room for the ecstasy rippling through my body. I gasp as he stretches me, the feeling of fullness like nothing I've experienced before.

"The head is almost in," he murmurs.

"Just the head?" I shift my body, suddenly unsure if I can take all of him. His body trembles as he loses his grip on control, and he sinks down, impaling me.

Fuck.

FUCK.

I can't move. Can't breathe. Can't even think. So fucking full. I sob his name, raking my nails over his neck, pulling him down as I stretch up to meet his lips.

"Fucking hell," Dylan rasps, his eyes rolling back as Henry bottoms out, stretching me to the max. Henry's hips freeze, allowing us to get used to the fullness as he ravages my mouth, his tongue pushing past my lips with a savage need, drawing me in for a kiss that makes my toes curl. As if some unspoken current runs between them, they all begin moving at once, six hands and three cocks doing their best to absolutely wreck me. By the time I manage to focus on one feeling, another comes along to override it, dragging me higher and higher as they fuck me senseless. I go limp as a noodle, losing all sense of time and space, making it impossible to do anything but ride the tide as the tsunami builds. As one, they all thrust inside me, their cocks pulsing with need, their grasp on control slipping through their fingers like sand. I squeeze around them, stars blooming behind my eyelids as I feel every ridge, every vein, as they grow impossibly harder. They pull out, and thrust again, filling me until I'm sobbing their names. Henry stops moving, allowing Dylan to pull out halfway, so he can pulse the head of his cock over my G-spot while Theo keeps up his rhythm behind me. Henry shifts, using one hand to lift my nipple to his mouth, sucking hard, urging me closer.

"Fuckkk," I groan, arching for him, the push and pull of three cocks and one mouth becoming too much for my body to contend with. Theo snakes a hand around my hip, delving between my legs, giving me exactly what they all know I need.

"Come for us, beautiful," he whispers, his breath hitching as I squeeze around him.

I sob his name as he circles my clit, my world splintering as all three thrust at once, pushing deep, nearly splitting me apart as ecstasy flays me alive. I scream, no longer capable of words, my body convulsing between them, as they lose themselves in my flesh.

"Holy fuck," Henry groans, his hips the first to stutter, starting an avalanche of erotic bliss. We're a gyrating mass of limbs and torsos, cocks pumping, pussy squeezing, wringing every possible drop of pleasure from each other's bodies as the of three of them come inside me together for the first time.

"Holy fucking god," Dylan groans, kissing me gently, his cock the first to slip out.

"I don't know what I was expecting, but it wasn't fucking that," Theo pants, slowly pulling his hips away, careful not to hurt me as he pulls out.

Henry rolls me onto my back, lifting one of my ankles over his shoulder as he thrusts into me, his cock still hard as a rock.

"Henry," I groan, rolling my hips. I try to act like I don't want what he's giving me, but I fail completely. "How?" I ask instead, giving in, lifting my hips to meet his thrusts.

"I'll always be hard for you, Isla. I'm always going to want one more fuck. One more chance to push our cum back inside you where it belongs. You have no idea how much it turns me the fuck on to fill you until you're dripping and then watch you push it out so I can stuff it back in." He rams into me, his neck cording as he struggles for control. "Tell me you don't like it, and I'll never do it again."

How can I say no when it's one of the most erotic things I've ever experienced? Instead, I pull his face down to mine, fucking his mouth with my tongue as my body matches his rhythm. Both of us descend into madness together, melting into each other as we coax out one more orgasm. Henry falls on top of me, both of us struggling to draw in breath, our bodies wrung out in the best way possible.

"Fucker always has to have the last word, doesn't he?" Theo gripes, pushing Henry off me. Henry smacks him playfully, moving to the side to let Theo and Dylan take his place. They scoop me into their arms, cherishing the post-coitus glow, murmuring sweet nothings in my ear.

If I had known this was what it would be like, I would never have questioned them. I would have dove head-first into this relationship and never looked back. I would have married them the day they showed up on my doorstep. This feeling of bliss is unlike anything I've ever known, a love I never thought I'd find. Who knew all it would take was getting my life ripped out from under me and starting over again?

67

SEPTEMBER

After focusing on the brewery and putting off wedding planning for far too long, the guys and I have a three-day weekend planned with the goal of picking out a venue. Today, we're taking a ride on the Jacobite train to see if there's any way it could possibly work for the ceremony and reception. Tomorrow, we're going to the top of Ben Nevis, and on the third day, we'll be touring the Glenlee, a decommissioned century-old merchant ship that was turned into a wedding venue. Jack and Charlie had questioned me relentlessly about why I didn't want to get married at the castle, but their wedding was so special, and I don't want to trample all over that memory.

HENRY and I are sitting in the back of Cam's old Defender, Theo is driving, and Dylan is working away on his laptop in the passenger seat, music blasting out of the open windows, on our way to Fort William Station.

"If I had known what this was going to be like back here, I would have suggested renting a car," Henry grumbles, his knuckles white on the back of our tiny bench seat.

"That would have been an excellent idea," I admit. I've never ridden in the back and didn't realize quite how bumpy it would be. "Do you need a little distraction?"

I bat my eyelashes at him, placing my hand obscenely high on his thigh, using it to boost myself up so I can reach his mouth. He grunts as my lips crash into his, wrapping his hand around the back of my neck and pulling me closer.

"Better?" I ask, tugging playfully on his lip with my teeth.

"Not yet." He pulls off his shirt and throws it to the opposite seat before wrapping his arm around my waist and pulling me into his lap, my ass landing on top of a very solid erection.

"Jesus Christ," I whisper, leaning back against his chest and resting my head on his shoulder. He slides his free hand up my stomach and between my breasts, circling the base of my throat. He tightens his arm around my waist, pulling me down as he presses his hips up, grinding his cock against me.

"Henry," I moan, half in protest, half begging him not to stop.

"You know they won't care," he says, his lips against my ear.

"Yeah, but *I'll* care when your cum is sliding down my thighs as we're boarding the train."

"Fuck, Isla." My words have the opposite effect I intended. He rucks up the front of my dress and slips his fingers inside my underwear, sliding one thick, callused finger along my slit. "I think you'd be dripping anyway, sweetheart," he rasps, pushing his middle finger inside me. I arch against him, grinding on the heel of his palm as he fucks me with his finger. God. "You're so goddamned pretty when you fall apart for me," he murmurs, pulling his finger out, circling my clit, then pushing it back in to tease my G-spot. He does this over and over again until I'm bucking against his hand, desperate to come. We go over a particularly big bump, and his finger jams deep. Blinding pleasure rocks through my body, followed quickly by the urge to pee. Fuck.

"Liked that, did you?" he chuckles, his breath against my ear, sending goosebumps careening over my skin. He repeats the movement, pressing against my G-spot as he drags the pad of his finger back and forth.

"Henry, you need to stop. I'll make a mess," I pant.

"Then I'll clean it up. I'll lick it off the goddamned floor if I have to."

I tremble in his arms as waves of ecstasy crash over me.

"Fuck me," he groans. "You're irresistible." He reaches between our bodies, unbuttons his pants, and pulls out his cock. Tugging my panties to the side, he notches himself at my entrance and slowly slides in, keeping his finger pressed to my G-spot. My body goes taut, blinding pleasure pulsing through my system. He keeps his finger moving as he fucks me, the pressure growing to an almost unbearable point.

"Why the fuck does it smell like sex in here?" Theo asks, jerking the car to the side of the road and twisting in his seat to look at us.

"Come for me," Henry whispers, his breath hot against my ear. I clench around him, gasping as he uses his other hand to massage my clit, his thrusts slowing.

"Isla, look at me." Theo's demand has my gaze snapping to his as my world explodes, those rich chocolate eyes my only tether to reality. I come hard, desire dripping from between Henry's fingers as he coaxes me through my orgasm. Dylan turns to watch, his teeth lodging in his lower lip, pupils blowing wide.

Henry pulls my knees wide, hooking my legs around his, angling himself toward the front of the car. "Show them how pretty your pussy is when you're dripping for me." He moves his hands to my hips, holding me still as he fucks me hard. "Give me one more, Isla. Please."

"I can't," I pant, my eyes rolling back as aftershocks rock through me. "What about them?"

"They'll get a turn later. Another," he demands, sliding his fingers up and down my slit as he fucks me.

"Henry–"

I clamp my mouth closed as he positions his second and fourth fingers on either side of my clit, his middle finger sliding back and forth over that sensitive bundle of nerves. I sob his name, anchoring my hands on his thighs to steady myself, my hips meeting every thrust. The tide starts rising, his punishing pace forcing me higher and higher, tears streaming down my face as he pushes my body to its limits.

"Fuck this, I want you looking at me," he grinds out, lifting me off his cock like I weigh nothing, turning me around, and impaling me. One hand dives between my legs, and the other grips my chin in a punishing hold, keeping me still.

"I need to see your face when you come," he says softly, holding my gaze as I move my hips. "That's it, ride me hard, Isla." I grip his shoulders, pressing my knees into the bench seat, bouncing up and down on his cock. I squeeze around his shaft, gripping him with everything I have. He grunts, pressing his fingers harder against my clit, encouraging me to grind against them, his dark blue gaze entangled with mine. I'm close, but it's Henry's whimper that sends me careening over the edge. He grips my ass, holding me still as he roars, emptying himself deep inside me as we come together. I collapse against him, my entire body trembling.

"Fuck, Isla." Henry cups my face, leaning back to look at me. He wipes under my eyes with shaking hands, his cock still pulsing inside me, tiny shocks of pleasure shooting up my spine. He gently lifts me off him, setting me on my feet. "Give me your underwear."

"What? Why?"

"They're wrecked anyway, Isla." He holds out his hand, waiting.

I stand and shimmy out of them, placing them in his palm. He grips my hip and pulls me between his legs, gently wiping his cum from my pussy and thighs. I bite my lip as he wraps the scrap of fabric around his cock, gripping his shaft and jerking it up and down. I've never seen anything quite like it, his abs contracting, his hips thrusting up into his hand, like he can't help but chase the pleasure.

"Stop showing off," Theo grumbles, rolling his eyes. He motions for me to sit before turning around and pulling onto the road.

"Never stop showing off," I murmur, my gaze glued to his crotch as he tucks his cock back inside and zips up his pants. "What are you going to do with them?" I ask as he stuffs my underwear in his pocket.

"Use them to jerk off," he says honestly, a wicked grin on his face.

"One of these days, I want to find out how many times you can come before your dick goes limp."

"Why not today?"

"How will your brothers feel about that?" I ask, catching Theo's eye in the rearview mirror.

"They can have their fun first. We're booked into a two-bedroom suite tonight. It'll be perfect."

"Did you guys hear that? Any complaints?" I ask.

"No, but you really have no idea what you're getting yourself into. You won't be able to walk tomorrow," Dylan says, the keyboard keys still clacking away.

"It's a good thing I have three strong guys to carry me around, then, isn't it?"

68

By the time we get to the Fort William train station, my thighs are a sticky mess, but I weirdly like it. There's something naughty about not wearing panties and having cum drip down my thighs while I'm standing in line. God, that's so fucked up.

The train pulls in right on time, a massive black and red beast billowing smoke from its maw. It's gorgeous. Dylan checks his confirmation email and leads the way onto the train. After a quick stop in the bathroom to clean myself up, he ushers us into our own little compartment. There are six seats with a small table between them and a wooden door with glass windows that can be closed for some semblance of privacy. The seats are upholstered in a rich brocade, with wood and gold accents everywhere you look. It feels like we're on our way to wizarding school. I love it.

"I didn't realize we'd have our own little spot!" I exclaim, sliding in next to the window.

"It was the same price as four seats in the first-class car, so I figured some privacy would be nice since we'll be stuck here for six hours," Dylan explains, smiling in response to my excitement.

"Does anyone else think this will be too small for the wedding?" I ask, drumming my fingers on the table. I don't want to feel cramped; I want everyone to be able to dance and have fun.

"There's no need to make a decision now," Theo says, grabbing my hand from across the table. "Let's just relax and enjoy the time away from our responsibilities."

"Oh, I have been enjoying myself," I assure him, biting my lip as I think of how Henry's cock felt pounding into me earlier.

"Stop right this second," Theo growls, his pupils blowing wide.

"Stop what?"

"Thinking about fucking us."

"I–"

"Don't lie, Sunflower," he growls, cutting me off.

I snap my mouth closed, trying not to laugh. "It's not like we could do anything in here, anyway," I say, gesturing to our cramped quarters.

"Is that a challenge?" he asks, his eyes flashing.

"No!"

"You're sure?" Dylan asks, grabbing my hand and pressing it to his crotch. He's hard as a rock. I tug up his shirt, and sure enough, the head of his cock is peeking out of his waistband.

"Do you need a little help?" I ask, cocking an eyebrow, my mouth already watering. I have no restraint when it comes to them.

He shakes his head. "Theo first."

I look over at Theo, raising my eyebrows in question. He crooks his finger, beckoning me, a challenge in his eyes. As I slide under the table, the train starts moving, jostling me against the wall. I grab on to Theo's leg and nearly faint when I see the way his hand is wrapped around his cock, tugging on it. I cover his hand with mine, sliding it up and down his shaft as I get comfortable between his knees. I swipe the tip of my tongue along his slit, lapping up the drop of precum. His hips push forward involuntarily, sinking the head of his cock past my lips. He cups the back of my head, holding me still as he fucks my mouth, his movements uncoordinated and jerky.

"Fuck, Isla. Watching you in the car absolutely undid me," he groans as he thrusts into my mouth. "I swear if you had just touched my cock, I would have come in my pants."

"You should have told me; I would have liked to see that," I mumble around him, taking him deep, hollowing my cheeks as I pull back. His hips flex, trying to keep his cock in my mouth, but I let him pop out, worshipping his swollen head before taking him deep again. I remember a time when I hated giving head, but there's something about the three of them that makes me crave it.

"Jesus fucking Christ," he pants, his fingers digging into my scalp as his restraint slips. I reach inside his pants, palming his balls, tugging on them before following the ridge of flesh up the back until I get to his taint. I press firmly as I take him into the back of my throat, swallowing around his thick shaft.

"Fuck," he bites out, his entire body stiffening. I hum around him, milking his cock with my mouth. I press harder and he suddenly comes to life, his hips bucking against me, his hand tightening in my hair as his cock pulses in my mouth, shooting cum down my throat. I swallow greedily, not letting up on the suction until he's spent. I pull away slowly, cleaning him with my tongue as I go.

"My turn," Dylan grinds out, a dangerous edge to his voice. He helps me from under the table and pulls me into his lap. His cock impales me without warning, shocking my system, sending waves of pleasure rocking through me. Henry sits down next to us, blocking the view of anyone who might pass by outside our compartment.

"I wish I could chase you, Isla. I would catch you and fuck you against the window for the world to see," Dylan whispers in my ear.

"I can try to get away from you in here." When he doesn't say anything, I launch myself across the table before he has time to act. He stands, latching onto the back of my neck with one hand and my thigh with the other, holding me down and slamming into my pussy.

"Fucking hell, Dylan," Theo mutters, both he and Henry standing to shield us from anyone that may happen to walk by. I grip the opposite edge of the table, giving me the leverage I need to keep myself from slipping off the other side. He slides both hands underneath me, one cupping my breast and the other cupping my pussy, holding me tight against his body as he fucks me senseless. Between the thrill of his demeanor and the threat of getting caught, I come almost immediately, my pussy convulsing around his cock, coaxing him to orgasm. He jerks me back against him and thrusts hard, the head of his cock pulsing deep inside me as he spills his seed.

"I swear you have a magic cunt," he pants, his lips moving against my ear as he slowly thrusts back and forth, wringing every drop of pleasure he can from our bodies.

"That's what they all say," I quip, wincing when I realize what came out of my mouth while his cock is still in me. Dylan growls, pulling out and flipping me over before ramming back in.

"Not any fucking more, they don't." He cups the back of my head in his palm and crushes his lips against mine in a rough, punishing, absolutely perfect kiss.

"Someone is coming!" Henry hisses, his eyes wide. He pulls my underwear from his pocket and tosses it to me. I wiggle them on, smooth my dress, and sit back down. Dylan is buttoning his pants when we hear a knock on the door. A middle-aged woman opens the door wide, smiling politely at us.

"Ms. MacLeod?"

"Yes?" I smile, trying to look innocent as I attempt to smooth my hair.

"If you'd like a tour of the first-class car and the dining carriage, now would be the best time."

"Yes, that would be nice, thank you." I smile at her, hoping to God it doesn't smell like sex in here.

She looks at the guys like she's trying to solve a puzzle. "Your brothers can stay if you'd like; this will only take a few minutes."

"They're brothers, but not *my* brothers," I correct. "They're part of the decision, so I'll need them to take the tour, as well."

She nods primly and motions for us to follow her, giving us a very thorough tour of the different train cars and facilities. The tour only takes about ten minutes, and we make a quick pit-stop in the dining car to bring some snacks back to our compartment.

"It's too cramped," I say rather bluntly once we're alone, slathering my scone with clotted cream and jam before taking a giant bite.

Theo nods in agreement. "It would be impossible to dance, and we'd be limited in how many people we could invite.'

"It's unique. Gorgeous, honestly, but we'd be giving up too much," Henry says, sipping at his tea, the cup tiny in his giant hand.

"What do you think, Dylan?" I ask.

He doesn't answer until he's finished typing our comments into his notes app. "Same. I love the idea of it, but I just don't think it will work for us."

I duck my head, hiding my smile, loving the juxtaposition of his nerdy side coming out to play right after he bent me over the table and absolutely railed me.

"Thank god we all agree," I sigh, snuggling into his arms as we watch the fall colors race by.

69

When the guys told me we had a two-bedroom suite for tonight, they failed to mention that it was in the beautiful Ivernochy Castle Hotel. After dropping off our bags, we order four picnic meals from the hotel restaurant and take them to the banks of the loch to enjoy the sunset while we eat.

"I've been thinking," Henry says, holding a grape up to my mouth. "I think we need to save our little challenge until we get back home–I still want you to be able to walk tomorrow."

I bite the grape in half, a wicked grin pulling at my lips. "I've been thinking about it too, and since I'm already a little sore, it should just be you coming. Tonight."

He swallows hard. "Just me?"

I shrug. "That was the point, right? See how many times you can come before your dick goes limp?"

"Yeah, but when I said it, I thought I'd be inside you, Red," he protests, tucking a strand of hair behind my ear.

"You will be. Inside my hand, inside my mouth..."

"Fuck me," he breathes, a blush creeping into his cheeks. "What are you going to do? Just lay me out on the bed and have your way with me?"

"Precisely."

"You two have fun. Dylan and I are saving ourselves for the gondola tomorrow," Theo says, handing me a piece of bread layered with cheese and jam.

"Are you serious?" I ask, blanching.

"Maybe not with that reaction," Theo says, raising his eyebrows. "If you're uncomfortable with it, then I'm sure we can manage to behave ourselves."

"We'll see what it's like tomorrow," I mutter, my heart racing. The thought of hanging high up in the air, swinging around in the wind, doesn't seem romantic. If I'm being honest, it makes me sick just thinking about it.

"Have you started planning the grand opening of the brewery yet?" Dylan asks, changing the subject. He's lying back on the grass with one arm tucked beneath his head, completely relaxed.

"I've been more concerned about brewing the first beers I'll be offering than planning a grand opening."

"When do you think you'll have them ready?" he asks, turning toward me, blocking the sun with his hand to keep it out of his eyes.

"I'm not sure. This is my first batch, and I want to make sure everything is perfect before I open."

"Just let us know when you're ready and we'll take care of everything else."

"You'd do that?" I ask, my voice cracking. I've tried not to show it, but getting the brewery up and running has been incredibly stressful. There are so many small tasks that still need to be finished. The guys have been great about helping, but I'm the only one who can make the final decisions, and it has definitely started wearing on me.

"Of course we'd do that," Theo says, exasperated.

I sink into the grass, months of stress and uncertainty melting away. "Thank you guys. So fucking much. I don't know what I'd do without you."

"You'd continue being a fucking badass, that's what," Theo says, leaning back on his elbows. Henry maneuvers himself to rest his head on my stomach, all of us gazing up at the color-changing sky.

"Can you believe how much has changed in a matter of months?" I ask them softly, blinking back tears, trying not to ruin the peacefulness surrounding us by crying.

"I think I'm speaking for all of us when I say it's been the best year of our lives, Isla. I'm not sure anything could top it," Henry says, reaching up to take my hand and bring it to his lips.

I NEVER DREAMED that I could have this. That I deserved it. Never in a million years could I have imagined I would be lying in the shadow of Ben Nevis with my three lovers, scouting out wedding locations. We lie there here in silence, watching the pinks and purples slowly leach from the sky. I shiver in the chilly air, and Henry immediately jumps to his feet, scooping me into his arms. I snuggle into his warmth as we walk back toward the hotel, relishing in how he makes me feel so small and cared for. Like I'm the treasure he's been searching for his entire life.

Safely ensconced back in our suite, Dylan and Theo kiss me goodnight, leaving Henry and me in our own bedroom.

"We can just go to sleep, Isla. I know it's been a long day," Henry says, pulling the sheets down and fluffing the pillows.

"Do *you* just want to go to sleep?" I ask, craning my neck to look up at him.

"You know the answer to that, but it's not just about me."

I plant my palm on his chest, pushing him down on the bed. He goes down easy, his gaze never leaving mine. I unbuckle his belt and pull it from his pants, wrap it around his wrists, and bring them up the headboard to secure them.

"Fuck, Isla." He tilts his head back, watching me as I work, the long column of his throat bare and irresistible. I straddle his waist and run my tongue up the side of his neck, peppering kisses along his jawline.

"You're so good-looking it hurts," I murmur, dragging my tongue over his collarbone, dipping into the hollow at the base of his throat.

He swallows hard, his hips already pushing off the bed, desperately seeking friction.

"It's absolute torture not to be able to touch you," he rasps, struggling to free his wrists.

"Let me enjoy your body, Henry. You have no idea how much pleasure it gives me to pleasure you." He groans, his breath hitching as I start to unbutton his shirt.

I drag my nails down his stomach, his muscles jumping under my touch. God, he's so damn pretty. I move down, straddling his thighs, taking a strangled breath before unbuttoning his pants and pulling down his zipper. He lifts his hips, allowing me to pull the fabric down, revealing skin tight black boxer briefs. Fuck. I trace the waistband with my fingertip, my pulse ratcheting up when he sucks in a breath through his teeth.

"You have no idea what I would do if I could touch you right now," he groans, lines bracketing his mouth as he struggles for control.

"Tell me." I slip my fingers beneath his waistband, pulling it down one millimeter at a time.

"I would pin your wrists above your head and lick my way down your body."

"Mmmhmm." I groan as I reveal the swollen head of his cock slick with precum. The muscles between my legs spasm, desperate for him.

"Then I would push your knees to your ears and feast until you're screaming."

I grip his thick shaft, and he rewards me with a quick intake of breath, his hips pressing up into my hand.

"Do you like that?" I breathe, watching as I work my hand over him, more precum leaking from his tip until it's dripping down his shaft, a tiny waterfall of pure, unadulterated lust. I lick him clean, swirling my tongue over his head, memorizing his taste and the velvety feel of his cock under my tongue.

"Jesus Christ, Isla," he hisses, his cock swelling impossibly larger, his body trembling as he wrestles for control.

"Do you think I can get you there by just licking?" I slide my tongue from the base of his cock to his frenulum, flicking my tongue back and forth.

"Isla, please," he pants, his neck cording as his body goes taut. I sweep my tongue around his head, then back down, sucking on his balls before making my way back up again.

"For fuck's sake, Isla."

"I want to see, Henry." Those words are all it takes for him to slip. He groans, his balls pulling up to his body. I watch as his cock pulses, cum shooting from the tip to snake over his stomach. God, that's fucking hot. I take him in my mouth, sinking down, holding still as he fucks the back of my throat, his grunts working up a frenzy between my legs. I need him. In me. On me. All over me. The second his hips stop stuttering, I sit up and unbuckle the belt, stripping my clothes as fast I can, desperate for him. He reads me like a book, his moan of mindless need matching mine. I turn away from him, getting on my hands and knees, then drop my chest and head to the bed, waiting for him to plow into me.

"Fuck, Isla. You so pretty when you're needy." He licks me from clit to ass, palming my cheeks and spreading me wide. He growls in appreciation, and my body responds with a flood of desire down my thighs. "Your pussy is crying for me." He licks them clean, kissing and biting as I push back on his face.

"Tell me what you want, Isla."

"I need your cock inside me, Henry. Please."

He lines his cock up with my entrance and slams inside, bottoming out before pulling out and doing it again. He sets a punishing pace, ramming into me, giving me exactly what I need. Wrapping my hair around his fist, he pulls me upright until my back is against his chest, commanding me to look into the mirror on the wall. He moves his hand from my hair to my neck, sliding his other one down my stomach and between my legs, circling my clit, holding me still as he fucks me, his cock hitting my G-spot with every thrust.

"Look at me," he commands, his grip on my neck tightening. My eyes meet his in the mirror as I surrender to him, feeling completely safe in his capable hands. I hold his gaze, not doing anything but focusing on how he's making me feel and the rising wave of pleasure that's about to wipe us both out.

"Come with me, Henry," I whisper.

"Not yet," he rasps, his breathing ragged. He presses me down on the bed, hiking my hips up with both hands, then slides his thumb down my crack, circling my ass hole.

"Henry," I moan, pushing up into his hands, encouraging him.

"You have such a pretty ass," he breathes, pressing his thumb inside me. I rock against him, practically delirious with the need to come. He bends down, burying his face between my cheeks, tongue fucking me until I'm sobbing into the mattress. "Let me fuck your ass, Isla. Please. I don't know if I can last another day without knowing what you feel like."

"I don't care what you do, Henry. I just want to come." I cry out in protest as he climbs off the bed, but he's back in twenty seconds, setting a dildo and a vibrator on the bed. He folds a pillow and positions it under my hips, then pulls my legs straight. Straddling my thighs, he slowly pushes the dildo into my pussy, turning it on once it's all the way inside me.

Holy fuck.

He grabs the second toy and turns it on, placing it in my hand.

"Hold this between your legs, sweetheart."

I lift my hips and sneak my hands between my legs, pressing the vibrator against my clit.

"Oh god," I pant, my hips thrusting against it, the tide rising by the second. Henry crosses my legs, ensuring the dildo stays put, and then squirts lube onto my ass, spreading it before fucking my ass with one finger, then two, making sure I'm ready. "I'm close, Henry," I whisper, my words muffled in the sheets, my entire body tensing, trying not to come before he's inside me.

He inches forward until his thighs are hitting my ass and then leans over me, notching his swollen head. He pauses there, slowly stretching me wide enough to take him. Once the head of his cock pops past the tight ring of muscle, he sinks into me with a groan.

"This is going to wreck me for life," he moans. If only he knew that there are fireworks exploding behind my eyelids, pleasure pulsing through every single cell in my body, overloading it until I can barely breathe, barely think, can't do anything but push back and take every single millimeter of his cock inside me. I squeeze around him as he pulls back, trying to keep him in.

"Oh fuck, Isla. I wanted to make this last, but the way your ass is strangling my cock is going to absolutely end me." He slams back in, rutting into me, both of us beyond words as we're swept into a tsunami of ecstasy neither one of us can comprehend. I scream his name as I come, and he shouts mine, his voice cracking as he empties into me.

70

enry must have carried me to the other bedroom at some point during the night because I wake up sandwiched between Dylan and Theo. The weak light of early autumn mornings bathes us in a golden glow, dust motes dancing in the air over the bed. I stretch, my muscles deliciously sore from yesterday.

"How are you feeling, Sunflower?" Theo murmurs, his hand stretching over my stomach and pulling me flush against his body.

"Wonderful."

"You're not sore from yesterday?" he asks, cupping one of my breasts and snuggling his face into the crook of my neck.

"I don't think so."

"Good." He smooths my hair back from my face, kissing my cheeks. "Do you think we'll still be doing this in forty years?"

"Doing what?" I ask, my gaze tracing Dylan's sleeping face.

"Finding risky places to have sex."

"I hope so," I laugh.

"Maybe that's the way we'll go out," Dylan mumbles, opening those big brown eyes and blinking at me like an owl.

"Morning," I whisper, leaning forward to kiss him. He cups my head, pulling me closer.

"Finally!" Henry barrels into the bedroom, clutching three cups of coffee in his large hands. "I was beginning to wonder if the three of you would ever wake up."

"What time is it?" I ask, confused.

"It's after ten, and I'm ready for breakfast."

Damn. I don't know the last time I slept that late.

"Did I finally tire you out?" Henry asks, setting the coffee on the nightstand and climbing on top of me, pressing his lips to my ear. "I never thought I would find someone who could keep up with me. I always thought something was wrong—that I wanted too much, too often. You proved me wrong. Thank you, Isla." I wrap my arms around his neck and hug him tight, letting him pull me into his arms.

Dylan and Theo both sit up, sipping at their coffee, bleary-eyed. Henry sits and pulls me into his lap, handing me my coffee. I'm not going to lie, drinking my coffee in the lap of a smoking hot man may just be my favorite thing ever.

"As soon as the three of you get ready, we can head up the mountain. There's a café at the top where we can eat breakfast," Henry says.

Dylan, Theo, and I share the extra large shower, taking turns stepping in and out of the double showerheads. This is the first time I've showered with them that we haven't ended up doing something sexual, and as dull as it sounds, there's something so intimate and vulnerable about sharing a shower. It has me feeling all gooey on the inside. I'm the last one out of the bathroom, thanks to my unruly hair. Dylan kneels and helps me pull on my boots, lacing them up quickly. He pulls me to my feet, keeping my hand in his as we walk out the door.

It's only a ten-minute drive to the parking lot and a short walk to the gondola. I can't help but giggle when another couple and their two small children are ushered onto the same gondola as us. The mother is carrying an infant strapped to her chest, only the baby's tiny nose peeking out. A little boy, maybe three or four, clings to the dad's leg, studying us.

"Hello," I say softly, waving at the boy. Dylan and Henry smile at him, but Theo keeps his trademark scowl, and I have to elbow him in the ribs before he terrifies the poor kid.

"Did you know Ben Nevis is the biggest mountain in Scotland?" the boy asks.

"Really?" Henry asks, crouching down so they're on the same level.

The boy nods vigorously, his eyes lighting up. "It's a volcano from thirty-five thousand million years ago. It exploded in the largest explosion ever, and now it's only a mountain."

"That's amazing!" Henry says, his eyes sparkling.

"What's your name?" the boy asks Henry, moving several steps closer.

"Henry."

"Why do you talk funny?"

"I talk funny, do I?" Henry laughs. "I'm from the United States. Do you know where that is?" The boy nods but doesn't say anything. "Do you want to know the tallest mountain in the United States?" Henry asks. The boy nods again. "Its called Denali."

"But it's not bigger than Ben Nevis, right? Ben Nevis has to be the tallest mountain in the world!"

Henry bites his lip, doing an impressive job of hiding his smile. "I'm not sure, little man. I'll have to find out."

"Otay." The dad grabs the little boy's hand as we arrive at the top. "Bye, Henry!" he calls, waving as he exits the gondola. The parents smile, and the mom gives a little wave before leaving.

"Well, that was just about the sweetest thing I've ever seen," I say, taking Henry's hand as we walk off the platform. "You're going to be such a good dad someday."

"Only if it's mine," he says nonchalantly.

I freeze, looking up at him in shock.

"I'm kidding!" he laughs, wrapping his arms around me and leaning close to my ear. "Do you think I would be pushing their cum back inside you if I really felt that way?"

"Don't say stuff like that in public," I whisper, my cheeks flaming.

"Why not? You're so goddamned cute when you blush."

I shake my head. "It's too freaking early for this."

"You'll feel better once you get some food in your stomach."

We step outside the gondola building, and I see the view for the first time. It steals the breath from my lungs. This is it. This is where I want to be married.

Dylan takes one look at my face and grins, the corner of his eyes crinkling. "We have a winner, don't we?"

I nod, turning in a circle and taking in the 360-degree view of my country. Sometimes, I forget about the beauty of where I live. The rain and wind get to me. The bitterly cold winters settle into my bones. But this—*this*—God. I can't even describe the feeling of *home* that roars through my blood. Some ancestral part of me is tied to this land. Even the ripping wind can't change my mind that this is the place.

"Please say you guys feel the same thing I'm feeling?"

"I only need to look at your face to know this is it, Sunflower," Theo murmurs, wrapping his arms around me from behind me and resting his chin on my shoulder. Dylan and Henry nod in agreement.

"You're sure? It's going to be freezing. There will be snow on the ground. It could be foggy," I warn.

"We're sure, Isla." Henry and Dylan each take one of my hands, and the three of us stand there, soaking in the absolute rightness about this place. My full body shiver is what finally interrupts the moment. Theo takes off his jacket and wraps it around my shoulders, practically dragging me toward the lodge. The restaurant is cozy and warm; shining wood and soaring ceilings take center stage. We completely forget about our plans to hike to the summit. Instead, we sit by a window with an incredible view, eat the amazing food, and sample a ridiculous amount of whiskey they keep bringing around on a little cart.

We decide that we don't need to see the ship and instead plan to make a detour to the fairy pools. I open my phone and scroll through some holiday rentals, hoping to find something fun for one night.

"Have the three of you ever ridden horses?" I ask, feeling foolish for even having to ask.

"Where do you think our love of going fast comes from?" Theo asks, grinning.

"You're serious?"

"We're from Tennessee, Sunflower. Of course, we know how to ride horses. Do you?"

"*Do I?*" I shake my head in disbelief. "I don't understand how we've never talked about this before."

"We've been a bit busy since the day we showed up on your doorstep, Isla. Nobody has had much time for riding horses."

"That's true. I do ride. I don't have my own horse, though. I sometimes ride Jack's, but it's been forever."

"Why are you asking if we ride?" Dylan asks, moving the conversation along.

"I have an old family friend who owns a farm not far from the fairy pools. She rents out rooms for guests. Kind of like a bed and breakfast."

"Book it," Henry says, standing up and stretching. "Do you guys want to head back down?" I can't help the way my gaze slides down his body, snagging on the prominent bulge in his pants. I stand, allowing Theo and Dylan to go first so I can talk to Henry.

"What's happening there?" I ask, biting my lip as I trace the outline of his cock with my eyes.

Henry clears his throat and adjusts himself, his cheeks red. "I was thinking about you riding a horse."

"Hm."

"Naked."

"Henry!" I slap his arm, laughing. "Do you know how uncomfortable that would be?"

"Without a shirt then?" he asks hopefully.

"You're hopeless."

"Hopelessly in love with you," he says, putting his arm around me, his hand casually resting on my ass.

"Do you think you'll still be like this when you're old and gray?" I ask as we hurry to catch up with the guys.

"There will never be a day when I don't think about railing you, Isla. I may have to pop a little blue pill, but I'll get the job done."

"Oh, so I'm a job now?" I tease.

"Yeah, and I'm the CEO-DYD."

"What does that stand for?"

"The chief executive officer of dicking you down." I roll my eyes, biting my lip to contain my smile.

"Don't you dare roll your eyes at me, Isla MacLeod." He scoops me into his arms and follows Theo and Dylan onto the empty gondola, a dangerous glint in his eyes.

71

The gondola door closes, the tension inside ratcheting to dizzying heights within seconds.

"We have twelve minutes," Dylan says, pulling out his phone to set a timer.

"Did you time it on the way up?" Theo asks, looking at him incredulously.

"Don't look at me like that. You should be thanking me." Dylan shrugs off his jacket, folds it, and places it on the bench.

Henry sits down, pulling me down onto his lap, his cock pressing into my ass.

"Twelve minutes isn't long enough," I protest, my heart galloping.

"It is if you're already wet," Dylan says, dropping to his knees in front of me, waiting until I nod my consent before he pulls down my leggings and runs one finger along my slit. "Fuck, Isla," he groans, sliding his glistening finger into his mouth.

Henry motions for Theo to take his place. Dylan pulls off my boots and leggings as they switch places. I should have worn a dress instead of having to be bare-assed in a–I lose all train of thought as Theo pulls me down onto his lap, his cock impaling me.

"Jesus fuck, Isla," he groans, his hands shaking on my hips. Dylan pushes me back against Theo's chest and pushes my knees wide, kissing his way from my breasts down my stomach.

"We don't have time, Dylan," I pant.

"Yes, we fucking do." He circles my clit with his tongue and sucks hard. He doesn't stop until I'm chanting his name, begging for him to let me come. He walks forward on his knees and unzips his pants. Wrapping his fist around his shaft, he taps it on my clit several times before notching it at my entrance, slowly pushing in on top of Theo's cock.

"Fuck," I whimper, clutching Dylan's shoulders as their cocks stretch me. I glance up to see Henry sitting on the opposite bench, his cock in his hand, slowly stroking himself.

"Come here, Henry."

"I can wait till tonight, sweetheart."

"No. Now," I demand. He walks to my side and waits for me to tell him what to do. "Stand on the bench, one foot on either side of me." He does exactly what I ask, then looks down at me, waiting for further instructions. "Hands on the glass." I lean back against Theo, shifting to the side so my head is against his shoulder, and watch Henry lean against the glass, his cock only inches from my face. "Now fuck my mouth like you mean it."

"Isla–"

I wrap both of my hands around his shaft and pull him to my mouth, sucking on the head of his cock like it's candy.

"Fuck!" His legs shake, forcing him to lock his knees, his hips stuttering as I use every trick I know to make him fall apart.

Theo reaches around my hip to rub my clit, and my moan must be a green start flag because they all begin fucking me at once. Henry cradles the back of my head in his palm, pushing the tip of his cock in and out of my mouth, dragging it over my lips. I hollow my cheeks, sucking on him hard with the next push of his hips, and he gives in, sinking into me until his balls are touching my chin. I groan around him as Theo slides his finger back and forth over my clit, keeping rhythm with his and Dylan's cocks. The adrenaline has my body tensing almost immediately. Dylan and Theo pick up their pace, one pressing in while the other pulls out. I scream around Henry's cock as they switch up their rhythm, both pushing in at once, and Henry careens over the edge, jets of cum hitting the back of my throat. He pulls out just as I start to orgasm, latching onto my nipple, pleasure and pain mixing as he sucks hard, shooting me into outer space. Both Dylan and Theo grunt in unison, their hands tightening on my hips as they ram inside me, coming hard. Henry waits for Dylan's cock to slip out before taking his place, sliding his thumb over my clit, and then down my slit as Theo pulls out. He gathers their cum and pushes it back in.

"You're so fucking pretty like this, Isla," Henry murmurs, his nostrils flaring. "Freshly fucked. Rosy cheeks. Stretched pussy." I can't even be embarrassed when he's looking at me with such reverence. He pulls my panties from my leggings and slips them over my feet, pulling them up my legs before helping me with my leggings and boots.

"Three minutes to spare," Dylan announces, looking at his phone.

"That has to be some sort of world record," I say, only moving from Theo's lap long enough for him to put himself back together. I cuddle against him for the rest of the ride in a state of post-coital bliss, my head in the clouds.

"So, what are everyone's wedding must-haves?" I ask once we're back in the truck and headed to our farm stay.

"I want Lorna's kids to be the flower girl and ring bearer," Henry says, not even needing to think about it. "They can pull Summer in a tiny wagon so she can participate, too."

"Done." I can't help grinning. This man will make the best father one day, and the more I get to know him, the faster I want it to happen. Fuck me. "Dylan?"

"I want it to be fun. I've been to too many weddings that end up being formal and stuffy. I want people to think back and remember what a great time they had for the rest of their lives."

"I agree. What about you, Theo?"

"I want us to write our own vows," he says, meeting my gaze in the rearview mirror.

Dylan and I groan in unison. "I'm not the best with words, Theo."

"Your entire existence is poetic, Sunflower. I'm sure whatever you come up with will be utterly flawless."

"You have way too much faith in me."

"And me," Dylan echoes.

Theo shrugs, refusing to back down.

"What about you, Isla?" Dylan asks.

I take a moment to think. I was never that little girl who dreamed about her wedding, so all of this is brand new to me.

"I want to incorporate my family tartan into the wedding, and if you're willing, I want the three of you to take my last name," I blurt out, finally giving voice to what I've been thinking about for the past few weeks.

"Why?" Theo asks softly.

"Because the three of you belong here. You should have the MacLeod name if you want it. There is so much life, love, and history behind the name, and it would be an honor for my family if you took our name." I look between them, realizing I probably shouldn't have done this in the car. "You don't have to. Only if you think it's right," I stammer, nerves getting the best of me.

"I don't speak for all of us, but for me, it would be an honor to be part of the Macleod clan," Henry says, his eyes shining.

"I agree," Dylan says, his grin nearly splitting his face in half.

"Theo?" My stomach knots, knowing that out of the three of them, he's the one who would take issue with it.

"I would move mountains for you, Sunflower. What's a little name change?" He catches my eye in the rearview mirror, holding my gaze for a second to let me know that he means every word.

. . .

WE SPEND the rest of the ride discussing all the other little decisions we need to make: colors, flowers, food, drink, and music. I take notes on my phone, writing down each of their preferences with the hope that I can come up with something that represents all four of us. As we pull into the farm drive, I tuck my phone away, knowing the next time I take it out, I'll be taking pictures of us riding off into the sunset.

72

FEBRUARY

As I watch Lorna and Charlie walk down the aisle through the fat swirling snowflakes, I can't help but be thankful for every decision I've made that led me to today. They're so beautiful in their thick gray-blue gowns and hooded capes. All the guests are standing and looking back at me, making it so the only thing I can see is Father Calum at the opposite end of the aisle. I smooth my hands over my dress, fingers pale against my family's tartan. Initially, I was going to use the tartan as an accent, but when the guys told me they would take my name, I decided it needed to be a focal point. The dress, made from my favorite MacLeod tartan, is a muted brown with gray-blue and sage green. There's a matching green, silk-lined cloak clasped around my shoulders to keep me warm.

"You still have time to run if you're not sure," Jack says from beside me, taking my hand.

"I've never been more sure of anything in my life," I murmur, smiling up at him.

"That's exactly what I needed to hear, Isla. I'm so proud of you." He pulls my hand through the crook of his elbow, drawing me to the head of the aisle.

The first heartbreakingly beautiful violin notes of "Our Song" by Elton John float over us, and I can't help the tears that come to my eyes. I try to blink them away, but they overflow onto my cheeks, dripping off my chin as we walk down the aisle. This was the exact reason I chose not to wear anything but waterproof mascara and lipgloss today. I may act like a tough bitch most of the time, but these men have made me a puddle of goo on the inside. Jack turns to face me as we reach the end of the aisle, cupping my face in his hands and wiping my tears away with his thumbs.

"I am so goddamned happy for you, Isla." He sniffles, wiping at his face, trying to hold himself together.

My chin wobbles, and I choke out a laugh. "Thank you for being you, Jack. I truly don't know if I could survive without you." His lips tremble as he smiles, but he pulls himself together, standing straight and walking me the last few steps to Father Calum's side. I take a deep breath and look up slowly. My heart tumbles in my chest as I see my guys for the first time. They're standing on the other side of Father Calum, dressed in brown suits that match the tartan peeking from their pockets, the colors complimenting their features perfectly. They look gorgeous. I meet each of their eyes, butterflies attacking my stomach, my pulse racing. I blow out a shaky breath and push back my shoulders, determined to get through this without making an absolute fool of myself. But then I see Theo's chin tremble, and all bets are off.

I desperately blink back tears, determined to get through this without falling apart. I turn toward Charlie and Lorna, hoping they'll give me the support I need, but they're no better. Mascara streams down their faces, blotches of black dotting their eyelids. Holy fuck. I pull a tissue out from between my breasts and clean up Lorna first, then Charlie, giving her the tissue to dab at my cheeks. I give them both quick hugs, laughing with them before taking a deep breath and turning back toward the guys. The sun breaks through the clouds at that moment, shining down on their gorgeous smiles, joy radiating from them. There are no questions in their eyes, no signs of doubt or regret.

"Isla, Theo, Dylan, and Henry, are the four of you ready to begin?" Father Calum asks. We all nod, and he greets our family and friends before inviting Theo to say his vows. Theo swallows hard and steps forward, taking my flowers and handing them to Charlie before taking my hands in his.

"Sunflower, I knew you were the one from the moment you knocked that croissant out of my mouth. The world fades away in your presence, and I am left with only the sound of your voice, the warmth of your touch, and the light in your eyes. You are the quiet in my chaos, the steady heartbeat in my chest. With you, I am both grounded and free. I love the way you see the world, how you find beauty in the simplest things, how your laughter fills the room, and how your kindness touches everyone around you. There is no need for grand gestures, no need for perfect words. It is enough to simply be with you, share this life, this love, and know that I have found everything I will ever need in you."

Fuck. I am not going to get through this without becoming a sobbing mess.

"Dylan, your turn." Father Calum smiles at him encouragingly.

Dylan is surprisingly confident as he takes my hands. "Freckles, there's a silent understanding between us that needs no words, only a glance, a touch, a shared breath. In you, I find the calm I didn't know I was missing, a sense of belonging that feels as natural as breathing. You are the moment before sleep when everything is quiet and still, and the world feels just right. I love the way your presence lingers long after you've gone, how your laughter echoes in my thoughts, and how your kindness softens the edges of my day. Being with you is like coming home to a place I never knew but always longed for. You are my peace, my challenge, my joy. In the space between us, I find a love that is steady, unhurried, and true. A love that simply is."

Father Calum wipes at his eyes as Dylan steps back. "Henry."

Henry trades places with Dylan, his hands swallowing mine. "Red, I found my anchor in you, a quiet strength that steadies me, a light that brightens every corner of my world. You are the warmth in my coldest days, the calm in my fiercest storms. With you, I have learned what it means to be truly seen, to be loved without conditions, and to love without fear. Today, I offer you my unwavering support, my patient heart, my open ears. I promise to stand by you, in moments of triumph, in times of doubt, in the quiet moments where words are not needed. Together, we will build a life woven with laughter, strengthened by trust, and colored with the joy of countless shared adventures. Isla, you are my beginning and my end, my constant, my love. Today, I give you all that I am, and all that I will ever be, now and always."

"Isla?" Father Calum takes a tissue from his pocket and wipes his nose, motioning for me to begin my vows.

I take several deep, shaky breaths, trying to tame my emotions so that I can get through this without sobbing. "Dylan, Theo, Henry, each of you adds something invaluable to my life. Dylan, you bring a quiet strength that grounds me. Your calm presence allows me to find peace when life gets overwhelming, and even in your silence, I feel the depth of your love—a steady, unspoken support that I know will always be there.

"Theo, you are my foundation, the one I can lean on without hesitation. Your strength and reliability give me the confidence to face whatever comes our way. You're the one who lifts me when I'm down, who stands by me in every challenge, and who helps me find the courage to keep moving forward.

"Henry, you are the spark that keeps me on my toes. You challenge me to think differently, to embrace new ideas, and to see the world as a place full of possibilities. With you, life is never dull—every day feels like an adventure, and you remind me to find joy in the unexpected.

"I am the person I am today because of the three of you. You have shaped, supported, and loved me in ways that I didn't even know I needed. You've made my life richer, more complete, and more beautiful than I ever imagined possible."

Father Calum steps forward, asking each of the guys if they'll take me as their wife, and then asks me if I'll take each of them as my husband. I'm practically bursting with joy as I slide a ring onto each of their fingers. They take turns sliding their rings on my ring finger, the three thin bands nesting together beautifully.

Father Calum takes our hands, brings them together, and begins wrapping a length of tartan around them. "May the road rise to meet you, may the wind be always at your back. May the sunshine be warm upon your faces; may the rains fall soft upon your feet. And until we meet again, may the gods hold you in the palm of their hands." He looks up from our hands, a giant grin on his face. "You may kiss your bride."

Henry is the first to crush his lips to mine, murmuring "I love you" over and over against my mouth, tears streaming down his face. Dylan is next, his lips soft and insistent on mine, cherishing this moment. When Dylan finally steps away, Theo picks me up in his arms, spinning me around. The joy on his face brings fresh tears to my eyes. He sets me back on my feet, pressing his forehead to mine. "Thank you isn't enough to express my gratitude, Isla. Thank you for saving me. Us. I will spend every day of the rest of my life showing you how grateful I am." He cradles the back of my head in his hand and presses his lips to mine, dipping me down, taking my breath away. When everybody starts cheering, he pumps his fist in the air, laughing against my lips. With him on one side and Dylan and Henry on the other, we run back up the aisle to the sound of Bruno Mars' "Marry You."

We make a beeline to the gondolas, the photographer snapping pictures as we climb inside. The doors close, shutting out the cheers, enclosing us in our own little bubble.

"Ready for the best twelve minutes of your married life?" Henry asks, shrugging out of his jacket with a grin.

AS THE FOUR of us pile into the limo, the driver congratulates us and slips me a note. I peek out the back window, tearing up as I watch all of our friends and family waving goodbye, sparklers lighting up their smiling faces. I slide my finger under the flap and pull out the card.

· · ·

My darling Isla,

Thank you for letting me live vicariously through you. Your bags are packed, and everything is taken care of, so relax and have fun! I hope you have a fantastic time on your honeymoon.

Love forever, Charlie

P.S. Lach paid for everything–he said it's part of your wedding present, so enjoy yourselves!

THEO TAKES the card from me and reads it. "What is this?"

"Charlie asked me a couple of months ago if she could plan the honeymoon, but she never said anything else. I thought she had forgotten!"

"You really thought Charlie would forget about that?" he asks, handing the note to Dylan.

"Do you have any idea where we're going?" Dylan asks, looking out the window like the inky blackness will give him a clue.

"I have no clue. I guess we'll find out at the airport."

FIFTEEN MINUTES LATER, the limo drives right onto the tarmac, stopping at a small jet. This can't be right. The guys look back at me, their eyes as round as mine. A fight attendant rushes down the stairs, taking the suitcases the driver pulls from the trunk, while another comes to meet us at the limo.

"Good evening! My name is Katie. John and I will be your flight attendants tonight. May I help you with anything?"

"Can you tell us where we're going?" I ask, struggling to get out of the limo in my voluminous dress.

"I'm under strict instructions not to tell you until we land," she says softly, smiling her apology.

"Do we need passports?" I ask, my heart jumping to my throat in panic.

"Yes, Charlie has already given them to me. They're on board."

The sneaky bitch. God, I love her.

"Those are our clothes?" I ask, gesturing to the suitcases John is hauling up the staircase, the guys right behind him with the rest.

"Yes. Charlie said you'll have everything you need for the next three weeks."

"Three weeks? Are you sure you can't tell us where we're going?"

"Afraid not."

Jesus. I follow her to the plane, then up the stairs, holding my skirts high so I don't trip.

"Can you tell me how long the flight is?" I ask, crossing my fingers.

"That I can do. Four hours."

Four hours. That means it's still in Europe, which explains the bazillion suitcases since we'll need cold-weather clothes. I duck my head to enter the plane and then freeze. The sheer opulence is astounding. The main part of the cabin has four plush chairs facing each other and two couches beyond that, also facing each other. The guys are all standing there, hands in their pockets, looking out of place.

"What's back there?" I ask them, gesturing to the door behind them.

"A bedroom," Henry says, looking dazed.

My stomach jumps, my heartbeat taking up residence between my legs almost immediately.

Katie reappears with a tray full of champagne flutes. "Congratulations on your wedding. We're ready to take off once the four of you are seated and buckled. You're free to move around the cabin once we're at cruising altitude and the pilot turns off the seatbelt sign. I'll be in the crew quarters at the front of the plane. Please push the attendant button if you need anything." She waits for us to sit and buckle before handing us our champagne and disappearing back into the crew quarters. Two minutes later, the plane is taxiing down the runway.

"Charlie didn't tell any of you anything?" I ask, suspiciously studying each of their faces. They all shake their heads.

"She asked me what our schedules were like after the wedding, but I thought it was because she was going to have a party or something, not *this*," Dylan says, shaking his head in disbelief.

I think back, realizing how many questions Charlie asked me over the last few months. "I think she's been planning this since we set a date for the wedding. I told her we were going to wait to take a honeymoon, but she said something about it being the slow season and the perfect time to go on one."

Henry shrugs. "She's right. It'll be mayhem in the summer, especially with the castle opening to guests."

"Charlie knows best." My laugh turns into a strangled screech as the pilot accelerates, pressing me back into my seat. I'm not scared of a lot of things, but being twenty-five thousand feet up in the air in a tiny tin can will do it. As the wheels lift from the ground and gravity takes hold, it suddenly feels like the dress weighs a million pounds. I adjust the stream of air from the vent over my seat, aiming it directly at my face.

"Isla? What can I help with?" Henry asks, palming my thigh through my skirts and squeezing comfortingly.

I lean forward in my seat, twisting away from him. "Unzip me. Please."

He leans over his armrest and slides the zipper down. I shrug out of my sleeves, pushing the bodice down to my waist. I lean back and close my eyes, taking deep breaths as I concentrate on the cool air hitting my face.

Theo clears his throat. "Isla, what are you wearing?"

Oh fuck. My eyes pop open. "It was supposed to be a surprise," I wail. I ruined it.

"Oh, it's a surprise, all right," Dylan whispers, his gaze searing my skin.

I look down at the emerald green straps crisscrossing my torso, my tits pushed up to the heavens, jiggling with every little movement the plane makes.

"Don't stop there," Theo rasps, motioning for me to continue undressing. A swirling maelstrom of need edges out the nerves, and I latch onto it. I plant my hands on the armrests, lifting my weight from the seat. Theo leans over and tugs at the bottom of my dress, slowly sliding it down my body.

"Fuck me, Isla." Henry's voice washes over me like a thousand fingertips brushing my skin, plucking at my nipples, sliding between my legs. All three of them sit there staring at me, their eyes tracing the top of my stockings, traveling up my garters and to the straps that cross over to the opposite hip. Theo unbuckles, dropping to his knees and shuffling between my legs, his hands rough on my thighs.

"Theo, you're supposed to stay buckled," I say, pushing at his shoulders.

He buries his face in the vee of my thighs, inhaling. "If I die tonight, I'll die a happy man, Isla. The devil himself couldn't keep me from you right now." I give in, dropping my head back against the headrest as he slides his hands up my body, slipping his thumbs inside the cups of my bra to tease my nipples. I relax into the plush leather seat, my legs opening in invitation, his hips pressing into my thighs as he leans over me and crushes his lips to mine. He tweaks my nipples hard, and I arch my back, gasping against his mouth, He takes advantage, pushing his tongue between my lips. I roll my hips against him, desperately seeking friction, needing to feel his hard length between my legs. Growling against my lips, slides his hand over the arm of my chair until he finds the recline button and follows me down. I barely hear the seatbelt notification, too enthralled by the way Theo's making me feel, but Dylan seems to think it's his signal and crouches at the head of my chair, deftly unbuckling me and sliding me out from under Theo's body. Dylan swings me into his arms and carries me into the bedroom, tossing me onto the bed and staring down at me, his eyes dark with need.

"I'd tell you how fucking sexy you look, but you already know that, don't you?" He slides his fingers under the straps on my stomach, following them slowly down to my hips, squeezing my flesh as he goes, as if he's holding back some feral part of himself. "You make me feel things I've never felt before, Isla."

I take a shuddering breath. "Like what?"

He tugs at one of the straps with his finger. "I want to cut this off of you, tear your panties off, and bury my cock in that sweet heat between your legs."

"Do it," Henry whispers, his voice thick with need. "She wants it, Dylan."

Dylan pulls a pocketknife out and slashes through the straps in a matter of seconds before unbuckling his belt and pulling out his cock. I whimper as he presses his thumb against my clit through my panties, then fists the material, ripping it from my body. Climbing on the bed, he slams inside me with a groan. I bury my face against his shoulder, whimpering as he lights up my body, every nerve ending going haywire as he fucks me.

"Flip over so she's on top," Henry commands.

I look at him and nearly come right then. He's gripping his cock hard with one hand, precum dripping from the tip. Dylan dips his shoulder and rolls, adjusting my legs so I'm straddling him. He grasps my hips, pulling me down, grinding against me.

"Sit up, Isla."

I obey Henry's command, planting my hands on Dylan's chest and pushing myself up.

"Good girl, now hold still."

Henry's praise rolls through my body, a tsunami of pleasure crashing over me from my head to my toes. The bed dips as he positions himself behind me, my heartbeat ratcheting up as his arm snakes around my middle and draws me against his chest. I break free from his hold, lift myself off Dylan, and turn around, sinking back down onto his cock with a moan.

"Much better," I whisper, making quick work of the buttons on Henry's shirt before pushing it off his thick shoulders. I slide my palms over his muscles, the light creeping in from the main cabin burnishing him with a golden glow. He cups my jaw, angling my head before capturing my mouth with his. I desperately fumble with his belt buckle, jerking at the button of his pants before greedily pushing my hand inside and wrapping my fingers around his cock. I tug him closer, and he straddles Dylan's legs, closing the distance between us. I drag the head of his cock over my clit, rocking back and forth over the ridge. Henry groans, sitting back on his knees, his dark gaze anchored between my legs where Dylan's cock disappears inside me. He reaches out, dragging two fingers over the stretched skin of my pussy before sliding them in on top of Dylan's shaft. He pushes up on his knees, changing the angle of his hand so his fingers are hooked against the front wall of my pussy.

"Breathe, Isla. That's my girl."

I whimper as he drags his fingers over my G-spot, coaxing me toward orgasm. Dipping his head, he sucks one of my nipples into his mouth, pleasure streaking through my system like a shooting star.

"Fuck, Isla," he grinds out, breathing hard. He pulls his fingers out, sucking my desire from them before crushing his lips to mine, pushing his tongue into my mouth, sharing my taste with me.

Fuck.

He breaks away, cheeks ruddy, pupils blown wide. Dropping his gaze, he palms his cock, pushing it down between my legs, sliding it over my clit. He notches it at my entrance, pressing our bodies together as he pushes inside me. Dylan's broken groan nearly launches me over the edge. Because of the angle, only the first two inches of Henry's cock are inside me, but fuck does he make those inches work. My body shudders as I rock back and forth, the head of his cock sliding back and forth over my G-spot, bringing me close to the precipice before he clamps his hands on my hips, holding me still.

"How do you want Theo?" Dylan rasps from behind me, his fingers flexing on my ass.

"However, he wants me," I pant, dropping my head to Henry's shoulder, trying to hold on and wait for Theo. And then he's behind me, his thighs pressing against mine as he straddles Dylan's torso, his cock nudging against my ass.

"Is this okay?" he asks softly, kissing his way down my spine.

"Perfect," I mumble, pushing my ass out toward him, needy and desperate. I hear the sound of the lube bottle, and then Henry's spreading my ass cheeks, and Theo is coating me in lube. He slides his cock back and forth over me, chuckling at my gasp every time he passes over my asshole. He notches himself and pushes forward slowly, stopping every inch to allow me time to adjust. I sob when he fully seats himself, my body trembling with need.

"Look at how good you take our cocks," Henry whispers, his lips against my ear. "Like you were made for us."

I start moving, pushing back on Theo then forward onto Henry's cock, Dylan staying snug inside me the whole time. "

Take what you need," Theo rasps, sweeping my hair away from my neck and licking me from shoulder to ear. I ride them harder, high on the fullness. High on their praise. High on them. Henry holds me close, my nipples rubbing on his chest, adding to the chaos of sensations my brain is desperately trying to catalog.

"Fuck, Isla." Henry exhales a shaky breath, cupping my face in the tenderest of touches. I strain up to catch his lips with mine, hooking my fingers around the back of his neck and drawing him down with me as I relax, all three stretching me to my fullest. I whimper against Henry's lips, squeezing around them.

"I'm close," Dylan chokes out, his body straining beneath me as he tries to stay in control.

"Push your ass toward Theo, love," Henry murmurs against my lips, sliding his hands down my body, guiding my hips the way he wants them. "Good girl."

On the next thrust, his entire shaft slides along my clit, igniting a wildfire inside me. Oh god. I grapple for his hips, holding tight as I explode around them.

"Jesus fuck," Theo grunts, groaning as that tight ring of muscle strangles his cock, giving him no choice but to come hard. His hips stutter against my ass at the same time Dylan pushes up to grind against me, moaning as he surrenders control.

I can feel Henry holding back, waiting. He bands an arm around my back, pulling me up against him. Theo and Dylan slip out as Henry sits back on his heels, lifting me up and down on his cock, using my body like a fleshlight. He palms my ass, his fingers sliding in Theo's cum, pushing his middle finger into me.

"You're so goddamned beautiful," he growls, his gaze roaming over me as he slowly pulls me back and forth on his cock, palming my breast with his other hand.

I cling to his neck, barely able to breathe, my arms shaking. He growls his displeasure when my hold begins to slip, twisting to the side and laying me across the bed. He kicks off his pants and leans over me, holding my gaze as he rams into me. I don't stand a chance against him. His jaw clenches. His muscles ripple. His blue eyes never leave my face, bringing us to the edge together.

"Come on my cock, Isla. I want to feel you squeezing around me." My body obeys him immediately. "That's my girl. Just like that." He slams into me, pounding me down into the mattress, and then holds me there, rocking his pelvis over mine, the sudden pressure on my clit extending my orgasm. He covers my mouth with his, swallowing my scream, moaning as I scrape my nails down his back, his hips spasming as I latch onto his ass. "Fuck, Isla." He buries his face in the crook of my neck and thrusts hard, pouring his seed deep inside me. I sigh contentedly, squeezing my muscles around the hardness of his cock, enjoying the aftershocks of my orgasm.

"You better be careful, wife. Don't do that unless you're ready for round two," he chuckles against my ear, flexing his cock, making me gasp.

"Stop antagonizing our wife with your bionic dick," Theo mutters, rolling Henry to the side and gathering me into his arms. He carries me into the bathroom, setting me carefully down beneath the steaming hot shower spray. I relax against his chest, closing my eyes as the water sluices over us. If this is what married life is going to be like, I'm all in.

73

"Welcome to Switzerland, where the local time is 8 am."
I jerk awake, adrenaline rushing through my bloodstream. It takes me a second to realize that the plane isn't moving anymore and another second for it to register that all four of us are buck ass naked when the flight attendant could show up at any moment. I scramble out of Dylan's arms, and out of bed, flipping on the bathroom light and dragging the duffel bag nestled at the foot of the bed into the bathroom. I dig through it, praising Charlie as I pull out a change of clothes for all of us, along with toothbrushes, toothpaste, and a brush. I splash cold water on my face and then pull on a comfy, wide-legged sweat set in my favorite shade of green. I run the brush through my hair, brush my teeth, and then wake the guys, dodging their arms as they try to drag me into their warm embraces. There will be time for that later—lots of time.

"Ready to disembark?" Katie asks, poking her head into the main cabin, her eyes staying focused on me even when Henry ambles out of the bedroom half-naked.

"Can we have just a couple of minutes?" I ask, rubbing my hands over my face, trying to wake up.

"Of course. Let me know when you're ready, and I'll open the door. Would you like the note Charlie left you now or once we have you settled in your vehicle?"

"Now, please!" I take it from her, suddenly feeling wide awake. The guys congregate in the main cabin as they finish getting dressed, waiting for me to read the note aloud.

DEAR ISLA, Dylan, Henry, and Theo, Welcome to your honeymoon in Bettmeralp, Switzerland! Bettmeralp is only accessible by cable car and is located near Aletsch Glacier, the first UNESCO world heritage site in the Alps. You'll be staying in a small family-owned resort. The owners will check in with you upon arrival and take care of meals, activities, and anything else you may need. Bettmeralp offers every winter sport you can imagine, and the resort has a state-of-the-art spa, so you can choose to relax, be adventurous, or both. With the view from your bedroom, you may not ever want to leave your cabin ;) Do what makes you happy!

Love, Charlie

I LOOK up at the guys, feeling like a little kid. I don't think I've been this excited for a vacation in, well, ever. "Do you guys know how to ski or snowboard?" I ask, bouncing up and down on my toes with excitement.

They all shake their heads. "Tennessee isn't the place people go to ski," Dylan says, making a face.

"I'll teach you."

"How do *you* know?" Theo asks. "From what you've told us, it didn't seem like you ever took time off."

"Being the adrenaline junky I am, I used to go every day I had off during the winter."

"Why not this winter?" Dylan asks, his dark eyebrows drawn together.

"There was too much to do," I shrug. "I'm so behind on the

brewery that it didn't seem like I should be doing much of anything fun until it's finished."

"And look at you now. Three weeks to relax and have fun," Henry says, grinning. The way he said the word *fun* implies other things–dirty things–and has me clenching my thighs together.

"Which means I'll be behind three *more* weeks," I mutter.

"Oh, stop. You know the best time to open is in spring, anyway," Theo grumbles, rolling his eyes.

"Don't talk sense to me." I squish his cheeks between my hands and kiss him hard, spinning away before he can grab me. I knock on the crew door and tell Katie we're ready to go. She follows me into the cabin and opens the door, revealing a set of metal stairs leading down into a winter wonderland. There's a black SUV waiting for us, the windshield glinting in the morning sun.

"Jackets are waiting for you in the vehicle," Katie informs us, stepping to the side as we pull on the boots Charlie supplied before leading the way down the stairs. The guys hurry to help John and our white-haired driver pull the suitcases from the plane and load them in the back of the vehicle.

"Have a lovely honeymoon, Isla." Katie throws me a wink before climbing the stairs and closing the door. I turn in a full circle, in awe of the jagged peaks surrounding us, everything covered in a blanket of pure white snow. I thought I knew mountains, having grown up around them and lived among them my entire life, but this is different.

"We're going to learn to ski on *those*?" Dylan asks, a nervous edge to his voice.

"Snowboard," I correct automatically. "We'll just have to see what it's like. Those mountains are intimidating even for me. There will be plenty of other things to do," I remind him, wiggling my eyebrows suggestively.

"Dylan can sit in the chalet and wait for us," Theo says, rolling his eyes.

"Rude." I stick out my tongue at Theo and grab Dylan's arm,

pulling him toward the SUV. The driver opens the door for us, and Dylan slides in, making room for me and Henry, forcing Theo to sit up front. Theo starts to protest, but Henry only needs to lift an eyebrow to make him realize that's what he gets for being an ass.

"Fine," he grumbles, folding his arms over his chest as our driver gets in the car.

"Good morning, lady and gents. My name is Noah, and I'll be your chauffeur for the entirety of your trip. Bettmeralp doesn't allow cars, but I live in Grengiols, the town at the base of the mountain, and will be available to drive you anywhere you wish to go." He hands Theo his card. "Would you like me to stop for breakfast on the way?"

"Please! Or at least some coffee?" I ask, desperate for something to clear the fog from my brain.

He looks back at me, blue eyes sparkling. "Of course. I'll take you to my favorite place."

I'm a nervous wreck for the first ten minutes of the drive, but Noah expertly navigates the snow-covered hills, and I quickly become more comfortable. Sensing my anxiety, Henry drapes his arm around my shoulders, pulling me against his side. At the same time, Dylan grabs my hand, threading his fingers through mine, and squeezing tightly. I relax, enjoying the gorgeous scenery as we climb higher into the mountains. After about thirty minutes, we pull into the parking lot of a tiny chalet made of giant logs, a cafe sign hanging above the red door and about a foot of snow covering the roof.

"Ready for the best breakfast you've ever eaten?" Noah asks, opening our door and ushering us inside the tiny building. He seats us at a large corner booth and then disappears into the kitchen, returning with an adorable woman with rosy cheeks and gray hair pulled back into a neat bun.

"This is my wife, Elena," Noah announces proudly. "She doesn't speak English, but she will make you the best breakfast and cafe-kreme you've ever had." He grins broadly, then retreats back into the kitchen with Elena, presumably to help her make our food.

.   .   .

THE COFFEE COMES OUT FIRST. I sneak two sugars into mine, and it's hands-down the best coffee I've had in my entire life. About ten minutes later, Noah and Elena reappear, their arms laden with dishes: yogurt, granola, all sorts of breads, jams, butters, spreads, various cereals, cheeses, soft-boiled eggs, and a bowl of fresh fruit. It's like girl-dinner for breakfast, and I'm obsessed. Once they've laid everything out, Elena heads back to the kitchen while Noah drags a chair over to our booth and sits down, a mug of steaming hot chocolate warming his hands.

"Would you like some suggestions for things to do while you're here?" he asks, spreading a healthy slab of butter on a slice of bread.

"Please!" I exclaim, drowning a croissant in chocolate hazelnut spread.

"There's a train with a glass ceiling called the Glacier Express. The ride is beautiful during the winter months," he begins, taking a giant bite of his bread.

"We love trains," Theo murmurs, glancing over at me, his eyes dark. I hide my smile behind my mug, trying not to blush.

"There are numerous resorts that offer every imaginable winter sport. I can drive you to Interlaken for kayaking, curling, and hang gliding. Or there's a complex high in the mountains called Glacier 3000, with dog sledding, glacier hikes, and a suspension bridge between two mountain peaks. There's even a hot air balloon festival in a couple of weeks."

Elena comes out of the kitchen with a large box in her hands, and Noah grabs her a chair, placing it beside his. She sits, resting the box in her lap, listening to our conversation. When there's a lull, she nudges Noah with her elbow and gestures to the box as she talks to him. His blushes, and looks up at us bashfully.

"I apologize for this, as it may be considered inappropriate, but she insists. Elena's family has a custom of making a blanket for newlyweds. When she heard I would be your driver for three weeks, she insisted on making one for you. It's made from sheep's wool. She spun, dyed, and then knitted it just for you."

Elena hands me the box. I carefully pull at the tail of the brown velvet ribbon and slide off the top, unveiling a thick wool blanket knit with variegated yarn in shades of purple, green, and brown. It reminds me of the highlands in the summer, when the heather cascades over the hills. It's absolutely beautiful.

"Thank you, Elena, it's exquisite," I smile at her, hoping she understands.

Elena nods, grinning, then turns back to Noah, saying something while gesturing toward us with her hands.

"She wants to make sure I tell you this blanket is to bring you luck with conceiving. You place it on your bed until you have a babe, and then later, you can use it to keep your babe warm."

"Ah!" I carefully fold it back into the box and shove it into Henry's hands, ignoring his idiotic grin. The guys slide out of the booth so I can stand and hug Elena tightly.

"Thank you so much for your hospitality, Elena." She bobs her head, patting me on the shoulder before heading back into the kitchen.

"What do you say, kids? Ready to get on with your honeymoon?" Noah asks, waggling his eyebrows.

"Yes, sir," Henry says enthusiastically, tucking that infernal blanket under his arm. And then it dawns on me. I didn't take my birth control last night. Did Charlie even pack it? Jesus fucking Christ.

NOAH BUNDLES us into the cable car, then steps back onto the platform and lifts his hat, waving as we're whisked up the mountain. We stand huddled together for warmth, speechless as the breadth of the mountains comes into view. They're magnificent. The thought of flying down the trails on a snowboard sends a thrill down my spine.

"I think Theo was right," Dylan says, his cheeks pale. "I will happily sip hot chocolate down in the chalet while you guys risk your lives on these mountains."

I grab his hand, pushing up on my toes to press a kiss to his cheek. "You don't have to do anything you don't want to do."

"What if all I want to do the next three weeks is you?" he murmurs.

"I think I can handle that," I laugh, kissing him on the lips this time.

We're scrambling to offload seven minutes later, dragging our suitcases out of the cable car and onto the platform.

"Isla?"

I turn to find a person bundled up in so many layers that I can't tell if they're a man or woman.

"Hello! I'm Josephine. You can call me Jo. It's nice to meet you. I'm from the resort." Before I can say anything, Jo grabs two of our bags and carries them toward a sleigh attached to the back of a snowmobile, her boots crunching in the snow. We grab the rest of the luggage and follow her, stacking everything in a compartment behind the sleigh.

"Hop in! It's about a ten-minute ride from here. There are blankets in the sleigh to keep you warm!" As Jo fires up the snowmobile, we pile into the sleigh, and she drives us into a winter wonderland. We drive through the town, passing by snow-covered cabins and churches before climbing into a pine forest where everything sounds muffled, like that hush right before a storm. She cuts the engine as we pull up alongside a beautiful a-frame cabin, silence covering us like a thick blanket.

"Here we are! Your home for the next three weeks!" Jo struggles through the snow to get to the back of the sleigh. "The main lodge is just up this pathway if you decide you'd like to eat meals with the other guests." She gestures up the path to a large building perched on the mountainside.

We step out of the sleigh, sinking into snow up to our knees. The guys grab the rest of the bags and follow Jo and me up the steps and into the cabin.

"I have to admit that I've been looking for a reason to do a cabin like this for ages. I'm glad Charlie called and gave me the excuse," Jo says, slipping off her hat and goggles to reveal bright blonde hair and sparkling blue eyes.

"What do you mean '*like this*'?" Theo asks from behind me.

"You'll see," she winks, grinning at us.

Her smile is infectious, and I can't help but return it as I follow her into the main living area. I only make it a few steps before I stop short, my brain short-circuiting. Thick honey-colored beams soar above us, leading the eye to the far wall, which is made of one massive window, offering an incredible view of the mountains. It's spectacularly beautiful. Henry lifts me, shuffling forward several feet, and sets me down inside the room so the rest of the guys can come in.

"I really hope you like it here," Jo says, her eyes sweeping the cabin like she's trying to make sure she didn't miss anything. "I've always wanted to design something that would work for non-tradi- tional relationships, and when Charlie called me, I knew it was a sign. The other cabins are only suited for couples, so this was outside the box for us." She prattles on, but my attention is drawn by the cozy fireplace and the gigantic rug in front of it.

"I'm sure it's going to be perfect, Jo." I shiver as Henry sweeps his hand down my back intimately, letting me know exactly what he's thinking.

She leads us over to the kitchen, opening the fully stocked refrigerator.

"There are all sorts of drinks in here. Wine, beer, canned cocktails, water and juices. There's a coffeemaker on the counter and a kettle on the stove for tea and coffee. There's a full bar at the lodge, as well. You'll find a daily menu in the notebook on the dining table. You can come to the lodge to eat or we can bring your meals here, just let us know. If you decide you want to cook, just text me an ingredient list, and I can have it for you the next day. Charlie gave me a list of basics, but if anything is missing, we can get it for you." She leads us out of the kitchen to a door on the opposite side of the cabin. "Fresh wood will be delivered to your porch daily. Cleaning will come whenever you request it. We won't just show up to clean since so many of our guests want privacy. And now the pièce de résistance." She throws the door wide, revealing a large suite with a mammoth bed, easily big enough for six people.

"When we pulled up, of course I thought it was beautiful, but I was worried about the bed situation. You have no idea how much this means to us," I tell her, relief flooding through me.

"I'm so glad we could accommodate," Jo says, her eyes shining with pride. But this isn't even the best part." She steps inside the bedroom, walking to another door on the far wall. She doesn't say anything as she opens it; she just watches our faces. I nearly melt on the spot when I see the gigantic sunken jacuzzi tub

"Are you serious!" I squeal, walking to the edge and bending down, swishing my hand through the steaming water. Three weeks isn't going to be nearly long enough.

Jo shows us how to drain the tub and the panel on the wall that controls the water temperature and jets. Lastly, she shows us how to work the shower. The walls are made of stacked boulders, the showerheads buried into the walls and ceiling. There's plenty of room for the four of us to shower and do *other* things without hitting our elbows.

"Any questions?" Jo asks, walking back to the family room and perching on the armrest of a beautiful, tufted leather couch.

"I don't think so," I answer, shaking my head, still thinking about the tub.

"If you think of anything, it's probably answered in the notebook, but feel free to text me anyway. I'll leave you to 'unpack' now," she says, air quotes around unpack, giggling as she pulls her hat and goggles back on and steps out into the snow.

I don't even have the door closed completely before Dylan presses me against it, his hips pinning me in place. Theo approaches, but Dylan blocks him. "I don't want to share right now," he says roughly, boxing me in with his arms.

Theo holds up his hands and backs away. 'Fucking hell, Dylan. Isla, are you okay with us taking turns today?" he asks, the corner of his mouth twitching.

"Yes," I breathe, gasping as Dylan drags his tongue down my throat.

"I get her last," Henry says, his heated gaze capturing mine from across the room, promising all sorts of dirty things. I'm not sure how I'm going to survive three weeks of this, but I'm sure as hell going to have fun trying.

74

D ylan scoops me into his arms and carries me into the bedroom, slamming the door behind us with his foot.

"Let me at least shower off first," I gasp, melting against him as he nips at my collarbone.

"Why?"

"Because I'm pretty sure I still have jizz dripping out of me from last night."

"Is that supposed to deter me?" He sets me down, pushes my jacket from my shoulders, and tosses it onto the bed.

"I kind of thought it would, to be honest."

"I wouldn't share you if somebody else's semen bothered me, Freckles."

I lift my arms, allowing him to pull off my sweatshirt, and before I can blink, my bra is on the floor by my feet.

"Fucking finally," he groans, palming my tits, pushing them together, dragging his tongue from one to the other. I pull him closer, moaning as he pulls one nipple into his mouth, teasing with his teeth before sucking hard. He walks me backward until my knees hit the mattress, pushing me down. "God, you're beautiful," he murmurs, his gaze like wildfire on my skin. He takes his time unlacing my boots and pulling them off, then climbs up on the bed, hovering over me like a heartbreakingly beautiful fallen angel, coming to do all sorts of bad things to my body. When I can't stand it any longer, I pull his face down to mine, running my tongue along the seam of his mouth before sinking my teeth into his lush bottom lip.

"You want it rough?" he breathes, his pupils nearly swallowing his irises.

I can feel him change, ferality streaking through his system. He drops his hips onto mine, plundering my mouth as he grinds his cock between my legs. He pushes away from me suddenly, breathing hard as he towers over me.

"Get undressed," he says harshly, pulling his sweatshirt over his head and dropping it on the floor. I scramble to obey, kicking off my sweatpants and underwear, then peeling off my socks and flinging them into the corner of the room.

"Sit on your heels," he commands, stepping out of his sweatpants and wrapping his hand around his shaft.

"Yes sir," I say hoarsely, lust gripping me by the throat, moisture flooding between my legs as I get into position.

"Spread your knees. More." He tugs at his cock as he watches me, coaxing a drop of precum to the tip. "Now touch yourself."

Fuck. His gaze follows my hand as I drag it down the swell of my lower stomach and between my legs. I circle my clit slowly, biting back a whimper when the drop of precum falls to the wood-planked floor. I'm so far gone that I would lick it up without a second thought.

"Good girl," he rasps, his nostrils flaring. "Put a finger inside."

I lift up a bit, sinking my middle finger into my center, fucking myself with it. He walks closer, circling my wrist with his fingers and pulling my hand up to his mouth, my middle finger disappearing between his lips as he licks it clean.

"Again."

"Dylan." It comes out as a whine. I want his cock in my mouth.

"Again," he demands.

I push my hand back between my legs, sinking down on two of

my fingers this time, pressing the heel of my palm to my clit. He pulls my hand away before I get too close, dragging my fingers over his cock, wetting it with my juices. He groans as he slides his hand up his shaft, slipping easily over the head of his cock, his hips jerking in response. He plants his other hand on my chest, pushing me back until my back is on the mattress. He tugs my ankles, bringing my ass to the edge of the bed, and then drops to his knees, burying his face between my thighs. The first long drag of his tongue up my center has me threading my fingers through his hair and pulling him closer.

"That's my girl. Ride me," he mumbles, his baritone vibrating against my pussy, making me squirm. I clamp my thighs over his ears, lifting my hips, riding his tongue until stars explode behind my eyelids. He pulls away right before I come.

"Middle of the bed, on your hands and knees, facing the wall."

I scramble up, getting on my hands and knees in the center of the bed, pushing my ass out like a needy whore.

"Please, Dylan," I beg, my whole body trembling with the need to come.

"You're so pretty like this," he murmurs, ignoring my plea. The mattress dips as he gets on the bed behind me, palming my ass cheeks, squeezing as he spreads them.

"Jesus fucking Christ," he mutters. He grips his cock, dragging the head from my clit to my ass, spreading my desire. He bends over me, gripping the base of my throat with his hand before straightening and pulling me up with him.

"You're too fucking sexy, Isla," he rasps, running his tongue along the shell of my ear. He presses his hips forward, sliding his cock between my thighs, the head dragging back and forth over my clit as he thrusts. He slides his other hand over my stomach and down to the apex of my thighs, rolling my clit under his fingers as he slams inside me. I shudder in his arms, my pussy clenching around his cock, desperate to keep him inside me.

"You feel so good," he moans, holding still as he tries to stay in control. His hips jerk, and then he's pulling out of me, backing off the bed, pulling me with him. He turns me to face him, capturing my lips with his, guiding me backward to the patio door, pressing me against the cold glass as he thrusts his tongue into my mouth. Sliding a hand from my ass down to my thigh, he hitches my leg up and presses the head of his cock against my entrance, stretching me as he slides deep.

He feels so goddamned good. I push a hand between us, needing to put pressure on my clit, but he captures it before I succeed, stretching it over my head as he fucks me.

"Dylan, " I whine, bucking my hips against him, desperation taking hold.

"Not fucking yet, Isla. I don't want to rush this."

I drop my weight slightly, forcing the shaft of his cock to drag along my clit as he thrusts. He grips my jaw, pulling me up onto my tiptoes so only the head of his cock is inside me, putting pressure against my g-spot.

"Naughty girl," he breathes, running his nose along mine, his gaze glued to my lips.

I'm rewarded with a groan as I squeeze my muscles around him. A violent shiver wracks my body as the cold of the glass finally sinks deep enough to register. Dylan pulls out of me, bending down to suck a puckered nipple into his mouth before throwing me over his shoulder without warning. He walks into the bathroom, ignoring my shrieks as he punches buttons on the control panel. He steps into the tub and sets me down, drawing me into a passionate kiss before turning me around. He holds me against his body, cupping a breast with one hand, the other sliding between my legs. Walking me forward to the edge, he nudges my knees until I kneel on the seat, not moving his hand until he has me positioned exactly as he wants me. He pulls his hand away, no longer blocking the jet that's aimed directly at my clit. I moan, dropping down onto my forearms, my nipples brushing the edge of the jacuzzi as Dylan slams into me. I tumble head-first into the abyss. The first contraction of my muscles has me gasping for air.

"Yes, Isla. Good girl," Dylan praises, his hips stuttering against me, his fingers digging into my hips as he pulls me back on his cock, fucking me hard.

We come together in an explosion of desperate noises, our bodies slapping together obscenely as we fall apart. I come back to earth slowly, my eyes fluttering open to see Theo standing in the doorway, his cock in his hand.

"My turn, Sunflower."

75

Theo pulls me out of the tub, leaving Dylan in the water with a dreamy look on his face. Theo bundles me into a robe, guides me to the toilet to make sure I pee, and then scoops me into his arms, carrying me into the bedroom.

"We need to replenish some of that energy first," he murmurs against my temple, setting me down at the small table next to the window. He must have raided the fridge because the table is laden with all sorts of snacks plus two glasses of champagne, the remnants of the bottle in an ice bucket. He sets me on my feet, kissing me soundly before pulling out a chair for me.

"Do you want to take a break between sessions so you don't get sore?" he asks, feeding me a grape.

"That's probably the smart thing to do." I groan as the sweetness of the grape bursts in my mouth. "I saw some snowshoes on the front porch. Do you want to go for a walk?"

"I want to do whatever you want to do, Sunflower."

"That's hardly fair."

He shrugs, rubbing at the day-old scruff on his chin. "It's the truth."

. . .

IT TAKES us ten minutes to get dressed and another twenty to figure out how to strap on the snowshoes, but it's all worth it when we begin our trek through the pines, silence enveloping us as we walk side by side. The trees are the biggest I've ever seen. Even holding hands, Theo and I can't wrap our arms all the way around one.

"This is magical," Theo murmurs, pausing to gaze up through the pines.

"Yes, it is," I whisper, looking at him. I get as close as possible to him with these monstrosities on my feet and tip his chin down. Pulling a mitten off, I brush the snowflakes from his long eyelashes–those deep pools of amber pulling me in, drowning me.

"I love you so much." The feeling overwhelms me, tears pricking the back of my eyes. I choke out a laugh, embarrassed.

"Don't." His gloves hit the snow, and then he's pulling my face to his, brushing his lips over mine in the gentlest caress.

"I love you, too, Isla MacLeod. More than anything." I push up on my tiptoes, winding my arms around his neck, angling my head to deepen the kiss.

He groans deep in his throat. "This was a bad idea. I want you in bed. Beneath me."

The snow underneath one of his snowshoes collapses, causing him to lose his balance. Before I can blink, he's on his back in the snow, and I'm sprawled on top of him, his arms still banded around my waist.

"Fuck," he gasps, laughing up at the sky.

"Maybe it's a sign." I bite my lip, wiggling my eyebrows suggestively as I shimmy up his body so I can reach his mouth. He grins at me, his eyes sparkling as he tucks a stray strand of hair into my hat before drawing my mouth to his. The warm glide of his tongue along the seam of my lips has me opening for him, a small spark of need quickly turning into a roaring wildfire.

"You're right," I pant, breaking our kiss. "This was a bad idea." I squirm against him, needing friction.

"We're already on the ground. We may as well just do it here," Theo says, smirking at me.

"I'm not taking my pants all the way off in the middle of a forest, Theo! First, it's freezing; second, some of the other guests could walk up here and see us!"

"We'd hear them long before they could see us, but you're right, it's not smart to have your pants off when it's this fucking cold out."

I push off his body, planting my snowshoes in the snow and standing, pulling him up after me. Even in snow pants, I can see the outline of his cock, and I'm not going to lie, it makes me want to drop to my knees right then and there. I look up at him, blushing when I realize he caught me. Something in his face changes, a predatory focus gleaming in his eyes. My pulse jumps, and I take several shuffling steps back. He follows. The back of my snowshoes hit something, and he swoops in before I can fall, gripping my waist and lifting me onto a gigantic stump.

"These things have to go," he says gruffly, squatting to undo the buckles on my snowshoes before stamping down the snow beneath his feet and taking off his own. "Much better."

I can feel the warmth of his palms through my pants as he runs them up my thighs and steps between my legs, a predator capturing his prey.

"Do you have any idea how beautiful you are?" he murmurs, brushing his thumb over my cheek.

"Come here, Theo," I rasp, cupping the back of his neck and tilting my face up to him, welcoming the rush as he crushes his lips to mine. He grips my hips as he pushes his tongue into my mouth, pulling me tight against him, the hardness of his cock pressing between my legs. I moan, locking my heels behind his butt, rocking my hips against him, whimpering as he moves to my neck, his hand sliding beneath my jacket.

"Fuck, how many layers do you have on?" he grumbles, pressing his forehead to mine as he unzips my jacket and rucks up three layers before finally finding bare skin. "There you are," he murmurs. He cradles my head in his hand, leaning me back until I'm lying flat on the stump. He helps me pull my arms from my jacket, carefully spreading it out beneath me, and then he hikes up my shirts, sliding his palms over my breasts and burying his face against my chest.

"Fuck, Isla." He peppers me with kisses, biting the swell of my lower stomach, sliding his tongue along my waistband before unsnapping my snow pants and shoving his hand beneath my long underwear, tracing my slit over my panties. "Already wet for me? That's my girl." He drags his finger back and forth over the damp fabric, teasing me. Pushing his finger under the edge of my panties, he dips a finger inside me before bringing it to his mouth. "Goddammit. You drive me so fucking crazy." Pulling down the layers just enough to fit his tongue against me, he feathers it over that most sensitive spot. "Fuck, I need you," he growls, biting at my hips, then the dip of my waist before roughly sucking a nipple into his mouth.

I arch up to meet him, desperate for anything he'll give me, my body thrumming with need.

"Hands and knees," he says roughly, breathing hard.

I scramble to obey, the wood rough beneath my palms as I grip the edge of the stump. He wrenches my pants halfway down my thighs, exposing my ass to the cold air, then I hear him fumbling with his button and zipper. I cry out as he slams his cock into me, his moan of surrender igniting something hot and frenzied within me. I push back, meeting every thrust, taking him deep. A gust of wind blows through, clumps of snow falling from the branches, disintegrating as it hits our skin. Theo pulls out suddenly, manhandling me onto my back and pushing my knees to my chest. I watch him curiously as he stares at the naked parts of me, need blazing in his eyes. Then he's eating a handful of snow, crouching down to lick a path from my ass to my clit.

"Theo!" I shriek, trying to twist away from his icy tongue. He jerks my pants past my knees and pushes his head between my thighs, sliding his tongue over my clit before sealing his lips around it and sucking. Hard. I strain against him, sobbing his name as he eats me alive. He stands, turning me on my side and dragging my ass to the edge of the stump. Notching himself at my entrance, he slowly impales me on his rigid length.

"Fuck, you feel good," he groans, his jaw clenching as he wrestles for control. He jerks out, flipping me onto my stomach before slamming back in, covering my body with his own, keeping me toasty warm as he rails me. He pushes his hand underneath me and between my legs, putting firm pressure on my clit as he thrusts, forcing me to the edge.

"Theo!" I gasp, my eyes rolling back as my body succumbs.

"Come for me, Isla. Good girl." He slams into me hard, my pussy clenching around him as he comes with me. "Jesus Christ," he pants, dropping his forehead to my shoulder. "I didn't plan for that. I have nothing to clean you up with." He pulls his hips away slowly, sliding out of me and tucking himself back in his snow pants before carefully helping me up, pulling each layer up before zipping and buttoning me into my cocoon.

"I'm sure Henry will help me with that when we get back," I tease, biting my lip to hold back my laugh.

"Ha! He'll just try to stuff it back inside you like the monster he is."

"A very sexy monster with a breeding kink I'm starting to like." I sit on the stump as Theo straps me back into my snowshoes.

"Do you like walking around with our cum inside you?"

I nod, my cheeks heating.

"You like feeling it drip down your thighs?"

"Yes," I rasp, flooding my panties with a new wave of desire. Fuck.

"You like when he pushes it back in?"

"Theo, you need to stop," I whimper, squeezing my thighs together, desperate to stem the ache.

He looks at me, his eyes dark. "Come here, Sunflower." As I approach him, he walks backward, pressing his back against a tree, his snowshoes straddling the trunk. As soon as I'm within reach, he pulls me close, shoving one knee between my legs and dragging my heat up his thigh. I wrap my arms around his neck, pulling myself higher, crushing my lips to his as I ride his thigh and the seam of my snow pants until I combust, stars blooming behind my eyelids as I come.

"Good girl," he rasps, kissing me softly all over my face as I come back down to earth.

76

H enry is waiting for me on the front porch when Theo and I return. He's been there so long that he's standing in a puddle of snow, the fertility blanket wrapped around his shoulders.

"What are you doing? You're going to freeze out here."

"Wouldn't be the first time I've nearly frozen to death just to be with you." He grips my face, pulling my mouth to his. He groans deep in his throat as I sweep my tongue over his lower lip, and he swings me up into his arms, carrying me into the cabin before I can even take off my boots.

"Do you remember that day on the beach?" he asks gruffly, sitting me down on the bed and unzipping my jacket.

"Like it was yesterday."

"I would have been okay with getting hypothermia if it meant I could spend more time with you."

"I noticed," I laugh.

"I was in love you even then, Isla."

"You didn't know me, Henry," I protest, lifting my arms so he can pull off my sweatshirt.

"I knew everything I needed to." He glances down at me, eyebrows drawn together. "Why are you wearing a sweater *under* your sweat-shirt? Are you trying to kill me?" I meet his deep blue gaze, holding it as I pull the sweater over my head, revealing my long underwear. "Fucking hell, Isla." He climbs on the bed, pushing me flat, his hands diving under my shirt.

"Finally," he groans, dragging his palms over my skin, pressing his face into the softness of my stomach. "You were like a fiery-haired nymph running into that water. All milky skin and jiggling tits." He buries his face against my hip, hiding his grin.

"You looked?" I shriek, hitting him on the shoulder.

"I tried not to. But, god, Isla. You're the most beautiful woman I've ever seen." He kisses from freckle to freckle across my stomach and over my ribs, palming my tits and squeezing. He rucks my shirt up to my chin and slides his thumbs into my bra, rubbing circles over my nipples. "You will always take my breath away."

I laugh at the absurdity. "Have you seen yourself? Not a day goes by that I don't wonder why you chose me." I push a curl from his fore-head, only for it to fall right back into place. I slide my hand over his jaw, his five o'clock shadow like sandpaper against my palm. The tip of my finger fits perfectly in the divot of his chin. I glance up, meeting his gaze and my heart nearly jumps out of my chest with the intensity in his eyes.

"Jesus Christ, Henry," I whisper, my voice breaking. I squirm beneath him, pulling my arms from the long underwear and drag-ging it over my head. "Make love to me," I plead, need thrumming inside me, an unquenchable thirst. He cradles my face in his hands, his gaze roaming over my face, memorizing me.

"I love you, Isla."

The moment his lips meet mine, a jolt travels through my body, awareness puckering my nipples before spearing between my legs. I whimper into his mouth, scrambling underneath him, trying to pull his body down onto mine, needing as much of him touching me as possible. He pulls away, chuckling, ghosting his lips along my jaw and down my neck before swirling his tongue in the hollow of my throat. He pushes his hands beneath my back, unhooking my bra and throwing it to the other side of the room before pushing my tits together and pressing his face between them.

"God, I love them," he rasps, first sucking one nipple into his mouth, then the other, humming in satisfaction.

"Henry," I plead, arching beneath him, needing friction.

"Don't rush me, Freckles." He bites my nipple in punishment, sending a jolt of adrenaline racing through my system. He rolls it between his fingers, the immediate ecstasy dragging a moan from my throat. Pushing onto his knees, he unsnaps my snow pants before dragging me to the end of the bed and pulling them off along with my boots.

"You're like a tootsie pop," he says, pulling off another layer. I wonder...?" He slides my long underwear down my legs, "How many licks it takes–" He nips his way up my legs, peppering kisses across my stomach before dipping his tongue into my belly button. He groans low in his throat, burying his face in the vee of my thighs before grabbing my panties with his teeth and working them down. "–to get to the center?"

The callouses on his palms scrape over the tender skin on the back of my thighs as he pushes my legs wide. His teeth sink into his bottom lips as he stares at the mess of cum and desire between my legs. He drops to his knees and flattens his tongue against me, licking one line from my ass to my clit. I sink my fingers into his curls as I plant my heels on the edge of the bed, pushing my body up as I pull him closer.

"Fuck, Henry," I pant, rocking my hips, dragging my clit back and forth over his tongue, taking the pleasure he's offering me like a greedy, greedy slut.

"I had plans, Isla," he pants, sucking my clit into his mouth. "I was going to shower with you, take care of you." He pulls back, his gaze almost predatory as he spreads me wide. "Take it slow. But the second I saw you, all I could think about was burying my cock in your perfect pussy."

"Then do it," I beg.

I push up on my elbows, watching him as he jerks his sweats down, his cock springing out, precum already glistening at the tip. He shuffles closer, wrapping his fist around his shaft before tapping it on my clit. Clenching his jaw, he drags the tip along my slit, back and forth, that midnight blue gaze meeting mine as his cock catches on my entrance. He only needs to push forward the slightest bit, and he'll be inside me.

"Please," I whimper, groaning when he pulls his cock away and slides it up my ass crack, holding it between my cheeks with his hand as he moves his hips.

"God, I swear I could fuck every part of you."

"My knee?" I tease.

"You think I'm kidding?" He stands, dragging two fingers between my legs to get them wet before wiping them on his cock. Bending my leg, he holds me steady as he pushes his cock into the crease at the back of my knee. His eyes roll back, his mouth dropping open as he slides his cock back and forth. A wild pulse of lust shoots through me, watching him like that.

"Okay, okay! I believe you!" I laugh, sitting up, his cock only inches from my face.

I look up at him, at that perfectly chiseled face. Holding his gaze, I lean forward, the tip slowly pushing past my lips. I don't stop until he's touching the back of my throat, his nostrils flaring as he tries to keep his control on a tight leash. I hollow my cheeks as I pull back, moving my tongue against his shaft. He tries to pull away, but I follow him, swallowing around him as I try to take him even deeper.

"Is that how it's going to be?" he growls, wrapping my hair around his fist and pulling me off his cock, breathing hard. "I can't fucking decide if you're the bane of my existence or the *reason* for my existence." He crushes his lips to mine, our tastes melding into something positively sinful. "I brought something for situations like this," he says, releasing me and walking over to the dresser.

"What do you mean by *situations like this*?" I ask, mesmerized by his perfectly round ass cheeks.

"When you're being bad," he says, looking over his shoulder at me, a dangerous glint in his eyes. He grabs several things before sitting next to me on the bed. "Hold out your hands." I obey, and he drops a wand, a butt plug, and handcuffs into them. "For my naughty girl." He hauls me up into his arms and throws me into the middle of the bed, a wicked grin on his face.

77

I can't describe the thrill that races through my body as Henry crawls up the bed toward me, powerful muscles shifting, mesmerizing blue eyes ensnaring me, making it hard to breathe, hard to think. My breath hitches as his fingertips brush over my calf. The corner of his mouth ticks up, like he knows exactly what he's doing, before he lowers his lips to my ankle kissing and biting his way up my leg.

"Henry," I gasp, trying to haul his body over mine.

"You better get used to that feeling," he murmurs, moving his lips to my other leg. "I'm going to edge you within an inch of your life."

"Henry, no," I gasp, already desperate for him to fill me, to feel him deep inside where he belongs.

He grips my legs and flips me in one smooth motion, pulling my hips back so my ass lifts into the air. He turns on the wand and hands it to me. "Hold this on your clit. Don't come, or I'll have to punish you."

Punish me? God, why do I like the sound of that? I sneak my arm beneath my torso, slowly sliding the wand into place with a groan.

"Henry, Jesus. How can you give me this and tell me not to get there?" I ask, my voice breaking as my body fights the vibration, already on the verge of coming. I hear the squirt of a lube bottle, and then Henry is shuffling toward me on his knees, one hand spreading my cheeks while the other slides the butt plug along my crack.

"It's only until I get this in," he says, his voice strained as his cock presses against the back of my thigh.

I would give just about anything for him to slide into my ass right now, fill me up so I can strangle his cock and watch him fall apart. A gush of desire drips down my thigh.

"Fucking hell, Isla." He palms his cock, dragging it along my slit with a low moan. "Just the tip," he says, like he's trying to convince himself he can handle it. He notches himself at the entrance of my pussy, pushing until his swollen head nestles against my G-spot.

I whimper, trying to hold still, trying to be a good girl. He blows out a ragged breath, his fingers flexing on my hip before the cold silicone of the butt plug nudges against that tight muscle.

"Relax, Isla."

I release the tension in my muscles, fighting the urge to impale myself on him.

"Fuck, I have to feel you," he groans, dropping the plug to the bed and easing his finger inside me instead. I slowly sit back, taking more of his cock, more of his finger, rhythmically squeezing around them. I'm so close that all it would take is one word from him for me to explode.

"Isla." My name is a warning, a promise falling from his lips.

"Henry," I moan, rocking back and forth, fucking myself on his cock.

"Jesus fucking Christ," he hisses, pulling his finger out and replacing it with the butt plug, putting constant pressure on it until my ass swallows it, leaving only a cute round black diamond on the outside. He sits back on his heels with a growl, flipping me over and taking the wand from my hand. I squirm beneath him, the plug heavy and full, making me want–no need–more. He falls on top of me, keeping his weight on his elbows as he cradles my face between his hands.

"How does that feel?" he asks, the concern on his face doing funny things to my insides.

"Good," I whisper, hooking my hand around his neck and pulling his face down. He slides his nose along mine before sucking my bottom lip into his mouth. I arch up to meet lips, my body on fire for him. He pushes his tongue into my mouth, and I suck on it, kissing and biting until he pulls back, panting.

"Shower?" he rasps, his gaze drifting to my mouth. "We don't have to, but I'm dying to see you naked and wet, pressed against those rocks."

"Only if you fuck me in there."

He chuckles, powerful muscles pushing his body away from mine, scooping me up and carrying me into the shower. He turns the water on full blast, waiting until it's steaming before walking underneath the spray and setting me on my feet. The rock walls are slick, the steam hovering just above our heads, making it feel like we're in a rainforest. Henry backs me against the wall, planting his arm above my head, looking down at me with those intense ocean-blue eyes.

I suck in a breath, my heart hammering in my chest. He presses his thumb to my chin, opening my mouth before bending down and kissing me, sweeping his tongue over my lips. My knees tremble, and he snakes one long arm around my hip, his hand gripping my ass, holding me up. He pushes his middle finger between my cheeks, pressing against the plug. I jerk in his arms, a noise I don't recognize ripping from my throat.

"Do you know how close I am to dragging you to the floor and burying my cock in your tight little cunt?" he groans, capturing my lips with his before I can beg him to do exactly that. He drags his finger back and forth over the plug, sending lightning bolts of pleasure through my body. "Fuck. I have to see it again." He spins me toward the wall, pulling me back several steps before running his hand up my spine, putting pressure between my shoulder blades until I'm bent over, my hands gripping the wall for support. He crouches behind me, groaning as he squeezes and kneads my cheeks. I nearly jump out of my skin when I feel his tongue slipping underneath the edge of the plug, teasing sensitive nerve endings. My body jerks as ecstasy shoots up my spine, electricity cracking over my skin. He stands, pulling my body against his, my back to his chest, one large hand sliding up to palm my breast.

"Despite what it looks like, I brought you in here to pamper you, but I can't seem to keep my hands off of you," he rasps, squirting some body wash into his hands, lathering it before dragging his hands over my body. "I could stay between your legs forever, Isla. My own personal paradise." He turns me toward him, slowly spreading the soap over my back.

I push up on my toes, kissing him long and deep. After dragging my hand through the soap on my stomach, I grip his cock, twisting my fingers over his shaft in steady strokes. He breaks the kiss, moaning as he drops his head to my shoulder. As I push my hand back toward his body, I extend my finger and slide it past his balls, stroking the sensitive skin of his taint. He jerks against me, a broken groan of need echoing off the walls.

Fuck. That sound alone pushes me so close to the edge that I'm tempted to shove him down on the floor and ride him into oblivion. I keep stroking him, pushing a little further each time until I finally get up the nerve to reach around him with my other hand and slide my finger down his crack.

"I'm too close," he rasps, even as he pushes his ass against my hand, his body telling me everything I need to know. I slowly sink to the floor, and he follows just like I knew he would, stretching his body over me, his cock pressing between my legs.

"Make love to me, Henry."

"The handcuffs–"

"–Can wait."

He shifts to his hands and knees, hovering over me as he sucks first one, then the other nipple into his mouth. He sits back on his heels, sluicing the water from his face before dragging the head of his cock along my slit, barely dipping in before pulling out and doing it again. Teasing us within an inch of our lives.

"Henry. Now," I beg.

In one powerful move, he plants his elbows on either side of my head and slams into me, filling me so full I see stars.

"Fuck," he bites out, holding himself impossibly still as he tries to pull himself back from the edge.

I whimper beneath him, writhing against his body, needing friction. Needing to break his goddamn control. Holding his gaze, I slide my hand down his back, pushing my middle finger down his crack, circling the puckered skin, waiting for him to tell me to stop.

He doesn't.

Desire gushes between my legs as I slowly push my finger in, watching as his eyes roll back in raw, unbridled ecstasy. His groan is primal, goosebumps peppering my skin as he rams into me, then pushes back on my finger, milking his prostate. It's frenzied, bordering on violent, as we fuck each other, using each other to find the ultimate release. Henry pushes his hand between our bodies, pinching my clit, and I detonate like a supernova, galaxies of stars exploding behind my eyelids as I come forcefully. His hips stutter as my muscles clench around him, and I massage him with my finger as he roars his release. He thrusts deep, emptying himself at the entrance to my womb.

"You're fucking incredible, Isla," he rasps, cupping my face, kissing me gently, his cock still half-hard inside me. He rolls over on his back, breathing hard. "I think that was the best fuck of my entire life."

78

I'm still buzzing as I pull on a cute silk robe. The fabric is cool against my skin, helping dull the fire roaring through my veins. Before the guys came around, I didn't realize that good sex only makes you crave more. I'll be forever chasing that feeling.

Henry and I walk out of the bedroom hand-in-hand, the butt plug still snug inside my ass.

"Finally," Theo groans, rolling his eyes, trying to act annoyed despite the wide grin on his face. "We texted Jo that we'd like to have dinner here. We have a movie ready to go on Netflix."

"We figured you could use some downtime," Dylan says, handing me a bottle of water and kissing me on the cheek.

"Psssh." I twist the top off the water and take a long drink before walking toward the couch. I pause, taking a shaky breath as the fullness of the butt plug lights me up like a marquee, my nerve endings sparking. Henry holds my gaze, biting his lip, growling low in his throat.

"What movie?" I ask, walking as fast as I can away from him before I do something stupid. I plop down next to Theo, the whimper that exits my mouth causing all three of them to turn toward me.

"Sore?" Theo asks, his face creased in concern.

"I'm good," I whisper, snuggling into his side. I look at the screen to see *365 Days* queued up and ready to play. "Um. Have you guys watched this before?" I ask, looking between them.

"No, have you? It sounds good. I looked it up and it says it's a Polish thriller." Theo leans over and nuzzles into my hair, breathing deeply.

"Mm. Well, it's certainly thrilling," I chuckle.

"Why don't we watch something else since you've already seen it?" he asks, picking up the remote.

"Oh no, I could watch this a hundred times and still want to watch it again." This is fucking great. I couldn't have planned it any better if I tried. Dylan sits next to me, leaving Henry to sit on the floor. I open my legs as he settles his back against the couch, the inside of my thighs hugging his shoulders.

THE BEGINNING of the movie lures the guys into a false sense of action. Guns and mob bosses—no reason to suspect anything out of the ordinary. Then we get to the masturbation scene, and Dylan's jaw drops.

"Wh–What kind of movie is this?" he stammers, looking at me, his eyebrows nearly touching his hairline.

A funny sound comes out of Theo's throat as he watches the main character stick his cock down the throat of the flight attendant. "I swear I just saw his dick. Isla! Is this porn?"

I cover my face with my hands, tears leaking down my cheeks, my whole body shaking with laughter.

"Fuck, Red. Is this the kind of thing you watch when we're not around?" Henry teases, eyes sparkling.

"I don't need to watch stuff like this anymore. Not when I have it in real life," I smirk, winking at him.

Theo scrambles to find the remote, pausing the movie. He opens his mouth, but nothing comes out. He clears his throat, then tries again. "Is this a good idea?"

"Why wouldn't it be?" I ask.

"Dinner is being delivered in the next hour."

I shrug. "Text her and have her leave it outside. That way, we're not risking her seeing something she shouldn't." I would suggest pretty much anything that would get us to the bedroom faster at this point. The butt plug feels like a ticking time bomb just waiting to detonate.

"Good idea." Theo pulls out his phone and shoots off a text.

I take the remote from him and press play, hiding it between the cushions so he can't stop it again. I have to stifle my giggle at the first *'Are you lost, baby girl?'* It's ridiculous in the best way possible.

"Oh, I don't like this," Dylan mutters after a while. "He kidnapped her? Is this like a Stockholm Syndrome situation?"

"Just watch. Forget about the plot. It's not going to matter in a little bit."

"Of course the plot matters—it's a movie," Henry scoffs.

I bite my lip, holding back my grin. "Wanna bet?"

"Yes, actually. If I win, I get to tie you to the bed, and the three of us get to have our way with you."

I'd let them do that anyway, but I don't tell him that. "Fine. If I win, I get to peg you."

Henry's entire body shudders, his mouth falling open, pupils dilating. "Seriously?"

I hold out my hand, and he shakes it, narrowing his eyes as if he doesn't trust this situation at all. He definitely shouldn't.

The guys almost give up on the movie when the main character is mistreated, but they settle back in during a high tension shower scene.

"Oh fuck," Henry says, running his hands through his hair, probably starting to realize he made a big mistake.

Then we get to the point in the movie when the main character finally gives in, and her love interest immediately sticks his cock in her mouth and then plants his face between her legs.

"Fuck, this looks real," Theo mumbles, adjusting himself. He pulls me closer, stretching his arm over my shoulder and reaching down to grab my tit. He holds a finger to his lips as he rolls my nipple. I arch into his hand, looking back at the TV just in time to the woman getting railed on the deck of the yacht.

"Do you think Lach would let us borrow his yacht so we can make our own sex montage?" Theo asks, leaning close to my ear.

"I'm sure he'd be thrilled with that idea," I say, rolling my eyes.

"Where's the goddamn remote?" Henry asks, holding out his hand.

"Why?" I ask, blinking at him innocently, my eyes wide.

"Because I'm not going to sit here and watch two people fuck when all I really want to be doing is fucking you."

"What about the plot, Henry?"

"I don't care about the fucking plot."

Got him.

I fish the remote from the cushions and plop it in his hand. He presses the power button and turns to look at me, an absolutely feral look in his eyes. Rough hands grip my thighs, pulling my ass to the edge of the couch. He slowly pulls on the sash of my robe, groaning as the bow comes loose and the fabric slips to the sides of my body.

"I hope you're ready for this," he rasps, sliding his hands up the inside of my thighs.

79

My heart flip flops as Henry pushes his hands along the insides of my thighs, rough callouses tugging at my skin, firelight drenching us in an ethereal orange glow. The first brush of his lips over my pussy has me arching into him, greedy for his touch. I shove my hands into his hair, inky locks falling over my fingers as I pull him closer. I moan my approval as he flattens his tongue against my clit, expertly working me into a frenzy. Just when I'm about to come, he pulls away and stands up.

"One of you take my place. I have to grab something from the bedroom," he says, licking his lips.

I watch him as he walks away, the large, muscled expanse of his back shifting as he moves, his sweatpants riding low on his hips.

"Eyes on me." Dylan touches my chin, turning my head toward him as he moves between my knees. He pulls me upright, biting his lip as he slowly slides the robe off my shoulders. His hands trail after the fabric, a light brush of his fingertips over my skin. Goosebumps follow in the wake of his caress, chasing his hands as he molds me to his touch. He catches me before I can melt against his body, gripping my jaw and crushing his mouth to mine. I wrap my arms around his neck, pouring every ounce of need into the kiss. He groans against my lips, smoothing his hands down my back and under my ass, squeez-ing. I whimper as the plug shifts, fireworks detonating inside me, sparks of pleasure shooting up my spine. His fingers brush between my cheeks and he freezes, a broken groan coming from deep in his throat.

"What's this?" he rasps, exploring more, making me squeal. "Fuck, Isla." He closes the small amount of distance between us, jerks down the front of his sweatpants and impales me on his cock.

Holy mother of God.

"You feel so fucking good." He presses on the plug as he fucks me, his other hand gripping the back of my neck, holding me steady while he nips at my bottom lip. I glance over at Theo, my entire body shuddering at the stark need in his eyes. I drag my gaze to the bulge in his pants, wondering why he hasn't taken it out yet, but I don't have the chance to ask because Henry comes back with a small duffel bag. He clears off the coffee table and up-ends the bag, all sorts of sex toys falling out and bouncing across the surface.

Dylan feels my body's visceral reaction and turns to look, his mouth falling open.

"Did you raid a sex store?" he asks, eyes wide.

"There was a sale online. I bought everything that had a good review," Henry says, shrugging. "I couldn't sleep the other night so I took them all out of their boxes and charged what needed to be charged, so everything is ready to go."

Jesus Christ. I look at everything on the table and admittedly don't even know what half of it is.

Theo leans over and grabs a smooth pink dildo, a bottle of lube, and the wand from the pile. He doesn't even have to say a word for Dylan to back up and give him space.

"Get on your hands and knees, ass facing me," he demands.

I hold his gaze for a second, the independent woman in me wanting to do the exact opposite, but the good girl overrides her and I assume the position. I hear a breath shudder out of him when he sees the end of the plug nestled between my ass cheeks. I hide my smile against my arm, smug satisfaction quickly giving way to blinding pleasure as he tugs on it.

"Were you saving me a spot, Sunflower?" he asks, his voice husky.

"Ask Hen-" I'm cut off by the moan that rips its way from my chest as he pulls out the plug. He squirts lube into his hand, first spreading it along my ass crack and then grips his cock, pulling me to my feet as he slides the lube up and down his shaft. He sits down, his jaw clenching with barely restrained desire.

"Sit."

I look at him, trying to figure out what he wants me to do.

He taps his thighs. "I want what's mine, Isla. Sit."

My insides liquefy, lust pooling like a red-hot inferno inside my gut, need dripping down the inside of my thighs. I walk between his knees, looking at him before I turn and slowly and lower myself, his hands helping to guide me down. A tsunami of pleasure rolls through me as the head of his cock presses against my ass. He groans, pushing past that tight muscle, his hands flexing on my hips as he fully seats me on his cock. It feels so good it's making it hard to breathe. To think. Pleasure pounds through my system like a base drum, urging me to move, to rub, to do *something*.

"Lean back."

I relax into him, my back to his chest, his cock pressing deeper as he hooks my thighs on the outside of his knees, spreading me wide, all of my weight now settled directly in his lap. I see movement out of the corner of my eye and look up to see Dylan and Henry standing several feet away, waiting and watching, cocks hard and ready.

Theo picks up the dildo, sliding it along my slit before focusing on my clit. I tremble as he drags it down to my opening, teasing me, sliding it in hard and fast. My back bows, my tits bouncing as I struggle to breathe past the pleasure obliterating my senses.

Dylan must not be able to hold himself back anymore, because he steps forward, dropping between our legs, taking the dildo from Theo.

"Use this," Henry says, picking up something from the table and holding it out to Dylan.

"Henry, that's too big," I gasp, looking up at him and then back at the dildo. It's molded to look like a giant monster cock, with wide knobby bumps on the underside leading to a thick knot at the base.

"I promise it's not," he says, wrapping his hand around the middle of the shaft, his fingers barely touching. He steps forward, reaching around Dylan to drag the tip up and down my slit. "Do you trust me?"

"Yes," I sob, reaching between my legs to press the dildo to my center, grinding my clit over the ridges, so fucking desperate to come I could cry.

"Does that feel good?" Theo rasps, tucking his chin over my shoulder, watching as I pleasure myself. "I bet I'll be able to feel those ridges when Dylan fucks you with it."

Dylan notches the tip at my entrance, circling there, teasing me.

"Please, Dylan," I beg.

He pulls the dildo away, bending down so his face is between my thighs, breathing deep before licking a trail up my pussy, pulling my clit into his mouth, lapping at me with slow, measured strokes. I buck against his mouth, ecstasy spearing through me as Theo slides his hand around my torso and up to cover my breast, rolling my nipple between his fingers.

"Are you ready?" Dylan asks, looking up at me, eyelids hooded over those big brown eyes.

"Yes," I moan, trying to sink down on the dildo as he notches it at my entrance. He palms my thigh, holding me still as he slowly slides it inside me.

Theo shifts beneath me, groaning, his hands spasming on my hips. "Fuck that feels good," he pants.

I whimper, my body buzzing.

"Almost there," Dylan murmurs, his gaze glued between my legs, the knot on the toy snug against the outside of my pussy.

"I don't think—"

Henry drops onto the couch next to me, wand in hand, fitting it against my clit as he sucks one of my nipples roughly into his mouth.

Oh fuck.

A fresh wave of desire gushes between my legs, and Dylan pulls the dildo out, sawing it back and forth, coating it in my juices before pushing it deep, not stopping until the knot pops inside me, stretching me, pain morphing into an exquisite feeling of fullness. I don't have time to warn them before I explode, my entire body shaking as I come harder than I have in my entire life.

80

As I come down from the height of my orgasm, I latch onto Theo's deep, ragged breathing, matching my own with his as he's fighting for his life underneath me.

"You okay down there?" I ask, shifting in his lap, trying to look over my shoulder at him.

"Don't fucking move," he gasps, his hands flexing on my hips. I don't have time to come up with ways to torture him as Henry takes Dylan's place, dragging the head of his cock through the mess between my legs.

"Will we ever be enough, or will you only be happy with monster cock from now on?" Henry teases, eyes sparkling.

"Shut up!" I swat him on the shoulder but don't have time to say anything else before he shoves inside me with a groan.

"I just need to feel you for a second, love," he rasps, capturing my face with his hands, holding me still as he ravishes my body, my mouth, my soul. He pulls away, panting, wrapping his arms tight around my back, and then stands, pulling me off Theo.

"Sorry, man, my turn." Henry carries me to the rug in front of the fire, his cock still buried deep inside me, and carefully drops to his knees, making sure my legs won't get crushed before laying me down.

Stretching over me, he fucks me with long, measured strokes, holding my gaze, the intensity increasing with every push and pull of his hips. "I had to see you like this," he whispers, pushing a lock of hair from my forehead.

"Like what?" I ask, arching up to meet his thrusts, pressing my nipples to his chest, moaning as they drag against his skin.

"Absolutely ravished on a rug in front of the fireplace."

"Is it everything you hoped for?" I tease, reaching up to stroke his cheek.

"God, yes. I wish you could see yourself right now. Your hair looks like flames, and your eyes are greener than I thought possible. Your freckles are melting into the rosiness of your skin. I've never seen anything more beautiful."

Tears spring to my eyes. How can he—with his angled jaw, full lips, eyes the color of stormy seas, and inky dark hair falling in curls over his forehead—be saying that about *me*? I strain up to meet his lips. He follows me back down as I relax, tilting my chin to deepen the kiss, stilling his hips to focus on my mouth, his cock buried at the entrance to my womb. I groan as he sucks my lower lip into his mouth, squirming beneath him.

I feel more hands on me, and then Henry and I are being pulled apart. It's like an out-of-body experience as they pick me up, calloused hands brushing heated skin. My eyes flutter open as they lower me toward the floor, Dylan's hooded brown eyes watching my every move. Strong hands pull me down on top of a warm body, my back to their chest. Fingers grip my thighs, pushing them wide, spreading lube over my ass. Theo's moan has goosebumps racing over my skin as he notches himself and slowly slides into my ass. I whimper, sliding my hand between my legs. Henry's fingers are like a vise grip around my wrist, pulling my hand away.

"That's my job," he says roughly, straddling Theo's legs, slapping my clit with his cock before sliding the tip down my slit and impaling me with a muttered curse, his eyes rolling back.

"Dylan." I motion for him to come closer, not knowing what I want, only that I need him near me.

"Where do you want me, Freckles?" he asks, sliding his back and forth along his shaft with measured strokes, a bead of precum glistening at the tip.

"We need a proper wedding night, which means all three of you need to be inside me."

"Does a cock in your ass count?" Theo murmurs in my ear.

"Close enough," I answer, gasping as he flexes inside me. They work like a well-oiled machine, moving just the right way to allow Dylan enough room to crouch over me.

"Wait. This doesn't feel right." I know it's selfish to stop them when they're so close, but I want this to be perfect, and it's just not. Not when I can tell Dylan won't be comfortable in that position for long, and I can't even see Theo.

"What do you need, baby?" Dylan asks, stepping to the side.

"Can we stand? I want to be able to see all of you." Henry pushes away from me, stands, and pulls me up after him. "Tell me exactly what you're thinking so we can make it happen.'

"Theo, put your back against the wall," I instruct, waiting for him to take his place before turning to Henry. "Henry, pick me up. I'll wrap my legs around your waist. Now take me over to Theo."

He does exactly as I say, their cocks twitching beneath me, desperate to be back inside.

"Dylan, I want you on my side." I pull him into a kiss as he plasters himself against my body, his cock bobbing just beneath my ass cheek. I reach underneath me, gripping his shaft, pressing the tip of his cock to my pussy. I swallow his groan as he pushes into me, breaking the kiss, I twist toward Theo, pressing my lips to his as I grip his cock and notch it against my ass. He growls, pushing his tongue into my mouth as the head of his cock pops inside me. I whimper, squeezing around him hard.

"Jesus fucking Christ," he grunts, his hips stuttering for a second before he gets himself under control and slides the rest of the way in.

"Ready?" I ask, turning to Henry, feeling for his cock beneath me, and wrapping my fingers around his thick shaft.

"Always," he murmurs, his hands squeezing my thighs as he leans forward, capturing my mouth with his. I slide the head of his cock along my slit, getting it wet before notching it against my entrance and Dylan's shaft.

"Fuck, Isla," Henry breathes. I hold him steady as he flexes his hips, slowly sinking into me. "Nobody move," he pants, breathing deep, trying to reign himself in.

Dylan moans, his entire body trembling, control slipping through his fingers like sand. "I can't, I'm sorry," Dylan rasps, pulling almost all the way out before slamming back into me.

"Fuck, Dylan," Henry grunts, his breath hitching. "God damn it," he groans. He pushes his weight against me, forcing Theo harder against the wall, anchoring his pubic bone against my clit, and ramming into me hard.

Holy fucking god. It feels like every single molecule in my body is tearing apart, atoms splitting to rearrange themselves into something new. My entire world shrinks to these three men in this tiny cabin before it explodes, pleasure tearing through my body, my nerve endings short-circuiting as I try to contain the euphoria. The first spasm of my muscles sets off a chain reaction, sweaty limbs tangling, toes curling, fingers clenching, bodies straining, ecstasy sliding through our veins like molten honey. I slump back against Theo, my head lolling against his shoulder as I struggle not to collapse beneath the wildfire roaring through my body. I feel them flexing inside me, growing impossibly harder as any semblance of control flies out the window.

Theo is the first to crumble, hips jerking, fucking my ass with hard and fast strokes. Henry slams into me, pushing me back onto Theo's cock, seating him to the hilt. Theo groans, his cock spasming deep inside me. Dylan grunts, his head dropping to my shoulder as he surrenders, his thrusts uncoordinated as he spills his seed. Henry pulls me in for a kiss, rolling his hips against me, his cock so deep I swear he's rearranging my insides. He growls against my lips as I clench around him, my orgasm building to something unfathomable.

"Come with me, Isla."

I implode on myself. Pleasure pulling everything into a tiny pinpoint before exploding outward, drenching me in blinding ecstasy. I lock my legs around Henry's waist, squeezing tight, hanging on for dear life as pleasure rips me limb from limb, delineating my life into before and after this orgasm.

"Fuck," I pant, my forehead against Henry's shoulder. I can't seem to pull enough air into my lungs, my entire body shuddering with the effort.

"Breathe," Dylan whispers, tenderly smoothing my hair back from my face.

"That was—" I stop, realizing I don't have the words to describe it.

"The best fucking orgasm of your life?" Theo suggests. "I concur."

I giggle, twisting in his arms, pressing my lips to his. They all wince in pained pleasure as my muscles tense around them. I squeeze again, laughing as they scramble to pull out of me. All except Henry, who walks backward with me still impaled on his thick cock. I clench my muscles, enjoying the aftershocks of my orgasm.

"You sure you want to tease me, Red?" he asks, massaging my ass cheeks with his rough palms.

"No, I surrender," I whisper, wrapping my arms around his neck and pulling myself up to kiss him properly. He groans against my lips, his cock flexing inside me.

"Okay! Okay!" I pull back, wiggling out of his grip. He sets me down slowly, his cock dragging over my clit. I nearly climb back up his body, the need to fuck him until he can't keep it up anymore written into my DNA. That will have to wait. Tomorrow maybe.

I gingerly lead the way to the bathroom, sore in the best way possible. I walk straight into the shower, turning on all the shower-heads, queuing up a playlist, and setting my phone where it won't get wet. Dylan comes from behind, wrapping his arms around my stomach and pulling me into the still-cold water.

"Dylan!" I shriek, struggling in his grip.

"It's good for you," he murmurs, tilting his head back into the spray.

I stop struggling as the water warms, turning in his arms,

admiring the lines of his neck as the water runs over him. He must feel the heat of my gaze because he smiles before looking down.

"Did your wedding night live up to your expectations, love?" he asks, sweeping his thumb over my cheekbone.

I laugh as Henry and Theo crowd closer to hear my answer. "It was perfect. Better than I could have ever imagined." I twist a strand of my hair around my finger, biting my lip. "We do have a slight problem, though."

"What's that?" Theo asks, raising an eyebrow.

"Charlie didn't pack my birth control." Dead silence. "Somebody say something."

Henry clears his throat, color high in his cheeks. "What day of your cycle are you on?"

I pick up my phone, water droplets sliding down the screen as I pull up my tracking app. I hold the screen out to him as it's loading, letting him read me the news.

"One day until ovulation?" he asks, sounding choked.

"Oh, fuck," I whisper, glancing at the screen to confirm what he said.

Theo starts tapping a staccato on his thigh, his detail-oriented brain running through our options. "Is this really a big deal?" he asks, surprising me. "We're married. We have enough resources to support a baby. Plus, Henry has wanted to be a father since he was twelve."

Dylan squeezes me tighter, prompting me to look up at him. "Not having your birth control isn't a big deal to us, Freckles. But you're the one that matters. Your body, your choice. Always."

I take a deep breath, thinking of baby Summer and Lorna's twins. Would it really be so bad? "If it happens, it happens," I say finally, shrugging my shoulders, hardly believing the words coming out of my mouth.

"And what about when we get back home?" Henry asks, cupping my chin and turning me to face him, his gaze full of hope.

"You would fill the entire castle with our babies if you could, wouldn't you?" I ask softly, blinking back tears.

"Only if that makes you happy, too, Isla." He pulls me into his arms, pressing his lips to my hair.

I bury my smile in his chest as tears slide down my cheeks. "I'm starting to think it would."

x The End x

If you would like to read Penelope's story as I write it, come join our community on Ream! https://reamstories.com/daphneleigh

UNTITLED

ACKNOWLEDGMENTS

This book is dedicated to everyone that found me on Kindle Vella and encouraged me to keep writing! I will forever be grateful for you. xoxo

PENELOPE (SNEAK PEEK)

1

I tie a kitchen towel around my face and pull the pin on the fourth–and last–fire extinguisher, squeezing the handle and aiming it at the flames leaping up the wall. Deep down, I know it's a lost cause, but I hold my ground as they shoot higher, licking at the ceiling. I'll go down trying to save this place if I have to. My heart drops into my stomach as the fire extinguisher sputters out. I take a couple of steps back, ducking as a piece of drywall falls from the ceiling, landing in the spot where I had just been standing.

"FUCK!" I scream with everything I have, like that one word might save me. Save my restaurant. Save the last ten years of my fucking life that I've poured into this place.

I run to the sink, turn the water on full blast, and use the hose attachment to spray down everything I can reach, hoping to slow the spread long enough for me to come up with some brilliant idea. The fire department should be here in twenty minutes, but knowing my luck, this place will be burned to the ground by then. I don't see how a centuries-old building can withstand a fire like this.

"Pen!"

Sammy's voice rises above the crackling of the flames, the desperate edge slicing like a knife through my heart.

"Get out of here, Sam!" I scream, tears streaming down my cheeks—whether from the smoke or emotion, I have no idea. Maybe both.

"Pen! You stupid woman!" Sam is perfectly outlined in the door leading out to the dining area. His dark skin glows in the flames, making him look like some sort of vengeful god.

"Go make sure the fire department is on its way," I yell, squeezing my eyes shut as I blindly aim the stream of water.

"Not without you," he roars, edging his way into the kitchen, dodging debris as he makes his way to me.

"I'm not leaving, Sammy," I sob, my hand spasming around the sprayer, my muscles protesting.

"Then let me take your place. There are too many people who love you for you to go out like this. Nobody would even know I'm gone."

Fury engulfs me. "Don't ever say that again! I would care, Sammy. *I would care!*" My words are punctuated by a portion of the ceiling over the stove caving in, sending in a fresh burst of air to feed the flames. Sammy jerks the sprayer from my hands and douses me with water before turning it on himself. "You may hate me forever, but I'm not going to let you do this, Pen." He scoops me into his arms, gripping tight as I try to twist away from him.

"You're going to kill us both. Is that what you want?" I shriek, going limp in his arms, hoping my dead weight will loosen his hold. I'll sacrifice myself to this goddamned restaurant, but I'm not sacrificing him.

"Take her out of here," he yells, his voice harsh as he hands me over to Spencer.

"No. *No!*" I thrash in Spencer's arms, but he only grips me tighter as he carries me through the restaurant and outside.

"We have to go get him, Spence, please!"

"He'll come out before he gets hurt, Pen." His soothing southern drawl does nothing to stem the panic.

"He said nobody would care if he died, Spence."

"Hell-fire!" He sets me on my feet, gripping my hand to keep me from running, and yells for Liam. "Don't let her back inside," he instructs, making sure Liam has me before heading in to help Sammy.

"What's happening?" Jamie asks, skidding to a stop next to us, Archer on his heels.

"We came as soon as we saw the smoke," Archer says, worry creasing his forehead.

"Sam and Spence are in there," Liam says, fear written in every line of his face. "It looks like it's only the kitchen so far."

Both Archer and Jamie run inside, and I feel like my entire world is crumbling. They're my best friends, my family, my *everything*. I can't let them put themselves at risk for a building.

"It should be me in there, " I whisper, my whole body shaking as adrenaline kicks in.

"No, you shouldn't. The restaurant can be rebuilt, Penelope. We can't bring you back to life."

"But it's my fault," I wail, furiously wiping at the tears streaming down my face. "I just wanted some damn fish and chips."

"We'll get you your fish and chips, Pen, don't you worry," Liam murmurs, smoothing his hand over my hair.

"Do you really think that's what I'm worried about now, you fucking eejit?" I try to wriggle from his grasp, but he holds tight, his sea-chiseled body hard against my back.

"I'm not going to let you go, so you may as well quit rubbing your body all over mine," he says stiffly.

"I don't want them to die in there!"

"They're all trained in fire safety, Nel. They'll be fine."

"Yeah, so am I! It's my restaurant. I'm the one responsible. They don't need to be in there fighting for something that means nothing to them!"

"*You* mean something to them! They don't want to see you die in there, either."

We both jump as glass shatters, dark smoke billowing into the air.

"They need to get out of there, Liam. I could never live with myself if something happened because of me."

He turns me toward him, pushing his leather outback hat higher on his forehead, his dimples showing as he looks down at me. "Darlin', even if something did happen, they'd tell you it was worth it,"

The faint wail of the fire truck rises over the roaring of the flames, and I sag against him in relief. Liam hikes me over his shoulder and walks toward the front of the restaurant to meet them.

"You can set me down. I won't go anywhere," I protest, kicking my legs, knocking his hat from his head.

His chuckle vibrates through me. "You think I believe that, Darlin'? I'm not letting go of you until that fire is out, and I know you're not going to go and get yourself killed."

The firefighters make quick work of the flames, dousing the now roofless kitchen with jets of water until there are only smoking embers left. I run inside the second they give me the all-clear and stop dead in my tracks. The kitchen is absolutely decimated. Everything is burned to a crisp. There are only twisted hunks of metal where my livelihood used to be. Thankfully, the dining room is still standing with only light smoke and water damage. Not great, but it's salvageable. The guys are covered in soot, dousing any hot spots with buckets full of water. The wall between the kitchen and dining room is soaking wet, and I realize that they must have been spraying the wall down until the firetruck arrived. They risked their lives to save the dining room.

"Thank you," I croak, trying to hold back my sobs, my chin quivering.

Sammy comes to my side, crouching down. "I'm sorry we couldn't save the kitchen, boss."

"I don't care about the kitchen," I hiccup, throwing my arms around his neck. "I'm just glad you guys are safe."

"You were ready to die for this kitchen, Penelope," he reminds me, his voice hoarse from the smoke.

"That doesn't mean I wanted *you* to die! You don't owe me that kind of loyalty."

"You don't give yourself enough credit, Pen. You gave us a home. A life. We owe you the world." He wraps his arms around me, standing, my toes dangling in the air. "Let's get you home."

2

I wake up to sunlight burning through my eyelids, searing my retinas. I groan, stretching, slowly becoming aware of my surroundings. I prop myself up on my elbow and look down at the fabric twisted beneath me. What on earth? There are towels piled above and below me. My skin is filthy. The memory of last night comes roaring back.

The fire.

Tears start immediately. I sit against the headboard, dropping my head to my knees as sobs wrack my body. I don't even know where to start. The restaurant is my primary source of income, and now that the kitchen is gone, so are my summer plans. I'll have to call the seasonal hires today and tell them to look for something else. Fuck my life.

"Hey."

Archer is standing at my bedroom door, leaning against the wall, sweatpants slung low on his hips, his hair wet like it had just come out of the shower. I swallow hard, averting my eyes.

"Good morning," I croak, wiping at my cheeks, my fingers coming away with black smudges.

"How are you feeling?" he asks softly.

"Not great," I admit. "I can't believe I passed out like that. I don't even remember you guys bringing me back home.'

"Stress can do weird things."

I nod, sniffling. "Why are you here?"

"We were all so worried about the kitchen yesterday that none of us even thought about the bunkhouse until it was too late. I'm sorry, Pen."

Oh my god. The bunkhouse. It shared a wall with the kitchen. I was so worried about saving the dining room, that it never even cross my mind. "The whole thing burned? What about all of your belongings?"

He shakes his head, his lips pressing into a thin line.

Goddamnit. "Where did you guys sleep last night?" Where will they sleep tomorrow? Will they leave now that they don't have anywhere to call home? My heart thumps painfully.

"Downstairs," he says sheepishly. "I hope you don't mind. With the bunkhouse gone, we didn't have anywhere to go."

"No. I'm glad you stayed here," I murmur, my gaze wandering to the tattoo on his chest, tracing the outline of the coast of Maine down to his—

"No rush, but breakfast will be ready in twenty minutes. I thought you may want to shower first."

I squeeze my eyes closed, my cheeks burning. I nod, embarrassed, broken. Devastation consumes me without warning, a tsunami of grief tossing me around, battering me against the rocks. I bury my face in my hands, my body trembling. The bed dips, and then Archer's arms wrap around me, pulling me onto his lap.

"It's okay, Penny. I promise we'll figure something out." He rubs his hand in small circles over my lower back, soothing me.

"Don't say 'we,'" I sob. "You guys will have to find a job where you have somewhere to stay. I won't even have any money coming in this summer."

"If we stay and fish, you will," he objects.

"It won't be nearly enough, Archer. Most of what you catch is to supply the restaurant, and the restaurant writes your paycheck."

"We're not leaving, Penny. The five of us have already talked. We're not going anywhere."

"But—"

"No buts. We'll figure it out together once you've had a shower and something to eat." He stands, carrying me into the bathroom. My feet hit the cold tile, and then he's turning on the shower spigot, waiting for it to get hot before releasing me completely. "You'll feel better after a shower." He kisses my head, my hair so dirty it leaves a black smudge on his lips.

He was right. I do feel better after showering. I towel dry my hair and pull on a tank top and shorts before padding to the kitchen. The scene that greets me stops me dead in my tracks. Five sleep-mussed, warm-bodied, heavily muscled men in various states of undress are cooking in my kitchen and lounging at my dining table. I haven't had a single man in this house since I bought it, except for my brother, so this is an incredible shock to the system. Jamie's greeting dies on his lips as his gaze slides down my body, snagging on my nipples, which have decided to come out and play. This may be the second or third time they've seen me dressed in something other than coveralls, and they sure as hell have never seen me in a tank top and shorts.

"I—I'll be right back," I stammer, running down the hallway and pounding back up the stairs. I tear through my dressers until I find my baggiest pair of sweatpants and one of Lach's old sweatshirts. I try to walk back into the kitchen without being noticed, but all the guys look at me at me the second my foot hits the tile. Sammy turns away from the stove, lifting an eyebrow as if to say, 'We already saw what's underneath that, and we're not going to forget any time soon.'

"Good morning," I murmur, twisting the sleeve of the sweatshirt in my hands.

I get an immediate response from all five, varying nicknames makign an appearance. "I've been thinking about it, and we need—"

"Not yet. We can talk after we eat," Sammy says in his posh

English accent, shoving a big bowl of scrambled eggs into my hands and gesturing for me to take it to the dining table.

I set the bowl on the table, and Spencer walks up behind me, pulling a chair out and gently pressing on my shoulders until I sit down. He scooches me in, and Liam places a steaming cup of tea on the table in front of me.

"I could get used to this," I murmur, wrapping my hands around the mug.

"You may have to," Liam says, chuckling as he sits beside me.

Does that mean what I think it means? Have they talked about possibly staying *here*? In my two-bedroom, one bathroom, tiny house?

Would I even be okay with that?

Dumb question. I'm pretty much okay with anything when it comes to them. I've been harboring some serious crushes that have only worsened over the last two years. I've been trying to get a handle on it, but my heart refuses to cooperate with my head. So, until today, I've been giving them room. Staying scarce. Trying to put some distance between us so I have time to get over them. But being in a tiny island town on the west coast of Scotland doesn't lend itself to meeting anyone who would help me get over said crushes.

Jamie sits on my other side and loads my plate with food before the guys serving himself.

After two minutes of silence, I can't take it anymore. "You guys have obviously talked already. Let's hear what sort of plans you came up with."

"We'd rather hear your thoughts first," Archer says, pushing his glasses up his nose, those serious brown eyes pinning me in place.

"I don't have any thoughts other than panic at the moment, so, please, go ahead."

Sammy clears his throat when nobody starts talking, taking one for the team. "We know you're going to tell us to leave, but we're not going to, just to make that clear from the start.'

I take a bite of eggs, trying to hide my trembling chin.

"We think you should take the summer to do what you've been

saying you want to do for the last two years. Rehab the restaurant. With the kitchen gone, and with our help, we can start from scratch and build a state-of-the-art professional kitchen. We can strip down the dining area and revamp that as well. Most of it will need to go due to the smoke, anyway."

"But what about money?" I ask, my voice cracking, hopelessness trying to worm its way into my heart.

"We'll take turns fishing and we can use that money for the restaurant. Money will be tight, but we're used to that."

"No, you guys are used to soft beds and two restaurant meals a day," I protest, pursing my lips.

"We had lives before we came here, Sugar. We can handle it," Spencer reminds me. I've heard his stories about growing up in Southern Appalachia, so I know he's telling the truth.

"That still doesn't solve where the five of you are going sleep. With the bunkhouse gone, we're five beds short."

"We measured, and we can fit two sets of bunk beds in your guest room," Liam says, leaning back in his chair, the gold hoop in his ear catching the morning sun.

"And the fifth?"

"Don't you have a king bed?" Sammy asks, grinning.

I choke on my food. "You can't—"

"I'm kidding, boss! We'll take turns sleeping on the couch."

Fucking hell. So my options are firing them, having no income, and having nobody to help me fix the restaurant. Or letting them live in my house and help me rebuild. I know Lach would help me in a heartbeat, but I'm too proud for my own good. I don't want to take his money when I know I can do it myself. Well, by myself with the help of five burly men.

"Okay," I whisper, massaging my forehead,trying to ease the ache between my eyes.

"Okay to what part?" Jamie asks, his soft brown eyes alive with hope.

"You can stay and help me." I hold up my hand to keep them from talking. "Thank you for being here for me and offering to help. I appreciate it more than you'll ever know."

"Thank you for allowing us to stay in your house, Penelope," Spencer says, that deep southern twang sending goosebumps skittering over my arms.

"So, where do we start?"

3

"Penny! Where are you? I brought coffee!"

Millie comes barging into the kitchen with a drink carrier in one hand and a half-eaten scone in the other. She stops dead in her tracks when she sees the guys, her mouth falling open, utterly oblivious to the crumbs falling out and sticking to her pink lip gloss.

"Morning, Millie," the guys call out, smirking.

"Thank you, Millie." I take the drink carrier from her and wave my hand in front of her face, trying to snap her out of it.

"What?" She blinks at me dazedly, then abruptly goes into a tirade. "Why didn't you call me last night? I had to hear it from my neighbor! I'm supposed to be your best friend, Penny."

"I know, I'm sorry, Millie." I wrap my arms around her, hugging her tight. "You are my best friend. It was late, and I passed out the second I got home."

"No! I'm the one that should be sorry. I drove by the restaurant on my way here and saw the damage. What happened?"

"I wanted a snack."

"You wanted a snack," she repeats dumbly, her eyebrows lifting toward her hairline.

"I don't know what happened. I was using the fryer for fish and chips, and then the wall was on fire."

"Holy shite. I'm so glad you're ok. And at least it wasn't the entire restaurant, aye?" She takes another bite of her scone, her eyes narrowing as she looks between me and the guys. "Okay, well, I'm off to work. I'll stop by later and see what you need help with. Love you, Penny Lou Who." She blows me a kiss and then bounds back out the door, leaving a cloud of sweet-smelling perfume behind.

"Penny Lou Who?" Archer asks, looking at me over the top of his glasses.

"Long story," I say, waving my hand in dismissal.

"Any relation to Cindy Lou Who?" Sammy asks. "You have a nose just like hers." He swipes one long finger down my upturned nose.

"Leave me and my Whoville nose alone," I grumble, stomping out of the kitchen and up the stairs to change into my work clothes.

I'm standing in front of the still-smoldering ruins of the kitchen and bunkhouse, trying not to cry. Two of the kitchen walls are entirely gone, the roof caved in, and not a single scrap of the bunkhouse is left standing. One of my neighbors was nice enough to bring a dumpster by early this morning, so we get to work filling it.

After three hours of back-breaking work, soot covers all of us from head to toe. I sit down on a lump of metal that probably used to be the prep table, dirty and dejected.

"Hey, we've got this, boss," Sammy says, sitting beside me. "Tell you what. I'll go to the store right now and get what I need to make a delicious lunch. You'll feel better after you eat my food. I promise. Bring the crew back to the house in a couple of hours." He pats me on the head awkwardly, and a minute later, I hear the rumble of the work truck, and he's pulling out onto the road.

Two hours later, the kitchen is cleared of debris, the dumpster is almost full, and somehow I feel even more hopeless than I did this morning. There's nothing left of the kitchen. Not one single spatula went unscathed.

"It'll be okay, Sugar," Spencer says, walking up behind me, warm hands squeezing my shoulders.

When I don't respond, he turns my body toward him and wraps his arms around me. I haven't been hugged by anyone other than Millie or Lach in so long that I don't know what to do, so I stand there, stiff as a board in his arms.

"Jesus Christ. Relax." He pushes on the back of my head until I rest it in the crook of his shoulder. I turn my face into his neck, his skin warm against my forehead, and I break. He gathers me close as sobs rack my body, making soothing shushing sounds, his lips pressed to my hair.

"We need to go meet Sammy at the house before the food gets cold," I mumble, hiccupping, refusing to let go of him.

"We will."

I pull back a little, wiping my sooty hands over my sooty face, ending up dirtier than when I started. "You give good hugs," I sniffle.

"It's because I'm short, Sugar. But thank you all the same," he says in his deep southern drawl.

"You're not short," I protest, craning my neck to look into his gray-blue eyes.

"Maybe not to someone that's five-foot-one, but I don't know many people that consider five-foot-eleven to be tall. I make up for it in other ways, though, don't you worry."

I pull away from him, my cheeks on fire. "I—I'm not worried," I stammer. "Why would I be worried?" My voice cracks, and I'm suddenly wishing a hole would open up beneath my feet and swallow me whole. He looks at me, tilting his head, awareness flashing in his eyes.

"I was teasing. Sorry if that made you uncomfortable," he says gruffly, his gaze sliding down to my lips.

"So you *don't* make up for it in other ways?" I ask, my mouth working faster than my brain. Fuck. I tilt my head toward the sky, closing my eyes. *Breathe Penelope. Fucking breathe.* "Will you round up the guys so we can go back to the house for lunch?" I ask him, not daring to look him in the face.

"Sure thing, Sugar, but for the record, I wasn't lying."

The house smells incredible. "What are you making?" I ask as we walk into the kitchen, trying not to ogle a shirtless Sammy as he stirs something in a pot on the stove.

"Oxtail stew." He turns toward me, full lips pulling into a grin. "You'll love it."

"I'm sure I will. It smells amazing." I squeeze my hands into fists to prevent myself from doing something stupid like reaching out and running my hands over his skin. He looks so soft. And warm. I clear my throat, reeling myself in. "I didn't know you could cook."

He shrugs. "I haven't needed to since working for you, but I'm glad to have the chance now. I don't want to forget everything my mother taught me."

"My stomach is glad you have the chance, too," I laugh.

The timer on the oven dings, and he takes out a tray of freshly baked, yeasty rolls.

"I didn't make these, they were frozen," he says apologetically.

"I think we'll survive," I tease, grabbing what I need to set the table.

Jamie walks into the kitchen, looking over Sammy's shoulder to see what he's making.

"God, that smells amazing." He runs his hand up Sammy's arm, squeezing his bicep gently before sitting at the table.

I look at the spot on Sammy's arm for a little too long, trying to puzzle out what I just saw. Sammy hands me a trivet to set on the table, interrupting my thoughts. The six of us dodge and swerve around each other as we grab drinks, and then we're all sitting down, talking over each other as we serve ourselves. The table quickly descends into silence as we start eating, all of us appreciating an incredible meal after hours of hard work.

Once finished, I sit back, watching as the guys clean their plates. The silence quickly turns into them making jabs at each other and then sharing stories back and forth, laughter filling the tiny space.

I like this—a lot. I didn't realize how lonely I was living here alone.

"We need to talk about meals," Archer says, rapping his knuckles on the table to get everyone's attention. "I assume all of us at least know how to make one meal?" We all nod. "Perfect, what do we think about taking turns making dinners? Lunches can be leftovers or easy things we can grab on the go. Sandwiches, cheese and crackers, stuff like that."

"I'll take the extra day every week," I offer, liking the idea of being able to cook for them.

"Perfect. Is that settled, then? Anything else we need to discuss before we get back to work?"

"How are we going to handle grocery shopping?" I'd love to be able to say I could handle it myself, but just thinking about it gives me anxiety.

"We can make a weekly list and go shopping together every Sunday," Spencer suggests, tipping back in his chair and locking his hands behind his head.

"We should be able to get most of the fresh stuff out of the garden at the restaurant." I stand and walk over to the kettle to make myself another cup of tea. "I just realized it's my responsibility now since the kitchen staff won't be around to take care of it."

"No," Liam says, except with his accent, it sounds more like 'naur.' "*Our* responsibility. If we're all eating from it, we can all help take care of it."

"Let me know if anyone thinks of something else we need to discuss. Should we draw names to see who cooks tonight?" Archer asks, looking around at us.

"Let's start tomorrow night. I want to take you guys out to the pub as a thank you." I push my hand through my hair, tucking it behind my ear.

"Thank you for what, Pen? We're just doing our job," Jamie says, patting me on the back.

"Fixing my screw-ups isn't your job, Jamie," I say softly.

I know he's just trying to help me feel better about everything, but those are the last words I want to hear. Am I just a job to them? Their boss? Are they hanging around because they're still getting paid, have somewhere to sleep, and have a full belly? Or are they staying because they care and want to help? I'm too much of a chicken shit to ask, so, per usual, I guess I'll just spend the next two months over-thinking it. Fuck me.

"Don't do that," Archer says, nudging my chin up with his knuckle so I'm looking him in the eye. "We're not going anywhere, Pen, and it's not because you're paying us. It's because you've been there for all of us the last few years, and now it's our turn to be there for you."

4

I should be showering, but I'm watching the guys hose off in my backyard instead. Being the tallest, Sammy is the one holding the hose. The guys strip down to their skivvies, yelling as they step under the cold water, goosebumps immediately breaking out over their bodies. Spencer must make a crude remark because Sammy sticks his thumb over the end of the hose and directs the spray at his face. I can't tear my eyes away as he tips his head back and laughs, his teeth nearly blinding in the sunlight. He's so beautiful it almost hurts to look at him. All that taut, dark skin painted over thick muscles—

"Darlin', if you're going to stand there watching them, do you mind if I use the shower?" Liam asks, poking his head through the crack in the bathroom door.

I startle, pressing my hand against my heart as I turn toward him, cheeks flaming. I peek at him through my eyelashes, then squeeze my eyes closed when my gaze catches on a bead of water sliding down his chest.

"Sorry. They just look like they're having so much fun. Give me five minutes, and the bathroom will be all yours."

"Fun, hey?" he asks, biting his lip and winking before pulling the door closed, leaving me to wallow in embarrassment.

I take the quickest shower of my life, towel off, pull on my robe, and call down to Liam before crossing the hallway to my bedroom. The bed creaks as I sit down and towel-dry my hair before raking through an air-dry serum. I get lost in thought, and the next thing I know, Liam opens the bathroom door, clenching a towel around his hips, steam clinging to his skin. He looks up and sees me sitting right there, in full view of the bathroom door, as if I was waiting for him like some peeping Tom.

"Sorry," I croak, ducking my head, but not before I get a good eyeful. My mouth dries up like the Sahara Desert.

"Sorry for what?" he asks, shaking the water from his shaggy brown hair, droplets raining down over his chest.

"I wasn't planning on sitting here like a creep when you walked out of the bathroom. You deserve privacy."

"I don't even know what the word privacy means anymore," he chuckles. "Thank you for letting me use your shower."

"You're welcome," I whisper as he turns to walk down the hallway, trying not to notice the way his muscles taper down his back or the gnarly mark on his shoulder blade.

"What is that?" I ask, walking over to him without realizing what I'm doing, tracing my finger over the bumpy skin.

He shivers under my touch, going preternaturally still. "It's my family's ranch brand," he says softly. "Everyone in my family has one. It's the mark we give the cattle on our ranch.'

"Did it hurt?" I ask, running my finger over it again, fascinated.

"Yes," he says, his voice hoarse.

Liam POV

I swallow hard, refusing to say what's on the tip of my tongue— that I would gladly re-live the pain every single fucking day if it meant she would be standing close to me like this, running her fingers over my skin.

I've made it three years. Three years of pretending not to notice the glances she casts my way. Three years of not returning them. Three years of flushing cheeks. Three years of wondering what *other* places might flush.

This is going to be the year that breaks me.

When I opened the bathroom door and saw her sitting on her bed, practically drowning in that fluffy white robe, those wide hazel doe eyes drawing me in, I almost fell to my knees and confessed right there. I don't move a single muscle while she examines my shoulder, terrified I won't be able to control myself if I turn and meet her gaze, that I won't be able to resist those rosebud lips for one single goddamned second longer.

As badly as I want her, I know I can't ruin this—whatever this is. I can't risk losing her. Yes, she's my boss, but she's become so much fucking more than that. I would sell my soul for this woman without a second thought.

"Did you use my body wash?" she asks, leaning closer, her nose skimming my neck. "You smell good."

Fuck. Me. I take a deep breath, then curse myself when it's only her I can smell. "Yeah," I say roughly, "We'll have to grab some regular soap when we go grocery shopping."

"You don't like the smell?" she asks, a hitch in her voice.

I steel my shoulders, clenching my jaw before I turn and plow my hand between her legs to find out what she really smells like. I bet it's cotton candy. Or peaches.

The second she lifts her hand from my shoulder, I stalk down the hallway without looking back. I know without a shadow of a doubt that if she sees my face right now, she would know exactly what I'm thinking. She'd see it in my eyes...and other places. Once I'm out of view, I press my back against the wall, taking deep, shuddering breaths as I try to wrangle my body under control. There's no room for mistakes in this house, no way to hide the effect she has on me. At least in the bunkhouse, there were multiple showers, so I had plenty of time to tug one out when I needed to. That's not going to be so easy here.

Sam passes me on his way to the bathroom, flashing a sympathetic smile. "It isn't going to be easy, man."

He can say that again. Pen's tinkling laugh floats down the hallway, and jealousy pricks at my heart. I immediately slam the door closed on that emotion. There's no place for jealousy in this house. Groaning, I scrub my hands over my face. I'm so fucking screwed.

Twenty minutes later, I'm sitting on the couch dressed in the only clean clothes I have. I hear Penny's faltering step on the stairs, and when she starts talking to herself, I get up to see if she needs help. My heart stops in my chest. Gone is the Penny that wears gaudy coveralls and chicken print wellies. This is *Penelope*.

"Is this too much?" she asks, smoothing her hands over a cream-colored dress with tiny yellow flowers, billowy sleeves extending just past her elbow.

When I just stare at her, she lowers her gaze and starts fiddling nervously with the charms on her chunky necklace. I clear my throat and try to talk, but nothing comes out. I try again.

"You look—fuck." My voice cracks, and I drag my hand over my face, mortified.

Her dark eyebrows almost hit her hairline and she giggles, her eyes sparkling as she pads down the stairs on bare feet, her cute little toes painted a peachy pink.

"You forgot to put your earrings back in." She holds out her hand, three earrings nestled in her palm. "Want me to help?"

"Yes, please," I croak, nearly choking as she stops on the last stair, a cloud of her scent enveloping me. I try to hold my breath while she puts my earrings in, but instead, I find myself inhaling deeply through my nose, trying to breathe in as much of her as possible.

"You look nice," she murmurs, her gaze sliding down over my crisp white t-shirt and jeans.

"I'm glad you think so because this is all I have." I grab my hat from the table by the stairs, worrying the brim, keeping my hands busy so I don't do something stupid like touch her.

"We'll have to fix that. I can take you guys shopping this weekend

—it'll be like a reverse Pretty Woman!" She jumps up and down excitedly, her hair bouncing just above her shoulders.

"You need to save your money, Penny."

"Insurance will pay me something eventually, and you guys need to replace the possessions you lost. I know the living situation sucks, but you at least need *some* autonomy." She tucks her knuckle under my chin, lifting it, running her fingertips over my two-day-old stubble. "Maybe some razors, too? God knows I could use one, too. I don't know the last time I shaved." She pats my cheek, smiling at me before heading into the kitchen.

I sag against the wall, letting my head thump against it as I close my eyes and will my heartbeat to calm the fuck down. It's difficult when she put the image of her shaving into my head. I don't even care, honestly. She could turn into a hairy beast at night, and it wouldn't change how I feel. But now I can't stop thinking about lathering her up with shaving cream and—I ram my hat on my head and walk outside. I need to get my head on straight before we go out tonight, or I'm liable to trap her in dark corner and ask her what I am to her. I need to get a fucking grip.

5

Our local pub is part of a gorgeous hotel and restaurant here on North Uist. It's my favorite seafood restaurant in Scotland. We supply them with the bulk of their seafood, so I know what we eat tonight will be fresh. Should I be splurging like this when I have a kitchen to rebuild? Probably not. Are the guys and their loyalty worth it? One thousand percent, yes.

As the hostess seats us, I look around at the guys, wondering what I did to deserve them. Why are they choosing to stay when they have nowhere to live, and money will be scarce? I haven't even thought about what it will be like having all five of them living in my house long-term. If I'm being honest, I'm not upset about having the opportunity to find out. I have three years of pent-up feelings to work through, and if yesterday was any indication, some of them may have the same problem. We can finally get everything out in the open, for good or bad.

"Are you doing okay?" Spencer asks, reaching under the table and squeezing my leg, his calloused fingers brushing against the inside of my knee.

I want to cover his hand with mine and drag it between my legs. I clear my throat, ignoring my sky-rocketing pulse. "Yeah. I'm good." I glance over at him, and the second our eyes meet, I can't fucking look away. A lock of dirty blonde hair has fallen over his forehead, partially obstructing his steel-blue eyes. The two-day-old scruff on his cheeks adds a mysterious edge to the smile pulling at his lips.

"Thanks for asking," I say breathlessly, looking away. I pick up a langoustine and de-shell it, terrified that if I meet his gaze, he'll be able to see what I'm thinking.

"So, what's the plan, Boss?" Archer asks, taking a bite of butter-drenched shrimp.

I'm like a deer in headlights as I watch him lick the butter from his lips, his gaze burrowing into my soul like he knows exactly what's going through my head. His smirk all but confirms it.

I don't answer right away. I take my time dipping my langoustine in butter, meeting Archer's gaze as I take a bite.

"I'll have to go into town and get a permit tomorrow," I say, watching his eyes darken as I lick the butter from my fingers. "Do any of you happen to have building experience?"

Spencer and Jaime raise their hands.

"Perfect. Can the two of you make some sketches so I can turn them into the building inspector? Once they're approved, we can get a supply list going and order everything."

"No problem," Jamie murmurs, his gaze glued to my lips, making me self-conscious.

"Do I have something on my face?" I ask him, wiping my mouth with my napkin.

"No. I'm just not used to seeing you like this. Sorry if I was staring." He smiles, his eyes crinkling, not embarrassed in the least.

"Okay, well, once the supplies are delivered, I'm going to order new appliances, which hopefully will arrive as we finish getting everything built."

"What about the bunkhouse?" Liam asks, tipping his chair back onto two legs.

"If all of you are okay with it, the bunkhouse will be the last thing we rebuild. I want to get the restaurant back up and running as soon as possible so we have some money coming in. Does anyone have any objections?" I look around the table at them, biting my lip to hold in my smile as all five vigorously shake their heads. "Okay. Good. That's our plan, then. Spencer and Jamie, you guys will stay with me tomorrow. The rest of you can take out the boat. Once the materials come in, we'll put the fishing on hold so all six of us can work on rebuilding the kitchen.

"Wouldn't it be better to hire a contractor?" Archer asks, the sole voice of reason at the table.

"It would, but that's not exactly in the budget."

"What about your brother?" he asks.

"What about him, Archer?"

"You know Lach would have a crew down here tomorrow if you told him what happened."

"I'm not asking him for money." I refuse to ask for help when I know I'm perfectly capable of figuring it out on my own.

"It's okay to ask for help, Nel."

"If you don't want to help, just say so." I snap my mouth closed before I say something I'll regret.

Archer throws his hands up in a sign of surrender. "Fine. But you know he'll be upset when he finds out what happened."

"That's for me to worry about."

Archer clenches his jaw, jerking off his glasses and scrubbing his hands over his face before downing his beer in several large gulps, frustration rolling off him in waves.

I pull my credit card out of my pocket and slap it on the table. "You guys finish up. I'm going for a walk on the beach to clear my head." I stand up and walk away before they can protest. This isn't the first time Archer and I have butted heads, and it definitely won't be the last. It's hard to stay mad when I know he's only looking out for me.

The wind whips around me as I make my way down the path to the beach. I smooth my hair out of my face, wondering for the hundredth time what I was thinking when I cut it all off a month ago. It's not even to my shoulders now, and I still can't pull it into a ponytail. It's the absolute bane of my existence.

"Hey! Wait up!" Liam's voice carries on the wind, that Australian accent bringing a smile to my lips.

I stop, waiting for him to catch up. "You didn't need to follow me, Liam. I wanted you guys to finish eating."

"I wasn't hungry anymore."

Well, that's a damn lie. He's *always* hungry.

"How are you *really* feeling?" he asks softly, walking beside me.

"Devastated," I answer honestly, too exhausted to come up with a better answer.

"Fuck, Penny." He grabs my wrist, pulling me toward him and wrapping his arms around me, squeezing tight. "I'm so sorry."

I squeeze him back, my cheek against his chest, breathing in leather and sandalwood.

"We'll build it back better than it was," he promises, his lips moving against my hair.

I close my eyes, basking in the comfort and intimacy of the moment. "I know," I whisper, my voice breaking, tears leaking from my eyes. I'm stronger than this, damnit.

He leans back, cupping my face in his hands and wiping away my tears with his thumbs. "Chin up, Buttercup."

I give him a watery smile, my eyes drifting down to his lips before I pull away and continue walking to the beach. He grabs my hand, threading his fingers through mine.

That simple touch has my entire body lighting up like a goddamn Christmas tree. I glance over at him, his hat casting half of his face in shadow, his bottom lip caught in those straight white teeth. God, the man is fine. He turns toward me suddenly, his gaze roaming over my face.

"Penny, I—"

"Incoming!"

That's the only warning we get before Sammy barrels into me like a freight train, scooping me into his arms and running toward the water.

WANT TO KEEP READING? I post all of my WIP manuscripts at reamstories.com/daphneleigh xoxo

Printed in Great Britain
by Amazon

62532173R00285